INTERFACE

Tony Batton

Interface
First UK Edition v.003

Copyright © Tony Batton, 2016
All rights reserved

First published in 2016 by Twenty-First Century Thrillers

The right of Tony Batton to be identified as author of this
work has been asserted in accordance with Section 77
of the Copyright, Designs and Patents Act 1988

Find out more about the author at:
www.tonybatton.com

When Tom Faraday joined internationally renowned CERUS Biotech, he thought he'd landed his dream job. A chance to work with their famous CEO, William Bern, perhaps to change the world.

But Tom has found himself in an organisation in crisis. The company bet the house on a radical biotech project, only to be blocked by a government with reasons of its own. Now CERUS is running on vapour and the corporate vultures are gathering. Bern isn't one to go down without a fight. He's turned things around before, and he has a plan to do it again.

The problem is, twenty-five years ago CERUS made a similar mistake. And if history is repeating itself, Tom might be the only one who can stop it.

for Sarah

ONE

THE BUILDING WAS NOT WHAT it seemed to be. The site was called Eastwell, but there were no signs and the name did not appear on any map. From the road it looked very little like an advanced research facility and considerably more like an ageing warehouse, with rough concrete-block walls and a corrugated metal-sheet roof, both painted a colour best described as 'peeling grey'. There were two double-height roller doors, but no windows. The whole site covered a patch of waste ground two hundred metres by four hundred, enclosed by a high, well-maintained metal fence. It was surrounded by dense woodland and there was only one access route: two kilometres of unmade road. Eastwell looked like what it was: a place that discouraged visitors.

Yet today, thought Dominique Lentz, there are many.

She stood in one of the two doorways, hands on hips, glaring through her thin-rimmed glasses. Two minibuses, six vans and three large four-wheel drives were parked inside the metal fence. Like the warehouse they bore no decals. All the number plates had been taped over.

A dozen armed guards in black combat-gear patrolled a

notional perimeter, clearly more concerned with watching those already on the site than any outsiders who might try to gain entry. Around forty technicians clad in disposable grey overalls were now swarming over the site.

Her site. Though not for much longer, it seemed.

The captain of the guards had produced a set of instructions signed by Bern himself: wet ink on actual paper. Naturally, she'd immediately called the CEO's office. One of his team had confirmed she was to cooperate. Fully.

Lentz glanced at the list of requirements on her clipboard. *To be followed to the letter*, it said at the top.

Lentz didn't like being given instructions; she was usually the one who gave them. Muttering, she turned back inside, passing through the airlock door and then descending by a set of metal stairs to sublevel two: the first of the operational levels. The majority of the laboratory was underground, in part to shield the sensitive equipment from electromagnetic interference, but mostly to hide the operation from anyone who might try to eavesdrop. The work taking place here was far too valuable and too important. Which was why it was so nonsensical that Bern would want to stop it all. The instructions had used the word 'terminate', not 'put on hold' or 'suspend'. Could Bern really mean it?

One of the technicians walked past her, guiding a cart with three large filing boxes on it. Seeing her, he paused, seemed to think about saying something then moved on. Lentz stared at the boxes. She didn't have to read the yellow stickers to know that they read

PROJECT TANTALUS
STRICTLY CONFIDENTIAL
PROPERTY OF CERUS BIOTECH

CONTENTS MAY BE HAZARDOUS: USE EXTREME CAUTION

Lentz continued down the corridor, looking for Richard Armstrong. He'd taken the news as if it didn't bother him that much: as if he wasn't surprised. But for Lentz, the work was personal. She was thirty-one years old, so it was a little early for her to consider the project as her life's work, but there could be no doubt of its significance. There'd been talk of Nobel prizes and indecent amounts of money. And of course there was the research itself: the real reason she had got involved. It was a chance to achieve something incredible: to turn an exciting possibility into reality. A chance to make a difference. But now they were taking it away from her.

Armstrong stood waiting next to Laboratory One, hands in his pockets. "Hey, Boss. Looks like we'll get to go home early today."

Lentz counted to five before answering. "You think this is all a joke?"

"Don't mistake frustration for humour," he replied. "I gave them access to Labs Two through Seven, then they ordered me back up here. Said they didn't need me. Wasn't sure what else to do."

She shook her head and walked past him into Lab One, a large workspace filled with high white benches and lit by crisp bright lights. "These people didn't come to listen."

"I suppose it's not really surprising." He followed her into the room. "Not after what happened."

She spun, her shoes' rubber soles squeaking angrily on the tiled floor. "After *what* happened?"

"The *incident*. Obviously."

Her eyes narrowed. "What incident?"

Armstrong cleared his throat. "I assumed you knew." Lentz took a quick step towards him. He took a pace back, bumping into one of the workbenches and turning to look at it accusingly. "There was a problem with the testing," he mumbled.

"Insertion's not for several weeks. What are you talking about?"

"I heard a couple of the medical team talking in that canteen you never go to." Armstrong leaned forward, lowering his voice. "They told me it was brought forward."

Lentz shook her head. "I monitor every room in this site. The surgery isn't even built yet."

"It wasn't done here."

"What are you talking about? How could it happen *anywhere* with the chip not even ready?"

Armstrong crossed the room and glanced into the corridor, then closed the door. "They're saying four people died." His voice was barely a whisper.

She blinked. "We weren't ready. Everybody knew that. I would never have signed off on this."

"Maybe that's why they didn't ask you."

"Then who *did* they ask? I'm in charge of everything here so who authorised it?"

Armstrong raised his hands. "Nobody's saying."

"I can't reach Bern. His assistant said I need to come in and meet this Peter Marron to discuss a new direction for me at CERUS." She paused, hearing footsteps in the corridor. She waited while they faded away.

"The new HR director?" said Armstrong. "I met him last week. He's not someone I'd want to annoy."

"Neither am I." Lentz folded her arms. "And what can he do? Fire me? I'll just up stakes and take my work somewhere else."

Armstrong shook his head. "We're all under non-disclosure

agreements. They'll sue us if we even think about the project outside this building."

"But this doesn't make sense. If there was an accident, there would be an investigation."

"Isn't that why these people are here?" Armstrong shook his head sadly. "Perhaps it's for the best if we all just move on. You know how many people said this was a terrible idea. Who said this was a line we should not cross. Maybe they were right."

From the corridor came the sound of heavy-booted feet and shouts that the facility was to be cleared.

"We can't stop this now." Lentz shook her head. "You can't make people forget an idea."

There was a loud knocking on the door and a raised voice. "Dr Lentz? They need you outside."

"I think," said Armstrong, "that our new friends might disagree."

"You're so naïve." Lentz placed a hand on his shoulder. "Believe me, something like this won't stay undone forever. We may not have been quite ready, but times will change, technology will change." She paused. "And then that technology will change us."

TWO

TWENTY-FIVE YEARS LATER

IT WAS FRIDAY NIGHT AND the main hall of the Exhibition Centre on Level 69 was considerably over its recommended capacity. Nevertheless, the waiters managed to weave their way through the tightly-packed crowd, distributing glasses of champagne with military precision.

Wearing his best suit, Tom Faraday stood to the rear of the room, positioned so he could watch the entire scene. He took one of the offered glasses with a polite nod, but he didn't need champagne for the evening to feel special.

One month ago he had got the phone call. Three interviews later and his life was transformed. Instead of working seventy hours a week, ploughing out a path as a junior associate at a City law firm, he had been plucked from obscurity, head-hunted to join the world-renowned CERUS Biotech. He didn't even start until Monday, but here he was at the VIP launch for the company's new London headquarters, waiting for CERUS' famous CEO to make an appearance.

Tom's phone buzzed in his pocket. His flatmate Jo had texted twice already, eager to know if Bern had strayed off script as he was known to.

Hey loser. Want to do breakfast tomorrow morning? 7am? I'm away after that for the weekend.

Tom started to tap a response when a voice broke over the public address system, "*LADIES AND GENTLEMEN, PLEASE DIRECT YOUR ATTENTION TO THE STAGE AND WELCOME YOUR HOST, CEO OF CERUS BIOTECH, WILLIAM BERN.*"

Applause rang out as Tom watched a tanned, energetic man in his fifties bound onto the stage.

"Ladies and gentlemen, good evening." His amplified voice seemed to come from every direction at once. "It is my absolute pleasure to welcome you to the grand opening of our new head office, CERUS Tower, here in the heart of London's Docklands." Bern paused and leaned forward. "I want to thank you for taking time out of your busy schedules, especially on a Friday night. I trust someone is keeping your glasses full." He turned and waved his hand. The lights dimmed and a projection of CERUS Tower lit up the wall behind him.

"Why are we all here? Those of you who know me know that I would love to be revealing a big surprise. Something that would truly 'blow your mind'. But, unlike most of our projects, we could hardly keep this building under wraps. Over the last twelve months it has steadily come to dominate the Docklands' skyline. But while the exterior may be rather obvious, inside revolutionary features are woven into its very fabric. In terms of both design and technology it is a quantum leap." Bern made another gesture and the image converted to a graphic showing statistics proclaiming energy efficiency, structural strength and the building's carbon footprint.

"Our chief architect will be available to answer your questions later, but let me rudely steal some of his thunder by quoting a few numbers for you: 1100 feet tall, 90 occupiable floors, housing 95% of our UK staff in a single site. There are 10 express elevators, 4 gymnasia, 42 miles of air conditioning ducting, and 275 espresso machines." Another gesture, and the image zoomed in to the reception hall, clad in glass and aluminium, filled with smiling CERUS employees.

"But in the end, why do we have a building except to provide the perfect environment for our people? It's become a cliché to say that people are your most valuable asset, yet here at CERUS we've walked that talk and created the most revolutionary work space anywhere in the world. Which brings me to..."

Tom was watching the presentation, so he didn't see the figure approach, just felt a finger tap his shoulder and turned to see a short man, somewhere in his fifties, the barest remnants of hair clinging to the back of his skull. Around his neck he wore a CERUS photo ID card, but it was obscured by his party invite tag. All Tom could see was that his first name began 'Ric'.

"You're in legal, right?" said the man, clutching an empty wine glass. He swung his gaze around, as if someone might be watching. As far as Tom could tell, the entire room was looking at Bern.

"I start on Monday," said Tom, with a smile. "Look, do you mind if I..." He gestured at the stage, but the man ignored him.

"I need to speak with you. It's important."

"Of course. I'm not on the system yet, but give me your email and I'll set up a time for us to chat."

The man frowned. "I want to report something. Is there somewhere we could speak?"

"Why don't you call me for an appointment on Monday? I'll give you every assistance then."

The man shook his head agitatedly. "I can't have anything on the system. Right now they won't have a clue that..." He seemed to hesitate. "Look, never mind." He turned and slipped away into the crowd.

Tom turned back to the front just as the CEO finished his speech.

Bern cleared his throat and said, "I'll take a few questions now." He looked around the room, almost like it was a challenge.

"How's the view from the top?" asked a man near the back.

"I'll assume that's a specific question about my office, rather than a prompt for abstract thoughts about business leadership," said Bern. "And the answer is, truly amazing. My apologies that, for security reasons, I can't take you all up there to show you."

"What do your staff think of the new, predominantly open-plan working environment?" asked a woman at the front.

"I won't pretend it's not a major adjustment for some. But it maximises use of light and space, and it really drives collaborative working. Also, most of our office-designated floors will use hot-desking. So anyone can have a window seat – if they get in early enough."

"Does it really make sense to have R&D on-site with your office functions?" said a woman in the middle of the crowd. "No other biotech company operates that way. Why not base yourself on an industrial park?"

Bern smiled. "I've had that same question many times." He nodded to the room. "And the answer is that we're not like other tech companies. We want our best people together, be they in research, finance, legal or marketing. And remember, this is not a full-scale R&D facility; we perform preliminary research and technical simulations, most of it done on computers. It's all about having the brain power and the computing power in one location so they can interface."

"Speaking of working together," said a man nearer the front, "there have been a lot of rumours about technical problems with the building. Is it all going to fall down on us?"

Bern frowned. "Any project of this size encounters problems. We have broken new ground with this building. Despite the challenges, our team of advisers have guided us through the maze and we completed on spec, on budget, and on time." He raised his glass. "And I, for one, will happily be moving in to my office full-time from Monday."

There was applause from most of the room. As it died down a thin man wearing glasses shouted out, "I don't think anyone will argue it's an impressive building. But can you afford it? How about these rumours of systemic financial problems at CERUS, linked with a succession of R&D failures?"

Bern smiled broadly. "Does a company in financial trouble throw a party like this? Now, this evening was meant to be a launch party for the building, not a forum for self-interested journalists to grandstand so let's move on--"

"And how about the rumours of CERUS' more dangerous interests in speculative science? Are you itching to get back into nanotech?"

Tom watched as four large, suited men started quietly making their way through the crowd towards the man who'd called out these questions, but Bern waved them off. He looked directly at the bespectacled figure and, when it came, his reply was liquid velvet. "We are, indeed, a company centred on speculative science. Someone has to stand up high and look into the wind. To see where we need to go next. We wouldn't be where we are now if the last generation hadn't done exactly the same. Now, you may think it's smart to point out failures, and use that as justification for not taking risks. But I see that as a big problem." He paused. "And do you know what's worse?" He looked around the room, as if inviting an answer. "Our politicians are just the same. We need leaders who have the vision to support and enable ground-breaking research."

"At any cost?" asked the man.

"In my experience the cost is usually worth it, in the long run. You can't stand in the way of progress. We should all embrace it. And then we might just change the world." Bern spread his hands wide. The audience obliged with a thunderous round of applause.

"Now, I'd better wrap this up, otherwise nobody is going to get a chance to sample the obscenely expensive catering. Just one last thing before I do." He tapped the lectern and the lights dimmed again. "When ships are launched, we usually smash a bottle of champagne over them. I know this building is not a ship. But, quite frankly, it could be mistaken for a spaceship so..."

Futuristic synthesiser music swelled around the room and from somewhere above a champagne bottle on a white cord lowered to hang just behind Bern. He grabbed it and raised an eyebrow to the crowd. "Maybe we should have done this outside."

There were some nervous titters.

Bern held the bottle high. "I name this building CERUS Tower." And he let the bottle swing towards the stone wall behind him.

It struck and bounced off. There was a moment of awkward silence.

"That didn't happen in rehearsals," said Bern. The crowd laughed obligingly. He stepped forward, gripped the bottle's neck and swung his arm in a forceful arc. Champagne and glass erupted, and the crowd cheered. A waiter rushed forward and handed Bern a towel. He wiped champagne from his hands, and turned back to the lectern.

"Ladies and Gentlemen, have a wonderful evening." He held up his glistening hand. "The drink really is on me."

Tom watched him leave the stage then turned away to look for the people he'd earmarked to talk to that night. He left his half-finished champagne on the table and started towards one of the senior lawyers who'd interviewed him.

Someone tapped him on the shoulder as he passed and he turned, half-expecting to see the nervous man he had spoken with earlier. Instead it was a slender woman in an elegant black dress, her matching stilettos spiking into the floor. She was cradling a glass in each hand, cognac from the sharp smell in the air. "Enjoying the party?"

"Wouldn't have missed it for the world," he said politely, about to turn away again.

"Isn't it bad luck when the bottle doesn't break?"

He was drawn to her smile, blood-red lips against a pale complexion. "I think that only works for ships. A building is hardly going to sink." He found himself unable to look away. "So, what brings you here tonight? Do you work at CERUS?"

"I suppose you could say I freelance. Disposals and terminations, that sort of thing." She held up the two glasses and grinned. "Toast to new beginnings?"

"To the building?"

"And your new job."

Tom frowned. "How do you know I'm new here?"

The woman smiled, extending a glass to him. "In my line of work, it's imperative to assess people quickly and accurately. And I *assess* you as needing a drink."

Tom blinked, taking it from her. "If you know I'm new, you know I'm not going to be much use for introductions. And if you wanted a word with the boss, Mr Bern's probably left already. I understand he's got a helipad on the roof."

Her eyebrows raised. "I'm not interested in him. Or anyone else here for that matter. I just want to share a drink with you, Tom."

"How do you know my name?"

She extended one elegantly manicured finger and tapped at his chest. "Your ID." She raised her glass and clinked it against his. "C'mon, Tom. Relax and have a drink with me. It's a party. What's the worst that could happen?"

THREE

EARLY MORNING SUN CREPT OVER Monaco. On the deck of the *Excelcium*, one of the many yachts anchored in the harbour, William Bern sat sipping orange juice as he watched a small motor boat approaching.

Soon there was the sound of footsteps on the internal staircase, then the familiar figure of Neil Bradley walked onto the deck. As always, he wore a suit that looked more expensive than he ought to be able to afford. Bern's eyes were drawn to the briefcase in his right hand. "Couldn't this have waited?"

Bradley placed the briefcase on the table. "I wish it could. I'm not the bearer of good news."

"Few people have been recently. What's happened now?"

"Gregory Stone called me yesterday to withdraw from the deal. He's got wind of the rumours. Doesn't think you'll be around to deliver in six months' time."

"He wishes." Bern shook his head. "Still his timing could be better. What does this mean for our numbers?"

"If we can hold off the liquidators for more than three or four months, I'll be stunned. And the moment that happens, we lose the Tower."

"I'd sooner blow it up." Bern eased back in his seat and adjusted his sunglasses, which were considerably more expensive than Bradley's suit. "We'll go to the banks. Or a suitably intelligent investor." He stabbed his forefinger on the surface of the table. "People believe in me."

Bradley took a deep breath. "You brought me on board to establish partnerships, find new sources of finance. But you have to understand: you've failed too many times. And all those run-ins with the government? People remember."

"How could they even know? Every project was classified."

"Rumours get out. And now people *don't* believe in you, William."

Bern snorted. "So you weren't up to the job I hired you for."

"I do have one idea, but I'm not sure if you're going to like it."

"Don't be coy, Neil."

Bradley reached into the briefcase and withdrew a grey card file. He slid it slowly across the table. "An old project you might remember."

Bern flipped it open, then stifled a laugh. "Where did you find this?"

"I've been trawling the archives."

"Deep diving would be more apt. I thought all these records had been destroyed."

"It seems the team were not as rigorous as they led the regulator to believe."

Bern ran his finger over the name. *PROJECT TANTALUS*.

"I understand the name was a joke about success always being out of reach?"

"I recall it was an accurate descriptor."

"Perhaps not any more," Bradley said. "I've had someone review the file. There are synergies with other research CERUS has done: research that might give you the missing piece to make this work."

"After what happened last time you think I want to touch that again?"

"I thought CERUS was, in your words, all about speculative science."

"There still has to be money in it."

A slow smile spread across Bradley's face and he produced another file from the briefcase. "I may have a customer. One not so... constrained... by the regulators."

Bern opened the file. "Viktor Leskov?"

"He's from Kazakhstan, although now operates out of Moscow. Made his money exploiting mineral rights."

Bern started to turn the pages of densely printed text.

"He has money. And we have a product that he wants." Bradley paused. "Or we could have a product he wants, if we decide to take a chance."

Bern closed the file. "You're telling me the best way to deal with our solvency issues is combining an illegal project from twenty-five years ago with an illegal project from this year?"

"I'm not telling you anything. I'm just doing what you hired me to do: present you with options."

"And if I decide to proceed?"

"Mr Leskov would be delighted to meet with you."

FOUR

THE ALARM CLOCK GOING OFF sounded like a police siren in Tom's aching head. He reached out a hand and smacked at it, taking three attempts before he stopped the piercing noise. Blinking to clear his vision, he sat up in bed and immediately regretted the manoeuvre. The room lurched as waves of pain stabbed though his head and nausea threatened to overwhelm him.

Quickly Tom lay back down, breathing in short gasps. He looked around his room, seeing his suit hanging on a hook behind the door. His phone, watch and wallet lay on the bedside table. The curtains were drawn. Everything looked as it should.

But he didn't remember getting here.

He'd been at the party, talking to the woman in the black dress. What was her name? He grasped for it and came up with nothing. Just how much had he drunk? Groaning, he made a second attempt to sit up. He reached across to grab his phone, but his hand jerked clumsily and it clattered to the floor.

From the other side of the door there were footsteps and a voice called out, "You there?"

Tom tried to reply, but his mouth felt impossibly dry. All he managed was a grunt.

"Are you all right?" The door was shoved open and Tom saw Jo glaring at him with a mixture of concern and annoyance.

"Just feeling a little worse for wear," he mumbled hoarsely.

Jo frowned. "What time did you get in?"

"Don't remember."

"Serves you right after standing me up."

Tom blinked. "It's only 7am. Look, maybe next week would be better."

She snorted, pulling her hair back into a ponytail. "Always another time, right? For now, though, some of us have to get to the office."

"Why do you have to go to work? Is something wrong?"

"I think that question should really be directed at you. Want an aspirin?"

Tom took a slow breath. "Don't worry. I'll get something if I need it."

Jo gave a shrug. "Well you'd better get moving if you don't want to be late on your first day. Anyway, I have a train to catch. Bye!"

She was gone before he could reply. The thump of the front door closing jarred Tom's head. He groaned again.

On the floor his phone vibrated. Taking a deep breath, he reached down and grabbed it. His eyes widened. He had twenty-five messages. Most of them from Jo.

Where are you?

Coming home tonight?

Guess I'll see you in the morning. Don't forget, breakfast @7!

Hey, Tom, it's 8. Are you OK? Call me.

Tom, hope you're OK. I'm really sorry but I'm going to have to leave in half an hour, with you or without you.

Hey, Tom. Got here safe and sound. Really hope you're OK. Call me.

Tom, do I need to start calling hospitals?

He stared at the screen. Was this a joke? He pinched the bridge of his nose between thumb and forefinger, trying to think more clearly. Just how much had he drunk? He'd never felt this bad in his life. Was it something he'd eaten?

Muttering, he stumbled into the kitchen and put on the kettle. With his other hand, he jabbed the television remote, searching for the morning news. He was just opening a packet of dark roasted Colombian when the sound came on. He promptly forgot the coffee as he stared at the screen.

He changed to two other news channels then checked the TV Guide.

Glancing around, he saw Jo's newspaper folded on the kitchen table. Shaking, he picked it up.

Today was Monday.

Today was Monday but he couldn't remember a single thing about the weekend.

Not one single thing.

FIVE

KATE TURNER PULLED IN FRONT of two slower-moving members of staff and wedged her VW Beetle into the last space in the Business Week News car park. Clutching her laptop and a very large café latte she strode into the building, waving her identity card at the security guard and slipping into the lift just as the doors slid shut. Three floors and sixty seconds later, she was sliding her chair up to her desk, docking her laptop, and simultaneously finishing a final touch of lip gloss. For a moment, it looked like she had arrived unnoticed.

"Afternoon," said a voice from behind her.

She forced herself to breath evenly. "It's only 9:15, Geraldine."

"I've been at my desk since 7am."

Kate turned and saw the frowning figure of the editor-in-chief, standing in the doorway of her office. Her arms were folded: never a good sign.

"Don't you have a column to deliver?"

"It's nearly done," Kate lied smoothly. "Ten minutes."

Geraldine sucked in her lower lip and stared at Kate for several seconds, then she jerked her thumb over her shoulder. "My office."

The tiny room was filled with stacks of lever-arch folders. Kate squeezed between them and sidled to a chair. "Run out of shelf space?"

"Company reports." Geraldine sat heavily in her chair, which creaked in protest. "I like to cast an eye over what they're saying about themselves, though it's what they don't say that's more interesting. Occasionally it yields something that gleams." She paused. "Or stinks. Either's good."

"Aren't these things available online?"

"I prefer the paper." Geraldine steepled her fingers. "You started so promisingly here, Kate. Made a name for yourself with that pharmaceuticals exposé. But lately you're just coasting. The column's been pretty much paint by numbers for the last twelve months. A good journalist makes the story." She pointed to the folders. "And it doesn't always just fall in your lap."

Kate leaned forward. "You know where I was on Friday night."

Geraldine drummed her fingers on the desk. "Are you going to tell me you met Bern? Did he agree to an interview?"

Kate sighed. "He was surrounded by PR people and minders. I couldn't get anywhere near him. And then he left early. Don't suppose you've come across a clue about CERUS' supposed financial issues in all of this," she said, gesturing at the files.

Geraldine rolled her eyes. "You want to do a piece on their difficulties? That's the worst kept secret in business."

"Yet nobody's run it as a story."

"Because nobody has anything concrete. And CERUS' lawyers would shred them."

"Ah, but they don't have what I have: an inside source. Someone with a long history at CERUS and an axe to grind. I think he overheard me being nosy and realised I was a journalist. Didn't talk much at the time, just asked for my card. Did a whole Covert Ops thing about not being seen together and walked off.

Thought maybe he was drunk or about to put security on me, but he called the next morning. Said he'd checked me out." Kate flicked her hair from one shoulder to another. "He liked that I have a science background."

"I thought you dropped out of your chemistry degree?"

Kate shrugged. "I usually leave that out of my public bio."

A faint smile appeared on Geraldine's face.

"I am going to meet with him. This afternoon."

"Then why are we discussing this now?" Geraldine threw her head back. "It's money, isn't it? A disgruntled employee wants to spill the beans and he wants something in return."

"He hasn't said yet, but you're interested, or we wouldn't still be talking." Kate paused. "I think the story isn't that they're in trouble. It's *why*."

Geraldine closed her eyes for several moments. Finally she opened them. "OK, meet with him. I'll give it my endorsement for now."

"You won't regret this."

"I hear that line five times a week. Make damn sure you're right."

SIX

TOM SAT AT THE KITCHEN table, staring into a cup of black coffee, trying to clear his head. The coffee didn't smell right and there were too many tiny swirling eddies on the inky surface. Brownian motion, they called it: random movements caused by the collision of tiny particles that you couldn't even see. Did coffee always look like this or was it time to descale the kettle?

Tom sighed. Had he come home Friday night having drunk so much he'd given himself alcohol poisoning and slept until Monday? Had he had one of those alcohol-induced blackouts his friends had laughed about at university? And hadn't Jo checked on him? His door hadn't been locked so how could she have missed him lying comatose in bed? So when had he come home? After Jo had left on Saturday morning but presumably before she got back on Sunday night. Where had he been in between?

He took a sip of the coffee. The bitter taste rasped on his tongue and he felt his head starting to clear. But something about the taste was wrong; there was a faint suggestion of something metallic. A memory flashed into his mind. He had broken his nose once. He remembered waking up after the operation to reset it with an odd taste in his mouth.

He banged the coffee cup down and stood up, running his hands over his torso, dreading what he might find. But nothing seemed to hurt. His hands shifted to his lower back and he wrenched off his shirt.

No bruises on his wrists, no marks on his arms as if he'd been in a fight or someone had held him down. There was just a faint mark in the crook of his elbow. Was that a spot or a bug bite or a mark from a syringe? He looked closer, but couldn't be sure. Had he injected drugs? Why would he do that when the most he'd ever tried before was one joint at university?

The woman in the black dress. She was the last thing he could recall. Had he gone home with her? He would have to ask around at work, see if anyone saw them leave together.

At work.

And it suddenly hit him. It was Monday, not Saturday. Monday. His first day at CERUS Tower.

Should he call in sick? *Could* he call in sick and not get fired? What would he even tell them? What if everyone had seen him roaring drunk at the party and knew it was just a hangover? He closed his eyes and considered how he was feeling. He didn't feel ill exactly. Just *off*. He took a gulp of coffee. That was certainly helping.

There was no reason to think he'd suffered anything worse than the world's worst hangover. No point turning bad to worse and getting fired before he'd even started his new job.

He shook his head. Time to get to work.

SEVEN

WILLIAM BERN GUIDED HIS ASTON Martin DB9 through the automatic gates of his country estate. Five walled acres of beautiful countryside in leafy Berkshire provided a perfect setting for a classic Edwardian house discovered, acquired, restored and decorated by his wife, Celia. His only contribution had been to pay for it. In his wife's words, he was always too busy trying to change the world. Well, he was about to play to form.

He parked and crunched across the gravel to the front door. Celia stood there, immaculate in a long black dress. "I thought you had meetings today in Monaco," she said, touching the silver chain around her neck. "What's going on?"

Bern pecked her on the cheek. "Let's have a drink and I'll explain."

"A drink?" She raised her eyebrows. "It's ten in the morning? Even for you that's early."

"Trust me: you'll need it."

They took the drinks trolley out to the veranda and sat for a while holding large glasses of cognac, looking out at the carefully manicured lawn and the orchard beyond.

Bern took a sip and cleared his throat. "I'm afraid, my dear, that I haven't been entirely truthful with you. Those rumours running around, the ones I've been furiously denying. CERUS is on the brink. We're way overextended: there's no way to prop things up any longer. We've got three months."

Celia's eyes narrowed. "The whole company? How is that possible?"

"You've heard the expression 'a house of cards'?"

She sighed. "Then we walk away, start over. It's not like either of us ever need work again. We can travel, spend more time on my charities."

Bern shook his head. "It's not just CERUS. We're in just as deep."

She put her glass down. "What have you done, William?"

"We've been struggling since the government put a block on nano research. We over-invested, overcommitted to what we were certain was going to be the next big thing." He took a deep breath. "I had to put everything up to guarantee borrowing by the company or CERUS would already have failed."

Celia's lips tightened. "And you didn't tell me? You didn't *ask* me?"

"I didn't want you worrying. I knew I could sort it all out and you would never know." He paused. "I've always managed it before."

She leaned back in her chair, took a slow sip of her drink. Her face was a mask. "You said *almost* inevitable."

"A new member of my team, Bradley, has come up with a possible solution."

Celia shifted in her seat. "Bradley? Have I met him?"

"I don't remember. Anyway, he's not important. But the idea is." He slid two grey folders onto the table.

Celia read them in silence, her lips tight. "I thought this was all behind us. I thought all the papers had been destroyed."

"The auditors weren't as thorough as they believed."

"And this Viktor Leskov? He might be rich, but can you trust him?"

"He's probably asking the same question of me. As long as our interests are aligned we can do business."

They sat in silence for several moments. Finally Celia drained her glass. "Is this wise?"

"I realise that I'm asking a lot."

"It should come as no surprise that I'd rather go to prison than go broke."

"You say that--"

"Protect yourself: protect us. I trust you to do what you need to." She smiled. "We're a team, William. Don't forget that."

Celia watched him drive away, then dialled a number from memory. It was answered immediately.

"Well?" said a man's voice.

"I think," she replied, "we can assume things are in motion."

"He doesn't suspect?"

"He's just doing what he does. What he has to do."

"You sure about all this?"

"I've never been surer. He's going to get exactly what he deserves."

EIGHT

TOM MOVED WITH THE CROWD through the high-ceilinged tube station, then out into glaring daylight. Around him suited figures fanned out, making their way towards their buildings for the start of the day. Above, seagulls wheeled and cried, the air filled with the faintly salty odour of the Thames. The great river looped around the Isle of Dogs and passed CERUS Tower.

Tom paused and looked up. It was going to be quite something to finally work here, especially since he would be one of the lucky few with his own dedicated office. Around him a seemingly never-ending stream of people were flowing in apparently random patterns, like the particles on the surface of his coffee. He waited for a gap in the crowd then began to walk, but something suddenly caught his eye. As if someone had moved at the exact same time, aping his movements. He stopped, puzzled, prompting a curse as a woman nearly walked into him. He apologised, spinning around and holding up his hand to fend off the glare of the sunlight.

Around him was a sea of faces. Nobody seemed to be paying him particular attention. Had he imagined it? Was he suffering some sort of drug-induced paranoid hallucination? Or had he just had too much coffee? With a sigh, he let the crowd carry him to the Tower, only to find a long queue snaking out of the lobby.

For the first time that day, he smiled. Today everyone was going to be late.

Tom stood patiently as the line shuffled forward. The acres of glass that clothed the Tower were offset on the first ten storeys by a feathering of steel plates, each the size of a large window, but sticking out at nearly ninety degrees, not unlike the fletching on an arrow. It was an odd ornamental feature, but not unattractive, he mused as he let his eyes roam over the building.

Finally, the queue started moving more quickly and soon he stepped into the lobby and saw what must have caused the problem: the automatic turnstiles were out of order and a line of harassed-looking security guards were admitting people through a service gate, checking their ID cards with handheld scanners.

"Problems?" he asked as he produced his card.

The guard flickered his eyebrows like he'd already answered that question a few hundred times. "Doing our best, Sir." He held out the scanner and there was an angry buzz. Frowning, he looked at it and held it out again. There was another buzz.

"I *do* work here," said Tom. "Or I will do if you'll let me in. It's my first day: don't really want to be any later than I am already. With the queue, I mean."

"Sorry, Sir. The access database keeps dropping out. Another joy to go with the turnstiles."

Tom suddenly felt a wave of pain stab through his head. He put his hand to his forehead, rubbing at his temple.

There was a soft beep from the scanner.

"Good morning, Mr Faraday," said the guard in a relieved tone. "You can proceed. Just make sure you keep your card with you at all times."

Tom forced a smile and walked towards the bank of lifts. He

emerged from the lift on Level 84 and walked into his new office for the first time. It was far from the largest on the floor, but the entire external wall was glass and, through it, he had a stunning view over London. Even with the recent incursion of other skyscrapers, there were few other buildings with such an outlook. What was it Bern had said? *From the top, we can see the future.*

There was a sharp knock on the door. His secretary, Samantha, walked in, clutching her day-planner as if someone might try to pry it from her. "Mr Bradley wants to see you in his office."

Tom stepped behind his desk. "I only just got here. What's it about?"

"He needs you to run a meeting. He's been diverted on to something for Mr Bern."

Tom coughed. So much for easing himself into things. "Sure. Where is he?"

"Up two floors. I suggest taking the stairs: it's amazing the lift got you here at all."

"I just need to log in."

"Don't keep him waiting. Oh, and don't forget to take your ID card or you'll get locked in the stairwell. The building keeps track of you through your ID, but if you don't have it... Well, people keep getting stuck in all sorts of places."

Tom quickly entered his password on the computer system. He felt a slight tingle in his fingertips as he typed and flinched back, wiping his hands on his jacket to earth the static. The screen jumped and an error message appeared.

Perhaps they had been hasty in moving in to the building. He looked under his desk for the computer terminal and crouched low to reach the reboot button. As his finger hit it, he felt the blood rush to his head. He had a brief moment of intense alertness, then suddenly pain was lancing through his brain, like it was burning. His tongue felt immense in his mouth, as if it would choke him.

He jerked back from the computer and fell sideways. He just had time to notice the CCTV system, a large fish-eye lens sparkling in the corner, before darkness took him.

NINE

BRADLEY ADJUSTED HIS SHARPLY PRESSED suit as he descended in one of the express lifts to Level 60: the first of the technical floors. He had given up waiting for the lawyer and told his assistant to cancel the meeting. There were more important things to deal with: things that he could share with only a chosen few.

The heads of each of the research and production divisions were now located on Levels 59 and 60, with their teams in the floors below. The idea was that the layout would help the team leaders to work openly and cooperatively together, sharing ideas and innovations.

The lift juddered twice then finally reached Level 60. Bradley rolled his eyes as the doors opened slowly. The building still had many teething problems: they should not have been moving in yet, but everything had been planned assuming things would be ready. The old lease for the old premises had expired: the old networks and phone lines had been switched off. Even if they hadn't, it wasn't Bern's style to delay. However, the building faults were nothing compared to the disaster on CERUS's horizon.

Bradley stopped at a touch screen, held his security pass over a reading device, and called up a plan of the floor. At least that was working. He turned right, heading to the office of Ed Holm, Head of Technology Research. A sign on the door proclaimed 'STOP! TRESPASSERS WILL BE ELECTROCUTED!' Bradley walked in to find himself amid chaos.

"Can it wait?" Ed Holm asked, looking up from the two laptops in front of him. "I'm kind of in the middle of something."

Bradley looked around the room. Boxes and boxes of files, bursting open and spilling their contents, covered the floor. There were a number of computer cases, routers and a multitudes of cables, plus a media player sound-dock and a rather neglected-looking bonsai tree.

"How did you make a mess so quickly? You only moved in today."

Holm removed his tiny circular-rimmed glasses and wiped them on a cloth. "Actually I've been moving stuff over for weeks. Didn't want my gear getting muddled with that of the great unwashed."

Bradley sighed. "Did you get my message?"

"What message? Oh, the one about a meeting tomorrow? Can't we deal with whatever you want then?" His phone beeped and he glanced at it. "Where is Armstrong? He's supposed to be briefing me on the Phase 3 analysis."

"This is important."

"Everyone thinks their stuff is important."

"We meet tomorrow at 7pm on Level 90. Bern will be there."

Holm blinked. "Really?" His tone was suddenly cautious.

"You recall that confidential side project? I need a plan to take it forward."

"Well, I have a *theoretical* production timetable for you."

"Good. Be prepared to explain it." Bradley turned and left, with Holm staring after him.

Bradley headed next to the opposite corner of the floor and the office of Professor Stefan Heidn. Heidn's office was a marked contrast to Holm's: files were neatly arranged on shelves and a bookcase held a number of medical texts and journals. A high-end stereo and record turntable were set up in a cabinet; classical piano music was playing softly.

"Neil, good morning." Heidn, his long grey hair brushed back, walked over and offered his hand.

Bradley shook it. "Professor, good to see you. Has the move gone smoothly?"

"No complaints. I hired my own movers so they would be more considerate with my possessions, but then our overzealous security team wouldn't let them in. I had to go and speak to them personally about it."

"You can't blame them," replied Bradley. "There are plenty of things in here we'd like to remain unseen. Did you get my message?"

"I did indeed. Very clandestine."

"Can you attend?"

"A secret meeting with our CEO? At which my presence is demanded?" Heidn patted Bradley on the shoulder. "I wouldn't miss it for the world."

"You don't want to know what it's about?"

"And spoil the surprise?" He ran a hand through his grey hair. "Besides, I'm pretty sure I can guess. I've been at CERUS a very long time. Few things that happen here surprise me anymore." He sighed and added, "Those years of experience make me think the wise course would be to forget the whole thing."

Bradley shrugged. "My job is just to present the choices. Others make the call."

The professor nodded. "However big this company gets, only one man ever makes the decisions."

"Let's hope he makes the right one."

TEN

KATE ARRIVED AT THE WEST London shopping plaza ahead of schedule. It was the kind of second-tier mall that aimed to be gleaming and aspirational, but had failed to attract the better retail chains. Now a heavy London grime had settled in every corner and Kate's shoes stuck to the grubby floors as she made her way through the lunchtime crowds, looking for the food court.

As arranged, she bought two cappuccinos and sat at a table tucked away to one side. There she opened a newspaper and waited. Five minutes later, a man emerged from the crowd and stood at her shoulder. His brown suit looked as ill-fitting and uncomfortable as he did; he kept touching his wire-frame glasses with a nervous twitch.

"Were you followed?" he asked.

Kate indicated the chair opposite. "I very much doubt it." She passed one of the coffees over to him as he sat down. "In my experience big companies have a lot of worries on their plate. They don't usually have the time or inclination to set covert operatives watching their staff."

He narrowed his eyes. "If they knew about me, they would,

but I've been careful."

"And that's great, but now the truth should come out," Kate said. "Shareholders, employees, the public: they shouldn't be lied to. If the financial situation is as dire as many suspect then it's time to--"

"CERUS has made plenty of mistakes with its finances, but I can assure you they are not its biggest mistakes." He shook his head. "I wanted to talk to you because you have a platform *and* your background is in science. You'll understand what I'm about to tell you and you'll know how to turn it into a story that everyone else can understand."

She gripped his hand. "Mr Armstrong, I don't know what you know, but if I can possibly help you, I will."

His eyes narrowed. "You realise this could be *dangerous*."

"If you're so concerned, why not involve lawyers? Or the police?"

"There's a CERUS lawyer so new he can't be part of the system. I started to speak to him at the launch party, but... I changed my mind. He seemed like a good kid, but can you ever really trust a lawyer?" He laughed bitterly. "And if I go to the authorities, this story is *never* getting out."

"This all sounds very dramatic, but you have to understand that without evidence of whatever it is that is concerning you so much..." Kate raised her hands.

Armstrong looked around the food court, then reached into a pocket and removed what looked like a watch case. With a practised motion he flipped open the case. Inside was a small glass vial, filled with a cloudy green liquid.

Kate leaned forward. "What's that?"

"Nano," he said. "Intelligent nanites in liquid suspension. Automated particles on a molecular scale."

She looked closer. The liquid almost seemed to be glowing.

"You're kidding."

"What I hold here could be the basis for creating functional systems beyond the microscopic, with applications spanning biology, chemistry, physics and engineering. The nanites just need to be programmed."

"You got them from CERUS? I thought that project was shut down?"

"My company is good at many things, but permanent deletion of valuable research is not one of them."

Kate stared more closely at the vial. "Of course I could be staring at food colouring and glitter. It's not like I can see the actual nanites."

Armstrong nodded. "Now you're talking like a scientist. Ten thousand of them stacked would be thinner than a sheet of paper: so impossibly tiny, yet they could change the world."

"Why would the company risk it? Why would Bern risk it?"

"Before we talk any more," he said, "we need to agree how this is going to work."

Kate sat back, clearing her throat. "I want to be clear that our funds are limited."

Armstrong laughed. "You think I want money? Ms Turner, you've misunderstood me. This is about technology changing us. And whether we should allow it to." He paused. "Or perhaps whether we can even stop it."

"So, what *do* you want?"

"I want to make things right." He paused. "And I don't want anyone dying. Not like last time."

"What?"

He slid the vial across the table. "A gesture of my good faith. Do some research, Ms Turner. You need to understand more about the company and its history because if it's about to make mistakes, it won't be the first time. Then if you still want to, let's talk again."

ELEVEN

TOM BECAME AWARE OF THE sound of heart monitors and the smell of disinfectant. Around him a swirl of light and noise coalesced into a hospital ward, with several patients sleeping in beds to either side. He blinked and tried to sit up, but realised he was swathed in electrodes and wires, a drip in his left arm. His tongue felt like a dry sponge.

"Careful now," said a man's voice. A doctor walked quickly over and scanned the electronic display next to the bed. "Welcome back, Tom. How are you feeling?"

Tom's head was pounding. He coughed, trying to get moisture into his mouth. "Can I get a drink?"

The man produced a white plastic cup and held it to Tom's lips.

"Thanks." Tom coughed as the cold water softened his tongue. "Where am I?"

"The Royal London Hospital," said the doctor. "You were brought here yesterday after you collapsed."

Tom shook his head and winced. "My head hurts."

"You have a nasty lump where you hit your desk, although thankfully it's nothing serious." The doctor paused. "It seems you fell over."

"I was feeling under the weather. I think I had a bit too much to drink at the weekend."

The doctor frowned. "When you say a *bit too much to drink*, could you be more specific?" The doctor lifted his pen and started jotting notes on his clipboard. "Times, quantities? Did you take any narcotics?"

"To be honest, I don't remember much about the weekend."

"We've run some tests and nothing showed up, but if you know you took something you really should tell us." He hesitated. "We're not interested in reporting drug use to the police, if that's your worry."

Tom shook his head. "I really don't remember"

The doctor started to say something, but behind him an alarm began ringing. He strode quickly away.

Tom watched a nurse walked across to his bed. "You have a visitor," she said. Tom turned towards the door, expecting to see Jo. Instead a grey-haired man in a neat suit walked up to him. His face seemed familiar.

"Mr Faraday," said the man with a smile. "Good to see you're awake. I'm Peter Marron. We met during your CERUS interview."

Tom frowned. "HR, right? What... Why are you here?"

Marron turned and looked at the electronic display next to Tom's bed, a small frown crossing his face. "Hell of a first day. How are you feeling?"

"Like I've got a very sore head. Only just woke up."

"What happened exactly?"

"I was enjoying the view from my office and then... I guess I fell and hit my head. I'm not sure how." Tom sat up a little in his bed. "Does the head of HR turn up every time a CERUS employee is in hospital?"

Marron gave a broad smile. "You're a new member of our

team, and we want to make sure you're OK. I know we're a big operation, but everyone's important." He leaned forward. "Especially those on the top floors."

"I'm sorry to have caused a fuss."

Marron pulled the privacy curtain into place. "Tom, let me be honest. We've had enough bad press about the building already; the last thing we need is some story about a design fault causing an injury. You didn't trip on a rug or something, did you?"

"Nothing like that."

"I don't mean to pressure you. I just like to manage issues for Mr Bern before they become problems." Marron interlaced his fingers. "What did they say is wrong?"

Tom blinked. "The doctor ran some tests, but nothing came of it."

"Well, that is good news." Marron looked around with a slight furrowing of his brow. "But this place doesn't have the time or money to spend digging too deep. Tell you what, why don't we get you checked in to somewhere a bit more agreeable?"

"I'm not on the company health insurance yet. Haven't done the medical."

Marron waved a hand. "Don't worry about that. The company needs you at a hundred percent. Remember what I said during the interview: the future of the business depends on people like you." Marron patted Tom on the shoulder. "I promise, once you're finished at the place I'm sending you to, you won't know yourself."

TWELVE

BERN HAD BEEN IN THE back of the van for more than hour. There were no windows, so he wasn't sure the hood was completely necessary, but the team of bodyguards had been politely insistent. At least the seats were comfortable.

The bodyguards had ignored his repeated attempts at conversation. Eventually he had given up and sat back, with nothing to listen to but the rattle of the engine and the grinding of the suspension, and with continual changes of direction he quickly gave up trying to work out where they were going. Finally he heard the handbrake being engaged and the van came to a stop. Then the hood was pulled from his face and he was guided out.

He was inside a large, apparently disused warehouse, amongst rusting machinery and piles of rubbish. In front of him was something very large and angular covered in dust-sheets.

"Good morning, Mr Bern," said a voice from above: a Russian accent, laced with overtones of Eton. "My apologies for the manner in which you were brought here. I prefer to stay under the radar for certain meetings."

A man, probably in his late fifties, walked down a set of metal stairs from the gantry above. He wore an immaculate pale suit. Two large men walked behind him, also wearing suits, although they looked more like their choice of clothes was an order rather than a choice. There were four other men, similarly attired, standing by the doors.

"Viktor Leskov, I presume?" Bern asked.

The pale-suited man reached the bottom of the stairs and extended his hand. "It is good to meet you. I've followed your career with great interest, but I did not think we would ever do business."

Bern shook the hand firmly. "Mining was never an activity we had much to do with, although my broker always said it was a good investment. But I hear you've diversified."

"I like to think that my other areas of interest are also good investments." Leskov pointed to a rough table and chairs. "Let's talk." He snapped his fingers and one of the large men produced a flask and cups, pouring hot, black coffee for them.

"Bradley briefed me on your discussions to date. He said you need a new kind of system interface."

Leskov gestured to one of his men, who reached into a case and placed a small black box on the table. "I'm looking for a fully bi-directional neural interface to communicate with this hub."

Bern slowly reached forward and picked it up. "What is it designed to control? A vehicle? A weapon system?"

Leskov smiled. He snapped his fingers. Three of the large men moved and began cutting cords connected to the dust sheets, which slid away to reveal a sleek black-grey helicopter. "It's not officially in production."

"How many passengers does it carry?"

Leskov followed him to stand next to one of the side doors. "Up to ten. But it's more comfortable for six."

"And why do you need a neural interface for this?"

"Because it is no ordinary helicopter. We're going to market it as a security vehicle for high-net-worth individuals. The weapon systems are a discretionary extra. But it is fully stealth capable, has active and passive radar, and a range of other sensor equipment, plus sophisticated autopilot and threat evasion systems and six ejector seats."

"Not ten?"

Leskov flashed a smile. "Like I said, it's more comfortable for six."

Bern tapped the door of the helicopter. "How much did this cost?"

"Close to two hundred million US dollars. We expect the unit price to fall once we enter production," he paused, "but not by much. It's not really a vehicle for those who have to ask about the price tag."

"So it's fully featured. Why the need for an interface? Considering the cost."

Leskov raised an eyebrow.

"If I don't know why you need it, I won't be able to build it."

"It takes a crew of three to fly it to full capability and those three pilots need extensive training. It's a logistical nightmare finding one suitably discrete pilot, but three? We need to reduce the number."

"To one?"

Leskov smiled. "To zero." He paused. "At least on-board. With your interface a single pilot could fly the craft and operate all systems – and do it all from another location entirely."

"So it would be a passenger-carrying drone?"

"I don't like that term. It makes my clients nervous. We're talking about a system whereby the pilot is on-board – just not physically. The sensor cluster would be his eyes and ears."

"So you already understand how the interface would work.

45

You know it wouldn't just be a headset you wear."

Leskov nodded. "We like it because it will exercise a degree of control over the subject. Those we select as pilots aren't going to be running off to a competitor."

"Just what has Bradley shared with you?"

"His conversation was frank. Knowing the financial state of your business, is this not a time to be frank?"

"I suppose it is. You have the full schematics for the aircraft?"

"Ready for you to take with you. Presuming you can meet the timetable."

"That depends."

Leskov looked at Bern carefully. "I didn't expect to find you so cautious. Perhaps you'd prefer to stick with a project with less personal risk."

Bern smiled. "I'm not cautious, Mr Leskov. I'm negotiating." He paused. "And the higher the price, the less cautious I will become."

"Ah. That I understand. Although in this case I am going to tell you what I will pay, and you can take it or leave it." He smiled. "My offer is one billion US dollars. For that I expect a demonstrably viable candidate. And full schematics, source code and nanite production equipment. In the next sixty days."

Bern closed his eyes, counting slowly to ten. As if there was any decision to make. He opened his eyes and extended his hand. "We have a deal, Mr Leskov."

THIRTEEN

THE PRIVATE AMBULANCE GLIDED SMOOTHLY up the bush-lined red-sealed private road, then slowed as it approached a large building that looked like a cluster of period houses squashed together. It pulled up under a huge shelter that extended over the road, and Tom's wheelchair was lowered out. Two smiling nurses appeared to greet him then wheeled him inside and along several corridors. The place seemed deserted. Eventually they left him in a large first-floor room with an expansive view across the grounds. He gazed out of the window for several minutes before he heard footsteps and turned to see a man wearing a white coat, a stethoscope, and a broad smile.

"Tom, great to meet you," said the man, shaking his hand. "I'm Dr Chatsworth. I'll be in charge of your care while you're at the Angstrom Clinic."

"Nice place. I'm glad work is paying for it." Tom nodded back the way he had come in. "I haven't even seen another patient."

Chatsworth smiled. "Our patients demand absolute privacy. And we want to make you feel you have our undivided attention while you're here."

"But why am I here?"

"After your incident, we've been tasked with making sure that you're in the best possible health. The more candid you can be about what happened to you, the better I can help you."

"Why do you say that?"

"Because a capable, athletic young man rarely just falls over in his office and knocks himself unconscious."

Tom narrowed his eyes. "How does that all work with patient confidentiality? Won't you be reporting back to my company, given that they're paying for all this?"

"Please be assured, Tom, that we will only disclose information to CERUS with your explicit permission. They may be footing the bill, but all they're entitled to is a breakdown of tests and other expenses, unless you say otherwise."

Tom sighed. "Well, it's not like I've got anything to hide. It's just... I had a strange weekend. Strange in that I can't remember any of it. From Friday night to Monday morning it's a blank."

"What do you mean?" asked Chatsworth.

"Friday night, I was at a party. I had a few sips of champagne and a cognac, but that is all I remember drinking. In fact that's the last thing I remember at all. I woke up on Monday feeling dreadful. Maybe I had more to drink after that. It's not like me but..." He shrugged. "I'm pretty sure I didn't trip over in my office. I think I fainted."

"Why didn't you mention this when you were taken to A&E?"

"I didn't want to make a fuss. Like I said, it was the first day in my new job and I wanted to make a good impression."

Chatsworth nodded. "Well, first things first. Let's run a few tests."

◇ ◇ ◇

Tom awoke feeling different. He was lying in bed at the Angstrom clinic. It was dark outside, but the curtains were open and a figure was standing at the window.

"How long was I out?" he mumbled. Then he saw he was not talking to one of the clinic staff.

"Hey, loser," Jo said, turning to face him. "I am struggling to decide whether to hug you or shake you for not telling me what had happened. You should have gone straight to the doctor. You should have told me to call an ambulance."

Tom began to struggle upwards, then noticed the bed had automatic controls. He tapped them and slowly raised himself to a seated position. "Yes, well hindsight is a wonderful thing. Although it's not like they've found anything wrong with me so far."

Jo put her hands on her hips. "Aren't you the one who said your mother should have gone to the doctor sooner, and if she..."

"Yes, thanks. I'd rather not think about that right now."

"Well, at least you're in the right place." Jo looked around. "CERUS must really love you."

"Let's hope this place's medical care is as good as its accommodation. How did you know to find me here?"

"I'm still listed as your next of kin - they gave me a call." She reached into her shoulder bag. "I've brought you a couple of magazines and a book, but given that you seem to have two hundred TV channels and on-demand movies I doubt you'll get round to them."

"Quite right," said a voice, "since he shouldn't be here too much longer." Dr Chatsworth walked into the room holding a tablet computer, smiling at Jo then Tom. "I've got the results of the tests. Would your friend care to step outside while we discuss them?"

"You've already got results?" asked Tom. "That was fast."

"Efficiency is part of the service, now about your visitor..."

"Jo's as good as family. You can speak in front of her."

"Well, then I have good news, with a twist." Chatsworth jabbed at the tablet screen. "We ran a full spectrum analysis on your blood and urine. We also put you through an ECG and MRI and we've been monitoring your heart function for the last eight hours."

"Eight hours?" asked Tom. "What time is it?"

"He fainted again?" asked Jo.

"No, no," Chatsworth said. "We had him under a general anaesthetic."

"For tests?" Jo asked.

"Some of the scans required Tom in a consistent state of inactivity. It's the most reliable path."

"So what did you find?" Tom asked.

"You're in good health. Nothing to suggest the problem will reoccur."

"Why do I feel there's a 'but' coming?"

"We think we know what caused it." Chatsworth turned the tablet to face Tom. It showed a scattergram. "This is a breakdown of your bloodwork. There are statistically significant flags for a Methamphetamine derivative."

"I took meth?" Tom took a deep breath. "Are you sure?"

"As far as we can be. The markers typically only show up in the blood one to three days after consumption."

"And that's what caused the problem?"

Chatsworth shrugged. "Everyone reacts differently. Also, there could have been a contaminant in the drugs. Now I'm sure I don't need to say that taking this type of substance is risky enough at the best of times--"

"I didn't *knowingly* take it," Tom said abruptly.

"Someone gave it to him," Jo said, "against his will."

Chatsworth raised his hands. "I'm just a doctor. I can't speak to how you came to ingest it. If you wish to notify the police, I can confirm to them that you had Methamphetamine in your system but unless you can demonstrate that you didn't take it purposefully..." Chatsworth seemed to hesitate. "It's really up to you. I know how sensitive employers get about that type of thing these days."

Tom frowned. "You're sure I'm OK now?"

"We'll monitor you overnight and you should come back for daily checks for a week or so, but we've seen nothing to give us cause for concern."

"So I go back to work?"

"As soon as you feel ready." The doctor's phone chimed. "If you'll excuse me."

Jo watched him leave. "Isn't he the slick operator?"

"You don't like him?"

"He sure came up with answers fast."

"Isn't that what he's supposed to do? Look, all I know is that he said I'm OK. I think I caught a break here." Tom smiled. "And shall I tell you what else is a good thing?" He picked up a leather-bound folder. "This is a hospital with room service."

Chatsworth returned to his office on the far side of the clinic, then closed and locked the door. He started-up his computer, logged into an encrypted voice service, pulled on a headset then dialled a contact. "The set-up is complete and the subject should be viable. There appear to be no adverse side effects from the procedure."

"Excellent," replied a soft, metallic voice. "Any difficult questions?"

"He seemed to buy into the story."

"How about the loss of consciousness?"

"He thinks he just fainted. Of course it was always a possibility with Phase One. But we're beyond that now."

"Good. I trust you did not run him through an MRI, as agreed."

"There didn't seem to be any need. What was the concern there?"

"You don't need to know. Are you ready to proceed?"

"Yes. The tests will start on his next visit."

"Keep me advised."

Chatsworth disconnected the call. Something about that voice gave him chills. He wondered, not for the first time, if he had made a mistake getting involved with this project.

FOURTEEN

BERN'S LEVEL 90 PENTHOUSE WORKSPACE had, he liked to think, the finest views in London. When coming up with requirements for his 'statement' office, Bern had asked that the architects 'let go of their inhibitions'. The room was triple aspect and, if you included the luxury private apartment, took up fully half of the floor. His boardroom accounted for most of the other half, with a small reception area that housed his personal assistant and a security guard making up the balance.

Bern threw his coat on a stand and stretched his neck. He gave a passing glance at the angular steel sculpture his design team had spent weeks sourcing, then walked the not inconsiderable distance to his desk, deviating only slightly to skirt around the Persian rug that had cost fully half as much as his Aston Martin. He took his seat, then suddenly became aware he was not alone: he looked up and saw CERUS' head of HR, clad in his usual plain grey suit.

"Didn't see you there," Bern said with a frown.

Marron shrugged. "That would be the preferred title of my autobiography."

"Planning on writing one?"

"Writing, maybe. Publishing, no."

"Are you here for the meeting?"

"I wasn't invited. As you are well aware."

"Indeed. In fact I know it was arranged with the utmost secrecy, yet you clearly know all about it. What should I read from that?"

"That I'm doing my job."

"What about the work you've had taking place up on the roof? I haven't been able to land there since the party."

"Also me doing my job."

"I saw workmen carrying up a large number of metal rods but, when I went and had a look, I couldn't see any change."

"Exactly my intention."

"And also a large number of steel drums, which I *could* see. They look a bit out of place."

"They won't be there much longer. As you know."

Bern nodded distractedly. "Was there something we needed to discuss?"

"There was an incident with an employee earlier who fell in his office."

"Is it going to be a problem?"

"I believe I've managed the situation appropriately. He's at a private clinic."

Bern blinked. "Good. We don't need any complications right now. "

"I'd better go so your secret meeting can take place. I hope CERUS' most brilliant minds come through for you."

Bern watched Marron vanish into the shadows. *So do I*, he thought.

Bradley followed Heidn and Holm into Bern's office then locked the door. The CEO nodded to them and gestured towards a conference table across from his desk. They all sat and watched while Bern poured himself a glass of sparkling mineral water.

"You are familiar with our last set of financial results?" he said. "Those that suggest the company is tracking on target for the year."

There were nods from around the table.

"And also the rumours that have been circulating? About how CERUS is about to fail?"

More nods.

"The latter are a more accurate representation of our current status. And regrettably it's too late to contain the problem. The whole company will be lost if we don't produce a miracle in the next sixty days." Bern took a deep breath. "Thankfully, this miracle doesn't have to be something *new*. Two months ago I tasked Neil to trawl the archives for something we could do again, but *better*."

"Intelligent nanites?" Holm asked, adjusting his glasses. "That's why Bradley had me looking at those? I may have produced a null batch in the lab, but monetising the project... that's a *long* way off."

Bern nodded. "True. And yet nanites may provide a way to transform a much older project."

Heidn ran his fingers through his long grey hair. "You mean Tantalus?"

"This is what I was looking at?" Holm said. "I just saw some code. What exactly is it?"

Heidn cleared his throat. "Tantalus was a Greek demi-god, famous for his eternal punishment in hell. He was made to stand in a pool of water beneath a fruit tree, the fruit eluding his grasp, the water always receding before he could drink. It's where we get the word tantalize." Heidn leaned back in his chair. "The name was a joke but it became a challenge – a call to beat the odds and prove that it could be done."

Holm waved his hand in irritation. "Thanks for the story, but I don't care about the name. What was the project about?"

"An interface. A point where two systems would meet and interact. Man and machine."

Holm gave a snort. "A brain-computer interface? Twenty-five years ago? Did you even have computers then?"

Bradley sighed. "They had electricity and instant coffee too. Stop being ridiculous."

"But there are plenty of BCIs now. You can get headsets for game consoles that respond to brain pulses."

"Not like this one," Bern said. "This is a fully functional bi-directional neural interface. The computer doesn't interpret what you want it to do. It *knows*. The possibilities for such a system... It would be paradigm shifting."

"If it was so revolutionary – and I grant you it would have been twenty-five years ago – why did you stop work on it?"

Bern scratched his ear. "The client pulled their funding. Plus we lost one of the lead scientists. Tragic accident."

"What was so special about this old BCI headset over all those we have now?" asked Holm.

"It's not a headset," Bradley said. He slid a file across the table.

Holm flipped it open and whistled. "A computer chip implanted into a person's *brain*? Jesus."

"It was the only way back then." Bern paused. "It's not how we plan to do it this time."

"Wait," Holm said, "I thought we were just bouncing ideas around. You're saying we're actually talking about doing this?"

Bradley stood up and tapped a nearby section of wall. It slid back to reveal a display panel showing the CERUS logo. "A little while ago Mr Bern tasked me with looking at how old projects and new customers might interface, so to speak. One came up." He tapped the display and a wire-frame image appeared and rotated. "We have to make the interface talk to this."

"A helicopter?" Heidn asked. "You want us to make some type of auto-pilot system?"

The image moved to one side and a stream of specifications began scrolling down.

"Not just any helicopter," Holm said. "This is an airborne command centre." He paused. "Russian?"

"Yes," said Bern, "but not military. It's being developed by a private enterprise. For private customers."

"Look at the sensor array," Holm muttered. "That is quite a piece of hardware."

"I'm glad you approve, because we need you two geniuses to programme and implement it with a test subject."

"Hang on a sec. We've gone from hypotheticals to concrete plans to testing this on actual people in the last five minutes!"

"It's a requirement of a deliverable we've committed to," Bern said.

Holm whistled again.

Bradley nodded. "This time the process will be surgery free. The nanites will build the 'chip', which won't actually be a chip in any case. Let's call it a node. Anyway, it's not key-hole surgery. We're just talking an injection; the risks are minimal."

Heidn stood up. "We are supposed to be changing the world, William, not helping some rich man fly his helicopter. Tantalus was always about changing the way people interact with computers: getting rid of keyboards, touch-screens, even speech recognition and replacing it with something that works at the speed of thought."

Bern inclined his head. "I want what you want, I assure you.

Occasionally necessity dictates that there are some intermediary steps. And this one is necessary to secure the financial future of CERUS so that we can achieve our loftier goals."

"We'd have to go through years of preliminary tests," Holm said. "And who'd agree to be a guinea pig?"

"You just do your part and let the rest of us worry about those things. All I'm asking is *can it be done*?"

"Do we have your word that you intend to take this further?" Heidn asked. "That this isn't just a cash grab to prop up your retirement fund?"

Bern stood up. "I plan to take this *much* further." He looked around the room. "We have an opportunity to turn CERUS' problems into a defining moment. And those who come on board will be rewarded handsomely."

"I don't care about the money," Heidn said. "I want my work to *happen*."

"Hold on there," Holm said. "Some of us aren't indifferent to financial rewards."

"They will be success-based and most generous," Bradley said. "You won't be disappointed. In return, we require your complete attention and discretion: this project is not to be discussed outside those in this room."

"So you know the plan, you know the stakes, you know the rewards," said Bern. "Go make it happen."

FIFTEEN

DANIELLA LAWRENCE HEARD THE RASP as the ancient and overworked air-conditioner struggled against the midday heat. Outside the grimy window a huge cotton tree loomed over the open-air cafeteria, offering only the suggestion of shade. She stared at it for a moment, thinking she really ought to get some lunch, and then that she ought to try to service the air-conditioner. But there was too much other work to be done.

She leaned forward and focused through glasses that had been fashionable twenty years ago. In front of her were six test tubes, racked and housed inside a vacuum-sealed chamber. Six control strains of the Ebola variant that had arisen in central Sierra Leone. Various Big Pharma companies had provided test batches of candidate anti-virals and though Daniella didn't have much love for big business, in this situation she would take all the help she could get. So far it hadn't proven enough. She needed to add some variations of her own and find the one small change that would make all the difference.

Behind her, a man cleared his throat.

Lawrence turned and saw the director of the clinic standing in the doorway. By his standards, Dr Kimoto's smile was less than broad.

"Dr Lawrence," he said, "do you have a moment?"

"I'm just writing up this batch." She nodded to the test tubes.

"I'll keep it brief. If you please." And he walked away without waiting for a further response. She shrugged, following him down a corridor stacked with boxes of supplies, and into his office. He closed the door firmly and indicated the seat opposite his desk. "Your work here has been exemplary, if a little unorthodox." Kimoto took his own seat. "You bring a perspective I've not seen before in a virologist."

"I'm just trying to make a difference. Like everyone else here."

"And nobody appreciates that more than I. Of course the challenges we face are many, but we do still have procedures and processes. We are accountable. And that means I have to maintain oversight." He raised his eyebrows questioningly.

"Has there been a complaint about my work?"

"In the three months that you've been here? Not one. It takes a rare talent to come into a new research environment, shake up all the systems, and not put anyone's nose out of joint." He paused. "Quite frankly I'm amazed you haven't risen to a higher station in your field."

"I like to stay in the lab."

He shrugged. "Still, I was curious about your previous work. You've moved around a great deal."

"I've always gone wherever the need is greatest."

"And why did you come here to our humble facility?" He spread his hands. "To help others?" He paused. "I placed a call to a former colleague of mine at University College London. He read medicine at the same time as you at Edinburgh. Roxburgh was his name; I'm sure you remember him?"

Lawrence shifted in her chair. "I can't say it rings a bell."

"He remembered someone by your name. Someone who

looked quite different."

Daniella shrugged. "Perhaps his memory is as bad as mine."

"The Daniella Lawrence my colleague knew at Edinburgh had only three fingers on her left hand. Now, either you grew them back or you aren't who you say you are." He patted his palm on his desk. "Shall I keep digging? It's confusing, because your knowledge and skill are no fraud, even if your papers are."

Daniella let out a slow breath. "Do you know how many hospitals and missions I've worked in over the last twenty years? None of them have asked these questions. None of them cared when I was so good at my job." She sighed. "I'll leave tomorrow if you want, though I'd rather stay a few more days: then I can put the project in shape to be handed over."

"What I'm worried about is whether the trouble in your past is likely to follow you here."

Daniella let out a long breath and smiled. "They don't even know *to* look for me."

He blinked several times. "Then, Dr Lawrence, keep on doing what you do. And I will say nothing further about this. To anyone."

"I appreciate your discretion."

"And *we* appreciate your hard work." Kimoto lowered his voice. "But perhaps it would be wise to appear a little less brilliant so that you don't arouse anyone else's suspicions."

"I'll keep that in mind." She stood and turned to leave.

"Before you go, your mail arrived." He handed her two medical journals wrapped in clear plastic and a copy of the *Financial Times*. "Do I need to know why you pay a small fortune to get the *FT* delivered every day?"

She grinned. "I like to keep abreast of current affairs back home. Let's just say that no one knows to look for me, but that doesn't mean I don't intend to watch them."

SIXTEEN

KATE EASED BACK IN HER chair, staring at the finished copy of her report spread out across the dining room table. Her eyes stung from a lack of sleep and too much coffee. In the day and a half since meeting with Armstrong, she had called in favours, accessed internet databases that were not readily accessible, and reviewed hundreds upon hundreds of pages of information. From all of this she had begun to draw a picture as startling as it was alarming. Now, she just needed approval to publish.

A bell in the hall clanged loudly. Kate padded down the corridor and pulled open the front door. Geraldine stood there holding two bottles of red wine, her expression weary.

"I've come to see if you've really been working or just painting your nails and watching soap operas."

"If only." Kate frowned. "You brought *two* bottles?"

Geraldine pushed past her. "I wasn't sure how tedious this was going to get. Maybe two won't be enough."

Kate closed the door and grabbed one of the bottles. "Your enthusiasm is so motivational."

"It's been a difficult week." She sniffed the air. "Did you order food? Or is there a chef next door?"

"Thai. It's in the kitchen."

"Then why are we standing here?"

Five minutes later they had assaulted the various dishes and Geraldine was on her second glass of wine. Kate sipped hers slowly and tapped the folder in the middle of the table. "When you're ready, boss."

Geraldine folded a crispy duck pancake together. She made a gesture for Kate to carry on.

"It's finished. Just needs your approval." Kate put down her glass. "But it turns out the real story's not CERUS's financial troubles."

Geraldine let out a sigh. "Oh great. Another disgruntled employee trying to push an exposé on Bern's personal life. Nobody cares, Kate."

"If it was that, I would have told you over the phone. Look, Richard Armstrong has been there from the start. He knows things. CERUS *is* in financial trouble, but the *real* story is what they're going to do to avoid it." Kate leaned closer. "Armstrong said they're looking to old research: projects that were shut down."

"The story people will want to read," Geraldine said, "is a thirty billion company failing."

"Not when they hear why the old research was shut down. People died."

"How? When?"

"He hasn't told me yet," Kate said. "I don't think it was recent."

"You don't *think*?" Geraldine slapped the folder. "What the hell is this if you don't *know*?"

"I've searched through every story relating to CERUS: everything from the last twenty-eight years." She paused. "And I found nothing."

"So Armstrong is lying." Geraldine took a long drink of wine.

"Wonderful."

"I don't think so. The one thing I did find was a lot of rumours about their earlier work involving bio modification and bio compatibility: about synthesising materials that work harmoniously with the human body."

"Like a hip replacement? Crazy *and* boring."

"That's one example. Or a pacemaker. The important thing is that Armstrong's a career scientist, not a lawyer or a marketer. He *could* know about something that was hushed up. And there *is* one relevant death on record: one of the scientists on a nanotech project. Dr Dominique Lentz. Given her areas of expertise I think she might have worked with Armstrong."

"Kate, those are some interesting bits and pieces, but it isn't a story. You haven't give me a single hard fact about any of these things being connected. Sure, people in suits going to prison always sells." Geraldine shrugged. "But this is still all conjecture."

"Actually, no, it isn't." She turned around to unlock a chest of drawers. From the top one, she removed a black metal box. She flipped the combination lock to the correct code and opened it to reveal a padded interior. From within, she lifted a small glass vial and placed it on the table.

Geraldine peered closer. "And what is that? Some sort of chemical?"

"Nanotech."

Geraldine flinched back. "You're kidding."

"Inert nano is pretty common now - it's simply a change to the way a material works on a nano scale. With inert nano, you can increase conductivity, reduce friction coefficients, but the change is a fixed one."

"So this is inert nano?"

"No. Armstrong said it was the other kind - intelligent nano. It changes reactively, based on data received and interpreted: the particles can adjust to variations in circumstance, including what is happening to other particles. They can talk to each other, adapt, and change. They communicate. At least they can once they're programmed."

"Presuming the scientists are right. Can these things learn? What if they lose control?"

Kate shrugged. "That is of course the principal reason intelligent nano is banned. That nanites might get to the point they can make their own decisions – evolve their own programming. And yet the potential for things like smart drugs, manufacturing, computing is undeniable."

Geraldine reached out and picked up the vial. "This guy, Armstrong. He was one of the nanotech team?"

Kate nodded. "And he's a company man. Twenty seven years." She picked up her glass and took a long sip. "He says he's not after money: claims it's just about stopping the research before it gets out of hand like it did twenty-five years ago."

Geraldine's eyes narrowed. "If there's even a grain of truth in this, it's a huge risk for him to speak to you." She paused. "Despite his reluctance to go to the authorities, I think it's our duty to inform them. And this," she waggled the vial in the air, "is stolen property. We can't keep quiet about it."

Kate sighed.

"So let's be publicly loud, say, in a lead story." Geraldine stood. "If we're doing this, we can't afford to sit on it. First thing tomorrow, get on the phone and set up another meeting with Armstrong. Get the story: the whole story." Geraldine leaned over and picked up the folder. "And you know what? I might even read this." She hefted it in her hand and frowned. "Or at least some of it."

SEVENTEEN

DESPITE EVERYTHING THAT HAD HAPPENED to him since Friday night, Tom refused to miss his mother's anniversary. He usually went alone, but Dr Chatsworth and Jo had been adamant that it was not a good idea. In the end, they had compromised. Jo collected him from the Angstrom Clinic first thing in the morning in her reconditioned Mini Metro, which alternately stuttered and purred its way down the private road and out of the gates. A quick stop at a florist and they were heading northwest towards the M40.

Two hours later, they were sixty miles outside of London in the tiny Oxfordshire village of Kingsford. They parked and Tom walked ahead. The gravestone was a simple granite slab, located at the rear of a walled field, opposite the small church. Tom's mother lay amongst the former school teachers, farmers, stockbrokers and shopkeepers of the small rural community that had welcomed her into its heart in the months before her passing. He stood looking around the carefully tended plots.

Her death had been uncomfortably like the chaotic last few days. It had all happened so quickly. One moment she had been in perfect health, the next they were diagnosing her with terminal cancer. She had been based in the south of France at the time, in an old run-down villa in the mountains, while Tom lived in London during term-time, studying Law at University College London. After the diagnosis she had reluctantly moved back to the UK, taking an experimental course of treatment at a private hospital. Less than nine months later she was gone.

Of course with hindsight he'd realised that she must have been feeling unwell, but why had she never mentioned at the regular health checks she'd always gone to? Surely they couldn't have missed how ill she was if she'd given them any indication. Or maybe the health checks had been to do with her illness in the first place. Maybe the illness wasn't new at all and his mother had decided not to burden him.

He wished he could go back and notice something, or say something to get her to confide in him. Of course it would have been hard, but nothing could have been harder than suddenly losing his only family. His father had died when Tom was only a few months old and both his parents had been only children. Jo was the closest thing he had to family now. He glanced over his shoulder and saw her standing at the edge of the graveyard, her hands in the pockets of her coat.

Tom knelt by the gravestone and brushed aside a couple of stray weeds that had started to encroach. Then he removed the daffodils – plain and simple, as she always preferred – from their wrapping and placed them loosely in the small vase at the front of the grave.

"Happy birthday, Mum," he whispered.

Then he stood and walked back to Jo.

They stopped at a roadside café on the outskirts of Oxford. Tom cast his eye over the menu and ordered a huge all-day brunch.

"Your appetite hasn't suffered from the poking and prodding they've been doing at the hospital then," Jo said, as she chose a tuna salad.

He shrugged. "What can I say? I feel great. Getting the all clear from the clinic was a huge relief."

She frowned. "All clear? Really?"

"You were there. You heard the doctor."

Jo drummed her fingers on the table. "I heard what he said. I just... I can't believe you're not more freaked out."

The waitress reappeared and placed two large mugs of coffee in front of them. Tom waited until she had returned to the kitchen before speaking. "Freaked out about what?"

"Someone gave you hard drugs. They could have killed you."

"We don't know that I didn't choose to take them."

Jo pulled at her ponytail. "Seriously? Tom, that is so not you. It's just not possible."

"OK," he said. "But why would anyone give me drugs if I didn't agree in some moment of drunken idiocy? I wasn't robbed. I wasn't assaulted. I wasn't cut into pieces for my organs and spare parts."

Jo made a face.

"I could have died or suffered life-changing side effects, but that didn't happen. What's more my brand new employer has stepped in to cover the best medical care money can buy."

Jo sniffed. "Whatever happened started at that party. Maybe CERUS are keen to look after you for more than simple liability reasons." Jo shook her head. "The whole thing stinks."

Tom hesitated. "The HR director did make some comment about having had a lot of bad press on the building: said he wanted to avoid a story about a design fault causing an injury."

"Well there you go. All about protecting their interests, not yours."

"But what do you expect me to do? Go poking about asking questions? What if CERUS finds out I've taken drugs? What if they've got CCTV footage of me getting high with this woman in the black dress and they just don't want trouble over it happening in their sparkling new office building where every square inch is meant to be monitored."

Their food arrived and they ate in silence for several minutes. Then Tom cleared his throat. "Look, I appreciate your concern, Jo. But I feel like I've had a lucky escape. Now's not the time to go pushing my luck."

"Fine, but I think it's a mistake."

EIGHTEEN

CELIA BERN SAT AT THE best table in one of the best restaurants in London. To her left a huge window looked across at Tower Bridge, the two floodlit towers rising high above the Thames. Behind it was the Tower of London, location of the original 'watergate': predating the US scandal by several centuries, it always amused her American friends. But she was not meeting a friend today.

She sipped from a glass of Chardonnay and surveyed the restaurant. City types were wooing clients all around, with the odd celebrity for colour: all mid-level movers and shakers. She moved in higher circles and intended it to stay that way.

A young, smartly-dressed figure approached her table. "Mind if I join you?" he asked in a tone that suggested he fully expected her to say yes.

Celia looked up and gestured with one carefully manicured hand. "Have a seat."

Neil Bradley slid smoothly into the chair opposite. "Isn't this a little public?"

"Excellent acoustic dampening, very hard to be overheard, plus," she pointed at the window, "I like the view."

"The bridge?"

"And the Tower. That's where they used to deal with traitors, you know."

"I hope you don't think of us in that way."

She laughed. "I'm sure neither of us would want our head on a spike." She beckoned to the sommelier, who poured Bradley a glass of wine.

"What's good here?" he asked.

"Everything. Order what you like. William's paying."

The waiter reappeared and they ordered. She selected roast partridge in a clementine sauce; he chose herbed venison cutlets on a bed of couscous. Alone again, they clinked glasses.

"So," she said, "you have an update for me?"

Bradley nodded. "He met with the customer yesterday. It went well."

"Say what you will about William, he always has been a salesman."

"And we've got the scientists on board."

"No protests?"

"None that money and professional ambition couldn't overcome." Bradley shrugged. "Are you sure *you* want to do this?"

She smiled. "Such concern for my welfare. Something I've not seen from my husband in a decade."

Bradley's eyes flickered. "Then he's not as smart as I was led to believe."

Celia tipped her head. "You're cute, Neil, but right now I need you to be sharp."

"OK. Although why not just divorce him?"

She drained her wine glass. The sommelier immediately moved to fill it but she waved him away. "I haven't shared the photos with you, Neil. I don't feel any need to, but I'm sure you'd find them diverting. All of them young, mostly blonde, all tanned and... supple, I think is the word. I could just leave him but believe me when I say he has very good lawyers. It wouldn't be quick and he'd make it ugly. I want it all on *my* terms." She paused. "There's also the little problem that he has lost most of his money. By which I mean *my* money. I need those coffers replenished. Once the new Tantalus project is up and running, all I have to do is threaten to reveal it to the government and... well, I'm sure he'll see it my way. Either he can give me CERUS or he can give up his freedom *and* CERUS. I shall delight in watching him chose."

NINETEEN

IT WAS NEARLY 2AM BUT Richard Armstrong was not asleep. He sat in bed, working on his laptop, reviewing yet another set of recent data from Project Tantalus. Downstairs, his dog barked at something outside, most likely a fox, but Armstrong didn't even look up. There was so much to do, so much data to process and catalogue, and then to hide.

He rubbed his forehead and looked at the empty whisky glass on the bedside table. Next to it was the cheap mobile phone that he'd bought especially for his plans. The reporter had been trying to contact him. She'd be better prepared this time, he was sure. He was about to make her career, to change her life, but how would it change his? Things would get ugly, no doubt; CERUS would try to discredit him, to dig up skeletons in his past. And of course there were a few. But *he* wasn't what mattered. What they were doing couldn't be allowed to continue. The world needed to know. He would live with the consequences.

Armstrong's laptop beeped. His internet access had dropped out. A quick diagnostic revealed the router was operational, but had lost its net connection. It would probably need a manual reboot, which meant a trip downstairs. Sighing, he put the laptop down, padding to the top of the staircase. His hand flicked at the light switch.

The light did not come on.

He frowned again and moved carefully down the stairs in the darkness. Perhaps something electrical had flared and tripped the fuse for downstairs, though usually it popped when that happened, triggering a barking frenzy.

"Hey, boy?" he called out. "You all right?" He moved into the kitchen and froze. In the moonlight streaming through the window he could see his dog lying on the floor.

Before he could move, someone spoke from behind him. "Take a seat, Richard. At the kitchen table." It was a woman's voice. Educated. Calm.

He spun in shock, but was blinded by the flare of a torch. Behind it he could just make out the silhouette of the intruder: a slender figure a little shorter than him. "Who the hell are you? What have you done to my dog?"

"I'm someone who wants to talk to you." She waved the torch. "And for what it's worth, I would never kill an animal: your dog's just sleeping."

"I'm calling the police." He began to move towards the phone on the kitchen bench. In the partial light he didn't see how quickly she moved. In less than a breath she'd caught his left arm and was twisting it sharply behind his back; he felt the joints strain and threaten to crack. He started to scream, but her elbow drove deep into his stomach and all he managed was a gasp.

"You're not calling anyone." Her voice was perfectly calm. She pushed him roughly into one of the seats at the kitchen table then took a step back.

His head spun with the rush. "There's money upstairs. I have a gold watch--"

She took the seat opposite him. "I didn't come here for your watch."

Armstrong felt his stomach knot. "I don't know who you think I am. I'm just an engineer."

"I know exactly who you are. And who you work for."

He swallowed. "I'm not permitted to talk about that."

She raised an eyebrow. "You want to play that card?"

"My employer takes secrecy very seriously."

"It's a pity you didn't."

Armstrong felt the temperature in the room drop.

"You've been collating company data off the servers. Who have you given it to?"

He shook his head. "No one. I mean, that's not true."

She leaned forward, putting her elbows on the table. "What did you do with the nanites?"

He felt his breath sticking in his throat.

She rolled her eyes then leaned back, reaching into her lightweight jacket. She took out a pistol fitted with a silencer and placed it on the table.

Armstrong blew out a hard breath. "You expect me to believe that's a real gun?"

She shook her head. "You're really not grasping this situation." In a fluid motion she picked up the weapon and pulled the trigger.

Even with a silencer, the gun was loud. Armstrong felt a hot, scorching sensation across his leg where the bullet had missed him by a hair's breadth.

His voice started to crack. "I found out that CERUS has restarted nano manufacture." He looked at the brown burn mark on his trouser leg. "What's to stop you shooting me once I tell you?"

"I promise that if you answer my questions, I will not shoot you with this gun. I also promise that I *will* shoot you if you don't."

Armstrong swallowed. "I wanted to know why I'd been left off of the team involved in all the hush-hush important meetings, so I started digging."

Her eyes narrowed. "Did you share what you found with anyone?"

"I've passed no details across yet."

"I'm pleased to hear it."

"But somebody should," he hurried on. "This project is like Pandora's Box. We have no idea where it will lead." Armstrong shook his head. "And you're too young to know what happened last time."

She smiled. "I'm not actually."

He frowned. "But--"

She slid the pistol back in her inside pocket, then pulled out a different weapon. "This is a tranquilliser gun. It's what I used on your dog." She aimed it at him and raised an eyebrow. "What I *said* was I wouldn't shoot you with the other gun."

And she pulled the trigger.

The woman watched the dart hit Armstrong in the neck, his shock turning immediately to stupor. It only took seconds for him to fall unconscious. She laid him gently on the floor, next to his dog. Then she turned the oven and all the burners on the gas cooker on, leaving them unlit. Next, she placed a small black box with an antenna and single switch by Armstrong's foot. She opened the door to leave then, with a sigh, she walked back and dragged the dog out, closing the door behind her. She hid the dog in a bush away from the house. Then she walked away, pulling out an encrypted cell phone and dialling a number from memory.

A man's voice replied. "Identify."

"It's Alex," she said. "We caught him in time."

"Good. Clean up and leave."

She ended the call, then dialled a second number and pressed send.

Behind her the night lit up with the blossom of a huge explosion, but she did not react. She just kept walking.

TWENTY

THE SUN SHONE OVER DOCKLANDS, though in the distance Tom saw a cluster of dark clouds. This time the CERUS security gates were fully functional, as were the lifts; in moments he was walking into his office, giving his desk a slightly wary glance. With careful movements he eased into his high-backed chair and let out a slow breath.

He'd returned to the clinic for an early morning check-up. Chatsworth had seemed pleased with his progress. They still wanted him to return daily, but the doctor stressed it was merely a precaution.

Samantha appeared at the door. "Morning," she said. "How are you feeling?"

"Better thanks," replied Tom.

"Try not to run before you can walk this time!" She smiled. "Your new company mobile is in your desk drawer by the way."

"What meetings do I have today?"

"I don't think you have anything yet. We didn't know if..." she hesitated, "*when* you'd be back."

Tom frowned. "I spoke to an engineer at the launch party. I think he wanted to meet this week. Hasn't he been in touch?"

"Nobody contacted me, but I can look him up if you like."

Tom sighed. "He didn't give me his name. I'm pretty sure his nametag said 'Ric' if that helps."

Samantha shook her head. "We have 25,000 staff. I'll need more than that."

"Yeah, but we're only talking the 100 or so CERUS staff who were at the party: a male engineer whose name started 'Ric'... Can't be too many of people who fit that profile."

"I'll go and have a look for you. Anything else?"

Tom closed his eyes. Perhaps he should just let this lie. Perhaps he shouldn't poke around for answers he might not like. He opened his eyes. "I also want to see the press photos from the party."

Samantha looked puzzled, but shrugged. "I'll see what I can do." She turned and left.

Tom slid open his desk drawer and picked up the mobile, noting it was fully charged and ready to go. Then he eased back in his chair and turned to the keyboard and shiny oversized monitor: ultra hi-res to display multiple pages of legal documents simultaneously. He reached out a hand to log in, but the screen winked on, flashing 'Good Morning, Tom.' He knew it was simply reading the ID card he carried, but it was still a little unnerving. He glanced over his messages; he'd only been with the company a few days, but already there were hundreds.

"Do you have a moment?" called a voice.

Tom looked up and saw Peter Marron smiling from the doorway. "Of course."

"It's good to see you, Tom, but should you be back in the office so soon?"

"I'm doing fine. I really appreciate the company covering the clinic to make sure, though."

Marron raised a hand. "No need to thank us. And believe me,

it was as much in our interests as yours."

Samantha reappeared. "Excuse me, Mr Marron. Tom, I worked out who the engineer was: Richard Armstrong."

Marron blinked. "Why were you asking after him?"

Tom shrugged. "I spoke to him at the launch party." He turned to his secretary. "Is he free to meet?"

"He seems to be out of the office today. I left a message for him to call you. As for the press photos, they're not available without authorisation from the executive team." She nodded in Marron's direction and strode away.

"Press photos?" asked Marron. "I thought this was the legal department?"

Tom took a deep breath. "I'm trying to reconstruct my evening. After my fall I'm having some memory lapses. I thought the photos might spark something."

"Well, I think we can do better than the press photos. I'll arrange for you to view the CCTV footage."

Tom smiled. "That would be great."

TWENTY-ONE

BERN STEPPED OUT OF THE lift on Level 64. Unlike the buzzing floors below and above, this one was quiet. Few CERUS ID cards even permitted access. In fact, as far as the system was concerned, Level 64 was not open for use. Temporary floor-to-ceiling screens divided the lobby from the rest of the level. Across the screens were notices reading RESTRICTED ACCESS: AREA AWAITING COMPLETION. And yet, in the middle of the screens, there was a high-specification security door. Bern approached it and placed his hand on the scanner. With a chime, the door swung inwards. Beyond was a self-contained research facility. Two labs, several small rooms, a tiny kitchen and a bathroom, all set up to allow its occupants to work undisturbed twenty-four hours a day. Bern walked into the largest lab, which was humming with the fans of a dozen high-powered servers and the steady suck of high-capacity air-filtration units. In one corner stood a gleaming black cylinder, twice the size of a dustbin: it was the most expensive piece of equipment in the room.

"Hey, Boss." Holm, clad in jeans and a navy t-shirt, walked over from one the workbenches. "Come to check on the geniuses?"

"I was told you had something to show me."

Heidn stood up from a desk at the far side of the room, his grey hair looking more than usually dishevelled. "Is Bradley coming? We don't want to do this twice."

"He had a call. And I'm not waiting."

Heidn glanced at Holm. "We're making good progress, thanks to how well-resourced we are here."

"Whatever you need." Bern shrugged. "Any questions about what's keeping you so busy?"

"No more than usual, but I'll let you know if anyone develops a particular interest." Heidn walked over to the shiny black cylinder and patted it. "Current yield on the nano vat is fifteen per cent, but we'll improve it."

"How long per batch?"

"Twelve to fourteen hours. We haven't managed to get them to coalesce any quicker, but it's acceptable in any case."

"Given how much time and money we've spent on this over the years, I'd have thought we'd do better."

"That's a reflection on not focusing on building intravenous nanotech. A significant portion of our research has been *wasted* on the synthesis of nanomaterials for the Resurface Project." He ran a hand through his grey hair. "We need to get back to work of real importance. We could be refining our understanding of how to use the nanites as a delivery mechanism to boost bodily functions or block undesired processes: we could be delivering controllable, tailorable treatments for cancer and heart disease."

"Personally, I want to get back to the truth nano," Holm said. "Chemical-free sodium pentothal: what's not to like!" He paused. "Well, other than the side effects, but--" Holm cut himself off, adjusting his glasses. "Anyway, back to our project. As intelligent nanites are inactive until they're coded that is where my magic comes in. I've parsed the helicopter operating system and I'm working on APIs with the nanites' base code. The bigger task is updating those clunky old Tantalus protocols, but I've been able to re-use a lot of code, even some of the interface systems used in this building." He turned to a desk and picked up a black box the size of a shoebox, with a small touchscreen display. "This control box effectively simulates how the interface will connect with the helicopter." He smiled. "Now, we just need to recreate it in our test subjects. We're trawling through the possible candidates, but it's hard getting quality subjects to volunteer these days."

"What are you telling them?"

"That we're developing a new type of brain scanner – the next generation in CAT scans – and that we need to inject a contrast dye during some of the testing for comparison purposes."

"But won't they notice if the nanites activate?"

"We're hoping they won't really understand what's going on. And once we demonstrate to the customer that they're viable, we just wipe the nanites by activating the fail-safes so that the node they've built becomes inactive. Then we thank the volunteers, they go on their way and everybody wins."

"But what if they ever get ill?" asked Bern. "Wouldn't the node show up on a scan?"

"It's not metallic so it's very unlikely. At the most a doctor would think it's a shadow or possibly a small benign tumour: ones of that size are not uncommon and, given the location, unlikely to need further investigation. If a subject did have brain surgery in that specific location, then I suppose it might be an issue but it's most unlikely anyone would realise what the node was, let alone connect it to us. No, the key thing is making sure we stay in control of the nanites. We've left some of the safety measures the government insisted on when they were involved in the previous project, like all our nanites can be deactivated by remotely sending a specific code, although it must be used with great caution because it's likely to cause temporary paralysis in the subject." He held up a remote control. "A controller like this can send out the right signal over a five metre range."

"We also added our own safeguards," Heidn added. "Each active nanite emits a coded trace signal, at a very low frequency well outside the range of normal detection equipment. Should any of our nanites get stolen, we'll be able to track and retrieve them."

"And where are we going to perform the process once we have the subjects?" Bern asked.

"The key thing is that we keep them separate from this building. The name of CERUS must never be mentioned. No employee except the special lab teams must ever see them." Heidn adjusted his glasses. "Above all, it would help if we could bring some other team members in. There's just too much work to be done in the time. Something has to give. Would you prefer it to be the timeframe or the team size?"

Bern narrowed his eyes. "I'll involve Marron. I think he can make a difference."

"We need engineers and scientists, not help hiring from HR: we can give you names."

"Marron knows people. And security."

"He seems to *run* security," said Heidn, shaking his head.

Bern was about to answer when a soft alarm sounded. The heavy door opened and Bradley walked through. His face was grim. "Sorry to keep you waiting, but I had a call from the police. There's been an accident. Richard Armstrong was killed in a gas explosion at his home last night."

Bern sighed. "Were we planning on using him for this project?"

Holm turned away, scrubbing a hand over his face. "This is terrible."

"We're all sorry this has happened, Ed," said Bern, "but we have to keep moving forward."

"William, really," said Heidn. "Give us a moment."

Bern shook his head. "We don't have that luxury. This project is bigger than any of us: than all of us."

TWENTY-TWO

GEORGE CROFT WAS WHISTLING AS he walked up to the door of the elegant Georgian House, just a couple of streets over from Regents Park. He had enjoyed a very pleasant lunch at the Ivy and was feeling convivial. He placed his palm on the panel next to the door and heard it click open. Stepping into the deeply shadowed interior, he removed his coat and nodded towards the familiar form of the guard standing to attention halfway along the hall.

"Good afternoon, Mr Croft. How was lunch?" the guard asked.

Croft smiled, marvelling at how the guard could look so relaxed with an automatic weapon swinging from his hip. "Any news?"

"She's here," he said quietly. "Has been for more than an hour."

Croft's smile vanished. "Then I'd better not keep her waiting any longer." He placed his palm on a matt black panel on the wall and a pair of double doors swung open. "Wish me luck."

Stephanie Reems sat in Croft's chair, speaking rapidly into his phone. She glanced up as he walked in and waved him into the visitor's seat opposite her. She looked, thought Croft, considerably greyer two years after her appointment as the head of MI5. Although she was his immediate superior, he saw her in person only a few times a year, mostly on social occasions: that she had come to see him without an appointment was significant. Reems cradled the receiver and frowned across the desk at him. "Nice long lunch, George?"

Croft glanced at his watch. It was nearly 4pm. "I was with the Chief Commissioner, maintaining interdepartmental relations."

She shook her head. "It's the twenty-first century. I can't believe that business still revolves around flexing your expense account. And isn't he your second cousin?"

"On my mother's side. Which is why I was given the detail in the first place. From experience I know he's usually more pliable after a decent meal."

"Then I look forward to your report." She eased back in his chair. "I understand you called my office this morning."

"Yes, Ma'am. Although I expected to come to you."

"I was in the area. What was it about?"

"Someone on a watch list has come to my attention. Richard Armstrong, an engineer at CERUS Biotech, died yesterday. A gas explosion." He reached across his desk and tapped a card folder. "It's all in here."

Reems nodded and flicked through the pages. "Looks like an accident."

"Isn't that what I'm supposed to check? I'll liaise with the Crime Scene Investigation Unit: visit the scene, and conduct my own analysis. And I'll dig into Mr Armstrong's recent activities, speak with CERUS: see if anything pops."

"I suppose that sounds sensible."

He paused. "Ma'am, is there something I should know? You'd usually just tell me to get on with it."

"CERUS has very expensive lawyers. They won't take kindly to you poking around." She stood up. "Get things underway, but keep it low key. No one else in the department must know about this unless you consider it absolutely necessary. You report to me and me alone."

TWENTY-THREE

KATE PARKED HER CAR AND switched off the lights, but didn't move to get out. Instead, she just sat and stared at the police cordon ahead, staffed by a number of officers. She shouldn't be here, staring at what was left of Armstrong's house. She knew what Geraldine was going to say when she finally started answering her boss's calls: that it was an accident. That accidents happen, even in suspicious circumstances – and that *this* accident meant the opportunity was over. But she'd promised her boss a story. She's promised herself a story: something jaw-dropping to get her career back on track. Armstrong might be gone, but the story wasn't. She just needed a new source. Maybe, with Armstrong dead, someone else might be running scared at CERUS and would be willing to blow the lid with sufficient monetary persuasion. She just needed to find that person.

She unclipped her seatbelt and stepped from the car.

"Can I help you, Madam?" asked a clipped voice from just behind her.

Kate spun to see a uniformed policeman frowning at her. She hadn't realised any of the officers were so close. "I'm press." She reached into her pocket and produced her ID card.

He took it from her and examined it closely, then removed a device from his pocket and seemed to swipe it.

"What's that?" she asked.

"Just for our records," he replied, handing the card back to her.

"That's rather hi-tech." She glanced around and noticed that none of the other officers were close to them. "Can I go take a look?"

He tilted his head to one side. "We finished the press conference earlier and there's no more access to the scene until the morning."

"Look, I got stuck in traffic and my editor will kill me if I don't--"

"Your ID says you work for a business journal. I wouldn't think you'd normally cover accidents."

"Was it an accident?"

His eyes narrowed. "Why do you ask?"

"It would be a better story if there was foul play. You know, I've spoken to a lot police officers over the years and there is something not quite right about all this. About you. You behave more like a detective and it's interesting that none of the other officers seem to want anything to do with you. I wonder what would happen if I called one of them over here to talk to us both about our ID."

His smile vanished. He pulled a phone from his pocket and listened to it, although Kate had not heard it ring. "If you'll excuse me, I have something to attend to. Good talking to you, Ms Turner, but I suggest you go home now."

She watched him walk to the cordon and speak to the policewoman on duty. For a moment she considered marching over and asking her own questions. She was exactly who she said she was and, as a reporter, she was entitled to attend a scene like this and be curious.

Only, of course, she wasn't just a reporter being nosy: she was a reporter who'd planned to write an exposé based on the evidence of the man whose house had just blown up with him in it. Now wasn't the time to push her luck. Kate turned, got back into her car and drove away.

A few blocks on, she pulled up to the curb and dialled Geraldine's number. "I've just been to his house," she said the moment the call was answered. "I couldn't get into the scene, but I had a weird conversation with someone in a police uniform who wasn't like any cop I've ever met. His ID code was 633-751. Do me a favour and look him up."

"Kate, what have you done?"

"I need to find a new source at CERUS. When we met, Armstrong said something about speaking with the new company lawyer. It's a start. And we still have the nanites."

"If that's what's really in the test tube. Could be green dye number five and some shavings of tinfoil. Maybe Armstrong blew his own house up because he's a nut." Geraldine hesitated. "Or maybe you're right. But if you are, this story just got someone killed. You're a scientist, why don't you look at our glittery little present and see what it really is? Though if it is something, we need to weigh the risks... not just the risk of the story but the risks of *not* bringing the police in."

Kate sighed. "You're right. Just... give me a day, OK? I'll see if I can find the lawyer – I'll tread carefully, I promise. If I can't find a new source by the end of the day, I'll reach out to a contact who still works as a researcher: get some time on an electron microscope and see what exactly Armstrong put in that test tube."

Geraldine was quiet for a moment. "I'll hold you to that promise. Keep me updated."

Kate disconnected the call and gripped the steering wheel,

breathing slowly. It was time to get creative about chasing the story.

TWENTY-FOUR

IT WAS 7:30AM WHEN Tom walked through the front door of his apartment.

Jo sat at the kitchen table eating a slice of thick, buttered toast. She raised a curious eyebrow. "Out all night? Anything you want to share?"

"Sorry to disappoint – just an early check-up at the clinic." Tom took a seat at the table. "I got the all clear. The doctor almost looked distraught."

"I'm sure you were a good source of income while it lasted." She looked down at a folder open on the table. "Come and help me with my Italian exam."

"How am I supposed to do that?"

She handed over a large sheet of paper with a list of words written in very small font. "Test me."

Tom's eyes flickered over the page. "I can't pronounce any of this."

"Say the English. I'll do the Italian."

"How will I know if you got it right?"

"We'll muddle through."

Tom tested her for what his watch said was fifteen minutes,

though it felt longer.

"You should give this a try," said Jo. She held up her textbook and turned to the description on the back. "*Learning a new language is a wonderful experience. Make new connections through the power of communication.*"

He snatched it from her and flicked through the pages. "I can see. Lots of nice pictures."

"Oh shut up, you. Why do I bother?"

Tom handed the book back and stood up. "Actually I've tried learning languages before. Never managed to keep any of it in."

"How you made it through law school, I will never know. I thought you had to remember hundreds of cases."

"Rote learning: most of it was gone a week later. You know, if I were to spend time learning a language, it would be Java or C++."

"You want to be able to talk to a computer? What would a lawyer need with that?" She laughed. "Just tap icons like everybody else."

Tom shrugged. "Maybe you're right. Anyway, *buona fortuna* with the test."

She tipped her head. "Oh, by the way, did you hear about that guy at your company whose house blew up?"

"What?"

She picked up her newspaper and handed it to him. "I'm sure everyone will be talking about it when you get to work. Read up on your way in."

◇ ◇ ◇

The Jubilee Line train jostled and bumped its way down the tunnel, but Tom was not aware of the jerking of the carriage. He continued to stare at the photo on the front page of Jo's newspaper. Richard Armstrong: the engineer from the launch party who had tried to talk with him. The story didn't say much: a faulty gas cooker, just him in the house. The police were investigating the scene but preliminary indications were that it was just a tragic accident.

He wasn't sure why the story was so unsettling. There was no reason to believe Armstrong's death was anything other than an awful coincidence. Yet the man had seemed agitated about something at the party. He could see his face vividly in his mind. What had he been trying to say?

The journey passed quickly, and almost before Tom knew it, he was back at CERUS Tower. He looked up as he walked through the entrance way, reflexively waving his card at the security gate and heading for the lift. Around him he could almost feel the building buzzing. Before he could reach the lift, he heard someone call his name. One of the security guards was hurrying over from the front desk.

"Mr Faraday! I was instructed to intercept you. Mr Marron asked that I take you to the CCTV suite."

Tom followed the guard to a service elevator. Heavy doors clunked together then they descended to Level Minus 2.

"I've not been below ground before here," he said as they stepped into a brightly lit corridor. "How far down does it go?"

She shrugged. "A ways. Along here, please."

At the end of the corridor she opened a security door and they walked into a room with a huge bank of display screens, the central one covering half the wall.

"I have the footage from the launch event ready," she said, typing onto a keypad. "If you care to look at the main screen."

An image of the function room on Level 69 appeared, with people setting up the stage and the lighting. The guard tapped the controls and the video accelerated then slowed as guests started to arrive.

"Anything in particular you're looking for?" she asked.

"I wanted to know who I spoke to. I'm having trouble remembering some details about the evening."

"Why don't I speed things up?" She tapped the controls.

Tom watched as people seemed to scurry into the room. He saw himself arrive and stand near the back. The security guard paused the footage as Tom spoke with Neil Bradley then with Samantha. The room suddenly got much brighter as Bern arrived on stage and began his speech. Then Tom saw himself talking with Armstrong, until the engineer abruptly hurried off. Bern swung the bottle of champagne and smashed it on the second attempt. When the CEO left, the main spotlights were turned off and the room dimmed again. Moments later, the woman in the black dress appeared.

"Pause it," Tom said, pointing at the screen. "Who is she?"

The guard adjusted the controls and zoomed in. "I can't get a clear image." Her hands danced over the controls. As the face got larger it seemed to pixelate. The guard sighed. "The resolution appears degraded. The lower light doesn't help. I can make the image larger, but not sharper."

"Is there another camera?"

"There are four in the room, but the others cover different angles."

"Fine. Roll it forward then."

Tom watched as the woman handed him a glass of what he remembered had been cognac. Then the image went dark.

"What happened?" asked Tom.

"I don't know," replied the guard. "That's all there is."

"I'm afraid," said a voice from the doorway, "that we've been having some teething problems with the CCTV system."

Tom turned to see Peter Marron walk in. "What about cameras elsewhere in the building?"

"I thought you just needed to see who you spoke with? Is there something else you were looking for?"

Tom closed his eyes. He seemed to be getting a headache, a pulsing in the base of his skull: almost a buzzing.

"No, not really. I guess I just thought it would all come flooding back, but apparently not. Thank you for your help, though."

"No problem. How are things by the way? Are you feeling better?"

"Just fine. The clinic have released me."

"Well isn't that good news! Were you happy with their care?"

"Nothing but the best."

"I'll be sure to mention that if I speak to them."

Tom arrived back at his office and closed the door. It was odd that he remembered meeting the woman in the black dress clearly, but absolutely nothing afterwards, not even leaving the party. How could his memory loss be so specific?

His phone rang. It was his secretary, Samantha. "I've got a call about your 11 o'clock meeting."

He frowned. "What 11 o'clock meeting?"

"I assumed you scheduled it."

Tom sighed. Perhaps this was an arrangement he had made at the party. "Put it through."

There was a click. "Hi, Tom, my name is Kate. I appreciate you taking my call. I'd like to--"

"Did we meet Friday night?" Tom cut in.

"You mean at the launch party?" A pause. "I *was* there."

"I'm so sorry I've not been in touch. It's been quite a week." He paused as a thought occurred to him. Could this be the woman in the black dress? "Do you deal in terminations?"

She seemed to hesitate. "You could say it's linked to what I do. Can you make 11am today?"

"I think I can move my diary around. Do you have a meeting room booked?"

"Why don't I buy you a coffee? There's a café on the corner across from CERUS Tower."

"I'll see you there."

TWENTY-FIVE

KATE CHECKED HER WATCH: 10:59am. She sat in the coffee shop, in a booth near the back with a clear view across the concourse. She recognised Faraday when he was still fifty metres away and stood to wave. He turned in her direction and wove his way towards her.

"Kate?" he asked, his expression suddenly hesitant. He looked a little disappointed.

"Hello, Tom," she said, extending her hand. "Thanks for coming."

Tom cleared his throat. "My apologies for not getting back to you. I had some problems with my computer and I lost my schedule."

Kate hesitated. "Oh... Ah... Never mind. It's all worked out, right?" she said, smiling brightly. She placed a crisp white business card on the table.

KATE THOMPSON
EXECUTIVE SEARCH

He let out a sigh. "I thought you worked at CERUS. I think there's been a misunderstanding. I've only just started this job and I'm not looking to move."

"No harm in having a conversation? Like we agreed, no?" Her eyes narrowed as Tom looked away and shifted in his seat.

"Sorry if I wasn't clearer, er, before but... well, I think it'd be a waste of your time."

"Most people are flattered to be headhunted."

He shrugged. "I was headhunted for my current role."

"A man of your talents, I guess that's no surprise. Still I imagine you'll be keen to keep your options open, given the things I heard at that party."

He frowned sharply. "What things?"

She let a smile play across her lips. "Why don't we do dinner? On me, naturally." He started to shake his head, so she quickly hurried on. "Come on, Tom. Some gossip about your new job. And, yes, I'll probably talk a bit of business too, but what's the harm? Don't you want to at least hear about other possibilities? There's an Italian Restaurant called Brocca opposite Baker Street Tube. Why don't we say 8pm?"

A battered grey transit van was parked across the road from the coffee shop. It displayed a business parking permit, although neither that, nor indeed its number plate, were genuine.

In the back, Harry Winston was eating a cold meat pie while watching the grainy video-feed from the three different cameras he had co-opted. There was audio as well, but the quality was proving very poor. He watched as Tom Faraday met with a woman who gave her name as Kate and claimed to be in recruitment. He noted a few bullet points down for his client's executive summary, although he would be forwarding a full package of audio and video too.

Winston swallowed the remains of the pie and threw the

wrapper on a pile of rubbish in one corner. Then he reached for a flask of tea and filled a large grubby mug. He loved these twenty-four hour surveillance gigs. It made him smile inside to think of the fees ticking up and up. This client was a little unnerving to deal with, but he was always clear about what he wanted and Winston respected that. He looked back at the monitors and saw that Tom was now leaving the coffee shop and heading towards CERUS Tower. He would soon be out of the range of his systems. Time for a short nap, he thought with a smile.

TWENTY-SIX

PETER MARRON'S OFFICE WAS SITUATED on the north-east corner of Level 88, looking out towards the Thames Barrier and Dartford Crossing. The rest of the HR team worked in an open plan area spread creatively across the rest of the floor. Marron emerged from the lift, hands in pockets, and walked through the floor, nodding to anyone who looked up. They could all see Marron's desk through the glass walls and he could see all of them – when he wanted to. He entered his office and closed the door then touched a control dial and the glass panels instantly became opaque.

He walked over to an oversized chess set on a coffee table in the corner of the room. A game was in play: the clean and elegant Staunton-design pieces poised between moves. Marron pulled his phone from his pocket and opened a message. It contained a move for white. He moved the bishop as indicated, then paused to regard the result: a single piece, a single move with repercussions throughout the board. He had a week to reflect before giving his response, which was good because he had other things on his mind.

He pulled out a second mobile phone and sent a short text:

Thanks for doing a great job. Then he turned to the interior wall on his right and produced a remote control, placing his thumb over its image scanner. There was a soft chime then a section of the wall swung inwards. Marron stepped through. The door closed silently behind him.

He had gone to great lengths to ensure the room behind the hidden door was no longer marked on any floor plans or schematics. It was a control room wired directly into the building's central computer and communications system, with its own network and power systems, completely separate both technically and physically from the building's main grid. The whole room was connected to back-up generators entirely unrelated to the main systems. He sat in the oversized swivel chair, looking over the various screens in front of him. From here he could see and control the entire building. If somebody sneezed in a corridor on Level 28, he would know. If CERUS Tower were a space ship, this control room would be the Bridge: just one that almost nobody knew about.

Marron turned to one of the terminals and opened an encrypted communications app. The call connected almost instantly. "Dr Chatsworth, why have you released Faraday from your care without informing me first?"

There was a pause. "You're not someone I like giving bad news to."

"I certainly prefer it to 'no news'. So the tests were negative?"

"Yes, but I wanted more information before updating you."

Marron sucked in his top lip. "Don't keep anything from me again." He closed the call and eased back in his chair.

His mobile vibrated: it was a text message from an anonymous forwarding service. It contained a string of eight digits. The digits themselves were irrelevant, but it meant something had come up. He slid his chair over to a different computer, pulled on a headset, and logged himself into a separate comms program. Then he dialled the sender of the message. It was answered immediately.

"This is Winston," came the reply, soft and metallic.

"What's happened?"

"Faraday had coffee with a woman. A recruiter."

A half smile crossed Marron's face. "Is that right?"

"Her name is Kate Thompson. She works for some small agency, not well known."

"Then she's probably not very good."

"At recruiting, probably not, since it's a cover identity. She's actually a reporter, real name Kate Turner."

"Does he know?"

"Not as far as I could tell. But they're meeting for dinner tonight at an Italian restaurant in Baker Street."

"You'll monitor them, of course."

"Sure. But it's hard to get sound remotely if they're in a crowded restaurant. And I've had no opportunity to go in and prep the place."

"Are you telling me I should hire somebody better?"

"I'll sort something out."

"I'm sure you will."

TWENTY-SEVEN

THE APARTMENT BLOCK WAS TWO storeys high and painted a functional mid-brown. In her ground floor unit, Daniella Lawrence forced the suitcase shut. She'd packed light, but still there were so many things she couldn't bear to part with. And she did not expect to return. Not after she'd read the paper that morning. It was time to activate her exit strategy. Or perhaps she should think of it as her 'return' strategy.

She'd managed to book a flight to Paris that left in six hours, but it was at least a five-hour drive to the airport. Four if you didn't value your vehicle's suspension. Three if you didn't value your life at intersections.

There was a knock at the door. She tensed and moved quietly to it. The knocking repeated, only louder.

"Who is it?" she called.

"Director Kimoto." His clipped tones were unmistakeable.

Lawrence moved closer. "Are you alone?"

"Yes." He sounded puzzled. "Why?"

She wrenched the door open and saw him standing on his own in the corridor. With a quick glance left and right, she pulled him inside and closed the door.

"What is going on, Dr Lawrence? A couple of the staff said you left in a great hurry. I thought something might be wrong." He pointed at the suitcase on the bed. "*Is* something wrong?"

"I have to go."

"Where? For how long?" Kimoto frowned. "I hope you're not leaving because of what I said the other day."

Lawrence shook her head. "There were always two reasons I might have to leave. Either *they* became aware of me. Or I became aware of *them*." She placed a hand on his shoulder. "Nobody is coming looking for me."

He gazed at her for several long moments, before bowing his head. "Then I wish you God speed. And I thank you for everything you've done for us. You have made a difference. You have saved lives; we will not forget that." He left, closing the door behind him.

Lawrence shook her head. Where she was going she would be trying to save more than a few lives. With Richard Armstrong dead, she had no choice: she could hide away no longer. It was time she risked the world discovering that Dominique Lentz was not dead after all.

TWENTY-EIGHT

TOM ARRIVED AT BROCCA AT exactly 8pm and found it packed. The manager smiled when he gave Kate's name, then guided him through the crowd. She sat in a booth near the back.

"Nice place," he said, as they shook hands.

"It's a favourite of mine. Very authentic."

The waiter handed them both menus and vanished. Tom studied the options. "It does look good."

She laughed. "Speak Italian, do you?"

"No, why?"

"They've given us the wrong menus."

He looked at the intricately printed sheets of paper inside their folder. Nothing seemed wrong.

"I prefer not to have to reach for the dictionary when I order," Kate said. She waved at the waiter. "English menus, please."

"Of course." He whisked the menus from them, and moments later Tom was staring at the contents of a new faux-leather folder. It looked exactly the same. Kate ordered for them both: pesto calamari, then broiled salmon, along with a bottle of Dolcetto.

"So why did you choose law?" she asked, holding up her wine glass. "I mean, aside from the money."

"Don't knock the money. We all have bills and student loans."

"Yes, but there are plenty of other jobs that pay well."

"Working with the law is one way to grasp how business works. It's one of the sets of rules that everybody has to operate within." He shrugged. "And I just didn't like adding up enough to be an accountant."

"And CERUS?"

"They made me an offer I couldn't refuse."

"But how do you feel about them keeping the company's financial difficulties from you when you were hired?" She paused. "Unless they didn't. Which would be even more interesting."

"I'm aware of the rumours, but, as far as I'm concerned, that's all they are."

"Maybe." She paused. "Talking of the news, did you know Richard Armstrong?"

Tom shrugged. "He was an engineer. It's a huge company and I've only been there a few days. Why would you think I would know him?" Tom felt his headache returning, stabbing at the base of his skull. Behind him, two mobile phones went off loudly. There were mutterings from diners and embarrassed rummagings as their owners protested that the phones had been on mute. Tom rubbed his temples.

Kate frowned. "Are you OK?"

"Just had a long day. So what did you think of the launch party?"

"Very impressive. The champagne bottle was unfortunate, but Bern knows how to step up to the moment."

"Did you happen to see me there with a woman in a black dress?"

"It was a Friday evening, there were a lot of women in black dresses. Why?" She folded her arms. "Someone skip out without leaving you their number?"

"I'm worried I may have done something that I can't remember."

She leaned forward. "Something embarrassing?"

He flinched back. "No, of course not. Look it's just..." He felt the pain in his head shift into something else.

It seemed like there was a fog around him, then suddenly he felt as if he were back at the party. He had the glass of cognac in his hand: he could taste it in his mouth. The woman in black was before him and he could see her face. She was smiling slowly, and he felt cold... A hand gripped his forearm and the scene slipped away. Kate's voice cut through the fog. "Are you all right?"

He jerked. "I'm fine." He realised his arm was tingling where her hand was on his skin. He stood up, almost hitting his head on a low beam. "I haven't been feeling well. The doctors said... I really shouldn't have come out for dinner. It's probably best if I go home. Sorry for wasting your time." He stumbled through the restaurant and out onto the street without giving her a chance to reply.

TWENTY-NINE

TOM STEPPED OUT OF THE restaurant into the cool night air. He shook his head, trying to clear it. The stabbing headache seemed to have gone, although he still had a faint tingling at the base of his head. Perhaps he should not have drunk anything. What a waste of time. Kate had nothing to tell him about the party and he'd probably embarrassed her by walking out during the meal. He glanced over his shoulder and could make her out behind the glass frontage of the restaurant, talking to the manager.

The Tube station was just across the road, but the air felt good so he decided to walk and turned down a side street, making his way south. There was a flicker of movement in the corner of his eye, but when he turned he just saw crowds of people walking in different directions. He continued down the alley. His phone buzzed and he pulled it from his pocket. Had he accidentally called someone? It was his new company phone too: just what he needed after everything else – inadvertently dialling a colleague.

"Give me your wallet, your watch and your phone," a low voice growled from behind him.

Tom started to turn, but a solid grip fixed on his shoulder and a sharp point jabbed into his lower back.

"Don't be stupid. And don't even think about calling out."

Tom felt ice rush through him. He nodded. He didn't fancy his chances of a passing Londoner being ready to come to his aid. The man grunted and pushed him against a wall.

"OK, turn around. Hand over the stuff."

Tom reached for his wallet, then slid his phone from its belt case.

"The watch too."

Tom hesitated. The watch had been a present from his mother. "It's just cheap junk: you don't want it."

The man looked irritated. "Just give it--"

There was a sudden flurry of black and a foot struck the man's wrist with a crack. He gave a scream and staggered back. The newcomer struck Tom's assailant again, kicking him in the stomach. The man doubled over, vomiting.

Confused, Tom looked at his rescuer.

It was Kate.

She stood over the groaning figure, breathing hard. "You OK?"

Tom gulped. "What the hell was that?"

"I thought you could use a hand."

"He had a knife. Did he drop it?"

She peered around on the floor and tapped something with her foot. "It was just a fountain pen."

The man groaned and hauled himself to his feet. Kate tensed as if about to lunge at him. He ran off.

Tom stared at the pen. "It felt sharp."

Kate grabbed Tom's arm. "Let's get out of here."

"What about that man? Shouldn't we report this to the police?"

"Not unless you want to spend all night giving a statement." She kicked the pen away. "He was just some opportunistic drunk."

Tom shook his head and let himself be led away.

They found a McDonald's and sat upstairs with burgers, fries and milkshakes. Tom was surprised to find he was intensely hungry.

"This wasn't quite what I had in mind when I invited you to dinner," Kate said, waving a French fry with a resigned expression.

"Getting mugged wasn't quite what I had in mind when I left," replied Tom.

"Are you OK? I mean, not just the mugging but... People don't normally walk out on me at dinner. At least not when I'm paying." She paused. "That was why I was following you: I'm not a stalker."

Tom shrugged. "It's been a tricky few days."

"With work?"

"Not exactly. Thank you for rescuing me, by the way. You certainly seem to know how to take care of yourself."

"I do a bit of Karate." She paused. "And when I say 'do', I mean 'teach'. But what do you mean 'tricky few days'?"

He sighed. "I was in hospital earlier this week after collapsing at the office. I think something happened to me at the party, but I can't remember. Nothing between Bern's speech on Friday night and Monday morning. I don't even remember how I got home."

Kate sat upright in her chair. "Are you serious?"

"I've had all sorts of tests. CERUS paid for me to go to some top private clinic. They've been amazing, given I've only just joined and hadn't technically even signed up to the health cover yet."

"Still, they made you go back to work already?"

"That was my decision. They didn't push me at all."

"And the doctors have no idea what happened to you?"

Tom hesitated. "They found traces of a toxin, said I might have taken meth."

"Oh," she said.

"I've *never* done drugs," Tom said angrily. "I've never wanted to. It makes no sense."

"But it could explain the memory loss. We ran a..." She paused. "I mean, I *read* a story about the side effects of legal narcotics: everyone reacts differently even to those. Who knows when it comes to an illegal one mixed with God knows what?"

"But I would never have agreed to take it." Tom sighed. "That was why I agreed to meet you for dinner. I was hoping you might have seen who I was talking to. If I could identify them, I might be able to find out more about that night."

"I'm sorry. I wish I could help more."

"And I'm sorry I wasted your time."

Kate smiled. "I try to take the view that few things are actually a waste of time. When you look back, unexpected opportunities often come from them."

THIRTY

CROFT SAT IN THE UTILITARIAN annex to Stephanie Reems' office, flicking through his report on a tablet computer. He had been waiting several hours, so by now he could largely quote it from memory. Reems was always busy, but today it almost seemed as if she was avoiding him.

Finally the receptionist cleared his throat and nodded that Croft should go through.

Stephanie Reems maintained several offices, but this was her primary centre of operations. Two floors below ground, there were no windows - just stone walls and heavy electronic shielding. Reems sat behind her steel desk, reading. She only half looked up. "Sorry to keep you waiting, George. Hell of a day." She indicated a seat in front of her.

"You've read my report?"

She shook her head. "I presumed you'd summarise it for me."

He forced a smiled. "Of course. As agreed, I looked into the circumstances surrounding Richard Armstrong's death. I inserted myself into the police team and analysed the scene first-hand, including conducting a number of interviews. I also undertook my own analysis of his recent comms usage."

"And what was your conclusion?"

"That this was not an accident." He paused to see if she would react. She did not. "We found three old phone SIM cards cut up in his rubbish. Pay as you go accounts. It suggests he was taking precautions to avoid having his calls monitored. As for who he called, there was only one unusual number: another pay as you go. We're looking into it."

"Perhaps he was having an affair."

Croft shook his head. "He wasn't married. Lived on his own with his dog. No reason to keep it a secret."

"Maybe the other person involved had a reason."

He shrugged. "We found the remains of a further mobile phone with the SIM card still in it. It was badly damaged, but the police believe it could have been a detonator."

"Or perhaps it was just a phone."

Croft shrugged. "The dog was also a point of interest. According to neighbours, Armstrong never let it sleep outside, yet the dog was found in the garden, unharmed. I took a blood sample and there were traces of tranquilliser."

"Perhaps it had been to the vet?"

"No record of that."

Reems puffed out her cheeks. "So what are you saying?"

"My task wasn't to solve the case, merely to consider whether there is one. I have a plausible and reasonable suspicion that this was foul play and that there should be a full investigation." He paused. "Which should start with CERUS."

Reems leaned back in her chair. "This is good work. Now I want you to archive the report. "

"What? Why?"

"Your conclusions are well researched and nobody could criticise you for reaching them, but they are based on incomplete data. Do you know why Armstrong was on the watch list?"

Croft swallowed. "My clearance isn't sufficient to access that information."

"And unfortunately I cannot change that." She gave a kindly smile. "But if you had the full context, as I do, you'd know that this is the appropriate outcome. I can tell you that the watch list is outdated: more than two decades old. If there were an issue, it would have been routed by me. It wasn't, which means there *is* no issue."

Croft stood up. "I understand. Thanks for your time." He turned towards the door, then paused. "I'm not the only one who thought this smelt funny, though. There were a number of reporters hovering around."

"CERUS is always newsworthy. I doubt they'll find anything you didn't."

THIRTY-ONE

MARRON PLACED THE HEADSET DOWN and glared at his computer. Winston had given him a full report about the Italian restaurant. All had seemed normal, then Faraday had suddenly walked out, only to be mugged. Or, rather, nearly mugged - this reporter had appeared to save him. Marron was half-tempted to think it was a set-up, so she could establish trust with Faraday - it was a play he might have considered - but Winston had not seen any evidence that was the case. Marron shrugged. He would still have to have her investigated, but right now he had more important matters to attend to.

He stepped out of the secret room, then left his office and headed towards the stairs. Emerging from the stairwell two flights up, he knocked on Bern's glass and steel door.

The CEO beckoned him inside, then returned to four grey folders that were arrayed before him on his stone desk. "I wanted to speak with you alone before we go downstairs. These people you've found, our four guinea pigs. Can we trust them?"

"We've done all the testing, all the profiling we can. I've done my part, but nothing's fool-proof."

Bern nodded. "What about Chatsworth?"

"He seems reliable, if prone to fits of panic. I'm watching him closely."

"And did the others welcome you to the team?"

"I'm not sure if 'welcome' is the right term, but nobody's complained."

Bern smiled. "They're probably too scared."

"You'd have to ask them. I like to think I'm pretty straightforward. Perhaps that's why I handle people-problems better than most."

"Speaking of people-problems, any fallout from Armstrong's accident?"

"There were a few questions, but everyone assumes it *was* an accident."

"Anything else that I need to know?"

Marron smiled. "No, William. Nothing that you *need* to know."

Bern nodded. "Then I guess it's time we got downstairs for our defining moment."

THIRTY-TWO

DR CHATSWORTH WATCHED AS THE last of the four vehicles parked in front of the Angstrom Clinic and began unloading. Everything was running on schedule so far. Their four new 'guests' were being managed by separate teams. The subjects wouldn't see each other's faces and his people would only see more than one of them if they absolutely had to. These were just some of the protocols that had been specified by Marron. One entire wing of the clinic had been cleared out and the operating theatre had been prepped, not that any of the subjects were aware of that.

The specifics weren't something the doctor liked to dwell on, but after today he would be paid and his involvement would be nearly at an end. At least that was what Marron had told him and, so far, what Marron had told him had always proved accurate.

Each of the candidates looked bored as, one by one, they were led into the building: the student, the science geek, the bankrupt businessman and the divorced housewife. Convenient, he thought, to reduce them to mere stereotypes. Smart, capable people who wanted to make a difference, but who needed the money. Except for the geek: if he'd known what this was really about, he would probably have done it for free.

Chatsworth returned to his office and confirmed via the secure link that all was on schedule. A glance at the monitor bank on his wall showed the subjects getting dressed in their hospital gowns, while medical staff went through a number of questionnaires and generally made everything appear normal. Chatsworth felt the sweat trickle down his neck. So many things could go wrong.

Signals from each of the teams indicated they were ready. He pressed a button and spoke to the rooms simultaneously. "Please proceed."

Four teams of anaesthetists got to work and within fifteen minutes the subjects were unconscious. Chatsworth, scrubbed up and ready, walked into the operating theatre, which now held the student. He looked up at one of the four cameras.

"Tower, this is Clinic. Are you receiving?"

In the laboratory on Level 64 of CERUS Tower, Bern, Bradley, Heidn, Holm and Marron sat watching the feed from the operating theatre. The student was rolled onto his front, his face fitting through a special hole in the padded table. They watched as Chatsworth opened a heavily padded case on a table set with instruments. Inside the case was a large syringe.

A boiler-suited man wheeled in a trolley with a large protective container marked with biohazard symbols. He unlocked the protective container and removed one of four ampules of green liquid. Chatsworth took the ampule and inserted it into the syringe. It clicked and the contents moved into the instrument's chamber. The doctor held it upright, and the green liquid almost seemed to glow, even as viewed on the video footage. Another assistant swabbed the back of the student's neck, just below the base of his skull. They watched Chatsworth check the syringe one final time then nod to the assistant.

"Commencing implant," Chatsworth said.

The injection took several seconds. All the patient's status monitors showed unchanged readings. Finally the doctor stood back, dropping the used instrument into a padded bin. He looked up at the camera. "Part one complete for Subject One."

"We expect to see results in the region of twenty-four to forty-eight hours," Heidn told his colleagues, leaning forwards towards the screen.

"I'll report back if there are any glitches or complications with administering Part One to Subjects Two through Four," Chatsworth said.

"Very good." Bradley pressed a button to disconnect the video link. "Happy, William?"

Bern nodded. "Excellent work. And I think congratulations are due to Peter for locating the subjects so quickly."

"Nonsense." Marron raised his hands. "I've played the most minor part. I'm just relieved the clinic was available so we had a discrete, credible location entirely separate from CERUS for our testing."

"What about this Chatsworth?" asked Bradley. "Did he seem a little twitchy to you?"

"We can trust him to supervise some injections and take his money," Bern said. "So I guess now we see if our two geniuses have been able to work their magic."

Heidn and Holm looked at each other, with a mixture of fear and optimism.

"We'll be ready," Heidn said, "presuming there are no last minute surprises."

THIRTY-THREE

THE VAN WAS PAINTED BLACK and bore a decal for KPS Services: plumbing, heating and electrical contractors. Yet it was not loaded with tools, piping and cabling, but rather a selection of powerful hand-built computers and network devices.

Kate sat hunched in the back with a man she knew only as 'Keith', the contact that a friend of a friend had once referred her to should she ever need to access electronic systems that were not meant for her eyes. She'd almost baulked when he'd told her how much he would charge, especially since he didn't look like the kind of 'contractor' who would provide a receipt. The only way Geraldine would even discuss reimbursement was if she got real results, so it was just as well 'Keith' appeared to know what he was doing. For the last hour he had been adjusting a small satellite dish and staring at streams of code running down one of his screens. It was almost hypnotic, if frustratingly slow.

"How much longer?" she asked, wishing she'd thought to bring a flask of coffee.

"Believe me," he said, "I don't want to sit in the back of this van with you any longer than I have to.

"What does the KPS stand for?"

"Duh? Keith's Plumbing Services."

"You realise your company name is effectively 'Keith's Plumbing Services *Services*'?"

He frowned at her. "You realise it's not a real company."

"Isn't it supposed to *look* real?"

"Do you want my help?"

"Never mind. Just keep hacking." Kate leaned back against the wall of the van. She had been ready to give up on Tom. Since their conversation after the mugging, she had made no progress. His story about not remembering his weekend had seemed like it had to mean something, but maybe it was just memory loss. It was all so nebulous – how could she possibly determine the truth?

Then she realised there was one thing she could confirm: how and when Tom got home. London now had CCTV everywhere and a quick walk past Tom's apartment block revealed two possible sources of the footage she needed. Normally, it would have meant trying to make a public access request or involving the police, either of which would mean a significant delay. Instead, she had called Keith.

Now they were parked across the road from Tom's apartment, using a parabolic dish to attempt to piggy-back on the carrier frequency of the cameras in order to follow the encrypted data tunnel back to the storage media - at least that was how Keith had explained it. Kate was reasonably tech savvy, but this was delving further under hood than she normally went.

"That's odd," Keith said suddenly. "I've located the file storage. But the period from Friday to Monday has been wiped."

Kate blinked. "You mean there's a fault?"

Keith tapped at his keyboard. "It can't be a malfunction; the data either side is perfect. It's been excised and deleted."

"Who'd have the capability to do that?"

"Someone like me," he said with a smile. He jabbed frenetically at his keyboard again. "Only they're not as good as I am. It wasn't properly wiped. Usual story, deleting a file just wipes the name and meta-tags. The actual content is still there until overwritten."

"And you can locate it?"

"Maybe..." He narrowed his eyes. "Yes. I think I have it." He switched on another screen. A camera view appeared, looking down the street, past Tom's front door. "OK, this is 8am on the Friday morning. Is that your boy, leaving in his suit?"

Kate peered at the screen. "That's him."

"When do you want to view next?"

"He was at the party until at least 9pm, so let's fast forward to around 11, and view from there."

They watched a very long time, skipping through in 2-minute chunks. Friday night turned into Saturday turned into Sunday. Still nothing.

And then finally they found it.

At 3am on Monday morning a white van pulled up outside the apartment block. Moments later a group of men carried a limp figure to the front door. Two men stood on guard as another opened the door and then they all disappeared inside.

"Let me see if I can enhance," Keith said. "See if we can make out some faces." He rewound to just before the figure was taken inside, tapped at some keys; a filter scrubbed across the screen, then again. The image sharpened. Keith zoomed in on the face of the unconscious figure.

"That's him," whispered Kate.

Keith restarted the footage. Nothing happened for ten minutes, then the door opened and the men left. Kate and Keith watched it all in silence, then rewound it and watched again.

"If that was when he came home, where was he all weekend?"

asked Kate.

Keith looked pale. "What are you sticking your beak into here? These look like serious people."

"You've done your part. I'm the one with her neck on the line."

He shook his head. "If you run this story, I'll come to the attention of whoever it was - and they'll want to know how you got the footage ."

She gave a snort. "That's not going to be happen. Besides, it's too late to be having second thoughts. We made a deal."

"Is your guy OK?"

"It seems that way."

Keith nodded. "Well, that's something." He reached forward and typed something on his keyboard. Progress bars immediately flicked up.

"What are you doing?"

"Deleting the footage, obviously. And *I'm* doing it *properly*."

"No!" She stood up but he quickly jabbed another key and the computer screen locked. "Why would you do that?"

"A basic sense of self-preservation."

"I need that footage. It's *very* important."

"It's already gone."

Kate took a step forward, her eyes narrowing. "Re-download it from the system."

"I wiped the original too."

She cursed, sweeping a computer onto the floor.

"Hey!" Keith shouted, making to get up. A murderous look from Kate kept him in his chair. "I thought you were a reporter: isn't this just a story for you?"

"Tom Faraday was abducted and you've just deleted the best, if not only, evidence."

"You can still tell him what you saw."

Kate ran her hands through her hair and then sighed. "With

your systems, can you tell if he's in the apartment?"

"I've been parked here all day, tracking everyone in and out. He's inside the building, so I'd presume he's in the apartment."

"And his flat mate?"

"She's out. Left two hours ago."

"Then I'm going to speak to him. There are things he needs to know."

THIRTY-FOUR

TOM STARTED UP HIS MEDIA player, then leaned back on the sofa and let out a contented sigh. He'd shared a quiet dinner with Jo before she went out to her evening climbing class, and now he was sipping a glass of mineral water and doing his best to relax.

His thoughts strayed idly to Kate. He could picture those sharp blue eyes like they were still in front of him, and he found himself wondering if her interests went beyond trying to headhunt him. But perhaps it was best if he kept things simple. He didn't need any more excitement for a while. Things finally seemed to be going back to normal: a bit of boring old normal was just what he needed. He was feeling better: no dizziness and the headaches had gone. It was time to focus on his new job... and perhaps indulge in a little binge TV watching at home. He grinned as Episode One of the *X-Files* started, something Jo had always said he should watch.

Although, if what he'd heard was true, the truth *wasn't* out there.

There was a loud knocking on his door. He frowned. Visitors had to ring the main bell to get access to the building before they could even reach his level. The *X-Files* theme music started playing and he looked around for the remote, but it was nowhere to be seen. The knocking repeated.

"Shut up already!" he shouted at the screen. As if in response, it went dark. He stared at it for a moment then moved to the door. "Who is it?"

"It's Kate. I need to talk to you."

He pulled open the door, and saw her standing, looking determined. "How did you get into the building?"

"I followed someone else. Can I come in?" She stepped past him without waiting for a reply. "We need to talk about what happened to you." She looked around. "I know how you got home after the party. And it was not under your own steam."

Tom blinked. "I'm sorry, what?"

"You were brought back by a group of men. I've reviewed the CCTV footage from cameras in the street and--"

"How did you see that? Are you with the police?"

"No. I'm a reporter."

Tom stared at her. "So meeting with me was all a ruse?"

"I was trying to get a story on CERUS."

"But you were on the recruitment company website."

She waved her hands. "It's a cover ID."

Tom folded his arms. "So, are you going to show me this footage then?"

"It was deleted before I could copy it."

"How convenient! So I'm just supposed to believe you? Right after you just admitted lying?" He shook his head. "I should have guessed when you mentioned Richard Armstrong's name."

"I got your name from Armstrong – well, indirectly. He said he'd spoken to a new lawyer at CERUS and I thought--"

Tom's brow furrowed. "Why were you speaking to Armstrong?"

"He was about to go whistle-blower on activities at CERUS: he was helping me write a story about them restarting intelligent nano research. Then he died."

"And, what? You're saying he was murdered? And I was kidnapped?"

"Functional nanotech could be worth billions. And you have to admit that what happened to you is difficult to explain."

"Life sometimes is, but I'm fine now. I've been checked over by the very best doctors."

She frowned. "What was the clinic you went to?"

"It's called the Angstrom. I've looked it up since and it's got a top reputation. Are you suggesting they're in on it now? Whatever *it* is. What about CERUS? Them too?"

"You should go to the police."

"With what? Your claims about some missing CCTV footage and a few half-baked conspiracy theories?" Tom closed his eyes. It was like there was a faint buzzing in his head: an itch somewhere inside. The ceiling lights flickered.

Kate glanced up. "I want to help you, Tom."

"And *I* think you should go," he said. "If I want your help, I'll ask for it."

THIRTY-FIVE

ON WILLIAM BERN'S COUNTRY ESTATE, Bradley watched as Celia drew back on the compound bow, her balance and form showing that this was not the first time she had practised archery. She released, the arrow speeding through the air, flexing and humming, before thudding into the target, some twenty-five metres away. It struck the outer bullseye.

Celia turned to face him. "I imagine it's William's head, so I never miss." She paused. "Although there are other possible targeting options."

"Remind me not to annoy you."

"You need to be reminded?" she said, hefting the bow and nocking another arrow.

"Probably not."

She raised the bow and fired in a single motion. The arrow struck, almost touching the first. "In which case remind *me* why we're meeting today. You weren't due to give me an update."

Bradley held up a large envelope marked 'Confidential'. "William has some documents he needs you to sign." He frowned. "Now I think about it, he was very clear he wanted me to come and oversee your signature. Do you think he has suspicions?"

She shook her head. "If he knew then we wouldn't be in any doubt. What are the documents about?"

"I'm just the messenger," he said with a shrug, "so I'd appreciate it if you didn't shoot me."

She gave a snort and placed the bow on a stand then strode over and took the envelope. Tearing it open, she removed a sheaf of papers. As she flicked through, a smile crossed her lips.

"Hilarious. He wants to transfer a number of assets into my name." She shook her head. "You know, it's no fun if he loses through stupidity."

"I imagine he thinks he's protecting himself. Because he thinks he can trust you."

"Then I suppose he is exactly where we want him. I'll sign these in a moment, but while we're out here, away from any microphones in the house, do you want to give me an update?"

"The four subjects have been implanted. Chatsworth informed us this morning that Stage One is complete."

"No complications?"

"The doctor seems on top of it. The four subjects are in an induced coma, ready to be moved from the clinic to the special facility at the Tower. Stage Two is next."

"After which we'll know if it works?"

"We should. Ed Holm keeps saying that the code is new and very rushed, but, as I understand it, it's built along similar lines to a number of other projects that CERUS has developed. He's simply patched in the helicopter protocols."

Celia frowned. "I don't like that these volunteers are getting caught up in all this."

"There was no other way. The buyer needs proof of viability. Without it he won't pay. But there's no doubt Leskov needs this product and he has no practical alternatives. As long as we deliver, he'll pay."

"We need to be ready to move quickly when the time comes. If we give him any room to manoeuvre, he'll use it. How about that Richard Armstrong man? Will that affect things?"

"He wasn't part of the project so it shouldn't impact our timelines, though now I'm sounding like Peter Marron."

"I didn't realise he was involved."

"Do you know him?"

"He's worked for my husband for more than twenty five years. I know he's officially head of HR but I think he manages most things William needs managing."

"Except for getting your signature on documents," Bradley said ruefully.

"Putting things in writing isn't really Marron's style," she said.

"Joking aside, is he likely to be a problem?"

"He just does what William tells him. It's William who provides the vision and *that* has always been the problem."

"Not for much longer."

"No," said Celia, with a smile. "Not for much longer at all."

THIRTY-SIX

FOR THE FIRST TIME IN a long time, Kate woke up before her alarm, too much on her mind to sleep. Within minutes, she was dressed and on her way to the office.

She left her car close to the entrance and made her way through security, the guard looking mildly confused to see her so early. She got to her floor then moved quickly across the office, her mind gearing up to plug in her laptop and check her emails, but she didn't even make it to her desk.

"My room, now!" barked Geraldine, appearing out of nowhere.

Kate forced a smiled onto her face, followed her in and closed the door. "Is something wrong?" She negotiated her way between the stacks of company reports to the metal-framed seat opposite Geraldine's desk.

Geraldine lowered herself into her worn chair. "You agreed you would keep me updated. How did you get on with verifying those nanites? "

"I got distracted with something else. Unfortunately, it didn't work out."

"What did you do?"

"I went direct to the CERUS lawyer, Tom Faraday. But it's all come to nothing. He doesn't want to be involved, even when I told him I had proof he'd been abducted."

"I said talking to the lawyer was a waste of--" began Geraldine. "Wait, did you say *abducted*?"

"I saw the aftermath on CCTV, when they were returning him, unconscious, to his apartment. The trouble is the person who was helping me access the footage deleted it when he realised that it could be dangerous."

Geraldine rubbed her temples agitatedly. "Well, there goes our evidence, though I suppose the nanites might yet check out." She opened a desk drawer and pulled out a card file. "Not to mention that I found out two things that could help us."

"How? I searched every online resource we have access to – and a few we don't."

"Call me a traditionalist," said Geraldine, pointing at the nearest pile of company reports, "but sometimes paper records are best. I went through the printed archives and I found a reference to a project cancelled by CERUS twenty-five years ago. It was called Tantalus and there was mention that people had died during testing. Officially nothing was ever confirmed and the relevant internet archives seem to have been stripped."

Kate rubbed her temples with her index fingers. "So what was the other thing you found out?"

"That the Angstrom Clinic has a surprising benefactor – one it took me hours of digging to uncover."

"How do you know the name of the clinic Tom went to? I never told you any of that!"

"I worked out which A&E he was taken to, then called in a favour with a doctor at the Royal London. They told me where he was sent on to."

"So who was the benefactor?"

"CERUS."

"You mean they donate to the clinic?"

"I mean that, hidden in layers of shell companies and secret trusts, they own it."

Kate's eyes widened. "So a company that we believe has done human testing sends one of its employees to a clinic it runs. And doesn't tell him."

"That's what it looks like."

"And they've tested something on Tom? Why would they do it?" Kate shook her head. "What was this Tantalus project about?"

"The file didn't say."

"If we're right, I know where the evidence must lie. In Tom. Surely a doctor not in their pay will be able to find some trace of it."

Geraldine snapped her fingers. "And I have a contact who can help with that." She pulled out her phone. "Get Tom ready. I'll tell you where to go tonight."

"How do I persuade him? Do I tell him the truth?"

"Tell him whatever you need to tell him."

Kate nodded, then a smile crossed her face. "Actually I think I know how to make this work."

THIRTY-SEVEN

TOM STEPPED FROM THE BUS across from Regent's Park as the sun was setting, casting a blood red glow on a row of terraced houses. The wine bar where Jo had asked him to meet her was right alongside: a modern, minimalist-decor place with exposed roof beams and a dark, polished floor. Jo waved from a table near the door.

"What's the occasion?" he asked as he sat down, seeing that she was already pouring him an oversized glass of Shiraz.

"Does there have to be one?" she asked. "I haven't seen you properly for days. Thought it would be nice to have a chat somewhere other than the apartment."

"It's just you usually have some plan. You're not trying to set me up with someone, are you?"

She held up her glass. "I wouldn't be that mean to anyone I know."

He gave a snort.

"So how are you?"

"Been at work all day today, and not one episode of falling unconscious and going to hospital to report."

She frowned. "So now it's a big joke? Are you really not going to try and find out more?"

Tom sighed. "That's what you want to talk about?"

"After our last conversation, you can't be surprised."

"I did try, but on balance I think I'm going to forget about it."

"So what *did* you find? Anything on the work security cameras?"

"Work was really helpful, but the footage wasn't. Too blurry to tell me anything and lots of cameras weren't even working."

Jo pulled at her ponytail. "In a brand new hi-tech building?"

"They've had teething troubles. Not exactly uncommon."

"Maybe they wanted to look like they were helping, but didn't help at all."

"OK, here come the conspiracy theories--"

"So you're giving up? Weren't you going to tell them what happened? Or go to the police?"

"I've thought about it some more and I really don't think I want to go there. I took drugs, Jo."

"Not voluntarily."

"The truth is, we don't really know." Tom rubbed his temples. "Look, work has been going well and I really don't want to jeopardise it. Whatever happened to me, I got home safe. Let's not forget that."

"If the people who did this were so benevolent, why didn't they take you to a hospital?"

"We don't know they didn't. Maybe I just can't remember."

Jo glanced towards the back of the room, then made a gesture to someone. She put her glass down between them. "Remember that I love you, Tom. And I wouldn't have done this unless it was in your best interests."

"Done what?" Behind him he heard someone clearing their throat.

"Hello, Tom," Kate said. "I know you won't be pleased with

me, but I'm worried about you. So I reached out to Jo."

"So you not only invaded my privacy, but you've been sharing your tall tales? Unbelievable," he said furiously, pushing himself to his feet.

"Too right," Jo said. "I can't believe you didn't tell me yourself what Kate saw!"

"What she claims she saw."

"We have a new theory, Tom," Kate said, "about why they took you. I think you've been experimented on. You were abducted so a procedure could be performed on you."

"What are you talking about?" He rubbed the back of his neck agitatedly. "That's just ridiculous. What procedure?"

"That's what we're trying to discover." Kate looked at Jo. "I found out that CERUS effectively owns the Angstrom Clinic."

Tom leaned back in his chair. "You're saying they're responsible?" He looked at Jo. "You really dragged me here to listen to this rubbish?"

Jo scowled at him. "She is trying to help you, you big idiot."

Tom stared at Kate. "There's an argument that I might not be able to trust CERUS, but I *know* I can't trust you."

"Then let's take trust out of the equation. You said you wanted facts. So let's establish them." She locked her fingers together. "Let's get you looked at somewhere completely separate from CERUS."

"There's nothing wrong with me. I feel fine." Tom turned to Jo. "You know she's a reporter, yes? She's just doing this to get a story on CERUS out of me once I feel I owe her."

"I don't think she is, Tom," Jo said. "I think she wants to help you." She paused. "And I think you should take her up on her kind offer and stop being so rude."

Tom gritted his teeth and spoke carefully. "I'm pretty confident I'm going to live to regret this, but if you can set it up, I'll do it.

And then you can leave me alone," he said to Kate, "and you can shut up with the conspiracy theories," he added to Jo.

Kate grinned, checking her watch. "We were hoping you'd say that. Let's go, shall we? They'll be ready for us by the time we arrive."

THIRTY-EIGHT

THE HARLEY STREET CONSULTING ROOMS were located a short cab-ride from the wine bar. Tom, Jo and Kate were ushered in a side door.

A grey-haired, well-tanned man shook their hands, but didn't look happy about it.

"I don't know what I was thinking when I agreed to do this off the books, but I guess you're here now, so let's get it over with."

They followed him down into a basement area. There were various warning signs about high voltages and magnets.

The doctor cast an eye over his shoulder as he gestured Jo and Kate into a room to the left while he led Tom into the one on the right. "You know the drill with MRIs?"

Tom nodded, removing his watch. "That's it. No other metal on me – or in me - that I know of. And I'd probably know since the other clinic ran one of these too."

"Then I expect it will be a formality. From there we'll move to blood tests."

"I'm sure this is all a complete waste of time," Tom said. "Not my idea." He glared over at Kate and Jo, who waved merrily from behind the glass in the next room.

The doctor's face showed the flicker of a smile. "I'll get everything done as quickly as I can."

Five minutes later, Tom was lying uncomfortably inside the giant superconductor magnet, waiting for the scan to commence.

"OK, starting her up," the doctor said, his voice conveyed over internal speakers from the room on the left where he'd joined Jo and Kate. "Just shout out if you feel any discomfort." The huge machine began to reverberate with a loud and steady banging. But even with that noise, the sound of Tom's scream was deafening.

The doctor slammed his hand on the emergency cut-off switch. "What's wrong?"

Tom scrambled out of the scanner, clutching the back of his head.

Jo opened the door from the viewing room and ran over to him. "What happened?"

Tom gasped. "The most incredible pain, a second after the scanner started up."

"Does it still hurt?" asked the doctor, hurrying in.

"It stopped the moment you killed the power."

"What would cause that?" Kate asked.

"It could only be something magnetic," said the doctor.

"And it's not like he's had a head injury and has any metal in his head," said Jo, with a laugh.

But Kate shook her head. "Not that he knows of."

Tom turned to the doctor. "Did you get anything before it was turned off?"

"I don't know. It takes some time to clarify the scan."

"Can we have a look?" Kate asked.

The doctor turned to a console and tapped on some keys. A fuzzy image appeared on a large monitor. "That's the initial scan of Tom's head."

"What's that bright spot?"

"I don't know. Might be a glitch."

"Or something metallic?"

"It's possible – especially given Tom's reaction to the machine."

"And if it is, where is that?"

"The base of the skull."

Tom's eyes opened wide. "There is no way this could have been missed." A dark expression crossed his face and he strode from the room, the door banging closed behind him.

"Where's he going?" asked the doctor. "I need to check him over."

"I expect he just wants some space," Jo said anxiously.

Kate shook her head. "I think Tom knows where he needs to go to get some answers."

"What do you mean?" Jo asked.

"If I were placing a bet," said Kate, "I'd say he's going to the clinic."

"Should we call the police?"

"And tell them what exactly? They'd either laugh at us or delay us for hours, by which time Tom could be in a lot of trouble."

"Then what do we do?"

"We follow him. He might need our help."

THIRTY-NINE

A WOMAN DRESSED IN AN expensive suit, her blonde shoulder-length hair elegantly groomed, stood drumming her fingers on the CERUS front desk. She flashed gleaming teeth at the guard on duty. "Daniella Lawrence. I have a meeting with Professor Stefan Heidn."

He typed her name into the system and it confirmed. "Would you please smile at that camera?"

The woman did as requested and was almost immediately handed an ID card with her picture on it, along with a printed guide to the building.

"Now, if you would just go through there," the guard said, gesturing to a personal security door on the right of the lobby. Her purse and laptop bag were scanned quickly and efficiently. All approved, the guard pointed her to a lift. She smiled, picked up her belongings and stepped in when the doors pinged open.

Only when they shut did Dominique Lentz adjust the blonde wig, which was itching furiously. On another day she might find quiet amusement in the disguise, but there was nothing amusing about what she was attempting to do. She had to know what Armstrong had uncovered. And in a company that guarded its secrets so jealously, the only place to look was the very heart.

She stepped from the lift on Level 40 and was directed to a waiting area. She sat in one corner and flipped open her laptop. It was drab and grey, but its internal mechanics were far from ordinary. She quickly picked up the public visitors' network, and the private company network, with its light encryption. As she scanned more rigorously, she saw there appeared to be nothing else. Puzzled for a moment, she realised that Marron had gone old school. The best way to prevent a wireless hack was not to run a wireless system. She would need a hard wire. Reaching back into her bag, she removed what looked like a power pack and plugged it into a nearby wall socket.

Now she could see what she had been looking for: the private security net. To anything with less than a supercomputer's muscle, it was probably unbreakable. Certainly Lentz and her laptop should stand no chance. Except that Lentz had a trick or two up her sleeve.

Her laptop carried an additional battery: a high-voltage capacitor designed to produce a brief spike of power – enough to overload the network and force it to reboot. She glanced around then entered the activation code. There was a soft hum as the pack discharged, then nothing more.

But all around, her screen told her, the network was crashing.

It was a crude form of attack and, of itself, achieved little. But as the network performed automatic disaster recovery and restarted, there was a brief window of opportunity when, unless specifically protected against, one could covertly piggyback on the reboot routines, sneaking in just before the barriers came down again. The system wouldn't fall for it twice, but once was all she would need. Her fingers flew over the keyboard, generating the necessary script, then she quickly uploaded it. There was a soft tone from the computer.

She was in.

Lentz's eyes flicked around the room. She wondered how long before Professor Heidn mentioned that he did not recall scheduling a meeting. Or maybe he'd turn up to greet her, assuming he had simply forgotten to put an appointment in his diary. She had to work quickly. She initiated a search of the company's primary research databases, but soon realised it was a pyrrhic victory. There was too much data and it wasn't indexed for searching: after several minutes, she still had nothing; if she stayed much longer discovery was inevitable. She was about to switch off when an auto-routine flagged that it had discovered files relevant to one of the search terms she'd used – Tantalus. The files included updated notes on 'Subjects One to Four': they were already at 'Phase One' of the 'testing stage'. Were they really repeating the mistakes of the past? She skimmed the files and found her answer.

Nanotechnology.

They were combining an old concept with a new solution.

She began to download the data, but saw immediately that there was a problem: the project files were many terabytes in size. Even if her laptop had been able to hold them, the network would have taken many hours to serve them up. The key elements, the most important folders, might be much smaller, but she had no way of identifying them.

This wasn't going to work. She would have to find another way.

But at least she had a starting point.

Smoothly, she closed her laptop and stowed it in her bag. She had to get away from this place before they realised what was going on. Walking to the small reception desk, she smiled at the man sitting behind it.

"Please pass on my apologies to Professor Heidn but I've been called back to my office."

The man looked at her, puzzled, but nodded, and then she was back in the lift, gliding towards the ground floor. Lentz forced herself to stroll nonchalantly past the security guard at the front gate. Several cameras would be on her, but they could have no recent image in their database and, with her disguise, it was very unlikely that they would recognise her.

A moment later, she was out and quickly vanished into the evening crowd.

FORTY

IT WAS DARK AS TOM stepped out of the taxi and glared up at the gates of the Angstrom Clinic, distractedly rubbing the back of his head.

"You sure you want me to leave you here, mate?" called the taxi driver. "It doesn't look very open."

"They'll see me," Tom said. He walked up to the gates and pressed the buzzer. An automated message played, telling him the clinic was closed to visitors. Cursing, he pulled out his phone: there were five missed calls from Kate and eight from Jo, plus various texts, all since he had left them. He ignored the messages and dialled Chatsworth's number.

To his surprise, the doctor answered. "Tom? Is everything OK?"

Tom took a deep breath. "I'm not feeling at all good. I was about to head to casualty, but I thought I'd see what you'd recommend first."

"You were right to call. I'm working late at the Clinic. Where are you? I can come to you now." Chatsworth's tone was worried.

"Actually I'm right outside. I wasn't far away so I came straight here. I didn't really think about the time."

There was a pause. "I'll get security to let you in."

An elderly security guard, who muttered something about missing a key moment in his favourite TV show, met Tom at the gates, then drove him up to the clinic in a small electric car. A few minutes later, Tom was being shown into an office.

Chatsworth got up to greet him, concern in his expression. "Tom, I thought you were on the mend. What's happened?"

"Actually, I have some questions," Tom said, taking a seat.

"I thought you said you were unwell. If it was just questions then--"

"What I want to know," he paused, "is what have you done to me?"

Chatsworth frowned. "We've discussed the programme of tests before, but I'm happy to run through it all again once we've discussed your current symptoms--"

"That's not what I meant."

"I don't follow."

Tom took a deep breath. "I had an MRI this evening."

Chatsworth swallowed visibly. "Why would you do that?"

"You said you performed an MRI on me."

"That is correct, but--"

"And now we both know that to be a lie. There's something in my head. Something metallic. The MRI had to be shut off: I was in excruciating pain."

Chatsworth cleared his throat. "That's impossible."

"I think you put that *something* there during the weekend I don't remember."

"Before you were admitted as a patient?" Chatsworth shook his head. "Perhaps you had a head injury when you were young? Perhaps some sort of metal plate was inserted?"

"But that would be on my medical records, so you would know. And of course it would have been detected the moment you did the MRI. Which I think we can agree you did not do."

Chatsworth seemed to hesitate. "Tom, you need to understand that I'm the face of the clinic, but I was not involved in your care 100% of the time. There were occasions during the tests that I left you in the care of qualified colleagues. This is all quite normal: we have a number of patients and we rotate our doctors to best suit our patients' individual needs. I believed an MRI was conducted, but it is possible it was not. Probably an error in the paperwork."

"But didn't you notice there was no MRI report? Or are you saying someone faked the results?"

Chatsworth blinked rapidly. "First thing tomorrow, I'll instigate a full investigation into it all. I know this is upsetting, but there really is no call for paranoia. Mistakes do happen."

Tom sucked in his lip. Perhaps this was plausible, but it felt wrong. "I know about CERUS."

Chatsworth went pale.

"I know they fund the clinic. If you don't want to talk to me, then I'm going to the police. One way or another I'm getting some answers."

Chatsworth's eyes flared and he shook his head. "I guess it's time you did know a few things." He walked over to his desk. "You should probably see this." He pulled out something and pointed it at Tom.

A hand gun.

Chatsworth shook his head. "I'm sorry." And he pulled the trigger.

Tom's heart leapt, but there was no bang, only a soft click and a stinging in his chest. Looking down, he saw a dart sticking out. Then everything blurred to black.

◇ ◇ ◇

Chatsworth moved to Tom's slumped form, checking his pulse. Then he hurried over to his computer and, hands shaking, connected a secure call, flagging it code-red. Marron responded almost immediately.

"Subject Zero is here," said Chatsworth.

"You said you'd discharged him."

"He claimed to be feeling unwell, but it was a ruse to get into the building," said the doctor. "He knows. Somehow he knows about CERUS. That we lied to him. He said he was going to the police. He said he had an MRI scan today. And it showed something metallic in his head."

Marron growled. "Where is Faraday now?"

"He's... sedated. I used the tranq gun."

There was another pause. A much longer one. "I'm sending someone over to tidy this up. They'll take Tom to a secure location. We'll work things out from there."

Chatsworth forced himself to breath more slowly. "I appreciate that."

"My resource will be with you in thirty minutes. Make arrangements for her to get in unnoticed."

FORTY-ONE

MARRON SAT IN HIS CONTROL room: the Faraday situation was one he would prefer to take care of personally, but the metrics on his screen were showing something wrong with his building and he was the only person who could investigate. He picked up one of his secure phones and called a familiar number.

"Yes?" answered a quiet voice.

Marron smiled. "Alex, I have a task for you. I need you at the clinic. Chatsworth is threatening to screw up the whole thing. He has Subject Zero with him, drugged. The doctor's finished his work with Subjects One to Four. And Zero didn't prove viable. We need to sanitise."

A pause. "I understand."

Marron frowned. "From your hesitation, do you disagree?"

"I thought Zero had other... relevance."

"Only to a point. There isn't time to manage him."

"Then I'll see it done. I should be there in twenty minutes."

"Update me when it's complete." Marron closed the call, turning back to his screen and the problem he was trying to unravel.

Two hours ago there had been a fault in the building network:

an overload that had caused a local re-boot. That such a fault could arise was not unexpected, but *why* it had arisen should be immediately apparent: there should be some identifiable triggering event. And there was nothing that seemed to fit the bill. Could the fault have been generated deliberately to create a distraction, to mask something else? If so, Marron couldn't see what the 'something else' might be. All the security systems, all the firewalls, seemed to be intact. No data tunnel of any form had been opened from outside the building.

To be absolutely certain, he ran a check on the system-data files. No file had been altered. But several had been accessed at almost exactly the same moment as the network had briefly gone down. He brought up the details: the files had been accessed from *within* the building.

Marron straightened in his chair. There were few people with the expertise and capability to break CERUS' interior security systems. A brute-force hack would have taken several thousand years. Whoever had accessed the files had insider knowledge of the system.

So what had they been looking for? It was still a vast ocean of information, almost impossible to navigate without very specific knowledge. But, as he checked, he realised that it had been navigated. The perpetrator had made an unfettered beeline for Project Tantalus. How had they even known to look? And who could have done this? Whoever it was had looked over everything related to the project. Even Subject Zero. At least some details weren't in those files, but it was still a substantial breach. He needed to know who had done it. And he needed to find them.

The fault that had triggered the reboot had manifested itself without a specific point of incidence: the whole subnet had failed. At first he thought he'd have to run analysis on everyone, but no.

It *had* to be a visitor or intruder. No employee would be brazen and stupid enough to attempt it. He set the system running a search of the CCTV footage from an hour before the incident, targeting visitors and scanning with facial recognition and pattern-matching software to identify suspicious behaviour. A dozen possible targets flagged. Most were known quantities: people who'd been doing business with CERUS for years. But two were new to his list. One was a man who was quickly identified as a representative of a local charity that CERUS wanted to align with. The other was a woman: *Daniella Lawrence*. He'd not heard the name before, although her face had a familiarity about it. He ran some broader searches and found several Daniella Lawrences of the same approximate age: a hairdresser, a teacher, a musician, and a medical doctor who worked in West Africa. This woman looked like none of them.

He isolated her activity in the CCTV footage. She sat, working on a laptop like it was an extension of her hands, occasionally glancing around. He zoomed in, the high resolution footage clarifying. There was something about her mannerisms, about those eyes, but he couldn't place it. Whoever she was, she knew what she was doing.

But so did he. He called up other CCTV footage and quickly viewed the same woman arriving. He saw the guard giving her the guide to the tower, the small souvenir booklet that every visitor was provided with. A memento of their visit. At least that was one of the guide's purposes. It also contained a paper-circuit tracking device that would activate once per hour for approximately a week and attempt to connect to a local network. If it could, it would send a message giving its GPS coordinates. Apart from those few seconds' of activity every hour, it was almost impossible to detect.

Marron smiled. If she still had the guide, he could find her.

FORTY-TWO

THE BARN WAS ONE OF a number of old outbuildings on the farm, located a few miles from Windsor, an hour west of London. Lentz had, years previously, struck a deal with the farmer to use the wooden structure for long-term storage of some old machinery. It wasn't an accurate description of what she did with the place, but the farmer had never seemed all that interested in the details of her activities.

She always checked on the barn when she returned to the UK, to make sure it was equipped and ready for her; today that care was going to pay dividends. She navigated the unmade road in the dim headlights of her twenty-year-old transit van: a vehicle that had once been white but was now several shades of dirty grey. Parking in the lane, she pulled out her phone and accessed a hidden wireless network. The barn's security system told her the site had not been disturbed.

Removing a heavy key from her pocket, she undid the oversized padlock and let herself in, strip lights flickering on and illuminating the space. It was full of old tractors and other farm machinery, very little of it ever likely to work again. Lentz pushed aside a deceptively light tractor wheel, revealing a trapdoor, and descended into a space full of equipment that was not so out of date and considerably more functional. She pulled dust sheets away to reveal a number of computer servers and three large computer displays. Every inch of wall space was decked with racking, all loaded with electronic components and mechanical parts, except for a single shelf on which stood a line of faded photos of two little girls and a child's remote-controlled car, decades old.

Lentz set her laptop on an empty desk and began scrolling through what she had managed to download from CERUS Tower. Unfortunately it was very little. She did not have enough to perform any useful analysis. She knew they were combining Tantalus with nanotechnology, but none of the specifics.

But she could guess a lot. It made her giddy and sick at the same time. The scientist in her almost couldn't contain herself: the humanitarian she had become wanted to scream.

Should she just go to the police? Last time that strategy had got her 'killed' – at least as far as CERUS was concerned. And to give her story any credibility she would have to reveal who she was, which was a can of worms she did not want opened. At this point, it was her one real advantage over CERUS.

So what should she do? She could try to re-enter CERUS Tower, but she doubted that would work. She was lucky she had got away undetected this time.

She opened her bag and removed the CERUS Tower guide, flicking through its pages. It was supposed to be a guide to the building, to the company, but it told her nothing she needed to know, just what they wanted her to know. As if it were more for their benefit than hers. She threw the guide aside and adjusted her wig, which still itched.

She needed to think laterally. Where else might CERUS data be stored? They were undoubtedly doing work at sites other than the Tower. Working at the old Eastwell site had taught her that Bern always planned carefully with special locations completely ring-fenced from the main operation. Nothing in the data she had downloaded indicated where the latest might be.

Sighing, she turned to her folders of publicly available data on CERUS Tower. The plans and specifications, down to power and sewer supply, were available for inspection at the local council offices; Lentz had made a nuisance of herself over the years, challenging the design plans at various stages. She hadn't been able to stop the Tower being built, but she'd made Bern's life difficult. And she'd archived a wealth of information about every aspect of the design of the building. Just nothing that would help her now.

So where else could she look?

And then it hit her.

Armstrong.

He had clearly been acting against CERUS. He must have acquired data and hidden it somewhere. Had they recovered it? Or was that why they'd blown up his house? Was it still somewhere among the ruins?

She palmed the van keys. It was worth a look.

FORTY-THREE

TOM WOKE WITH A GASP, sucking in a deep breath of air. It felt like he had been thrown into a tub of ice water, yet he was completely dry. Breathing hard, he looked around. He was still in the office at the clinic, but he was tied to the chair. He started to test his bonds, then something made him look up.

And he froze.

Chatsworth sat opposite. And he was dead. At least that was Tom's presumption, based on the grey of his skin and terrible bulging eyes.

The door opened and a woman walked in. Not in a black dress this time, as she had been at the launch of CERUS Tower, but Tom recognised her in an instant.

She looked at him with mild surprise. "You aren't supposed to be awake yet. This is awkward."

Tom was so angry, had so many questions, that they jammed in his throat. He coughed and managed to spit out, "You killed him. Why?"

"He had become a liability." She placed an electronic device with a keypad and display on Chatsworth's desk. "Don't go anywhere," she said, and walked from the room.

Tom assessed his options. He was tied up and still groggy, although his head was clearing fast. Perhaps he could negotiate a way out of this? But then he shook his head. She had basically admitted to murder in front of him. She wouldn't let him leave.

The woman returned, dragging a large metal cylinder.

"What is that?" he asked.

She placed it next to the desk then clipped the device to it. "It's an oxygen tank. I need an accelerant because there's no mains gas supply to this room." She tapped some numbers into the device and the digits 15:00 appeared.

"Three o'clock tomorrow afternoon?" he asked hopefully.

She turned to him. "Fifteen minutes. Sorry, Tom. I'm under instructions to clean up this mess."

"So you're just going to leave me here? To watch that countdown?"

She seemed to consider that, then reached into a pocket and withdrew a familiar item.

"This is the tranquilliser gun that the doctor used on you." She raised it and aimed. "I was told you were special: that we're alike. But I didn't see it at the party and I don't see it now."

And she fired.

The same click, the same sting, then he was fading, fading...

Tom woke with a start, still sitting in the chair. In front of him the red glow of the timer glared.

3:01... 3:00... 2:59...

In shock he sat up and immediately realised he was untied. For a moment he wondered why, then realised he had, again, woken up much faster than expected. She hadn't wanted to leave evidence of him being tied up, so that this looked like another 'accident'. Could that be enough to save him?

2:43... 2:42... 2:41...

He lurched over to the timer and looked at it closely. He couldn't quite say why but it *felt* complicated. There were several buttons of different colours, but no markings.

2:19... 2:18... 2:17...

Should he try to disarm it? Might he just set it off? Something in his head was telling him to have a go: that he could do this. He looked across at Chatsworth. If he did not act fast, he would be joining the doctor.

2:07... 2:06... 2:05...

He took a decision. With renewed energy he ran to the door.

It was locked. And the key was gone.

Gritting his teeth, he pushed hard. The door groaned in its frame but held. He tried again, throwing his full weight against it, but was thrown back onto the floor. There could only be a minute and a half left now. He thought back to when Kate had rescued him from the mugger. He remembered the flash of movement as she had kicked. So much power and accuracy. He had tried a few kicks like that since in front of his bedroom mirror, feeling like a fool but curious too. He tried to recall what it felt like, then kicked out.

He bounced off the door again.

1:10... 1:09... 1:08...

Adrenalin racing, he shook his head, drew in a deep breath and closed his eyes. He could see the kick in his mind. He watched how her leg moved: the exact way it extended and accelerated. He could do that. He could recreate it.

He kicked again.

The door burst open. With a whoop of triumph he leapt through then ran towards the emergency stairwell, bounded down two flights of stairs and out through a fire door.

Behind him a hot angry explosion blossomed.

FORTY-FOUR

KATE EASED HER VW BEETLE to a stop outside the gates of the Angstrom Clinic and turned off the tiny engine. It was a dark, cloudless night and the only illumination came from two rather feeble streetlamps.

"OK, now what?" she asked, looking at her watch.

"I still think we should call the police," Jo said. "After what we discovered in Harley Street--" She stopped as a motorbike glided smoothly out of the private road and past the Beetle, the rider turning briefly to look at them. The electric gates buzzed and began to close.

Kate shook her head. "Do you think Tom is confronting Chatsworth?"

"Probably. He looked pretty mad."

"Then we should get in there and stop him."

"You think they'll just let us in?"

"I didn't mean we should ask for permission--"

In the distance was the sharp, percussive bang of an explosion.

Jo threw herself out of the car and ran to peer through the gates. In the distance there was an angry red glow. She moved towards the gates as they clicked shut. "We have to get in there!"

"Actually maybe we *should* call the police," Kate said, also climbing out of the car.

Jo stabbed at the buzzer. "You call them! I need to find Tom!"

From inside the clinic grounds, they heard the pounding of someone running towards them, gasping for breath.

A moment later, Tom pelted into the dim illumination of the streetlights. He saw them and froze. "What are you two doing here?"

Jo gripped the bars. "We wanted to stop you doing something stupid." She looked back in the direction of the explosion. "What happened?"

"We need to get out of here. It's not safe. I'll tell you on the way." He glared at the metal bars and kicked at them. "Jo, do you have a hacksaw in your bag?" he called through the bars.

"Don't be ridiculous." She unshouldered her rucksack. "I do have ten metres of climbing rope, though."

"What on earth is that for?" asked Kate.

Jo shrugged as she pulled the rope out and slung one end over the top of the gate to Tom. "Just in case." She pulled the rope tight.

"Just in case of what?" asked Kate.

Tom started climbing: he hauled himself quickly over as Jo nodded approvingly. The moment he jumped down to stand next to her, shivering despite the mild night, she wrapped her arms around him.

He hugged her back for a moment and then pushed her firmly away. "Let's get out of here."

FORTY-FIVE

IT WAS THE EARLY HOURS of the morning. Marron sat in the back of the dark grey Ford Mondeo: a boring vehicle perfect for this mission. The car made its way onto the M4 motorway, heading west. Twenty minutes ago the tracer in the CERUS guide had pinged its latest location: a farm on the outskirts of Windsor. Whoever this woman might prove to be, he knew where she was. It was time to have a conversation.

With him in the car were two of his more reliable security staff, not part of the regular CERUS Tower security team. They were both gruff ex-military and more than capable with the range of weapons that they were carrying.

His phone rang: Alex's number. "Is it done?" he asked.

"There was a complication."

"What do you mean?"

"Chatsworth has been managed. But Faraday escaped."

"How is that possible?"

"I left him tranq'd in a locked room for the bomb to take care of, but now I'm looking at him, climbing over the gates of the clinic. I'm not sure how he recovered so quickly."

"Then why are we talking?"

"That would be the complication. There are two people with him: one is his flatmate, the other is the reporter."

"I thought he'd gone to the clinic alone."

"Apparently they followed him. I figured I'd best check with you before I act."

Marron muttered. "You're going to have to manage all of them."

"Is that kind of body count acceptable?"

"No, but what is the alternative?" He paused. "I want you to call in some support."

"I can deal with three civilians."

"I'm sure you can, but I can't take any chances. The reporter has already proven she has some self-defence skills, and Faraday is apparently less predictable than we believed. No mistakes this time, Alex."

"Working alone is how I avoid mistakes."

"Just do as you're told."

There was a pause. "I monitored their conversation. They're returning to his apartment."

"Then you know where to set up. Be there first."

"Understood."

Marron click the phone off. "How long?" he asked the driver.

"Twenty-five minutes, Sir," the driver replied, tapping a navigation screen on the dashboard.

"Make it twenty."

Nineteen minutes later, they pulled off the side road onto a gravel track, powerful headlights illuminating the way. They wound through a stand of trees and came to a halt fifty metres from a large wooden structure.

"This is the location," the driver said, "but it looks like an old barn."

Marron leaned forward, looking at the display on his phone. "The signal hasn't rebroadcast in the last hour."

"I see no signs of occupation. You want me to drive closer?"

Marron shook his head. "Let's proceed on foot."

The three men grabbed powerful torches and walked quietly around the building.

"Those tyre tracks look fresh," said the driver, pointing at the ground. "But it might not mean anything."

Marron walked over to the main door. There was a very large padlock in place. As he looked closer, he could see it was well-oiled.

"Is it a trick?" asked the driver. "Did she make it look like the signal came from here?"

Marron frowned. "If she knew about it, she'd probably just disable it rather than try anything more complicated. Perhaps she came here then went elsewhere."

"Want us to break in and have a look around? I've got tools in the car."

Marron sucked in his lower lip. "I'm not sure. Perhaps--" His phone rang. Another member of his team.

"The system raised a flag," the man reported. "The cameras we placed at Armstrong's house. The same woman who entered the Tower has just arrived there."

"Get a team in place, but don't do anything until I get close." Marron clicked the phone off and turned to the driver. "I need you to take me to Armstrong's house: the target is there."

"We could just torch this place."

"After we're done, you two can come back here and turn the place over, just in case. For now, let's get moving."

FORTY-SIX

IT WAS DARK WHEN KATE parked outside Tom's apartment building. The street was deserted. Tom sat staring through the window. He could almost feel the hum of the streetlights above him.

"We should just go to the police," Kate said. "That would be the sensible course of action."

Tom shivered. "Things in my head? Bombs killing people? The police will think I'm mad." He paused. "Or a killer."

Jo gripped his shoulder. "These people just sent a professional to kill you. The question isn't whether the police believe you, it's whether they can protect you."

Kate rolled her eyes. "C'mon. You think they'll do anything if they know he's spoken to the police?"

"All we know," said Jo, "is that whoever is involved wants Tom dead."

"They probably think they've succeeded," said Tom, his voice weak. "I just need to stop. To think about what to do next. Let's go inside and take it from here."

Jo nodded. "And hopefully the journalist can hold off calling her editor."

Kate sighed. "Believe it or not, I'd prefer to focus on us all getting out of this unhurt."

They made their way into the building and up the stairs to the second floor. Jo unlocked the door, ushering them all inside while Tom closed it behind them, sliding the bolt into place. He frowned at the keypad on the wall. "Didn't you set the alarm when you left?"

Jo looked puzzled. "I haven't been home all day, so it must have been you."

Tom jerked his head to Kate. "We need to get out--"

"Stay where you are," said a chillingly familiar voice.

He turned and saw the woman from the party: the woman who had killed Chatsworth and left him to die. Tom knew he ought to be afraid, but something overrode it. This woman knew what was going on: she must know who was behind it. She would give him answers. Tightening his fists, his heart banging in his chest, he threw himself forward.

But Kate moved faster, stepping forwards and driving the heel of her hand towards the other woman's throat. Tom's eyes could barely follow the movement. Yet the woman simply swayed back and caught Kate's wrist, twisting it sharply, horribly. There was a loud crack and Kate screamed in pain, falling.

Tom began to run forward, but another voice called out, "Stop right there!" A large man with a shaved head appeared in the doorway to Tom's bedroom, holding a silenced pistol.

Tom edged away, dimly aware that Jo seemed to have vanished. "What do you want?"

The woman took a step towards him. "How did you get away from the bomb? You should have been unconscious for an hour."

"I don't know what to tell you. What the hell did I do to deserve all this?"

She laughed. "You were born."

Tom was about to speak again, but, with a loud shriek, Jo charged from her bedroom, a baseball bat raised over her head. Everyone looked on, stunned, as she brought the bat down towards the gunman's arm. But she was not quick enough. The man spun away, his expression intense. He raised the gun.

And fired.

Everything seemed to move slowly. The impact hit Jo in the chest and she was knocked backwards. Tom leapt to catch her, but she was heavy, lifeless. She slipped through his arms, crumpling onto the floor. There was blood. So much blood. And she didn't seem to be breathing. He needed to do something. Then he saw her glassy, staring eyes, and he knew that it was already too late.

He screamed.

"So much for doing this cleanly." The woman reached inside her jacket and produced a similar pistol. She pointed it at Tom. "Look what I have to do now."

"No!" shouted Kate.

But the woman swung her gun away from Tom, towards her colleague.

The man with the shaved head blinked. "What are you doing, Alex?"

"Giving them a killer. Someone of no consequence." And she fired. The bullet struck him between the eyes: the back of his head exploded and he fell to the ground. A terrible silence, mixed with the smell of gunshot and blood, permeated the room. The woman shook her head as she raised the gun. "I'll make this quick."

Tom stared at the barrel: at her finger on the trigger.

He wanted to stop her. He needed to stop her.

He *would* stop her.

And something within him connected with that anger.

Something reached out. He curled his fists, digging his nails into his palms, drawing blood. Next to him Kate seemed to be shifting her balance.

He shouted, a cry of pure rage. But his voice seemed to have gone and all he managed was a hoarse gasp. In the next room there was a pop and a voice spoke, commanding and loud: *"...and now it's time to take a few calls...".*

Alex turned, confused. "Who else is here?"

Tom started to move, but again Kate was faster. She scooped up the baseball bat Jo had dropped and swung it at Alex's head. Alex started to react, to sway back from the blow.

But this time she wasn't fast enough. There was an ugly thunk as it connected with her temple and she fell to the ground.

FORTY-SEVEN

THE RUINS OF RICHARD ARMSTRONG'S house were immersed in darkness. Putting some form of lighting on would certainly have helped in the search, but it would also have alerted the small police team still stationed outside. Lentz stood up from where she had been scouring the remains of the kitchen and rubbed her back. For the first fifteen minutes, the smell of charred wood and melted plastic had made her want to gag, but she'd worked on regardless. Yet, despite her diligence, it all looked like a huge waste of time.

Had Armstrong hidden the data in a secret fire-proof safe? He'd always been so thorough, so careful, she couldn't believe he wouldn't have tried something of the sort. But if he'd been too careful she might never find it. And if she were to take steps to thwart CERUS, she needed a weapon: her weapon of choice was always information.

So where could it be? It had to be hidden but accessible, because he'd probably have updated it regularly. But she'd already exhausted everywhere obvious that hadn't burned down. What if Marron and his team had removed it already?

Her phone vibrated.

Lentz held her breath. One of the two motion sensors she'd placed on the damaged external doors had been triggered.

Someone else was here. One of the police? Had she been seen, despite her precautions? Would she be able to talk her way out of this?

"I see you there," said a voice with a clipped accent. "The police have this building surrounded. But then you probably saw as much when you snuck in."

She held her breath.

"I *can* see you. You're in the remains of the kitchen. Now do you want to tell me who you are and what's going on, or shall I come and get you?"

Lentz sighed. She would have to respond. "Who are you?"

A man appeared in the doorway. "Officer Croft, CID. And you?"

"Daniella Lawrence, journalist."

"For which paper?"

"I'm freelance."

"Do you have some ID?"

"Do you?"

He smiled and held up a warrant card in one hand, shining a torch on it with the other.

"Very convincing. I have a similar one that I bought on Amazon."

He gave a snort. "Now yours, please."

She reached into her pocket and pulled out a dog-eared plastic card, throwing it across to him.

He caught it and frowned. "So what are you really doing in here, Ms Lawrence? Because it looks like you're interfering with a crime scene."

"Actually I've been interfering with it for some time so I'm curious about why you only just came in. I think you were watching to see what I would do."

"You're not really a journalist."

Lentz smiled. "And you're not really a police officer because to see me in the dark you must have had some kind of thermal imaging camera. Why would you have one, and why would you be pointing it at a burned out house?"

"Fair point." He reached into his pocket and pulled out a gun. "Shall we start again?"

"Do you work for Marron?"

He frowned. "Peter Marron? Why would you think that?" He pulled out a badge and turned it towards her.

She squinted. "So your name *is* Croft. Security service. Huh."

"Your turn."

She sighed. "Look at my ID card again. It tells you all you need to know if you look closely."

He held up the small piece of white plastic in his left hand. "And what am I looking for?"

Lentz reached into her pocket and touched a button on a mini controller. Then she closed her eyes tight.

The surface of the card pulsed impossibly bright. Croft shrieked and, as Lentz re-opened her eyes, she saw him stagger backwards.

Then something unexpected happened. Croft dropped to the floor and fell silent.

In his place stood an older man with thin grey hair and an intense expression. Someone she'd hoped never to see again.

Peter Marron.

In his right hand was a cosh. He glanced at Croft then stepped over him and smiled.

FORTY-EIGHT

LENTZ WATCHED AS MARRON PULLED a gun from his pocket. Had he come alone?

"I'm not sure what you're doing here," he said, "but I'm going to need you to explain." He raised the gun and pointed it at her chest. "Who are you?"

She cleared her throat. "I'm a journalist, please--"

He cut her off with a laugh. "Yes, and I'm an astronaut. You just disabled this man with some type of flash-bang grenade, so stop wasting my time. Why were you at CERUS Tower earlier?"

Lentz froze. It wasn't just coincidence that Marron was here then. "I'm researching a story."

Suddenly his eyes narrowed and his smile vanished. "Ah... Now I know who you are."

"I don't think--"

He shook his head. "Despite your attempts to hide it, you clearly know me. You know to be afraid of me."

"You do have a gun."

He shrugged. "You can change your face, your hair, but your voice is the same." He took a step forwards. "So tell me, Dominique, how are you still alive?"

Lentz glared at him for several seconds before replying: "Because whoever tried to have me killed sent a rather pliable hitman." She paused. "I always assumed it was Bern."

Marron blinked. "William has always been the one with the grand vision. He relies on me to take care of the details."

"*Did he know*?" she growled.

"How does the cliché go? I'll be the one asking the questions. What information did Armstrong give you to get you back here?"

"You don't want to hurt me," she said. "You'll just bring the police stationed outside down on you if I scream."

"Possible, but I have a heavily-armed team outside. If we have to, we'll take them all out. Do you want their deaths on your conscience?"

She sighed. "My conscience has always been somewhat complex."

"Mine too. But let's get over the notion that you have a choice in complying." He pulled a capped syringe from his pocket.

Her eyes flickered.

He smiled. "This is one of the simpler programmes we've developed for our nanites, but one of the most useful. I can't think of anyone more appropriate to use it on. I like to think of it as truth nano."

Lentz smiled and lunged at him.

He fired without hesitation, the subsonic squeal of the silencer bouncing off the walls. The bullet struck her in the chest and she fell backwards.

Marron gave a grunt and walked forwards, poking her with his toe. As he did, she rolled and grabbed his leg, lifting it sharply upwards, throwing his balance. As his arms wheeled, she plucked the gun from his hand then shoved him back across the room. Before he could recover, she had the weapon aimed at his face.

"Body armour," she said, tapping her chest. "Ultra-light. And twenty-five years of martial arts training. I figured it would come in handy one day."

"I'll bear that in mind next time," he ground out.

She aimed the gun at his face. "I could just kill you now."

He blinked. "Go on then."

She glared at him, then punched him on the nose with a tightly curled fist. "If you follow me, I will shoot you."

Lentz kept low as she crept out of the door, moving to the cover of the trees next to Armstrong's garden pond. She had been sloppy and it had nearly cost her everything. She didn't even know how Marron had managed to track her down. She held her breath, watching the back door of the house. Marron would surely be calling his support team already, but the police meant they would have to act carefully.

Creeping forwards a few more steps, she nearly fell over two faded garden gnomes fishing in the pond. She rolled her eyes, moving around them. And then it struck her. Armstrong had always talked about spending time in his garden. For a techie, he loved to get his hands dirty, and part of that was the time he spent painting his prized gnome collection. He had said they were real collectors' pieces that most people ignored or laughed at.

Away from the house, hidden in plain sight. Could it be?

She picked up the nearest gnome and hefted it in her hand. It felt heavy and a tap suggested it was solid. She tried the other.

Also solid.

With a sigh she put it back, standing it carefully next to the first. They looked so sad, chipped and worn. Perhaps they got hit by the explosion. Her eyes roamed the pond. Something was sticking out of the water. She reached down and drew a third gnome out from under a clump of pondweed. It felt much heavier, water pouring out of it, the weight rapidly diminishing.

It was hollow.

She put down the gun and ran her fingers over the gnome's surface. No obvious hidden compartment. Was there a gap at the neck? She twisted the head gently and it lifted off. Inside was a small compartment containing a high-capacity solid-state drive.

From the house she heard footsteps. Marron's support team must have arrived.

Time to move.

Marron waited in the kitchen, wiping blood from his nose and glaring at the back door. He was joined by one of his men, who entered through the front.

"You took your time," Marron said.

"Sir, there's been a development with Alex. She was captured at Faraday's apartment. The police are attending."

"We can't let them interrogate her." He raised his eyebrows. "You know what to do."

FORTY-NINE

IT TOOK LESS THAN TEN minutes for the armed response team to arrive at Tom's apartment block, just as the sun was starting to rise. Shortly after that there were dozens of plain-clothes and uniformed officers swarming through the building, putting up cordons, trailing police tape as they went.

But Tom didn't care. The inspector in charge quickly moved them downstairs and took initial statements. A growing crowd of onlookers watched from across the street. Two officers secured a groggy-looking Alex inside a prisoner-transport vehicle. She locked eyes with Tom and gave him an unreadable stare before the door was closed on her. Tom turned away, watching as two body bags were carried out of the building. One of those bags contained his friend.

A policewoman tapped him on the shoulder. "You're going to be at the station for a while. Is there anyone you want us to call for you? Your partner? A relative or friend?"

Tom stared at where they were loading the body bags into an ambulance. He shook his head.

"This way then, Sir."

Tom and Kate were guided to sit in the back of a police car.

"Where are we going?" he asked.

"Charing Cross Police Station," the policewoman said, as she climbed in the front. "Say, how did you manage to overpower that woman if she had a gun?"

"The television turned itself on in the other room. Don't know why. It distracted her for long enough..." He took a long breath. "Where are you taking her?"

"Same place as you."

"I get the feeling the people she works for will try to get her back."

"I can assure you there's no chance of that."

His brows furrowed. "Well, officer, that's probably because you have no idea what you're talking about."

The woman blinked, then turned back to face front and the car eased away, following the prisoner transport.

Tom leaned back in his seat. Kate reached over and squeezed his hand, wincing as she did so.

"How's your arm?" he asked.

Kate looked down at the sling she was wearing. "They checked me over. It's not broken, just bruised. I said no to pain relief. I get hit worse in most karate classes."

"You saved both our lives."

"I'm just sorry that I couldn't..." She trailed off, her eyes glistening.

Tom closed his eyes and tried to shut out the world. In the space of a few days everything had changed. None of this should have happened. If he hadn't accepted the job, he wouldn't have been at the party, wouldn't have been in hospital. He would be just fine. And Jo would still be alive.

His eyes jerked open and he found he was breathing hard and fast.

"What's the matter?" Kate asked. "Are you sick?"

Tom looked around. They'd just pulled up near a set of traffic lights, behind the prisoner transport, which was blocked from proceeding by a van that had pulled out from a side road. "Something feels wrong." He narrowed his eyes. "Are these lights taking a long time to change?"

"Perhaps a little--" began Kate.

The doors of the van burst open and six men carrying automatic rifles emerged. Pedestrians nearby started screaming and running away.

"Assistance required!" the policewoman shouted into her radio. "Armed units respond."

The men moved to the prisoner transport. Two were carrying a heavy ram and they swung it at the back door. It dented but did not break. From the police car behind Tom's, two armed officers emerged and shouted a warning. They were answered by rifle fire and ducked for cover.

"Get down on the floor!" shouted the policewoman from the front of their car.

Kate obeyed but Tom ignored her, watching the two men throw down the ram. One of them swung a rucksack off his back and produced a round metal disc from it. He stuck it on the door and all the men stepped clear.

The disc exploded. Car alarms all around started ringing.

Tom pulled at the door handle, but it wouldn't open. "We have to stop them!"

"Sir, please stay in the vehicle," the policewoman shouted. "We need backup immediately," she said into her radio.

Through the clouds of smoke, Tom saw the men jump into the van, brutally clubbing the guards with their rifle butts, then grabbing Alex's slender form and carrying her out. They climbed back into their van then turned and pointed their rifles at the police cars. Tom threw his arm over Kate and ducked. Two gunshots hit the car. Then there was the sound of the van's tyres squealing as it sped away.

"I warned you, but you didn't listen," Tom shouted at the police woman, who was craning back to check on them.

"Stay in the vehicle," she repeated. Then she climbed out and locked the door, running over to the prisoner transport and climbing in the back.

Kate tugged at the door handle, but the door remained closed. She leaned close and whispered, "How did you know something was going to happen?"

"I can't explain it. Something just felt *wrong*. It doesn't matter now. We're not safe with these idiots. We have to go."

Kate shook her head. "If you hadn't noticed, she locked us in."

Tom reached for the door handle and pulled. It opened.

"How did you do that?"

"Maybe one of the bullets hit something. Look, you can stay here if you like but I'm going."

Kate sighed and nodded.

"We'll head for that street on the left." He pushed open the door then launched himself out, Kate scrambling to follow. He heard shouts from the direction of the prisoner transport, but they were already tearing off down the street.

FIFTY

IT WAS 7AM AND REEMS had already been in her bunker office for more than an hour, trying to digest the reports that had come in overnight. Croft had requested a meeting and now she was forcing calm into her voice as they argued.

He stood, eyes blazing, looking like he was not going to be assuaged. "Three incidents in one night. Three people dead, a prisoner liberated from police custody, and an MI5 officer – *me* – attacked in the line of duty."

"I presume you want to make a link to CERUS?"

"*A* link? How many do you want?"

"I mean one based on actual evidence. One that suggests they are in any way culpable."

"I can't believe I'm having to fight you on this. I don't understand it at all."

She glanced at a screen in front of her. "I'm not fighting you. But you're too close to the situation and you can't judge it dispassionately. You went into Armstrong's burnt out house in the dead of night without backup, for God's sake." She shook her head.

"So you're saying I should *ignore* what's happened?"

"We don't ignore anything, George. We *prioritise*." She gave a sigh. "So who is this Alex woman?"

"We don't know yet. She had no ID and she hasn't been flagged by facial recognition. Likely a professional."

Reems scratched her nose. "Do you think she was working with the other two and we didn't spot it?"

"It seems unlikely given that she was about to kill them when they overpowered her."

"And why was the reporter with the lawyer? Are they in a relationship?"

"I don't think so. Actually I met reporter at the Armstrong property. She seemed suspicious of me: her company searched my credentials."

Reems closed her eyes and rubbed her temples. "You're right, George. This is worth further investigation." She opened her eyes. "Go and speak with the reporter's editor: see where that leads you. But make sure you go home tonight. See your family." She paused. "How is your daughter?"

"I'm sure you don't need to be troubled with..."

Reems folded her arms. "George, please. I have some idea what you've been going through."

Croft looked away. "We have good days and bad days. We've just changed specialists but..." He sighed. "It doesn't affect my duties."

"Sometimes we get so caught up in trying to save the nation that we forget about life closer to home."

"I'll keep that in mind." He turned and left the room.

Reems watched the door close behind him. She locked it remotely before she picked up her phone and called a number by memory.

FIFTY-ONE

IT WAS BUSY ON CHISWICK High Road, the morning rush hour in full swing. Tom and Kate made their way slowly on foot, hidden amongst the crowds. Reasonably sure they weren't being followed, they walked into a Starbucks and ordered two cappuccinos.

"Isn't this a bit public?" Tom asked.

Kate shrugged. "We won't stay long. I just need to think of somewhere we can go."

"These people just rescued one of their own from a police convoy. You think you have somewhere safe from that?" He shook his head. "While you're with me you're in danger, but there's no need for you to be caught up in this any longer."

She reached forward. "Tom, what would you do by yourself? Go to CERUS? Go back to the police? We don't know what to do because we don't understand what's going on. Look, I'll find out what I can. Geraldine tracked down some paper records about projects CERUS did in the past that have been wiped from digital archives. Maybe there's something in there."

"Fine. But I'm still going my own way. I've had one friend killed already today."

Kate looked away, biting her lip then nodded, turning back to him. "Give me your phone first. They'll use it to track you." She handed him a business card and scribbled a number on the back. "This phone doesn't connect to me in any records. Get yourself a cheap, basic handset and call me, but only let it ring once. Then I'll have your number but no one will be able to track the call. If I find anything, I'll contact you."

Tom pocketed the card then he placed his company phone on the table. "Do what you like with this."

"Where will you go?" She raised a hand. "Wait, don't tell me. Just stay safe."

FIFTY-TWO

MARRON WATCHED AS THE WHITE Ford Transit van pulled into the warehouse. It was not the vehicle that had intercepted the police convoy; that was currently being compacted at a discrete junkyard, after the occupants had switched to the replacement. He was as sure as he could be that they had not been followed. Four armed men climbed out and stood aside. Then Alex stepped out.

He walked over to her, his expression a mask. "What a mess," he said quietly. "What a complete and utter mess."

She looked him in the eye. "Clearly I have much to learn."

"You said you could handle Faraday." He leaned closer. "Should I give you another chance?"

She didn't blink. "I won't let you down again."

"You have to do better..." He smiled then wrapped his arms around her, hugging her fiercely. "You had me worried for a moment. If you weren't my daughter, I swear I'd... How did they overpower you?"

"I think Faraday's interface might be working. The television suddenly turned on and distracted me. Next time I'll be ready. Next time I will bring him back."

"Actually we don't need Faraday anymore, so I need you to neutralise him. He's currently my second highest priority. He ran off in the confusion your rescue created." Marron reached into his pocket and pulled out an oversized phone-like device. "But he won't be difficult to locate."

She took the device and switched it on. A map lit up on the screen. "So what's the highest priority?"

"A complication from the past. Dominique Lentz is still alive."

Alex's eyebrows rose. "How is that possible?"

"She negotiated with the assassin. Which is very disappointing."

"That'll teach you to outsource. Will she be a problem?"

"I intend to make sure she isn't. You focus on Faraday. Do you want a team?"

"I work better alone. This morning certainly showed that."

"That was unfortunate." He scratched his nose. "Who shot our man, by the way?"

Alex gave him a direct look. "He misread the situation. What about Chatsworth? How are your friends going to react to that?"

"I'll handle it. Just get to Faraday."

Alex nodded. "I'll call you when it's done."

Marron was watching her walk away when his phone rang.

"Have you seen the news?" Bern asked. "What happened with Chatsworth?"

Marron took a slow breath. "The police are there, investigating the explosion, but they'll find no connection to CERUS, and we don't need the good doctor for Phase Two."

"Heidn and Holm may get jumpy. Who is supposed to have done this?"

"Some other disgruntled patient. The Angstrom's client list includes plenty of rich angry people. I'll be sure to drop that into the conversation if the police question me."

"OK. And Peter, is there anything I need to know?"

Marron smiled to himself. There was only one answer that Bern ever wanted: "No, William. Nothing that you *need* to know."

FIFTY-THREE

A TIRED SECURITY GUARD WEARING a uniform a size or more too small guided George Croft across the third floor at Business Week News. Croft was wearing a regular suit, but he felt the eyes of the building on him as if they all knew who he was. *Journalists*, he thought. Much too observant.

The guard led him to a corner office and knocked loudly just below a brass name plaque that read 'Geraldine Cartwright', Editor in Chief. A square-jawed woman with intense eyes opened the door and beckoned him in. He wove between stacks of folders and took the offered seat, noting that she did not look pleased to see him.

"I know you're a busy woman," he said, putting as much warmth into his tone as he could, "so thank you for making time for me. I'm sure it will come as no surprise that I want to speak to you about Kate Turner. Do you know where she is?"

Geraldine gave a sniff. "Is she under investigation?"

"She was a witness to a double homicide."

"Along with a roadside gunfight. And I've already given a statement to the police this morning about what I know. What exactly is MI5's interest in this? Don't you trust our boys and girls in blue to do their job?"

"We just want to speak to her. We're not clear why she fled before we could do that."

"Kate was nearly shot while under police protection: I think she just wants to stay alive."

"Where would she go? Is there a friend or relative we could contact?"

"If she's trying to avoid discovery, do you think she'd do anything so obvious?"

Croft shrugged. "Was Kate working on a story about CERUS Biotech?"

"She covered the death of Richard Armstrong – I believe she ran into you when she visited the scene. Although then you were merely a police officer. Congratulations on the promotion."

Croft blinked. "Ms Turner was with a CERUS employee, Thomas Faraday, when the incident with the police convoy took place. Was he helping with her story?"

"You'd have to ask her."

"We'd certainly like to." Croft frowned. "And how about Mr Faraday's location?"

"How am I meant to know that?"

He paused, then lowered his voice. "People are being surprisingly resistant to putting the necessary resources into this investigation, even now. I want to do something, but I need your help. And I think Ms Turner and Mr Faraday need *mine*."

Geraldine turned away, staring out of the window. She seemed to nod to herself. "Are you sure?"

"About what?" asked Croft.

"I wasn't talking to you." Geraldine tapped her ear. She stood up and stared at him. "But now I am. Why don't you follow me?"

She led him out of her office and down a corridor to what looked like a storage room. Geraldine opened the door with a smug grin. Inside, sitting on a chair and wearing a wireless headset, was a figure that he immediately recognised.

"Hello, *Mr* Croft," said Kate Turner. "Good to see you again."

FIFTY-FOUR

IT WAS LATE MORNING AND Tom sat on a wooden bench, staring across the Thames at the Embankment. He cradled his hands around a strong cup of tea and let his mind drift. Since the CERUS party, his frame of reference, his whole world, had been coming apart. He didn't know what to do next.

He *wanted* to make what had happened 'unhappen'. He wanted to rip those responsible apart as if, by doing so, he could tear space and time asunder and pull Jo back into life. She had tried to save them all, and for her bravery she had died. And there was nothing he could do.

So if he could not reconfigure the universe, he could at least deliver retribution. But as the urge flashed through his mind, it made him uncomfortable. Was it a natural reaction to the horrific events, or had Jo's death changed him? He could see the moment in perfect detail - it had been replaying over and over in his head like a film shot in high definition, every frame eerily specific. And he realised that since Jo died, he hadn't felt a fog in his head: all his confusion had been replaced with absolute clarity.

Was this what they called post-traumatic shock? Or was it related to what they had done to him? His mind was full of images, of things that he had seen. He looked to his left and saw the London Eye revolving slowly. When he closed his eyes, he could still see the scene. He could look in detail at any part of it. He blinked and shook his head.

He thought back to the Italian vocabulary he had helped Jo learn. Then the moment at the restaurant when there had been that confusion over the menus. Perhaps there had not been any confusion. He pulled a notepad out of his bag and wrote without pausing. A minute later he looked down at what he had: an entire page of English and Italian words. He knew it was correct. Every last letter.

He stood up, threw his paper cup into a bin and started walking, making his way along the footpath. They – whoever they were – seemed to have given him a perfect memory, then made him watch something he wished he could forget. He would find some way to use it against them. But right now, angry and alone, he didn't know how. He walked over to the railing, looking down at the thick grey surface of the Thames, London's first highway. The river knew where it was going. Tom shook his head. He had to go somewhere too. But where?

FIFTY-FIVE

DOMINIQUE LENTZ SAT IN THE basement of her barn hideout, ignoring a cold cup of takeaway coffee and staring at her laptop screen. She had been reviewing the documents on Armstrong's high-capacity pen-drive for several hours, but it felt like only a few moments.

Twenty-five years ago, after she finally got through the layers of security around him, she had confronted Bern about Eastwell. He had sworn that the mistakes that had been made would never be repeated: that all the research would be destroyed. And she had believed him. Had he been deceived too? Or had he lied? It was a question she intended to ask him.

But first she needed to know more, including why the project was being resurrected now. Was it just that the tech had advanced sufficiently that Tantalus was now viable? The insertion of the chip had always been the major problem: too great a likelihood of rejection, too much radiation and heat created by the chip. Nano implantation was genius – if you could get it right. But she doubted that was the only reason Tantalus was back in operation now. CERUS needed the money – the worst rumours about their financial straits were not even half right. Necessity might be the mother of invention, but desperate men also seized on desperate measures and this smacked too much of the latter.

They already had a customer lined up, but she hadn't been able to find out any more.

What she had discovered was that CERUS was already trialling the new Tantalus technology with four subjects. She spotted another file and, frowning, clicked on it.

Not just four subjects. There was also a Subject Zero, handled completely separately from the others. An employee of CERUS, not referenced in the main project files. If he wasn't in a lab setting like the others, might she be able to reach him? Even if she could, what would she say? What was her endgame? Was she trying to avenge an old friend or was she unbendingly curious to see if they had done it and how? Or was it just that this was the right thing? Her chance to make a difference. To atone, in a way that twenty-five years fighting Ebola had not. She shook her head, and looked in her bag of tools and spare parts. Whatever the case, it was time to get to work.

Three hours later she had created what she needed. She had 'kludged' the scanner together with Blutack and sticky-tape: half its components were cannibalised from other devices, including her oldest mobile phone. The scanner's performance would be variable and she suspected the battery life would be dreadful, but that wouldn't matter if it just worked. She slotted in a nine-volt battery: it beeped into action and started scanning for a lock. Three minutes later it beeped again. Lentz looked at the display and smiled.

He was in central London, near Waterloo.

FIFTY-SIX

"I KNEW YOU WEREN'T POLICE," Kate told Croft, folding her arms.

Croft shrugged. "So what *is* your involvement in all this? Is it just about a story?"

"It was. But it's not really one we can publish now that we've become part of it and seen what danger we're in because of it."

"We were unprepared last time: it won't happen again. If I make a call, I can have two armed units here to escort you to a safe house in half an hour."

"You say that, but can you trust your own people?" Geraldine folded her arms. "Just before you arrived, I received a phone-call from my boss. I was told not to help you. It was more than a suggestion."

"You *knew* I was coming? Who tipped you off?" Croft demanded.

"I don't know. Like I said, *someone* contacted my boss: he wouldn't be drawn on the details. I assume it's someone in Government – or the Security Service. If I knew for sure, you'd have already read about it in the papers."

"How does Tom Faraday fit into all of this?"

Kate glanced at Geraldine. "We believe he is absolutely central."

"Central in what *way*? And where is he now?"

"I'm not sure we can trust you yet. Before I tell you anything about Tom, I need you to help me. I want you to find out about an old CERUS project called Tantalus. It seems to have been wiped from the digital footprint, but Geraldine found some details in old paper records. We think it's relevant." She paused. "We believe it involves intelligent nano."

His expression darkened. "If that is true, we should be going in now and searching CERUS' labs."

Kate shook her head. "If you could even get the operation sanctioned, the Tower's got ninety floors. Good luck with finding anything before their lawyers shut you down or their security team destroy any evidence. If you dig a little, something may come up that will help us formulate a better plan."

"Fine. I'll see what I can uncover. What are *you* going to do?"

"Best I don't give you the specifics. I'll call you again, via Geraldine, and we can meet."

"How soon?"

"Yesterday, if possible."

FIFTY-SEVEN

TOM WALKED WEST ALONG THE Thames, past the London Eye, as seagulls wheeled overhead. He felt in his pocket and found the phone he had bought on Kate's instructions: a cheap handset without even a touch-screen. He put in her number, let it ring once, then hung up.

He looked up to find himself passing a funfair set up on the plaza. Even though he was in the very centre of London, the peeling, faded attractions had seen better days. It was early and the crowd was sparse. He noticed a basketball shooting game where you had to score three shots out of five. On a whim, Tom handed over two pounds and grabbed a ball. He used to play at college and felt reasonably confident given that the hoop was quite close.

The first shot felt OK, but banged off the back rim. Adjusting his stance, Tom shot again. It felt perfect, but still ricocheted off the back. He squinted at the metal ring.

"That basket is not full size," he said to the boy running the stall.

The boy shrugged. "Just take your shots."

Tom frowned and shot again. Another miss.

"Better luck next time," said the boy, with a smug smile.

"I've got two more shots."

"Sure, whatever. But no prize if you don't get three in."

Tom picked up another ball. He felt the grooves on the rubber: felt the shape, allowed for the weight. And then he shot.

Another miss. He ignored the boy.

He grabbed the last ball and threw it. It went in. He blinked and thought about how it had felt: thought about the motions.

"One of out of five. Don't give up the day job," said the boy.

Tom narrowed his eyes. "I think I'll have another go."

"Sure," said the boy. "I'll take your money all day."

Tom cleared his mind, remembering what had happened with his last shot, loading it back into his memory.

Swish. In.

He picked up the next ball and repeated the process.

Another swish. Another score. The boy looked uneasy now.

Tom picked up the third, fourth and fifth balls with the same result.

"Oh wow," said a little girl, watching with her mother.

"You cheated," said the boy running the stall.

"How exactly?" Tom gave the boy a smile. "I'll have that one," he said, pointing at a large cuddly monkey. When the boy handed it over, Tom turned and offered it to the little girl. "Do you want to look after him for me? If it's OK with your mummy?" He glanced at the woman, who smiled in a bemused manner. "He's too big for me to take back to work." The little girl shrieked with delight and grabbed the toy.

Tom walked away, feeling good, but wondering what on earth had just happened. As he walked, he realised he'd not had breakfast – or dinner the previous night either. He felt the back of his head. There was a buzzing sensation again.

It was now beyond any doubt. They had done something to

him. And whoever *they* were, and whatever that *something* was, it had enabled him to do what he had done at the fairground. He had remembered the basketball shot and then been able to recreate it faultlessly. Just as he had been able to recall the Italian words. Perfect muscle memory and perfect recollection.

He found himself in a small park, surrounded by offices. Across the other side was a small café. As he walked, he closed his eyes. He could still see the scene before him: an old man sitting on a bench, a woman in a brown coat tapping at a tablet, two school kids arguing, and on the edge of the scene a figure dressed in black, looking directly at him.

His breath caught in his throat.

Alex.

A chill swept over him and he opened his eyes. The figure had gone. He spun around and then he saw her, walking sideways to him, trying to approach from a less obvious angle. Suddenly aware that he had seen her, she broke into a run.

How did she always seem to know where he would be? No time to worry about that now. She was closing fast, her face set.

Tom ran.

His sprint took him past the old man on the bench, who flinched back, and then the woman in the brown coat, who had turned her tablet towards him, her eyes opening wide. *Was she with them?* He saw her eyes flick to Alex. In a flash, she pulled something from under her coat. She held it like a gun and pointed it at him.

No. Just behind him.

She fired.

He spun and saw the taser hit Alex in the chest. Her expression spoke of shock and fury as she collapsed to the ground, her body jerking. Tom stopped as the woman in the brown coat turned to him.

"Get out of here!" she shouted. "Your friend will be up and about in three minutes. I wouldn't wait."

Tom nodded. And ran.

FIFTY-EIGHT

BERN SAT IN HIS PENTHOUSE office, staring out of the window. Behind him, on a display screen, the story of Chatsworth's death was running on the early evening news. He turned back to the three men standing before him.

"So, Peter, do we have a problem?"

Marron folded his arms. "It's a tragic occurrence, but I believe Chatsworth's part in the project was largely over, so we shouldn't be impacted."

Heidn shook his head. "That's cold, even for you. He was a good man."

"As William has reminded us, this project is bigger than any one person."

"It isn't that he's dead, it's how he died," Holm said. "First Armstrong, now the doctor. Both killed by explosions? Can they really be unconnected?"

"The police haven't attributed foul play to either event," Marron said, "if that's what you're suggesting?"

"Has nobody else made a link? It seems to me it's rather staring us in the face."

"Trying to play detective can be entertaining, but is it helpful?"

asked Marron.

Holm glared. "It is if someone is targeting people on this project."

"Leskov has the resources," Marron said. "And he's one of the few people outside this room who knows about the project, but I can't see why he would want Armstrong or Chatsworth dead."

Holm coughed. "What if they were selling us out? I mean, there is a lot of money at stake and if Leskov found out..."

Bern shook his head. "I can't believe anyone linked to this organisation would behave in that way."

Marron sighed. "I certainly hope that's true. But I can look into it, if you want."

"Only to the extent that the project doesn't need you. That has to be our priority. So, gentlemen. How are we doing? Because some good news would be most welcome right now."

Holm cleared his throat. "The four subjects are safe on Level 64. Following Stage Two, we're seeing promising reactions from the nanites. Tomorrow we'll start some conscious testing. All seems to be on track."

Heidn nodded. "The nodes are forming well. I couldn't be happier with our progress."

Marron's phone buzzed and he raised a hand. "Sorry, I have to take this."

Marron stepped from Bern's office and into the stairwell before he answered his phone. "Is it done?"

"No," Alex replied. "He escaped again. And it appears our problems are combining. The reason he was able to elude me was that he had help. From Dominique Lentz."

"How did she find him? How does she even know he exists?"

"You tell me. You said she didn't get the project data."

"Not from her incursion here. Clearly I underestimated her."

"If she has the data that changes the paradigm dramatically." Alex hesitated. "Given these changes, I'll need that team after all."

"I have some people on standby; they'll be with you within the hour. Where is he now?"

"I don't know. The system isn't finding him very quickly."

"Be patient. As long as he doesn't go completely off grid, you'll get your trace."

"Do I kill Lentz as well?"

"Not unless it's your only option. I would very much like to question her."

"What about afterwards? She tasered me and I'd like to have a word with her about it."

Marron smiled. "Once I've finished, you're more than welcome to take it up with her at length."

FIFTY-NINE

AT ONE END OF THE Serpentine in Hyde Park stood an unremarkable café-restaurant: the kind that offered food well below the standard of its location. Tom sat at a corner table, facing out across the room, in plain sight of the other diners – safe for now, he hoped. He was tired and hungry and the large plate of paella, while bland, was warm and filling. He was already planning his dessert selection, but, as he glanced through the menu, his thoughts turned to how Alex had managed to find him. Had he been bugged? After making his escape, a thorough search of his clothing had revealed nothing that he could imagine was any kind of tracking device. To add to the mystery, there seemed to be more than one group pursuing him, and they were at clear odds with each other. Who was the woman with the taser and why had she saved him? Could he trust her?

A slim woman with salon-perfect hair and a glistening smile walked into the café and glanced around. She fixed on someone at a table near him and walked that way. Tom shook his head and smiled inwardly. He was obviously getting paranoid.

But then the woman stopped and sighed, looking lost. She turned to Tom and said politely, "Could I sit here a moment?" She stood tall, confident, her expression relaxed.

"Sorry, I'm waiting for someone," he said brusquely.

She shrugged and walked back to the entrance, but Tom felt her eyes casting over to him repeatedly. Next to him, a waiter cleared his throat. "Phone call for you," he said.

How would anyone know he was here? "Are you sure?"

The waiter rolled his eyes, motioning Tom to follow him to the end of the bar where he passed him the receiver. "Is this Tom Faraday?" asked a woman's voice.

"Who is this?" he replied, looking around. At the back of his head he felt the familiar buzz.

"I'm the person who saved your life earlier today with the taser."

"How do I know that?"

"Good point. To prove my credentials I'm going to tell you how they are keeping tabs on you. Although first we need to get you to safety."

Tom paused. "Where are you?"

"Close, but unfortunately the others are much closer."

Tom looked over his shoulder. "Why don't they just shoot me then?"

"Too public. You've chosen a good location. But they'll follow you until the circumstances are more favourable. And they can find you anywhere." She paused. "Meet me and I will explain everything."

"Wouldn't I be safer staying here?"

"That café will close in less than an hour and then you'll *have* to leave. Is there a woman there with you? A disarmingly attractive woman?"

Tom swallowed. "She asked to sit at my table."

"She's probably there to divert your attention. The others will be less obvious. You need to get out. You have to decide, Tom.

Life is about these moments: small choices that make a big difference."

He took a breath. "What do I have to do?"

"Put the phone down. Ask the waiter where the toilets are. Next to them is a fire exit. I've shut down the alarm, so just open it. From there, run north as fast as you can, until you see me."

"How will I know it's you?"

"I'll be the one who isn't shooting at you."

Tom heard a click then there was just static on the line. He wanted to believe her, but he could not bring himself to do so. There could be more than one group that meant him harm. He glanced at the woman waiting near the entrance, tapping on her phone. She was too alert, too coiled. He put the phone down, then beckoned to the waiter and asked where the bathrooms were. The man pointed directly behind him. Tom nodded and walked that way. Quietly, he opened the fire exit. No alarm sounded.

He stepped through and ran.

Lentz switched off the jamming device, the whining noise fading away. Too long active and they would trace her. Her scanner flickered back into life and she cursed as she saw the dot: it was in the wrong place. He wasn't running towards her but away. In his position she might have done the same. She could try to pick him up immediately but perhaps it was better to make sure he got away safely.

For that she needed a distraction.

In the café the fire alarm started ringing. The woman standing at the entrance ran over to the bathrooms, but was chased away by the café manager.

"My boyfriend is in there!" she protested.

"It's empty. You must have missed him go outside."

Cursing, she ran out, looking around, but Tom was nowhere to be seen. A second later and a figure was at her side.

"What happened?" asked Alex.

"He got out. I thought he was in the bathroom."

"The scanners went dark for thirty seconds. We assumed it was a glitch. And that you had a visual."

"I watched him go in. There was no other way out. The fire door was alarmed: we checked."

"It must have been deactivated."

"Then he had help. Who was the phone call from?"

"What phone call?" asked Alex. "Why didn't you flag it?"

"You were tapping all the lines. I assumed you were listening in."

Alex cursed. "Lentz is messing with us." She touched her earpiece. "Recalibrate the scan for a broader area. Assume he's at least 500 metres away. Find him. Fast."

SIXTY

THE GUESTHOUSE WAS LOCATED IN a shabby, run-down block half a mile east of Liverpool Street. It was not mentioned in any tourist handbook, not rated in any official hotel or accommodation guide, nor did it have a website. Tom had never been there; he had found it by randomly selecting a page from an old London A-to-Z, then strolling until he found something suitable. Its only sign had fallen from the wall, so it was a miracle that he located it at all. Less surprisingly, they had a vacancy. He signed in under a false name and paid with cash.

He couldn't be any more anonymous: he couldn't vanish any more completely.

And still they found him.

He woke in the middle of the night, his head throbbing, knowing something was wrong. Instinctively, he grabbed for his backpack, pleased that he had chosen to stay fully dressed. He moved to the door and listened. From three floors below there was the faint sound of footsteps in the entrance hall. Looking at his watch he saw it was 3am. He eased the door open a crack. Four figures were quietly climbing the central staircase. One was holding out something like a large smartphone. Tom eased the door closed again. He had prepared before he went to sleep and now, shouldering his pack, he moved over to the only window. With a sharp tug, he opened it and stepped out onto a metal fire escape. The air was cold and the fire escape wobbled disconcertingly, but he did not hesitate and began clambering down.

As he reached the ground, he heard a shout from above. He had been spotted. Throwing caution aside, he sprinted down the street. He was only twenty metres from the comparative safety of the busy main road when a van door suddenly opened in front of him. Tom froze as a figure emerged from the shadows: a woman he recognised.

The woman who had used the taser.

"Tom, you need to trust me."

He took a step back. "Who the hell are you? And how did you know I was here?"

"My name is Dominique Lentz. And I know a great deal more than simply how to find you, Thomas Faraday."

Behind Tom people were rushing down the fire escape.

The woman brought out a calculator-sized device from her pocket and pressed a button. Tom felt the faintest buzzing in the air. Behind him he heard a muffled shout of "I've lost him."

Lentz raised her eyebrows. "I've just jammed their signal, but I can only do it for about sixty seconds so we should get going."

"Where?"

She held the door open for him. "Somewhere safe."

He jumped in as she ran round to the driver's side.

"How are they tracing me?" he asked, as she started the vehicle and pulled away.

"It's what is in your head. The interface." She looked at him.

"From your expression, that's not a total surprise."

"It's been a strange week. How do you know about it?"

She reached the main road and merged into the traffic. "I know about it," replied Lentz, "because I designed it."

SIXTY-ONE

BERN BURST INTO THE LEVEL 64 lab, his heart pounding. The room was lit with pulses of red light, beating in time with a low-frequency siren. Waiting for him were a very serious-looking Heidn, Holm and Bradley. "What is going on?" he asked. "Who activated the alarm?"

"We have a problem," Holm said. "With the nanites."

"In the lab? A containment issue?"

"No. In the subjects." Holm ran a hand through his short hair. "The nanites are ignoring their programming. They won't stop."

Bern frowned. "I don't understand."

"Neither do we," Heidn said. "Everything was progressing perfectly. The nanites had created nodes connected to each subject's cerebral cortex, but after that they should have deactivated, awaiting further instructions. They did not."

"Then what are they doing?"

"They decided to anchor themselves more permanently to the brain. They're doing it by replacing brain tissue with a network of greater structural strength, but they're creating it from the raw materials available – and killing the subjects in the process." Heidn hesitated. "All of them."

"Then do something!"

Heidn cleared his throat. "We've already exhausted the options."

"Including wiping the nanites?"

"It won't make any difference at this point. They've already caused irreparable brain damage."

Bern pinched the bridge of nose. "How did you allow this to happen?"

"It happened so fast. By the time we understood what was going on, it was too late." Heidn shook his head. "We ran simulations. We made our best possible projections, but simulations can only take you so far. We always knew this was pushing the limits."

Bradley shook his head, his voice trembling. "Do you have any idea how Leskov will react if we fail to deliver this technology?"

"You are the one who *promised*," Heidn said. "We just undertook to try."

"If Leskov did kill Armstrong and Chatsworth, what's he going to do to us?" Holm asked.

Bern cleared his throat. "Can we start over? Commence with new subjects?"

"We could," said Heidn, "but we'd need to find them, vet them. And now we don't have Chatsworth or the clinic. Plus there's the rather big issue that we don't yet know how to stop the same thing happening again. It could take months to resolve. *If* it is resolvable."

"Maybe," Holm said, "we need to accept the reality that this isn't going to happen."

"I," said Bern, "am the only one who gets to say when something isn't going to happen." He placed his palms together. "Stay here. There's someone I need to speak to." He turned and walked out of the room. Behind him a life support system sounded an alarm.

It didn't slow him one step.

When Bern arrived back in his office, Marron was waiting for him. "You saw all that?" asked the CEO, as he sat at his desk.

"I did."

Bern looked at his phone. "Leskov's due his daily update. What should I tell him?"

"In my experience, one always tells rich people what they want to hear. If that happens to be the truth then so much the better."

"I'll bear that in mind." Bern narrowed his eyes. "Tell me you prepared for such a contingency."

Marron frowned. "We always handle that sort of information on a need to know basis."

"Yes. And now I need to know."

"Then the answer to that question is 'yes, *but*'. I authorised an additional test subject, known only to Chatsworth and myself. That test subject is still alive."

"That's great news. Do you know why?"

"It's not certain, but the answer is probably at an even greater level of need to know. I'm just protecting you, William. Let's just say that I chose someone I could observe easily: a CERUS employee. Unfortunately, there's been a complication there too and he is currently unavailable to us. I'm seeking to resolve the issue, but there are other players in the mix."

"We need him *here*."

Marron nodded. "I'll handle that. You should watch Heidn and Holm. I'm worried they're losing focus."

Bern sighed. "If only Dominique Lentz was still on the team. She wouldn't be throwing in the towel."

◇ ◇ ◇

Alex answered Marron's call on the first ring.

"Please tell me you failed," he said.

"We had him in sight, but Lentz helped him escape again. It's very--" Alex paused. "You're *glad* we failed?"

"The situation has changed. The other subjects are no longer viable."

"I see."

"Faraday seems to be unique and the scientists have to know why. I need you to bring him here."

There was a pause. "With Lentz helping him that may prove even more challenging than killing him. She seems to have found a way to prevent tracking."

Marron paused. "If we can't find him then we look for someone we *can* find and make him come to us."

SIXTY-TWO

THEY DROVE THROUGH THE NIGHT, apparently free from pursuit. Tom watched as Lentz nursed the old van through every turn and gear change. For the first half hour he had barraged her with questions: *Who is that woman who's been trying to kill me? Who are you? Are you working for CERUS or against them? Why are you helping me? What is this thing in my head?* She had just told him to wait.

Tom shifted in his seat and felt his head-covering crinkle. He was wearing a hat made of tin foil. Had he been less fatigued or grief-stricken, he might have laughed when Lentz asked him to wear it. Instead he had simply said, "Will this stop them tracking me?"

"Until I devise a more permanent solution," she had replied.

So he had put it on. Jo would have had a field day, he thought sadly.

Now he stared out of the window at the occasional streetlight, watching the reflections off the windscreen, listening to the knocking of the old diesel engine. He was tired and desperately hungry. But he was safe. At least for a while.

He woke to find that the van had stopped. The sun was up. And he smelt coffee. Lentz opened his door and held out a plastic cup.

"It's not that fresh or hot, but it is strong," she said.

He took it, nodding thanks. "Where are we?" The van was parked in the shadow of a large tree on a gravel road beside an old wooden building.

"My secret lair."

"I was expecting some kind of cave, but this looks like a barn."

"It's what's inside that counts. Come on, I'll show you."

Tom eased himself from the front seat and stretched awkwardly. "Are we safe here?"

She ran a hand through her hair, unkempt and shot through with grey. "As safe as we can be."

"I need to make contact with a friend to let her know I'm OK."

"In good time. We have lots to do first, Tom."

"Like answering some of my questions?"

Lentz pulled open the door of the barn. "Some of them."

SIXTY-THREE

THE PUB WAS CROWDED EVEN at 6am, though at this time of day it was more of a breakfast café. Its early-morning fry-ups were legendary in central London and, with Smithfield meat market only two minutes away, the odours of sweat, chopped meat and cooking oil layered the air in a combination that was frequently overpowering. A steady stream of customers arrived, ate and left.

Among the crowds, a slim figure wearing a cap and jacket stepped through the entrance. She glanced around then moved to a booth at the back and slid in next to a man wearing jeans and a grubby sweatshirt. He nodded but before he could speak a waitress appeared and pulled out her notepad. They ordered by pointing, which was what most of the clientele did, exhausted after coming off an all-night shift or having emerged from a nearby nightclub. The waitress smiled, yawned and moved on to the next table.

"This is your disguise?" asked Kate, once the woman had left.

"Would you prefer a high collar and dark glasses?" replied Croft. "And I'd take your cap off inside, unless you really want to look odd. Did you tell anyone about this meeting?"

Kate shrugged and removed the hat. "The only other person who knows where I am is Geraldine. And, while I may not always agree with her, I trust her with my life."

He looked around the room then locked his gaze on her again. "So what's the story, Ms Turner?"

"You go first."

Croft folded his arms. "At some point, we're going to have to start trusting each other."

"I suppose." She leaned closer, lowering her voice. "Richard Armstrong approached me. I think he'd worked on the Tantalus project twenty-five years ago and understood just how dangerous CERUS' latest experiments really were, but he died before we could discuss most of the details. I decided to look into who else might have been with the company that long and came up with a few names: Bern, obviously, and the head of HR, a man named Peter Marron. Then there was a scientist and former brain surgeon called Stefan Heidn. When I started searching those names, they cropped up in relation to another scientist: Dominique Lentz. She died twenty-five years ago, apparently in an accident, but I found archive photos of Lentz and Armstrong together; Lentz's responsibilities included project-managing work on neural interfaces. Then I started trying to figure out if what happened twenty-five years ago could help me figure out what was happening now." Kate paused. "So what did happen with Armstrong? How come you were monitoring the crime scene?"

"He was on an MI5 watch list but it's classified above my level of clearance. I couldn't find out why."

"So what *can* you tell me?"

Croft sighed. "I looked into the name Tantalus but I found absolutely nothing. Not in the police records. Not in MI5's databases."

"That seems unlikely if Armstrong was right and people died?"

"I agree. As I see it, there are two possibilities. One is that there was a system failure and the electronic records were lost or deleted. The other is that someone deliberately deleted them." He shook his head slowly. "What is this neural interface that Lentz was working on? Is it some way of controlling a computer with your brainwaves? Like a headset or pads taped to your forehead?"

"I believe it may have been more... invasive than that. An implant of some sort, though that's still just a guess."

"How does Tom Faraday fit with all this? Because he seems to be key."

"He is, but not out of choice. It started when he was abducted after the CERUS launch event. I had proof – CCTV footage – but... well, it was wiped and Tom has no recollection of the weekend. I think someone took him and experimented on him."

"And he didn't visit a doctor after he 'lost' an entire weekend?"

"He did. His name was Chatsworth."

"Oh."

"Anyway, his flat-mate and I persuaded Tom to get a second opinion."

"The doctor in Harley Street?"

"That's right. The test found something metallic in his head. Tom took off to confront Chatsworth, then everything went crazy."

"So you're saying he had some sort of experimental brain op? Even if it were keyhole surgery, surely that would have been apparent even without tests?"

"That's the part that doesn't make sense."

"And what does this have to do with nanotechnology?"

"I have no idea. All I know is that's what Armstrong was so worried about."

Croft leaned back in his seat. "Look, I'm on your side, but I need actionable proof. I need Tom. Do you have any way of contacting him?"

"Not that wouldn't risk others finding him first."

Croft sighed, looked around and stood up. "When you're ready to really trust me, give me a call."

"Wait." Kate reached into a pocket. "This is my gesture of good faith." She placed a small plastic box on the table. "It's what Armstrong gave me. He claimed it was intelligent nano. I was going to try to get it tested myself, but I'm sure you've got access to far better labs than I do."

Croft carefully picked up the box. "I'm not sure whether to hope you're right or wrong."

"There's one other thing I hoped you could follow up. If someone's making something like intelligent nano, they're usually making it *for* someone. There must be a customer."

Croft nodded. "Suddenly I'm not hungry." He pulled a twenty pound note from his pocket and threw it on the table. "You stay and enjoy. And try to stay out of trouble."

Kate picked at the two plates of bacon and eggs, but her brain was buzzing too much to concentrate on the food. It was time to go somewhere less public. She needed to speak with Geraldine and work out what to do next. In her pocket, she tapped her mobile: the one that Tom had called briefly from his new burner phone. She had memorised the number then deleted it. Now she, and she alone, could contact him if it became necessary. Standing quickly, she moved to the rear fire exit, which she'd noticed was standing ajar for ventilation. She stepped through and onto the street, slipping on her cap.

"Hello, pretty." someone said from behind her. A woman's voice.

Kate spun on reflex, her muscles corded, ready for action. A flurry of movement registered. Her arms lifted to block the incoming blow.

She did not succeed.

SIXTY-FOUR

TWO SMARTLY DRESSED FIGURES STOOD in St James' Park, wearing long overcoats and feeding the ducks.

"Why here?" asked Reems. "It would have been simpler to meet in my office."

"I wanted to give you a different perspective," said Croft, patting his briefcase, "when I update you on the CERUS situation."

"What update? I'm told the police haven't located any of the three persons of interest."

"They haven't. But I've been conducting some off-book investigations."

Reems frowned. "George, you know about my reservations. There's no need for us to make things even more complicated by treading on the police's toes."

Croft shook his head. "Why are you so resistant even now the situation has spiralled out of control?" He paused. "Why did you tell Business Week News to stay out of it?"

"What are you talking about?"

"The editor had been told not to cooperate, before I even got there. Very few people could have exerted that kind of influence:

fewer still would have been aware of a need to do so."

"And you think it was me?"

"I looked at your file. Twenty-seven years in the Security Service: an unblemished career during which you've risen to the highest levels. But there's a six-month spell when you apparently did nothing. Why does the blank part of your file coincide exactly with a CERUS project called Tantalus that also seems to have been wiped from the records? Curious that it seems to be cropping up now and *you're* the person who doesn't seem to want anything to do with it, no matter how many bodies pile up."

"That part of my file is classified for a reason, George. I understand your frustration and I sympathise, but you know you don't have the full story. Why don't you trust the person who *does*?"

"People are dying and CERUS is involved. We need to move on the Tower. And for that I need a warrant."

"Bring me proof and we'll go straight to a judge."

Croft reached into his briefcase and produced a metal case. He unhinged it and lifted the lid to reveal a small glass vial. "Intelligent nano. Produced by CERUS."

She raised an eyebrow. "Is it indeed?"

"The source is credible. Get it checked out." He closed the case lid and handed it to her.

"I will. But remember, all we have for certain is some glittery water and your determination to go digging into your boss's personal file. I'll look into these nanites, if that's what they are, but we're overdue a serious conversation about your future."

"So no warrant. Will you at least let me try to join up some of the dots?"

Reems glared at him. "Cautiously, George. Tread very cautiously." She turned away and left him standing by the water. When she reached the road, she pulled a phone from her pocket and dialled a pre-set number.

"We need to meet," she said. "Today."

SIXTY-FIVE

SEVERAL HOURS HAD PASSED AT Lentz's hideout and they had achieved a great deal. Outside nothing had changed, but inside the barn was now considerably less barn-like. The van had been moved inside so as not to alert any passers-by. They'd emptied it of its substantial amount of computing tech and brought up more from the hidden basement, which held a range of supplies and equipment, including large quantities of tinned food, bottled water and other long-life supplies. If necessary they could remain here for weeks.

Lentz was busily setting up and networking a phalanx of computer servers and laptops. Standing ready for connection were a number of other pieces of scientific equipment, most of which Tom could only guess the purpose of. "I'm not sure if you're a scientist or ex-special forces," Tom said, peering at the nearest contraption.

Lentz stood up. "Can't I be both?"

"You tell me."

She took a deep breath. "I used to work for CERUS. Before that I worked for the government. British Intelligence, to be specific. Technical field agent."

"That's quite a CV."

"It's had its low points."

"What have you been doing since leaving CERUS?"

Lentz paused. "Mostly I've been dead."

Tom raised an eyebrow. "But now you're not?"

"It's a long story. And if I'm going to tell it, I need more coffee." Lentz searched among some cardboard boxes then pounced on a small one and tore off the tape sealing it. Reaching in, she removed a percolator.

"Filter coffee?"

She looked at him. "I know you're probably an espresso child, but this is the best I have."

"I just haven't seen one in a long time."

"The way we do things changes when we learn better ways. Although sometimes better is a matter of perspective: something that is particularly relevant to your situation."

"What do you mean by that?"

She didn't reply, instead taking the glass jug over to a grimy looking sink and turning the tap. There was an alarming banging sound, but the water ran out clear.

"Well?" he said.

"How are you feeling, Tom? How is your head?"

"It's fine. Can I take this tinfoil hat off yet?"

"I need to perform a procedure first."

Tom flinched back. "Like the one that got me into this mess?"

"No, no. Nothing invasive." She emptied the jug into the percolator then added filter paper and coffee and switched it on. Coffee started to drip through almost immediately. "OK, the smell is enough for starters. Why don't you sit down and I'll tell you what I know."

Tom found a chair and lowered himself into it.

"Twenty-five years ago," Lentz said, "I worked for MI5. I had quite a promising career. But in a moment of madness I was tempted to join the private sector."

"You sold out?"

Lentz gave him a glare. "I was enticed to join what was then just an exciting start-up. The company was called CERUS Biotech and the men who recruited me were a silver-tongued young entrepreneur named William Bern and his head of research, Stefan Heidn. They had been commissioned to develop a Brain-Computer Interface, or BCI, and needed a technical team leader. It was a radical new idea, very expensive, very controversial."

"Brain-Computer Interface? Sounds like science fiction?"

"Twenty-five years ago, it was. Now, not so much, but the systems that exist are still rudimentary and unidirectional. The project, which was codenamed Tantalus, began well. Immodestly, we were brilliant and soon developed a solution: a microchip that could be wired directly into the brain. But someone authorised testing before we were ready and all four test-subjects died after implantation. As a result, the whole project was shut down. The client pulled the funding and ordered all the records to be destroyed." The coffee percolator had finished its cycle and Lentz paused while she poured them each a cup of the thick brew. "Despite this colossal set-back, CERUS' subsequent growth was stratospheric and Bern became a billionaire. Tantalus was forgotten until a few weeks back when something caused CERUS to start the project up again."

"But how? You said the files had been deleted."

"Apparently not. One of my former team members discovered this and was going to go public."

Tom swallowed. "You mean Richard Armstrong."

Lentz nodded. "I don't think he anticipated what he had stirred up." She sipped from her coffee. "From files he left behind I learned that CERUS has created a new version of Project

Tantalus using a radical approach. Instead of inserting a microchip, they were using another cancelled CERUS project involving nanotech to solve the problem. You see, the nano project wasn't cancelled because it had failed: it was blocked by the regulator – something that's happened to them quite a bit over the years."

"So what is Tantalus about?"

"Tantalus is about dealing with the problem of inefficiency in communicating with computers. Instead of using a keyboard or a touch screen or even speech recognition, you just think what you want the computer to do. Even today, 90% of the time you spend using your computer is wasted." She paused. "And I don't mean gaming, where 100% of your time is wasted."

"So they're going to sell it to computer manufacturers?"

"Tantalus has many uses, but the most lucrative are military in nature. And when I say lucrative, I mean enough to make even Bern salivate."

"So what's the crossover between nano and Tantalus?"

"Instead of inserting a chip, as in the original Tantalus, they're injecting subjects with a quantity of pre-programmed nanites, feeding them with raw materials and then allowing these tiny machines to construct the interface inside the subjects' heads. It's far more precise and doesn't involve surgery."

"But what's to stop the nanites getting out of control?"

"It's all in the programming of their base code. Kind of like Asimov's Three Robotic Laws on a micro level. There are certain things they fundamentally cannot do. But that doesn't mean the concept was infallible even through they've already been implanted in four new subjects."

"Three other people like me?"

"*Four* other people: volunteers who didn't understand what they were really signing up for. But before they started testing on the four subjects, there was an initial 'proof of concept' phase involving a Subject Zero."

Tom stared at her.

Lentz sighed. "You are Subject Zero."

SIXTY-SIX

STEPHANIE REEMS' JAGUAR XJ SENTINEL glided to a halt on the runway of the RAF airbase behind a large SUV with darkened windows, watched by four armed military personnel. Reems' bodyguard climbed out from his front seat and gave a hand signal. Immediately two men exited the SUV, one of them huge and bulked up, the other slim and wearing an expensive suit. The bodyguard opened one of the Jaguar's rear doors and the man in the suit climbed in, flashing a smile.

"Good evening, William," Reems said. Her bodyguard closed the door.

"Always a pleasure, Stephanie," Bern replied, as he sat next to her. "Although it's been much too long."

"Has it?" she replied. "I'd say it's not been long enough."

"Straight to the insults? No small talk first?"

"Nothing you say is ever small talk."

"And *I* don't doubt that national security threads through everything you say and do." He smiled. "If I may say so, you've certainly done well for yourself, coming from such humble beginnings."

Reems frowned. "I'd say the same, with a few zeroes on, except that the word is that your company is experiencing difficulties. And not just financial ones. "

"Are you asking as potential investor?"

"More as a stakeholder. And the name of your organisation keeps cropping up in security briefings. Why is that, William? What are you up to?"

"Inventing the future. It's what we do."

"But are you doing it by digging up the past? Because CERUS has made its share of mistakes before."

Bern shrugged. "I don't intend on repeating any, if that reassures you. I'm sure you don't either."

Reems glared. "If you cross the line, there's nothing anyone can do. You will give me no choice."

"Perhaps you should focus on catching criminals and terrorists."

"The things your company has done put you in both camps."

"You forgot to say *allegedly*," said Bern, tipping his head. "Anyway, it's never been a problem for you before. I've always liked the fact that you've shown yourself willing to embrace necessity in the name of progress."

"Says the man trying to make another billion from it."

"There's nothing evil about making a profit. And let's remember, it didn't used to be a problem for you."

"That was a different time." Reems sighed. "Or maybe not. Have you restarted Tantalus?"

"You know those files were destroyed."

"Do I? Were they?"

"Perhaps you should speak to your auditor. I'd assumed they were thorough."

"And what about intelligent nanotech? Is that back under development?"

He tilted his head to one side. "Wherever are you getting these ideas?"

"Just answer my question."

"I think I'm entitled to ask, before you continue with your fishing expedition, whether I should have a lawyer present."

"I thought if we talked one-to-one we might reach an accord." Reems shook her head. "Get out, William. This was clearly a waste of my time."

"As you wish." He put his hand on the door handle. "I'll bid you a pleasant evening, much as I know you probably wish that some unfortunate accident befalls me."

"I would not view it as unfortunate."

Bern started to open the door. "You know, I've only ever wanted to change the world for the better." He took a breath. "Someone has to be bold enough to try. It just doesn't always work first time round."

"I understand that. The problem comes with who you're asking to pay the price, because it never seems to be you, William. It never seems to be you."

SIXTY-SEVEN

TOM STUMBLED OUT OF THE barn, tripped on a branch and fell into the gravel. With a sigh, he picked up a handful, letting it slip through his fingers.

Lentz following him and placed a hand on his shoulder. "Tom, I know this must be difficult for you."

"It's nothing compared to losing my best friend." He stood up, shrugging off her hand. "I need you to explain exactly what they did to me. Why they chose me. But mostly I want to know what we're going to do about it."

Lentz gave him a long look, but nodded. "First things first. Come back inside and let's stop them tracking you."

She led him to a corner and a device like a fifties salon hairdryer; indeed, Tom strongly suspected that was how it had started life.

"So what are you trying to do here?" he asked, as he lay back, the metal dome encasing his head.

"The nanites contain a number of safety features. One of which is that each active nanite emits a coded trace signal, at a very low frequency, that suitably calibrated equipment can detect and track. I'm going to target the node, where the nanites are

233

clustered, with a pulse from an x-ray laser. Now don't move." She pressed a button and there was a sharp click. She looked over at the screen then turned round and smiled. "We're done. You are now untraceable."

"Just like that? Brilliant." Tom sat up, rubbing at the back of his neck, though there had been no pain, no buzzing even. "So what is this node thing?"

"It's like a junction box. The nanites they injected grew an implant in your head. It's made of biocompatible forms of carbon and silicon. They form a cluster, which performs the role of the original project's 'chip', with fibres extending into your brain, like roots from a plant."

"So no metal?"

"Definitely not. That was the problem last time. It conducted the heat too effectively."

"Then why is there something metal in my head?"

She looked at him sharply. "What are you talking about?"

"I had an MRI scan two nights back. Well, about two seconds of one, before we had to stop because of the pain it caused me."

"I ran a rudimentary scan before the using the laser, but I didn't process the results except as I needed." She slid her chair back to her laptop and began analysing a stream of numbers. After a few moments, she hit a function button and a diagram came up. "Get your head out of the device. Sit up," she ordered. She pushed his head forward, running her fingers through his hair, and hissed. "I don't understand."

"Then that makes two of us," Tom said. "Care to share?"

"You have no sign of recent surgery. Yet, according to the scan, you have a microscopic computer in your head, protected by a metal casing."

"But I thought--"

"There is no explanation for how it got there." Her eyes grew distant as she spoke.

"Surely the nanites made it?"

"They can't just make metal. They cannot transmute base atoms. They can fabricate compounds and structures from appropriate materials, but there is no way they could create it from carbon and silicon."

"Then what happened?"

"I've not been involved with this version of the project. Perhaps I've missed something." She stopped suddenly. "Unless..."

"What?"

She pushed his head forward and ran her fingers through his hair again, this time much more slowly. Her fingers circled to the back of his head moving lower and lower then suddenly freezing. "What is that?"

Tom reached up and replaced her finger with his own. "I don't know. A blemish or a little scar maybe? It's always been there."

"It *is* a scar, Tom. The last trace of a medical procedure. Probably from when you were a child."

"I don't remember having an operation when I was kid."

"I doubt you would if it happened when you were an infant, but somebody did something in your head. And they left you a little present: an old-fashioned silicon chip with a metal casing."

"You're not making any sense. So I *didn't* have any nanites put in my head, then?"

She shook her head. "You have the nanites – but from a separate procedure twenty-five years later."

"So I'm Subject Zero *and* one of the original Tantalus project subjects from the first set of experiments?"

"No. The original four subjects were adults."

"Then you've lost me."

Lentz sighed. "There's lots I haven't told you yet. You need to be patient while we figure this out."

"You mean there's more good news to come?" Tom snapped. He turned away for a moment. "How did you get mixed up in all this, if you now think it's so wrong that you're on my side?"

"My reason for doing this? That started a long time ago."

SIXTY-EIGHT

BERN WALKED INTO THE MASTER bedroom of his country house. Celia was out at a charity dinner, which gave him undisturbed access to his wardrobe and now a selection from it was spread across his oversized bed. He'd had so long to select these items, to pare them down to what was absolutely necessary, but still the choice was peculiarly difficult. As with everything related to this initiative, it needed to be perfect; he had to control the things he could control so that, when the unexpected happened, he was ready to take advantage of it. Because if everything went to plan, things were about to change beyond all recognition.

His phone rang and he frowned as he answered it.

"William, it's Stefan Heidn. Can we speak?"

Bern flipped open his suitcase and started packing a shirt. "Sure, go ahead."

"No, not on the phone: in person. I'm right outside your gates."

"You are?" Bern hesitated. "Is something wrong?"

"Can I come in?"

"Of course." He pressed a control on the wall. "Drive right up."

Bern clicked the phone off then immediately dialled another number.

"Peter, Stefan Heidn is here to speak with me. Is he a problem?"

"Not one that I can't manage. I'll be monitoring him."

Bern nodded to himself. "You know I met with Reems."

"Was that wise?"

"I don't think I had a choice. She asked a lot of questions. Do you have things under control?"

A pause. "There's nothing you need to know."

"I'm glad to hear it." Bern clicked the phone off and walked downstairs to the front door. Heidn's antique Mercedes drew up on the gravel and the professor stepped out, wearing a worried expression. "What's up, Stefan?" asked Bern, shaking his hand.

"Not here," Heidn replied. "Is there somewhere we can talk?"

"There's nobody here except a few of my staff, but sure, follow me. Would you like a drink?"

"I could certainly use one."

They took glasses of cognac down to a small rose garden a hundred metres from the house. Surrounded by tightly cropped hedges, they were safe from prying eyes and ears.

"So, what's up, Stefan?" asked Bern, sitting on an oak bench.

"Something unexpected," replied Heidn, dragging his foot through the gravel of the path. "Dominique Lentz is alive."

Bern shook his head. "Have you been drinking? Before you got here, I mean."

"A woman by the name of Daniella Lawrence came to the Tower for a meeting with me the other day, but I'd scheduled no such appointment. When I came down to investigate, she'd already left."

"So?"

"I was puzzled so I called up the CCTV footage - and it was

her. Twenty-five years older, wearing a disguise, but I *know* it was Lentz."

Bern ran a hand through his hair. "How can you be so sure?"

"I'm a details person. She kept drumming the desk with the fingers of both hands, one after the other. There was a distinctive pattern to it. I'm right, William. Beyond any shadow of a doubt. And you know they never found a body."

"The report said that was the ocean currents."

"Or maybe there was no body to be found."

Bern shook his head. "Assuming, for one moment, that you're right, why would she come back now?"

"Yes, that is the question." Heidn snapped his fingers. "I think she's trying to take back Tantalus. You know how frustrated she was when it was terminated."

"How could she even know that we're pursuing it?"

"I don't know. But if you remember anything about Lentz, it should be that it's unwise to underestimate her. I checked the system, and when she visited the Tower, she hacked the building network. Using twenty-five-year-old base code."

"Are you sure?"

"Who else could it have been?"

"Maybe Armstrong?"

Heidn gave this some thought. "Maybe," he conceded. "Or maybe they were working together. I ran my own searches of the system. There's evidence of a conspiracy, William." He paused. "And by that I mean other than the conspiracy we are all participating in. Marron is behind it."

Bern blinked. "Say that again."

Heidn gulped from his glass. "We've all been tricked."

"Peter Marron? Are you sure?"

"He ran a separate test program. Without anybody's knowledge. There was a Subject Zero. Nanites were implanted into Zero *prior* to our selection of Subjects One to Four. I have the data to prove it." Heidn shook his head. "Marron--" He froze. "Did you hear that?" He swung his head back and forth.

"Hear what?" Bern asked. "Seriously, Stefan, you don't seem yourself at all. Now--"

Heidn pulled a handgun from his coat pocket, swinging it in an arc. "Have I made a mistake?" Heidn stopped with the gun pointing in Bern's direction. "You seem awfully calm about all this."

Bern looked at the gun, his eyes wide. "Do I look calm now?"

"I never signed up for all this. I just wanted to be a scientist." He took a step back. "This needs to end, William."

There was a sudden movement as a flock of birds erupted, disturbed by something. The noise all but muffled the sound of the single gunshot.

SIXTY-NINE

LENTZ HAD BEEN SLUMPED IN her chair, silent, for such a long time that Tom jumped when she started speaking. "I had a twin sister," said Lentz. "Her name was Elena." She looked at her hands, took a deep breath, then continued, "When we were born, there was no indication of any problems, but at the age of two she was diagnosed with a rare degenerative condition. She was barely walking before she was in a wheelchair. I didn't understand what was happening: why we couldn't play like we always had. At first I thought she didn't like me anymore. Or that she was just lazy because she never wanted to do anything. But once I realised that wasn't the case, all I wanted to do was help. I kept asking why we couldn't use some magic and make her well again." She pushed up from her chair and started to pace the barn. "I was only five when she died. I kept asking why. And nobody could give me an answer. I refused to accept it for such a long time. Maybe I still do." She sighed. "It's always been the drive behind my passion to make a difference. And if you don't have a passion, it's hard to make a difference."

Tom shook his head. "I'm sorry I assumed you joined CERUS for the money."

She glared at him. "If it was money that drove me, I wouldn't have become a scientist, full stop. Given my interests I had to join an organisation like CERUS. My area of research is incredibly expensive. If it doesn't happen under the auspices of a well-funded commercial project, it simply doesn't happen at all."

She looked at the floor, scuffing a foot through the dust.

"After university, I got word of a government initiative in neural interfaces. One thing led to another and I was recruited into MI5's Special Projects Division. None of the work got very far, though. There were too many restrictions, too many protocols to follow and funding was insufficient. I realised I was going to have to go elsewhere if I were to succeed. That's when William Bern approached me." She gave a bitter smile. "He knew all the right things to say: all the buttons to push. Said he had this new project that I was perfect for."

"And the project was Tantalus?"

"Actually there were several things I ended up working on, including leading the initial stages of research on a nano material initiative with an even worse project name – Resurface." She rolled her eyes. "But, yes, Tantalus was the big draw."

"And you thought it was a good idea to fiddle with people's brains? Who shut you down? Bern? The government?"

"I don't know who was calling the shots. A team of armed men turned up with paperwork from Bern telling me to do as I was told and keep my mouth shut. I ignored that and I started asking questions. Too many it seems. And Bern wouldn't give me any answers. Kept fobbing me off with one of his execs, Peter Marron."

"The Head of HR?"

She laughed. "Yes, I'm *sure* that's what he is. Anyway, I took myself off on holiday to try and decompress. I hadn't given up. I really thought Tantalus would still go somewhere: that eventually we could use the research to help people. Maybe even people like my sister. I was pretty devastated to have it taken away from me. I knew I needed time to accept it: to adjust to the fact that I'd have to start from scratch with a completely different research direction. Marron was delighted to let me take some leave, so I booked myself into a little resort in the Cayman Islands for a fortnight. It seemed like the best decision I'd made in months – until someone tried to kill me."

"Yet you're still alive."

"I was both very lucky and very persuasive. The assassin wasn't expecting me to take precautions and he triggered the portable intruder alarm I'd rigged in my room. It gave me enough time to grab the small harpoon gun I'd hired as part of my diving equipment."

"Whoa! Bet that was a surprise for him."

"Especially since he just had a knife. The surprise bought me enough time to negotiate. It turns out most hired killers are in it for the money. Who knew? The only thing money couldn't buy was the identity of the person who'd hired him. Of course I now know it was Marron." She ground her teeth together. "Anyway, in exchange for a little extra money he helped me fake my death and go into hiding."

"Why didn't you go to the police?"

"I had no proof of anything. I knew that all I'd achieve was letting whoever sent the killer know I was alive." Lentz shrugged. "My parents were dead by then and I'd always been a workaholic, so it wasn't like I was leaving a lot behind. And I've found plenty of things to occupy me. The first year or two were the worst, but whenever I got bored, I moved somewhere new."

"So what brought you back?"

"I've always kept an eye on CERUS. When I read about Armstrong dying I knew it was no accident. He was such a boring, careful man. The chance of there being a faulty appliance in his house? Almost zero." She shook her head. "I can't believe what they did. What they're doing."

Tom shook his head. "So you came back, and you found me."

"CERUS didn't keep you as secret as they would have liked. I knew immediately you were different." Lentz interlaced her fingers. "And I've just realised exactly how."

Tom frowned. "What do you mean?"

"Only one explanation makes sense. You were picked to be Subject Zero in *this* version of Tantalus because of what was *already* in your head." She looked at him. "The chip they put in all those years ago meant you were perfect."

Tom blinked. "So you *are* saying they did trials on me as a child? That I wasn't just Subject Zero in the current project, but part of the old Tantalus?"

Lentz nodded. "That's exactly what I'm saying."

SEVENTY

TOM CLOSED HIS EYES, RUBBING his temples, feeling the buzz of electricity in Lentz's computers. "They put a chip in my head as a baby?"

"Twenty-five years ago. It must have been then or the scar wouldn't have healed so well."

"Why would my mother have allowed it? Did she even know?"

"She could have been deceived in some way. Heidn once suggested implantation in infancy would be optimal - it would allow neural pathways to form and strengthen as the brain developed. At the time I assumed it was just a theoretical discussion. Apparently I was wrong." She shook her head.

"So why didn't I die like all the adult subjects?"

Lentz shrugged. "Some difference in the way your brain accepted the chip probably. Heidn may have been thinking along the right lines after all – from a purely science-based perspective, I mean. Not a moral one, of course."

"But I've never had any abilities or whatever until now."

"They never progressed your programming. You had an inert chip."

"But how did they find me after all this time?"

Lentz shook her head. "Who says they ever lost you? Perhaps they've been watching you ever since? Why did you choose to work at CERUS, Tom?"

Tom let out a sigh. "I was headhunted. By Marron."

Lentz shrugged. "An appeal to vanity is hard to resist."

"So why go to all that trouble then try to kill me?"

"Either you didn't work out as a test subject. Or they didn't need you." She paused. "Or you became a risk like I did."

Tom swallowed. "Maybe they found out I've been talking to a reporter. She was in contact with Armstrong then, after his death, she approached me."

"Then she is in grave danger."

Tom gave a laugh. "Oh, she knows. We were both nearly killed by the assassin you saved me from. We'll need to get in touch with her soon, but there's something I need to figure out first. I'm fed up being clueless and defenceless, but there's a way I don't have to be." Tom tapped his head. "Exactly what can I do with this thing?"

"Now that, Tom, is the best question I've heard all day."

SEVENTY-ONE

KATE AWOKE IN A ROOM with two fixed metal beds, a door and no windows. It looked very much like a prison cell and there was no mistaking the heavily-reinforced door. Checking the time, she realised her watch had been taken, as had her other jewellery.

She stood up and walked over to the door then proceeded to bang, kick and scream for all she was worth. Approximately thirty seconds later, the door hissed and swung open. Two men dressed in black combat gear and wearing tinted helmets stood in the entrance, guns trained on her.

"What?" snapped the first guard.

"Where the hell am I? Why am I here?"

"We're not authorised to answer that. Are you unwell? Or thirsty?"

"I want to speak to whoever is in charge," Kate said, looking from one guard to the other, sizing them up. Their guns didn't waver.

"They'll speak to you later," said the first guard.

Kate gave them each a vicious glare then stomped back to her bed. The door hissed shut. She listened carefully. There was no further sound from outside, but even such a short interaction with her captors had told her several things. First, she was in a high-tech facility. This room was not really a prison cell but a secure store room. The door sounded like it was vacuum sealed. And it was probably soundproof, which meant they were listening in on the cell via hidden microphones. As for the guards, they were professionals, not thugs. They were polite and methodical. They didn't seem to want to hurt her, but they probably wouldn't be easily fooled.

Finally, she had seen their ID badges. The logo in the corner told her that they were in a CERUS facility, possibly even the Tower. Kate looked at the ceiling. Whoever had her hostage was probably watching and listening right now. He could have just had her killed, as he had obviously planned before. Now, he wanted her for a reason.

She stared at the door. What could she do before he arrived?

SEVENTY-TWO

THE BLUE PULSING LIGHTS TOLD Croft he was close to the scene. He guided his car around the bend then pulled to the side of the country road, parking on the grassy verge next to the three vehicles already there. A uniformed police officer met him as he stepped out of his car. The air was filled with wisps of smoke and the stench of charred rubber. The road bore heavy tyre marks, but it was their end point that immediately drew the eye.

The fire had clearly been burning for some time before being extinguished: all that remained of the car was a blackened shell. There was an ambulance parked alongside, but the crew were in no hurry. No lives were going to be saved here today. Six other police staff stood at a discrete distance, watching him with the eyes of people desperate to know more, despite having been told not to ask.

"Sir," said the officer, "we appreciate you coming so quickly."

"I'm not usually called to road traffic accidents. A Code Black? For this? Was another vehicle involved?"

"Not as far as we can tell, Sir. No passengers. It looks like the driver simply lost control."

"Then why am I here?"

"We weren't told. We presumed you *were*." The officer pointed to a twisted scrap of metal on the floor. "The call was triggered when we ran the number plate. We were ordered to stand down."

Croft frowned and crouched next to the remains of the number plate. He pulled out his phone, aimed it at the plate and selected a special app.

"We're going to need forensics to make an ID," said the officer, "but there's just the one body. No cameras of course. If there was a witness, they didn't stop."

Croft nodded. He pointed at one of the wheels, lying separate from the main wreckage. "Expensive car. What's that logo on the alloys? Jaguar?"

"Aston Martin," replied the officer with a half-smile. "Big difference."

The phone buzzed angrily in Croft's hand. He stood up, turning away to read the display.

He read it again.

"Bad?" asked the officer.

"Depends on your perspective. We're going to need to secure this scene. And you'd best get your superintendent down here."

"What?" The man tugged at his moustache. "Can I tell her why?"

"So I can brief her before the press conference."

The officer considered this for a moment. "Just whose car was that?"

Croft sighed. "Someone whose death will be headlining the evening news."

SEVENTY-THREE

HEAVY SPATS OF RAIN STRUCK hard against the glass, whipped by the wind, but inside CERUS Tower there was only the faint whisper of the climate control. Bradley stood in his office, trying to make sense of the phone call he'd just received. Throughout his time at CERUS, throughout his plotting with Celia, one thing had been ever present, dominating his goals: as constant as the Northern Star – or so he had assumed. Yet it seemed that was not the case.

There was a knock at the door and Holm and Marron entered.

"What's going on?" Holm asked. "Your PA wouldn't give me any information."

"Because I didn't give her any."

"What?" Marron asked. "I don't have time--"

"Where's Heidn?" asked Bradley. "He's supposed to be here too."

"Not answering his phone," replied Holm. "Is William not joining us?"

Bradley sighed. "I just had a call from Celia Bern about a call *she* got from the police." He paused. "Early this morning William's Aston Martin went off the road near his house and caught fire."

"What?" gasped Holm.

"There was a body inside, badly burned." He lowered his head. "They believe it's him."

"No!" Holm cried. "It must be a mistake."

"This is going to be all over the news within a couple of hours, but I wanted you to hear it from me first."

Marron walked over to the window and looked out. "We have to keep pushing ahead."

"Are you kidding?" Holm asked. "We can't just carry on, as if nothing has happened."

"William would have wanted us to. We can still save CERUS and his legacy." He hesitated. "And there's the little matter of what Leskov will do to us if we let him down."

"But he'd understand? Surely?"

"I think he will expect delivery on time. What do you think, Neil?"

Bradley swallowed. "I think he will respectfully ask that we continue."

"Whatever your views," Holm said, "you've forgotten one big problem with what we need to do next. We don't have any more test subjects. The last one died overnight."

Marron stroked his chin. "I've learned that William ran a prototype trial. There is a Subject Zero: a twenty-five-year-old male who has not suffered the problems experienced by the other four."

Holm blinked. "That's... unexpectedly great news."

Bradley frowned. "That doesn't make any sense. How did he get a separate trial moving so quickly?"

Marron shrugged. "William always liked to have a back-up plan, and he usually kept them to himself."

"But why would he have kept it a secret? And what's different about Zero that he lived?"

"I can't explain what Bern did, let's just be glad that he did it. I'm having Zero brought to the Tower as soon as possible."

"I'll speak to the Professor," Bradley said, "and ask him to get ready to run some tests."

Marron shook his head. "We can't wait for the old man. We need to push ahead with all possible speed: get this over and done with. Holm can figure it out. I have a task for you, Neil, that's going to take all your attention: I want you to assume the role of acting CEO."

"Aren't you the ranking executive?"

Marron snorted. "I'm no leader. The company needs someone who can steady the ship. Are you up to it?"

Bradley straightened. "I'll do my best."

"Good. You should make an internal broadcast: announce the tragic news and that, as a mark of respect, CERUS Tower is closing for seventy-two hours. We need the building empty." Marron placed his hand on Bradley's shoulder. "The fastest way to get this over with is to get Leskov to come to us. We'll use Zero to prove Tantalus works. Then we get paid, he leaves and it's all over."

SEVENTY-FOUR

MARRON GRIPPED THE SMALL PADDED case as he marched down the corridor on Level 71. He should have dealt with his prisoner much earlier, but his attention had been diverted by matters that only he could attend to. It meant he had very little time to obtain the reporter's cooperation, which was why he had brought the case.

The two armed guards standing outside the cell snapped to attention as he approached. Marron placed his hand on a panel and the cell door slid open. The small room was lit with dim LEDs and furnished with two single beds. On one lay his captive, her eyes immediately locking onto him.

Kate sat up. "I was wondering when someone in management was going to show up. How are you today, Peter?"

"Ms Turner. How nice of you to pay us a visit."

"I was going to say much the same. I don't suppose it's worth me mentioning that your men brought me here against my will. I'm getting a bit fed up of sitting in this room."

"It's been a busy day," said Marron. "But now I need you to perform a task for me. I need you to contact Tom, so I can help him."

"Help him? Or have him help continue your bizarre brain experiments?" She glared at him. "Why would I do that?"

"It's not about helping me. It really is about helping Tom. He's in great danger."

"From you," Kate said. "Your people, I presume, tried to kill him. I was there, remember."

"That was an unfortunate misunderstanding. No, Tom is going to die because of an unforeseen complication with our experiment. All our test subjects have died now except him."

"You're bluffing."

"If they were alive, would I be bothering with him? He can help us figure out what went wrong with the others. A small price to pay for saving his life in return."

"I'm not going to help you hurt him again."

"That's a pity, given that I asked so nicely. Because I really need the information."

"So, what? Are you going to torture me?"

Marron raised his eyebrows. "Nothing so inelegant. I'm going to use a more twenty-first century approach." He held up the padded case and flipped it open. Inside was a large glass syringe; a green liquid swirled within. "Working for this company gives me access to some rather unique resources. This has a very long technical name, but we usually refer to it as 'truth nano'."

"What, like sodium pentathol?"

"*Un*like it because this works: the nanites compel you to speak truthfully." He leaned towards her. "That is why you haven't been given any food. Potency is increased on an empty stomach. But I'd be acting unfairly if I didn't mention the side effects, and there are a number. It may bring on allergies. Some bloating. A slight chance of brain damage. Oh, and you may experience random, stabbing pains in your head, chest and stomach. I wouldn't call it torture, but it's certainly not pleasant." He watched as she shifted her position on the bed, weight now poised on the balls of her feet.

Then she moved.

She was faster than him, there was no question. But speed wasn't everything. She didn't have his experience or training. He swayed to one side, caught her arm and spun it behind her back.

"Did you think," he said, "I'd have come into this room alone if I couldn't handle you?"

Kate grunted but, though she struggled, she could not get out of his grip. "Can't blame a girl for trying."

"Unfortunately you learned to fight in a classroom."

"Maybe if I were speaking to Bern, instead of his trained monkey, you'd have found me more persuadable. You're just going to kill Tom and me. So it might as well just be me."

Marron shook his head. "I need Tom alive. And I need you to get to him."

"I've no way of contacting him."

"I don't believe you."

"Believe what you wish."

He held up the syringe "I'll believe what you say once this has worked its magic." He called to the guards to come in.

They took her arms, holding her down.

"Now hold still; this will hurt a little." He paused. "Then it's going to hurt a lot."

SEVENTY-FIVE

LENTZ WALKED OVER TO THE pile of items they had unloaded from the van and selected a large reinforced case, similar to the type used for transporting musical instruments. She popped the catches and flipped it open. Inside was a round metal hoop, a hand-span across. She gently separated the sides into two semi-circles and held it out to Tom. "Place this around your neck, and click it together."

"You want me to wear a collar?"

Lentz tilted her head. "Would you prefer a helmet?"

Tom coughed and took the metal pieces from her. They were smooth, a colour like burnished copper, and cool to the touch.

"Careful with it. I only have one other and it doesn't work at the moment."

"I'll be careful." He clicked the two halves together around his neck.

She checked the positioning. "So far, what abilities have you noticed?" she said.

"Flashes of enhanced memory. I played a game shooting a basketball and was able to replicate the shot several times, but I'm not sure if I could have kept going. It feels... inconsistent."

"The capacity of the chip alone is extremely limited and the data is stored very inefficiently, so you probably had 'data overflow'. If it is used more intensively, you risk the overheating problem that plagued the original experiment. But with this collar we move most of the processing outside the chip. Were you able to do anything else?"

"A couple of times I seemed to be able to *glitch* computer equipment - perhaps make things turn on or off."

Lentz reached forward and rotated the loop slightly again. "That's the key feature of the technology: interfacing with other computers and networks. This collar will amplify the ability." She reached into the case again and withdrew something the size of a matchbox, holding it out to him.

"What's that?" He took the item and rotated it in his fingers. It was made from the same material as the circle round his neck. It had a single switch and LED light.

"It's a hub. It clips on the back of the collar. It provides the interface with the necessary power. Should be good for twenty-four hours. I'm working on one that lasts longer." She took the hub from his hand, clicked it onto the back of the collar then pressed the switch. "OK, you should be up and running in a minute."

"What do I do then?"

Lentz pointed to a table in the middle of the room. "Sit there. And let the testing commence."

'Testing' was indeed a word that Tom would use to describe the experience. For nearly two hours he tried everything he could think of, all to no avail. He sat at the table, staring at a laptop screen, a cable running from the hub to the computer.

"So what exactly do you want me to do?" Tom had asked.

"Your goal is to control the computer. Make it do something. Anything. Open a webpage, create a new document: it doesn't matter what."

But two hours on and the only thing that had happened was that the laptop had gone into standby mode. Tom closed his eyes in concentration then opened them. The laptop screen stared back at him, unchanged. "How exactly am I supposed to do this? You've got to have some ideas," he snapped, his voice sharp with frustration.

Lentz sighed, sounding equally frustrated. "As I've said, *I don't know*. Think in different ways? Reach out in your thoughts and see if anything feels different? All I know is that it can take time for the new nano tech to make connections in your brain – for the software to learn and adapt. Once it works, you should be able to recall the path and do it again. Like with the basketball game."

"But I'm not getting any special feeling. I've been trying for two hours and zip."

"OK, OK. Let's try something else." Lentz walked over to the equipment pile and withdrew a battered metal case. She placed it on the desk and opened it to reveal a robotic arm. "This is a computer-controlled synthetic limb. I'm hoping you might find it simpler to manipulate. It will give you something specific and familiar to visualise." She reached over and plugged it into the laptop, then set it on the desk; it was not unlike an angle-poise lamp with a gripping hand. "See if you can make it move."

Tom closed his eyes again and tried to feel the robot arm, to sense its shape and form, to guide its movement; but it did not happen. After several minutes, he sat back. "I'm sorry. I can feel a slight buzzing around me. Nothing more."

Lentz shook her head. "Perhaps there were other explanations for the phenomena you've experienced. Maybe you were just lucky with the basketball shot. In our rush to reach the conclusion we want, we could be trying to impose a desired cause on an effect."

"Give me something to remember. A string of random numbers. Let's see if I can memorise them."

Lentz shrugged, grabbed a piece of paper and pen, then began writing a string of digits. She slid it across to Tom. "That's the first fifty digits of pi."

"Only fifty?" he asked, eyes fixed on the list. He gave the sheet back almost immediately, half-smiling. "OK, I'm ready to surprise you."

But Lentz cocked her head, frowning, then raised a finger to her lips. "We have company," she mouthed.

SEVENTY-SIX

TOM HEARD A VEHICLE CRUNCH to a halt on the gravel outside, the engine turning off. Lentz shoved Tom in the direction of a stack of old cardboard boxes.

"Do you get a lot of visitors?" Tom asked, as he crouched out of sight of the door.

"Not really. I prefer my privacy. Quit talking and hope they don't come inside."

The door to the barn rattled as someone turned the handle. "I don't know why we're bothering with this place," said a man with a rough and gravelly voice. "There's no way she'd be stupid enough to come back here."

"We're here," said a second man, "because the boss gave us orders. So shut up about it."

"It's not even locked. Can't be anything in here. Waste of time."

The door swung inwards and, through a narrow gap between the boxes, Tom saw two large men walk in, blinking in the half light. They immediately stared at the piles of new equipment.

"What the--"

"Look like a waste of time now? I'm calling this in."

The hub on the back of Tom's head beeped softly and he stifled a curse.

"Who's there?" The first man advanced on Tom's hiding place, a large pistol in his hand. "Get out where we can see you!" he shouted.

Lentz whispered to Tom, "Let me manage this." Then, more loudly, "We're coming out. Everybody stay calm." She stood up and beckoned for Tom to do the same.

The second man had also produced a gun.

"I don't suppose it's worth pointing out that you're trespassing," said Lentz.

The first man was looking around. "Check out all this gear."

"She's supposed to be some kind of genius." The second man leaned closer to the robot arm. "This looks like something out of *Terminator*."

The first man pushed his pistol forward until it was directly in her face.

I need to do something, thought Tom. And in his mind he sensed the artificial limb.

Then things happened quickly.

The robot arm swung and struck the second man on the wrist. There was a crack of metal on flesh and bone. The man screamed, dropping his gun. The other looked round on reflex and Lentz moved with him. She stepped inside his reach, grabbed his wrist and, with a sharp rotating movement, forced the gun from his grip. Continuing the same motion, she drove her elbow into his solar plexus and knocked him backwards, simultaneously taking the weapon and turning it to point at him. The second man had recovered and was looking for his gun, only to see the robot arm had picked it up and was shaking it in an agitated manner. He took a step back as Lentz calmly cycled her aim between them.

"Now, you two, let's start again. You can begin with how you found me."

SEVENTY-SEVEN

TOM STOOD IN THE DOORWAY as Lentz climbed out of the underground storage area of the barn, closing the trapdoor then kicking straw over it.

"I drugged them. It'll buy us several hours," she reported.

He stared out at the road. "No sign of anyone else yet. How did they find us?"

Lentz held up a small booklet. "The visitor guide for CERUS Tower. It contains a microscopic passive tracker that activates sporadically and tries to broadcast via any local network. Very hard to detect."

"So I guess we have to move on?"

"Marron will send more goons. He needs to get you."

"Because I know too much?"

Lentz shook her head. "Actually, no. He doesn't want you dead." She paused. "At the least not any more, based on what his thugs told me. It sounds like New Tantalus has gone off the rails. The main four test subjects have died from complications."

Tom swallowed. "What does that mean for me? Am I going to--"

Lentz placed her hand on his shoulder. "Listen, those two

idiots didn't know any of the details, but, you have to remember that you're different from the other four. You were chosen as Subject Zero because you already had the chip. That's what saved you. And it's because you lived that you're now in danger. Before, you were just a loose end; now *everything* hinges on you. You are the only real proof that a project costing hundreds of millions actually works."

"We can't keep outrunning them." Tom shook his head. "We have to go to the authorities."

Lentz laughed. "That's just going to be a different group of scientists who want to experiment on you. Your interface works. It's a paradigm shift, Tom. You have no idea of the implications: financial, military, political..."

Tom closed his eyes. "Hold on, we haven't proved it works."

Lentz laughed. "You controlled the mechanical arm."

He blinked. "Oh. I'm not sure if I can do it again."

"It will take time, and unfortunately that is something we don't have a lot of. At least not if we stay here."

Tom sighed. "I just need to send Kate a message, then I'll help you pack up."

Lentz shook her head. "The less she knows, the safer she is. We need to keep a low profile until we can figure out a plan."

"But--"

"It's not just New Tantalus that's gone off the rails." She tapped on her phone and showed him a news headline.

Tom stared, his mouth falling open. "Bern is dead?"

SEVENTY-EIGHT

CELIA BERN PARKED HER FERRARI across the entrance to the CERUS underground car park and climbed out.

Two security guards immediately ran up to her, waving their hands. "You can't put your car there," said one of the guards. "The building is closed to visitors."

She turned on him, eyes blazing. "Do you know who I am?"

"It doesn't matter who--" he began.

"Mrs Bern," said the second guard, jabbing the first with his elbow. "Perhaps we could find you a space? Or move it for you?"

Celia glared, threw him the keys then marched past. She had to fight her way through a steady stream of people leaving the building, eventually reaching the front desk.

A security guard the size of two men sat there, his expression placid. "Can I help you?"

She leaned towards him. "My name is Celia Bern. I want to see Neil Bradley. Immediately."

"I'll take things from here," Peter Marron said, appearing from a door behind the desk. "Celia, would you come with me?" He led her to a meeting room on the first floor. "Neil is just finishing up a meeting. He'll be down as soon as he can."

Celia sniffed. "Nobody is answering my calls. Nobody is telling me anything."

"There's been rather a lot going on." Marron placed a hand awkwardly on her shoulder. "I know this is a difficult time for you. And I'm very sorry for your loss."

She pushed him away. "Don't pretend that I'm some gooey-eyed twenty-year old. William had been cheating on me for years."

"I don't know anything--"

Celia raised a hand. "Don't bother. It doesn't matter anymore. It just wasn't supposed to be this way."

"No one could have predicted what's happened. It was just one of those freak--"

"You are *not* going to tell me it was an accident, Peter. I'm not in the mood to be handled. Was it the Russian?"

"I think perhaps you're getting a little carried away--"

"William was not destined to die in a random road accident." She closed her eyes. "I didn't want him dead. I wanted him to wish he was dead. I wanted him alive to suffer."

"Life doesn't always work like it should."

Celia opened cold, determined eyes. "William always trusted you. Now, I'm the one who's going to need your help. I'm stopping Tantalus – the whole project. With William gone, what's the point?"

Marron stared at her. "You're still grieving--"

Celia's eyes flashed angrily. "I am not grieving: I'm taking charge. Somebody is out there killing people. We have to go to the police with what we know. Before anyone else gets murdered."

"If you're right, you think the police can protect us?"

"We're more at risk if we do nothing. And it's the right thing to do." She looked into Marron's eyes. "I'll make sure you and the key team still get your bonuses. I'll pay them myself if necessary."

"They won't do us much good in prison."

"They'll do you less good if you're dead. And our lawyers have got us out of worse before. I'm going to need your support as I tell them upstairs, Peter."

"I understand." He pulled his phone from his pocket and looked at the screen. "Neil is free now – he's in the video conference suite. Follow me."

They walked to the express lift, and the doors slid apart. Marron turned to the control panel. "Level Minus 5." The doors hissed shut and the lift descended quickly.

"William never mentioned that the basement went down five levels," Celia said distractedly. "Why is the video-conference suite down here?"

"Something to do with isolating it from electronic interference." The lift slowed and the doors opened, revealing a dimly lit concrete corridor. Marron walked to the third door on the right. "This won't take a second." He walked in and the lighting came on automatically.

"What the hell?" said Celia. "What is all this?"

The walls were packed with weaponry: hand guns, automatic rifles, even a rocket launcher. Marron picked up a short rifle with a scope and calmly slotted a magazine into its chamber. "This is the armoury."

"Why do you have all these guns? It can't be legal."

"It's a security measure. Only registered operatives can use what's stored here."

"So where is Neil?"

"Actually I haven't spoken to him." Marron shouldered the weapon and aimed it at Celia. "William knew, you know."

Celia swallowed. "Stop it, Peter. What are you talking about?"

"William knew about you and Bradley."

"What?" She blinked rapidly. "He knew *what*?"

"About your little conspiracy. So he just slotted it into his plan."

"A lot of good it did him." She swallowed. "Did you kill him?"

"That's one theory." Marron clicked off the safety catch. "I'm sorry it's come to this, Celia. But this project is not going to be stopped."

The sound of the rifle firing, even silenced, was painfully loud in the enclosed space. Celia fell back, an expression of complete confusion on her face.

Marron walked over to her slumped form. "I would be the last one to kill William."

But she was already dead.

SEVENTY-NINE

TOM MADE YET ANOTHER TRIP, carrying a box of equipment from the barn and loading it into the van. The rusting vehicle was nearly full to bursting and creaked worryingly on its suspension.

Lentz shook her head. "Too much stuff, too little space. I've had no time to sort it. Don't get back home that often."

Tom stepped back, putting his hands on his hips. "Can I ask you a question?"

"*A* question?" she replied. "I don't think you've stopped since we first met."

He shrugged. "Why are you doing this? Helping me? Why come back at all?"

Lentz shook her head. "You know, I told myself that I wanted to stop CERUS. And part of me wants revenge. But then another part wants to see Tantalus work." She looked at him. "This thing you have, it has such wonderful possibilities. It will change the world in ways nobody can predict."

"What do you mean?"

"Do we really understand the human brain? We have theories and models - but we're still not even close to truly comprehending its inner workings. So how can we hope to understand the outcome of building an interface connected with it?"

"Didn't that occur to you when you signed up for the project?"

"Of course. But, as a scientist, I had to believe that some risks were worth taking if we're going to move forward as a species."

"Now you sound like Bern." Tom ran his hand through his hair. "If this works, will we become more or less human?"

"You tell me. Right now, you're the only one who really knows."

"I like to think I'm still the same person."

"But are you, given the things you can do now? When you moved that mechanical arm, were you moving something remotely or was it like it was your arm?"

"I'm not sure."

There was the harsh sound of a cheap mobile phone ringing. Lentz scowled and pulled it from her pocket.

"That's my phone!" Tom said.

"Did you do that?"

"Make it ring? No. Can I do that?"

"Then who has the number?"

"Only one person." Tom grabbed it from her and answered. "Kate?"

There was a pause, then a man's voice. "She's here."

Tom swallowed. "Marron."

"Excellent. I hate having to explain myself. Is Ms Lentz with you?"

"If you've hurt Kate I'll--"

"Ms Turner is fine. Mostly. Although you'll be flattered to hear she really didn't want to give up your contact details. Now, listen closely--"

Tom clenched his jaw. "How do I know you even have her?"

"I'd send you a video link but this phone is pre-industrial revolution. How about you have a very quick word."

There was a pause then a hoarse voice spoke, "Tom, just run. He won't hurt me"

Marron's voice spoke again, "I will actually, but for now she's fine. Come to CERUS Tower and she'll stay that way."

"So you can kill us both?"

"I have no intention of killing *you*, Tom. I want to help you. But I have every intention of killing your friend if you don't comply."

"I know what you did to me," Tom said. "Why would I ever trust you?"

There was a pause. "I'm sure Lentz has explained what she thinks this is about, but what she doesn't know is that you are in grave danger. The item in your head has proven unstable and we need to help you before it's too late."

"I suspect your definition of help and mine are somewhat different. I'll take my chances."

"I hope for Kate's sake you rethink that position. You have twenty-four hours. Come alone. If I even smell Lentz..." The phone clicked off.

Lentz looked at him. "We have to go. He's probably traced the call."

"It doesn't matter."

"Why?"

"Because he doesn't need to come here. I'm going to him."

Lentz put a hand on his shoulder. "Tom--"

"I'm going to rescue Kate. I'm going to stop him."

Lentz shook her head. "You're not thinking clearly. Kate made her own decision to get involved. In a few weeks, months, who knows what you'll be able to do. But now? What do you really think you can accomplish? "

He returned her look, his eyes hard. "I'm going to break into one of the most modern secure buildings in the world, protected by an army of security guards, save my friend and, if the opportunity presents, exact retribution on the people who experimented on me. Any questions?"

EIGHTY

THE WHITE VAN GLIDED UP the approach road to CERUS Tower watched by fifty pairs of eyes and twice as many cameras. It slowed as it approached the security barrier. Inside the glass front doors of the main building, Alex and a team of eight security guards crouched, waiting. She tapped her radio earpiece as she peered through a set of high-powered binoculars. "It's the vehicle he told us to expect. I see one figure inside. Can't make out the face, but it's his height and build."

Marron replied immediately. "Raise the barrier. Move Teams One and Two into position."

"He can't really believe you're going to release the journalist."

"I don't care what he believes."

Alex signalled and a guard raised the barrier. Two other guards waved the van towards a parking space in the pedestrian area immediately in front of the Tower. The vehicle manoeuvred smoothly over to it, as four other guards converged. Alex nodded with a smile.

There was a squeal of rubber and the van lurched from its path, accelerating towards the glass doors. Alex dived to her left, landing in a tight sideways roll, just as the vehicle exploded through the glass and skidded to a halt in the middle of the lobby. Alex looked around and saw that two guards had been knocked down and were not moving. Cursing, she unshouldered her weapon and crunched through broken glass to the front of the van, flanked by the six remaining guards.

"What the hell happened?" shouted Marron's voice in her ear.

"I don't know. He just went crazy." She signalled to the nearest guard. "Open it."

"Is he injured?" asked Marron.

The guard pulled the door open and leapt back. Seven weapons were instantly trained on the interior. A man sat at the controls. He was tied up and had clearly not been driving. He turned to her, eyes wide.

It was not Tom.

In one of a network of sewer-access corridors not marked on any commercial map, Lentz looked at her laptop screen with a smile. "Time to move, before they work out it was simply a distraction. Though I expect it'll take them a while to realise how I was controlling the van."

"I get the strangest feeling that's not the first time you've remote-controlled a full-size vehicle as if it's a model car. How did you even get a signal down here?"

"I'm running through a relay. It also means Marron will start searching somewhere else if he manages to trace the signal."

"Nice of one of our guests from the barn to stand in for me."

"It was the least he could do." She closed the laptop and placed it in her bag. "Ready to break into theoretically the most secure office building in the world?"

Tom puffed out his cheeks. "You suck at motivational

speeches."

"I said 'theoretically'. Marron's weakness is that he has an enormous building he is attempting to secure with no more than forty guards. He cannot possibly do that without the help of the technology, which he assumes is infallible. We just need to use that against him."

Marron burst from the lift into the chaotic lobby scene, the air thick with the tang of splintered metal and dust. Two dozen guards and technicians surrounded the van, pointing guns and scanners.

"There's no sign of Faraday," Alex said, striding over, her boots crunching on fragments of black glass. "We thought about the 'Trojan horse' scenario. But the tech guys have run infrared all over it. There's no space large enough for him to hide."

Marron cursed. "So who's the driver?"

"This is the good part. He's one of our men. You sent him to Lentz's barn hideout."

"He was working with Lentz?"

"He wasn't really the driver. He was just tied up in the driver's seat." Alex pointed at a system of hydraulics that an engineer was pulling out from under the bonnet. "A remote control system, and cameras, all relayed via a mobile phone call. Whoever it was could be anywhere."

"Lentz," spat Marron.

"You have to admire the ingenuity. But why bother?" She gestured at the van. "What did this achieve?"

"I don't know. Maybe she's trying to create a distraction. But they must be close. I'm going to activate a cell-phone jammer around the building. It should stop her using the same trick again."

"Good." Alex stepped back and spoke a series of orders into her earpiece, then turned back to Marron. "All cameras are operational, all scanners are active. Guards are sweeping the vicinity. Faraday won't get within 400 metres of this building without our knowing it."

Approximately forty metres directly underneath where Alex stood, Tom and Lentz had reached a grimy steel panel the size of a small door. It was held in place by hefty bolts that looked as if they hadn't moved in years. Lentz tapped the door with a smile. "Forget programming 'backdoors': you can't beat a physical one."

"How does Marron not know about this door?"

"I've meddled with the CERUS Tower design for years. I hacked their architects' offices and made a few modifications to the plans after CERUS approved them. Mostly for my own amusement. I had no idea it would all actually come in handy."

"Of course we still have to get it open."

Lentz pulled a battery-powered socket driver from her backpack. "I brought my key."

Tom stepped back as she got to work on the first bolt. "I went through all the building schematics on your laptop on the way here. A few areas are blank: on Level 88 it's about ten percent of the entire floor. What do you think that means?"

She glanced across at him. "Just focus on locating Kate. But first, give me a hand with this," she said, as she removed the last bolt.

Together they pried open the hatch. Tom peered through. "I can see a service lift. It says Level Minus 5"

Lentz stowed the power tool then held up a phone-sized

device and looked at the display. "We can go through the doorway, but stop immediately inside." They clambered carefully through. Lentz reached into her backpack and flipped open her laptop. Then she ran a cable into a socket in the wall.

"Not going wireless?" asked Tom.

"I need considerably more bandwidth. I'm activating my last back door."

"You left something in the system? Surely it's not still there after all these years? Wouldn't it have been overwritten even if it wasn't discovered? The Tower wasn't even built then."

Lentz's hands flew over the keyboard. "They moved the system from building to building. And my backdoor is hidden in millions of lines of code: on its own it looks like benign redundant instructions. And as for being overwritten, you're right: IT systems are normally replaced with next generation code within a few years, but although CERUS made upgrades, at its core it's still the same product." She paused. "Or at least I hope it is. The important thing is that modern protocols and attack techniques simply aren't relevant to this system."

"So it's impenetrable?"

"Unless you have the key." Her fingers rattled across the keys again. Her screen flashed red.

"That doesn't look like a good colour," Tom said.

Lentz sucked in her breath. "Maybe I spoke too soon. I think I only get one more chance before the alarm is triggered."

"Maybe you just typed something wrong?"

Lentz glared at him then typed again, more slowly and deliberately.

ACCESS GRANTED appeared on her screen.

EIGHTY-ONE

MARRON SAT IN HIS COMMAND centre, sixteen large monitors in front of him cycling through various views, his fingers drumming on the control panel. Of their quarry there was no sign.

"They're not here," said Alex from just behind him. "None of my teams have reported anything. He's either late or he's simply not coming."

"Then why the van?" asked Marron sharply. "No, they're here, but for some reason we haven't spotted them."

"Our guards are pros. How could he have got past them unseen? It's not like they could have flown in."

"No... But what about the other end of the building?"

Alex stared blankly. "Underground? There's no access that isn't covered by security. There would have been an alarm or at least a system error."

"Actually, there is an access route from the river not shown on any plans. It's a special addition I worked into the plans. If they didn't use that, I wouldn't put it past Lentz to have dug her own tunnel."

"That's impossible. She wouldn't have had time. And we'd have detected it being dug."

"Not if it was done during construction."

"Who would plan that far in advance?"

"Lentz."

"But there are cameras on the Minus Levels. Not as many as above ground, but surely something would have shown up."

"Perhaps I've become too reliant on tech." Marron sighed. "Take a team and do a sweep."

◇ ◇ ◇

The service lift rose smoothly, carrying the two people that Marron most wished to locate.

Tom looked about warily. "Did you switch off the security systems?"

Lentz shook her head. "Marron would have seen that immediately. Instead I looped the last thirty minutes of every system's analysis. So they'll appear to be receiving normal security data, but actually it's historic, not current."

"Just the analysis or the live video-feed too?"

"Both of course." She tapped her tablet. "We'll be on Level 45 in thirty seconds. The room will be ten metres to our right."

"There is one rather obvious problem."

"With the room?"

"No, with your looping the video footage."

◇ ◇ ◇

In the artificially lit underbelly of the Tower, Alex and her team of six guards had swept Levels Minus 1 through 4. Alex tapped her earpiece and spoke quickly. "One floor to go. Nothing so far."

"Oh crap..." Marron muttered.

Alex pushed open the fire door to the stairwell and began descending. "What's happened?"

"I know why they haven't shown up on the system. It isn't showing current footage."

"How do you know?" She reached the foot of the stairs and stepped into the corridor of Level Minus 5.

"I'm looking at the lobby. There is no van in it."

"Perhaps the guards moved it already?"

"Did they also replace the glass doors?"

Alex pulled a torch from her belt and walked forwards, shining it at a hole in the wall. "It looks like you were right: Lentz had her own tunnel after all."

EIGHTY-TWO

LEVEL 45 WAS A GENERAL administration and services floor, tucked between Level 44 catering and Level 46 Marketing. It was entirely unremarkable at first glance, but Tom and Lentz had identified one office on Level 45 as perfect for their plan. They walked into a small windowless room containing three computer terminals with high bandwidth connections to the building's network. A principal data-trunk for the Tower ran down one wall.

"How long do we have?" Tom asked, quickly unpacking equipment from his backpack.

"They may have already noticed the little matter of their wrecked lobby suddenly being fully restored," replied Lentz. "Let's just hope it takes them a while to get the system recalibrated." She ran a cable from her laptop and jacked it into the nearest terminal. The lights flickered and all three computer terminals beeped softly.

"Was that you?" said Tom.

Lentz looked at her screen. "I don't think so. I think it's a status alert."

"Signifying what?"

She tapped her keyboard then swore. "The security system has just been refreshed. It's good in that we can track the guards, but bad in that they can now track us too." She clicked on an icon and a cluster of red dots appeared on a number of small rectangles.

"What are those?"

"Live maps of active ID tags on a floor by floor basis." She pointed at the top left. "This one is Level Minus 5, where we entered. There are seven IDs moving towards the lift."

"We should have replaced the plate so they wouldn't know how we got in."

"It can only be reattached from the tunnel side. Anyway, right now I'm more concerned about them finding *us*."

Tom looked at the featureless door to their room. "There's no lock if they do."

"Just an electronic one, which I've already activated – with a little twist to confuse things. But it won't slow them much." She plugged a cable into a spare power point. There was an angry beep from her computer. "My backdoor might still work, but he's shut down the subnet that I used to gain access last time."

"Maybe I can talk to the computer?" He reached into his own bag and removed the collar and a broad, flat cable, one end of which he clipped to the hub.

"It's a complex system, not a simple mechanical appliance like that robot arm. I don't know what will happen. Perhaps it will feedback on you and render you unconscious." Lentz looked again at the screen. The dots from Level Minus 5 were now in the lift. "We've got three minutes, max."

Tom slipped the collar around his neck. "Then we'd better hope I can come up with something."

Peter Marron watched his displays. A simple reset of the security networks had been enough to clear the looping of legacy data, and now he knew where his enemy was. He wasn't sure exactly how Lentz had managed it, but he was now running multiple scans across all systems. If she tried anything else, he would know immediately. It meant the system wasn't working at peak efficiency, but better that it was under his control.

"We're in the lift, ascending," Alex said over the speakers.

"Yes, I can see," replied Marron. "They're still on Level 45."

"What are they doing there?"

Marron stared at the floor plan, showing two red dots in a simple office room. "I've got no camera coverage. I assume they're trying to access the system. I can't physically disconnect it from here, but I've activated further firewall layers."

"I'm about a minute away."

"They're not going anywhere."

At first, for Tom, there was just the darkness behind his eyelids, the faint hum of the building, the buzz of the network.

And nothing more. Frustration welled within him. He couldn't let his failure in the barn repeat. This had to be different.

In the barn he had tried too hard. He forced his breathing to slow, he tried to forget where he was. He counted backwards from a hundred. This had to work, or they were all done for...

And something changed.

It was still dark, but it wasn't *nothing*. It was a space with *dimensions*. He could feel his mind mapped out around him, intimate and familiar. Yet it was not enclosed, it was no longer just *him*. Ahead was another space: somewhere alien and unknown, but rich with information.

This was the interface in action. It was the Tower system ahead of him; he was visualising it with the interface, and he was on the verge of making a connection. All he had to do was reach out. With a rush of excitement, he moved his perspective forward.

And hit a wall.

With a jerk, Tom opened his eyes and stared at the computer display. "Something's not right."

Lentz walked up and placed a hand on his shoulder. "It was always a shot in the dark."

"That's not what I mean. I think I've got it working, but something is stopping me. It's like a wall of glass. I can see the system in front of me, but I can't move to it. I can't make the connection."

"Marron knows where we are. He might be trying to lock the system down." Lentz picked up her laptop. "They're about to reach our floor." She hit a key and the screen switched to a video view. The lift doors slid back and a familiar figure emerged.

Tom pointed at the screen. "That woman. It's always her."

Lentz reached into her bag and pulled out a taser and an automatic pistol.

"There's seven of them," he said. "We can't win."

"If you have a better plan feel free to share it."

Tom closed his eyes, and tried again to feel the system. He pressed against the barrier. It would not move, but as he pushed harder he found he could glimpse through it. He could just make out...

He sat up with a start, his eyes flying open. He pointed to the back wall. "Over there. It's not a proper access panel, but behind it is ducting large enough to accommodate us. There's a ladder system built into the wall."

"Where would we go?"

"Up. I've ID'd a room on Level 60 with a non-standard connection to the building's datanet. We might have better luck there."

"Certainly beats waiting here to be captured."

Tom nodded. "So, Dr Lentz, I don't suppose you would happen to have a power screwdriver in your magic bag, would you?"

Lentz smiled. "I just might."

Alex exited the lift on Level 45 and, with considerable impatience, led her team to the third office on the left. Her guards split ranks to stand either side of the door.

"Remember," she said quietly, "Lentz used to be a professional, so give no quarter, but Faraday must not be harmed."

Her team nodded sharply in reply.

"Now open it."

One guard pressed the door release. There was a hiss, but nothing else happened. The guard slapped the button again. Still no response.

"The door won't open," said Alex into her earpiece.

"Odd," replied Marron. "Let me override that for you. There you go."

The guard hit the button again, but still nothing happened.

"Nope," said Alex.

"Are you sure?" asked Marron. "My readout shows no issue."

"Perhaps your additional firewalls are causing interference. Or perhaps Lentz did more to the system than you realise."

"Actually, I think it's this," said one of the guards, pointing at the base of the door.

Alex looked and laughed.

"What is it?" demanded Marron.

"She stuck a pencil in the door track. Nothing like a low-tech solution to confuse us." With a grunt, she pulled it out and the door slid open.

The room was empty.

EIGHTY-THREE

THE SERVICE PANEL CLATTERED TO the ground and two figures clambered out.

"That was not comfortable for someone of my dimensions," Tom said.

"More comfortable than being captured by Marron, I'm sure," Lentz replied, looking around. "Where are we?"

"Ed Holm's office. He's one of the senior techies working on Tantalus. The connections to this office are higher bandwidth and they circumvent many of the system safeguards."

"Done with Marron's knowledge?"

"Who cares." Tom gazed around at the clutter. "Wow. How does he work in here?" He stepped between piles of paperwork and boxes strewn across the floor.

Lentz froze. "Are there cameras in here?"

Tom pointed up to his right. "There's only one and it covers the doorway. Stay away from it and they'll be none the wiser. Also don't make any unusually loud noises." Tom sat down and plugged his cable into the computer. "Now we just need a little bit of time."

Peter Marron had joined the team on Level 45 as they examined the room for the third time. The answers he needed were still not forthcoming.

"Your systems are lying to you," said Alex through gritted teeth.

"There's a trick we're missing. I know they were in here."

Ed Holm walked into the room. "You called for me? What's going on?"

Marron turned, his face breaking into a smile. "I need your help, Ed."

Holm looked uneasily at Marron, Alex and the guards, each prominently armed. "With what?"

"Subject Zero is in the building."

"He's here? You want to run some analysis?"

"Indeed I do, but first I need to find him."

"I don't follow?"

"Unfortunately the Tower's systems have become rather blind, deaf and insensitive when it comes to Zero."

"Can't we track the nanites in his body?"

"That function has been deactivated."

"How?"

"Dominique Lentz is with him."

"What? How is that possible? I thought she was--"

"If we find her, you can ask for details. What I need right now are ideas."

Holm rubbed his palms across his face. "If you can give me access to your central security systems, I might be able to figure something out."

Marron's phone beeped and he glanced at it. "Good. Because Mr Leskov has just confirmed he is on his way to the Tower to inspect the product. Which means we'd better have something to show him."

EIGHTY-FOUR

IN ED HOLM'S OFFICE, TOM leaned back in the large leather chair, staring at the middle of three oversized computer monitors on the desk.

Lentz was next to him, her fingers blurring over the keyboard. "OK, I've configured the system: you've got the best access I can grant. That's your cue."

Tom closed his eyes and took a deep breath. Once again the dark space was around him, filled with an eerie hum. He reached out carefully. It felt like before, but this time there was no wall in front of him, just a clear path. And yet still he couldn't move forward. He wanted to use the interface to extend his perception beyond himself, into the computer, but his mind resisted.

It felt *wrong*.

Perhaps he needed to sharpen his focus. He took a deep breath and tried to move his thoughts out into the system. Still nothing.

He had to find the key. The motivation to step over that threshold: to step outside himself. Tom was aware of Lentz standing next to him, yet she seemed a thousand miles away.

"If I had more time," she said, "then maybe I could come up

with a hack."

"Just a little longer." His mind wouldn't accept that it could reach into the computer. Something was telling him that if he went there he would lose himself. A bead of sweat formed on his forehead.

"We need to get out of here," Lentz whispered.

"I have to make this work. Just a few more moments--"

"You have no idea how long this is going to take. We have to get to safety."

"What about Kate?"

"This plan has gone from 'long shot' to 'suicide mission'. We'll have to find another way: regroup and try again."

"Marron will kill her."

"Tom, I'm disconnecting you. Killing yourself won't save her, and right now that's all you're likely to achieve."

Tom felt her reach forward in front of him, towards the cable. Without even knowing he was doing it, his hand caught her wrist. "That's not your call."

And something in him clicked.

At first it was just a point of reference in a shapeless mass. But it showed him the way.

He was at a junction: a connection to more substantive data. He opened his mind and let it flow through. He could feel it, almost taste it.

He opened his eyes. The screen in front of him blinked. A simple cursor prompt appeared. Then text started to scroll down the screen. Tom felt the collar humming around his neck. Information streamed from the computer along the fibre optic cable.

The Tower opened up to him.

He felt its thousand cameras become his eyes, its hidden microphones become his ears, its sensors become his skin. He was one with the enormous structure around him. And it threatened to overwhelm him. If he was to find what he was looking for he needed to filter: to constrain and limit. He needed a guide.

The Tower's systems were built around a hub. He could feel the processing core: powerful if not sentient. *What do you want to know?* it seemed to ask him.

He focused on one question. *Where is Kate?*

Images of her face flashed up in his memory and he found he knew how to pass them to the system. Powerful pattern-recognition algorithms kicked into play, searching for Kate's image among millions stored on CERUS' servers. Tom felt his mind riffle over the floor, not sequentially but somehow all at once. And in a blink he had found her.

He turned to Lentz. "Kate's on Level 71. In an internal storage room."

"Are there guards?"

"Two outside. Armed. I'll see if I can do anything to even the odds by the time you get there."

"Can I use the lift? Will it be safe?"

He concentrated. "Take the lift furthest on the right. I'll take it off the monitoring system."

She handed him a small radio. "This is encrypted and linked to mine. Use it and there's no way Marron can listen in." She turned to leave. "Will you be OK here?"

"Just go get Kate."

EIGHTY-FIVE

TOM CLOSED HIS EYES AND let his senses expand. One moment he was Tom Faraday, the next he was something... more. His senses reached out within the building. He could feel its systems, its power, its sensors, its doors and windows. He was a part of it. It was a part of him.

Yet again it threatened to tell him too much - a flood of information that would exhaust and overwhelm him if he went any further - and he drew back. This was not about feeling powerful: this was about using his abilities to help Lentz to rescue Kate. He might have found her, but the mission was not over yet.

He focused instead on one small part of the building: the area outside Kate's cell. The two guards were alert, professional and carrying automatic weapons. He'd told Lentz he would even the odds, but how? The central computer had records of an armoury in the basement. Could he guide Lentz there? It was a far longer journey than the few floors to Kate's prison cell: a far greater risk that she'd be intercepted. Even if she did make it there and back, even if she had a bigger gun, a firefight with two guards was still a risk. There had to be a better way.

And then he found it.

There was a system not listed on any of the specifications. Hidden in part of the ducting next to a laboratory on Level 61 were six gas canisters. Each contained anaesthetic gas of a kind regularly used in medical procedures. Carefully, he made adjustments to the air flow and began pumping the mix into the section where the men stood, quietly closing off doors to seal them in.

He noticed one of the men sniff the air, as if subconsciously aware something was wrong, but the gas was virtually odourless.

Tom permitted himself a smile. There were plenty more guards to deal with if they were to leave the Tower safely, but once Kate and Lentz were safe, Tom would handle them. And then he would find Marron.

Kate sat on her bed, looking at the wall, shame burning her from the inside out.

She had given up Tom's number.

She had tried to fight the truth nano, but she had lost. And lost quickly. Those *things* had got inside her head and taken apart every defence she could muster. They grated, they fought, they rearranged her very thoughts and memories. Within minutes she had found herself telling Marron what she knew. It was like someone else was controlling her speech, saying things she would never say. Whatever he asked, she answered. Finally the sensation faded, but by then it was too late.

There was a hiss and the door to the room swung open. But instead of a guard, a short, intense-looking woman stood there, a grim smile on her face. "Are you OK?" she asked.

"Who the hell are you?"

"My name is Dominique and," she stepped aside to reveal the

two guards lying slumped on the floor, "Tom sends his regards."

Kate's eyes widened.

"He tells me they're just unconscious."

"No offence, but how do I know you're who you say you are?"

Lentz held out an earpiece. "Ask him yourself."

EIGHTY-SIX

MARRON'S COMMAND CENTRE HUMMED WITH activity. Holm sat, mouth open, staring at the screens around him as they cycled endlessly through thousands of different video-feeds. "I have never seen anything like this."

"There *is* nothing like this," replied Marron with a slight smile.

"How many cameras do you have?" asked Holm.

"Nearly 10,000 in the building: several hundred more outside."

"And how the hell do you monitor them all?"

Marron tapped a key and an interface appeared on the largest screen. "I have multiple monitoring programmes running. They scan all the camera feeds and run configurable analysis algorithms."

"So how do you track somebody specific?"

"Using their ID card. I can track every card to within a couple of metres in real time." He paused. "Of course Zero is no longer carrying his card, but there are several other options for tracking people and usually the system runs them in parallel. The cameras can attempt facial recognition. Also, when the building is relatively uncrowded, all activity can be flagged and inspected. Unfortunately, Zero and Lentz seem to have vanished."

"And all the systems still appear to be operational?"

Marron nodded.

"Then there are two obvious non-exclusive possibilities. First, that they are moving within parts of the building that do not have camera coverage."

"Everywhere has coverage."

"Then we have to assume they have somehow taken over the system and instructed it not to show them."

Marron stared at the screens. "She hasn't co-opted my hardware, so what is she using? It would take considerably more than a laptop's processing power. Unless..."

"Unless what?"

"Zero is connected."

Holm blinked. "I'm sorry. What do you mean 'connected'?"

"If I'm right, his Tantalus interface is already operational. And he's using it to connect with the building. To control it."

"That would be way ahead of our most optimistic projections. Does he even have the latest code?"

Marron shook his head. "Lentz must have helped him accelerate things."

Holm adjusted his glasses. "I'm pretty sure I can stop whatever is happening, however they're doing it. It's quite simple really: a hard reset. We turn everything off and then turn it on again. It'll trigger a complete cold reboot."

"Won't they just re-establish control?"

"Maybe, maybe not. It'll give us both a window of opportunity to come out on top." Holm hesitated. "There is a risk attached. The whole building will be temporarily offline. *Everything* will shut down. All doors will open, as if it's an emergency. Also, if Zero *is* connected, rebooting could be... painful. If Heidn were here, he might have a better idea--"

"Forget Heidn; he's chosen to run off on us. And don't worry about Zero. A little pain can be character-building." Marron reached forward and tapped a key. On the central screen a view of the empty cell where Kate had been kept flashed up. Changing cameras, he saw the two guards lying on the floor in the corridor outside. "Apparently they have control of the lifts, cameras and who knows what else." He turned to Holm. "We have no choice. Reboot. Now."

Tom watched via CCTV as Lentz led Kate out of the cell and towards the lifts.

"What now?" Lentz said via the encrypted comms unit.

"Get to the ground floor," Tom replied. "I'll meet you there."

"Shouldn't we rendezvous with you on Level 60?"

"If I disconnect, I'll lose control of the system. I'd rather not risk us all being recaptured. If you can get out, you can get help."

"I have a contact," Kate said. "Someone who should be able to bring the cavalry."

Lentz nodded. "OK, Tom. But no heroics."

"As if," he replied. He turned back to the computer. He had so much control, but still he had not been able to locate Marron and the effort was making him weary. He began again at ground level, scanning each floor. But as he did so he began to hear a pulsing sound. It grew in pitch and volume, filling his senses. Within the sound seemed to be a command: an instruction that he could not refuse. Something about beginning again. A fresh start. A reset instruction...

He yanked the cable out of the computer, falling backwards off his chair. The back of his head was buzzing, the collar hot. He seemed to be swimming in fog. Gasping, he closed his eyes.

"Did it work?" Marron asked.

Holm looked at the computer screen. "We'll know soon enough. It's coming back online now."

Marron called up the building diagram. One item was flagged for attention: two figures in a lift that had started its journey on Level 71, but which had come to halt with the system reset. The lift camera activated and he saw Kate and Lentz frantically pounding on the controls. He permitted himself a smile: one problem solved.

Next, he analysed the recent data flows. They had been centred on an office on Level 60.

"That's my office!" cried Holm, leaning over Marron's shoulder. He backed away when Marron flicked him a stare.

"How irritatingly ironic." Marron clicked his earpiece. "Alex, get to Level 60. Zero is in Holm's office."

EIGHTY-SEVEN

NEIL BRADLEY SAT IN WILLIAM Bern's penthouse office, spreading his hands across the huge stone desk to feel every inch of its near-perfectly smooth surface. He had dreamt that one day he would experience this moment: to take the helm of a corporate giant. But not in these circumstances.

And even though he was acting CEO, he knew he was in control of very little. The plan he had been following with Celia had all but fallen apart in a slew of failures and death. Everything in his head was telling him to get out while he could.

Yet there was still the chance to make a great deal of money if he could just find a way through the next few hours. Subject Zero was in the building, so they could yet have their deliverable. Marron had been vague about where, ordering him to focus on managing Leskov. He glanced at his mobile - he'd got a text from Celia saying she was coming to the Tower, but there was still no sign of her. He had called Marron, but had received no reply. Muttering, he decided to check for himself. Logging into his laptop, he accessed the visitor records.

A red symbol appeared. He was locked out.

Odd.

He entered Bern's override code, but the system didn't respond. Perhaps Marron had shut it down when the building was evacuated? He needed to make sure he got to Celia first: he needed to make sure she didn't say something ill-considered – something emotional that might compromise their plan. The irony was that Bern had been the rock holding things together. And yet he had also been keeping secrets. How had he set up a Subject Zero so fast? It was almost like he'd known what Bradley was going to propose...

Bern's office phone rang. He swallowed and answered it. "This is Bradley."

"We will be with your shortly." Leskov's voice was heavily digitised.

"We're finalising our preparations for you. The building will be secure."

"I'm sure you believe that, but I'm not prepared to rely on you. I'm amending my travel arrangements. My team are sending you the details."

Bradley tapped his laptop and pulled an incredulous face as he read the message. "Will you get clearance?"

"We won't need it. Our ETA is one hour."

The call disconnected. Bradley picked up his phone to contact Marron, but suddenly the lights flickered then went out. A few seconds later, they came back on. Bradley frowned as he looked at his laptop and saw that the network was down.

He picked up the phone: it was dead too.

What was going on?

Another beep and his laptop chimed that it was reconnecting. He breathed a sigh of relief. A moment later, a message flashed up on the screen: *SYSTEM REBOOT. ADMINISTRATOR ACCESS RANK TWO ENABLED.*

Bradley blinked. That was way above his usual access. His

hands flew over the keyboard: the visitor-records interface filled the screen. He puffed out his cheeks and typed in Celia's details. The result was immediate.

She was not shown as having signed in to the building, but one of her cars was parked in the visitor car park. And facial recognition confirmed she had arrived an hour ago.

So where was she?

He saw an icon marked 'advanced' and clicked on it. A log of her movements appeared.

She seemed to have gone to a meeting room on Level 1 then she'd taken a lift to Level Minus 5. What was she doing down there? He scanned down, but the system said that she was still on that floor, in a storeroom.

What was down there? Some secret Bern had been keeping? He shook his head and stood up. He would go and find out for himself.

EIGHTY-EIGHT

TOM CAME TO, LYING ON the floor. He blinked, his vision blurry. The collar around his neck was very warm. The cable dangled uselessly across his chest.

In his head there was a vacuum: a void where the power had been, the connection to the system. He had been so careful not to lose himself in the sensation of control, but now it was gone completely and he felt shattered: it was as if his senses had been cut off. The ache was almost unbearable. The building no longer responded to his will. And that meant Marron was back in charge. Tom grabbed the end of the cable and looked up at the computer terminal. What had happened? He ran his hand over the back of his head. There was a strange tingling. He unclipped the hub from the collar and almost dropped it. While the collar was warm, the hub was searingly hot. He placed it carefully on the floor and, with a growl, pushed himself to his feet.

Could he reconnect? If he did, would the problem just happen again? Could he do anything to defend against it? He concentrated then something occurred to him: if they were controlling the system again, they knew where he was. He wondered how long he had, then he caught himself: better to think about what he could do with the time he had.

Alex's team arrived on Level 60 with a purpose. Eight men, all ex-special forces, fanned out around the office. Alex noticed in passing that the glass windows into Holm's office had been darkened so they could not see in. The only feature visible was Holm's infamous 'Trespassers will be Electrocuted' sign. She waved at two of her men. "Take the lead. We don't believe he is armed, but take no chances. And remember that he is not to be harmed." She pointed to the remaining men. "You six, follow in and fan out. I don't want any mistakes."

The lead two kicked the door down and leapt through. The other six followed. "He's not here," shouted one.

"What?" Alex moved to the doorway.

The sprinkler system came on. Alex stepped back reflexively. The men looked up, irritated. Suddenly there was a spark from one of the light fittings, as if it was overloading.

Realisation dawned on Alex. "Get out!" she shrieked.

But it was too late.

High voltage electricity, conducted by the water, flowed into the men. Their bodies jerked.

And they screamed.

Tom watched the scene impassively on the CCTV cameras that he once again controlled. He sat two offices to the right, plugged into another terminal, back in charge.

But this time things were different. This time he would not hold back. This time he would throw every resource he had at these people. They were not fighting fair, so neither would he.

Before plugging in, he had visualised what he needed to do. And he was beginning to realise how much he really *could* do. This was all in him, in the chip, though the distinction was becoming blurred. The chip was part of him: inorganic, calculating, clinical.

For a moment, he let the men writhe, the power flowing through them, twisting and jerking their bodies. But only for a moment. He wasn't a killer.

He turned the electricity to the room off.

Then he scanned the building until he found Kate and Lentz in a lift, stuck between Levels 58 and 59. They were safe. He would get them moving again in a moment.

But first he turned to his most important task: locating Peter Marron.

And yet still he could not do so. Marron was nowhere on any of the systems. If he was in the building, he was in some part beyond the reach of any of its sensors, so well hidden that even the system did not know where he was. Frustration welled up in him. The thought echoed in his mind then was processed and relayed through the building's tannoy system.

A single sentence: a statement of intent bellowed in a robotic voice, flat and emotionless. From the basement to the rooftop helipad, the voice reverberated.

Marron, I'm coming for you.

EIGHTY-NINE

TOM'S VOICE ECHOED IN THE air-conditioned air of Marron's control room.

Marron glared at Holm. "You heard him. Now find him!"

"Actually, I think I might have a way." Holm walked over to the nearest computer. "I'm presuming he has re-interfaced with the system from a different point. But he had to get there before he re-established, during which time the building would have logged his movements. If I can just access the buffer – which is within your private systems, and he does not control – then we can see where he went."

"If that works you're a genius. And Leskov won't have to kill us all."

Holm swallowed. He tapped the screen. "He's there: two offices away from mine."

Marron looked at the screen. "Your office faces north, yes?"

"Yes, but how does that help?"

Marron strode over to a cabinet and started pulling out equipment. He stepped into a webbed personal-safety harness and unravelled a long length of rope. "We just need to think laterally."

◇ ◇ ◇

Tom frowned. He was looking at a room on Level 88 connected to Marron's office - the same location he had previously noticed was missing from the building schematics. It had to be where Marron was, but Tom could not penetrate the room's systems at all. It wasn't just that access was encrypted: according to the system, there was nothing in the room. No wires, no air-con, no computers. He checked and re-checked but got no further. The doorway was a barrier he could not pass. He scanned the building but found no other clue until he started picking up an odd noise. A light double-thump from one of the levels way above him. Then a similar noise on the levels below the first. And so on down the building from floor to floor. Analysing the sound, the system told him that it was glass vibrating at low frequency, as if impacted by something padded. He tracked the noise down in a straight line for several floors before he realised that the next room in line was the office he currently sat in.

Alarm bells sounded in his brain, but it was too late.

Bullets shattered the window, aimed high, perhaps intentionally to miss him. Tom ducked to the ground as a helmeted figure swung in on an abseil rope, gun aimed unerringly at him. The figure moved as Tom crouched in shock and, with a fluid motion, pulled the cable from the computer and the collar from around Tom's neck.

Fire seemed to burn through every cell of Tom's body and he screamed. His hands and feet went numb, his legs and arms so weak he slid to the floor.

Straightening, the figure pulled off its helmet. "Good to see you again, Tom," said Marron.

NINETY

KATE STABBED THE LIFT BUTTONS for the twentieth time. "Can you not get it working?"

Lentz was glaring at a control panel she had opened in the wall. "The lift program went into safe mode when that system reboot happened. Until someone overrides it centrally we're not going anywhere."

"Great," Kate said. "Out of one locked box into another, smaller one."

"An elegant but unhelpful summary."

"Something has happened to Tom."

"A lot of things have happened to Tom." Lentz levered open an inspection flap and frowned at the wiring inside.

Kate swallowed. "I've just realised who you are. I saw your photo in an old news archive: you're Dominique Lentz." She blinked. "Aren't you dead?"

"I'd have preferred it if I could have stayed that way. And if I can't get us out of here, my death may prove to have not been so greatly exaggerated," Lentz sighed. "Unfortunately I've used up all my tricks for overriding the CERUS system."

"Then we need to get a signal out. I have someone we can call."

"What sort of someone?"

Kate raised an eyebrow. "They're MI5."

Lentz blinked. "You're working with *them*?"

"That might be overstating our relationship."

Lentz cast her a speculative look, but pulled an oversized mobile from a pocket. "You know, it's my experience that when you ask for help from MI5, it rarely comes on the terms you expect." She tapped at the phone and frowned. "The only certainty is that you'll regret asking."

"And you know a lot about them, do you? If you've been managing on your own for twenty-five years, I guess you're not used to asking for help."

Lentz shrugged. "It's all academic. This building now has cell-phone screening in place. No cellular wireless comms of any nature, in or out."

Kate folded her arms. "Surely someone as resourceful as you has a couple of tricks up her sleeve. We can't let Marron get away with what he's done." She gave a grimace. "And not just to me."

Lentz placed a hand on her arm. "Tom said you didn't talk until Marron gave you the right motivation. What did he do to you?"

"I'd rather not think about it. I can still feel them inside--"

Lentz hissed. "Truth nano? This is supposed to be about the future and he's trying to drag us back to the dark ages."

"Then help me stop him. I think the MI5 agent is someone we can trust."

Lentz nodded slowly. "You asked if I still had a few tricks up my sleeve, I recall." She sniffed. "Let's have a look, shall we?"

NINETY-ONE

THE EXPRESS LIFT ACCELERATED DOWNWARDS. Bradley stared at the screen on his tablet, exploring his administrator-level access. He was now scanning the CCTV footage from the time of Celia's arrival. He watched her drive up and park her Ferrari across the CERUS car park entrance. He saw her storm into the reception area and shout at the guard on duty. Then he saw Marron appear and steer her away. He took her to a meeting room and then to the lifts.

Why hadn't Marron told him she'd arrived? He searched again, but there were no further CCTV records of Celia and the system would not confirm Marron's current location. So much for administrator access.

The lift slowed then finally reached its destination. Bradley stepped out onto Level Minus 5. According to the floor plan, the storage room Celia had gone to was twenty metres along the corridor. Clenching and unclenching the fingers of his left hand, he walked towards it, noting the CCTV cameras and wondering why they weren't providing footage to the system. He reached the storeroom door and tugged at the handle.

It was locked. Smiling, he searched for the physical door

access menu on his tablet. The screen flashed red: *ADMINISTRATOR ACCESS - LOGIN REQUIRED.*

Muttering, Bradley realised the system had restored. His administrative privileges were gone. He knocked loudly on the door. "Celia?" he called.

There was no reply.

He shouted her name again. He tried turning the handle, jiggling it roughly, but it would not move. In frustration, he kicked the door, hard. It groaned in protest. Then he threw his whole weight at it. The door groaned again but held. He rubbed his shoulder then backed up to the far side of the corridor. Shouting, he charged at the door, focusing his impact on the mid-point, near the handle. With a shriek the lock split and the door swung inwards, Bradley stumbling through.

At first, his brain did not register what he was seeing.

A woman's body. Slumped face down on the ground. There was blood. Lots of blood - a gunshot wound in her chest.

His heart pounding, he brushed her hair aside and stared at her face.

Celia.

He took a step back, trying to digest what he was seeing. He had never seen a dead body before. He stood motionless for a long time, finally realising he was holding his breath. He let it go with a painful gasp and stepped away from the body, stumbling out into the corridor. He closed the door, though the lock was broken and it didn't shut properly, then he ran for the nearest stairwell and pounded up the metal treads. Reaching the ground floor, breathing hard, he pulled out his mobile phone and called a number on speed dial. But, as he held it to his ear, it beeped in error. Confused, he looked at the display.

No signal. There was no cellular network available: Marron's lock-down protocol. Muttering, Bradley reached into another pocket and removed a second, larger phone: an encrypted satellite phone. There was only one number programmed.

"What is it?" replied Leskov immediately.

"I've just found Celia Bern. She's been murdered. I think it was Marron. It *had* to have been him."

"Interesting. Perhaps Bern was also his handiwork."

"Do you still want to come here?"

"I need to be certain I'm getting what I'm paying for."

"What about Marron?"

"I'm more than ready to deal with him."

NINETY-TWO

TOM WAS PLACED IN STEEL handcuffs then escorted by a large group of guards to Marron's office on Level 88. Waiting there was a man he vaguely recognised and someone clad in a familiar black combat suit: the woman who had started everything.

"Alex. It's always you. Don't you have anything better to do?"

She smiled. "It's been quite a dance, Tom."

"Whatever they're paying you, you're not going to have long to enjoy it."

"You think this is about money?"

"That was exactly what I--"

Marron raised a hand and beckoned the man over. "Ed, do what you need to do."

The bespectacled man walked over to Tom. "I need to run a few quick checks on you before I run the installation. You're getting the final interface code. The codecs for the helicopter." Holm held a scanner near Tom's head. "I have a connection! And it's stable. Now please hold still."

Tom felt a tingle under his scalp and leaned away. "Or maybe I won't."

Marron coughed. "I have two friends of yours suspended in a lift more than two hundred metres up a lift shaft. Would you like me to lower them at a speed considerably in excess of the recommended maximum?"

Holm tapped something on the scanner. "OK, commencing transfer."

Tom felt as if someone had dunked his head in a cold bucket of water. The cold intensified, becoming like shards of ice. Then suddenly it was gone.

Holm nodded. "It's complete. I'm getting bidirectional data transfer. No conscious instructions at this point, but it should be enough for Leskov."

"Excellent," Marron said. "How do you feel, Tom?"

"Like killing you all."

Holm removed a blood pressure kit from a case and slid it up Tom's arm.

"Now you're concerned for my health?" Tom looked at Marron.

"Circumstances change. Now you're our main attraction."

"And you're going to use me to demonstrate the technology to your buyer. Then what?"

"That's all Leskov wants from you. Proof that the technology works. What *we* want is you to come back to work – only in a slightly different capacity. You'll find staying with us far more comfortable than GCHQ or Moscow."

"Moscow?"

"*Chez* Leskov."

Holm pumped up the blood pressure cuff and then let it deflate, making notes of the readings.

"Does he know the truth about me? That I'm *not* evidence that the project is replicable?"

Marron coughed. "I'll leave that kind of statement to the

scientists."

"I know why you selected me as your little back-up plan. And I know about the original Project Tantalus. I know I was your side-project that time too. I know about the chip, Marron."

Holm looked up. "What?"

Marron frowned. "Finish your tests, Ed. Alex, I need to speak to you." He beckoned her from the room.

Tom watched them leave then lowered his voice. "Look at the base of my head. I have a very faint, very old scar. I'm sure you have scanning equipment. Check it out."

Holm smiled. "Tom, I can understand your confusion and, under the circumstances, a bit of paranoia is really quite natural but whatever the case with your recent, er, co-option to our efforts, I can assure you that all the original Tantalus Project subjects were adults."

"Not all of them," Tom said. "It was hushed up."

Holm shook his head distractedly. "I should probably X-ray you anyway, for our records. Over here."

Tom walked over and sat in a chair under a blocky X-ray unit.

"If there was more time we could run a full CAT scan but this should suffice. Now hold still." Holm stepped away and jabbed a button. The equipment hummed and there was a loud click. The result displayed almost immediately on a nearby screen.

Tom watched Holm and waited for the discovery.

But it did not happen.

Holm stood back from the equipment, rubbing his palms together. "All perfectly normal. No chip or other unexplained object."

Tom stared at him, incredulous. "Don't be ridiculous. I had a scan only days ago. Of course it's there."

"Must have been a glitch," said Holm. "See for yourself." He turned the display screen to face Tom. "Anything metallic would be a bright white point."

Tom blinked. "What about the node itself?"

"That's not likely to show up as it's non-metallic. But it's definitely there. How else would the interface be working?"

"You people have no idea what is going on. You don't know whether your project has gone spectacularly right or spectacularly wrong."

Marron strode back into the room. "What's going on?"

"I did a quick X-ray," Holm replied. "Is that a problem?"

Marron stared at the image and a half smile crossed his face. "Not at all."

Holm switched off the screen. "Then I'm done here, Peter. We're looking good."

"Why don't you get up to Level 90? Apparently that's where all the action is going to be. I'll follow with Tom in a few minutes."

Marron closed the door after Holm. "I want, Tom, to make sure that you conduct yourself appropriately in our imminent meeting."

"Why would I help you?"

"Because it's in your own interests. Our buyer is not someone you want to disappoint."

"It would seem that I have what we lawyers call 'leverage'."

Marron snorted. "Viktor Leskov is a man of considerable means who knows what he wants and expects to get it. We have to deliver him a working interface or he is very likely to kill us all. Thankfully, he is also a man of his word: if we give him what he wants, he will pay us and leave. You could come out of this a very wealthy man."

"You think I care? You killed my best friend."

Marron sighed. "You're going to need to make a choice, Tom. You can either die in some misguided attempt to honour her memory. Or you can try to salvage something from the situation. Live to exact your revenge another day."

"Even if I were willing, how do you know it will work to his requirements?"

"When you've needed to do things, you've found a way. And believe me, you *will* need to do it."

Tom ground his teeth. "What do I have to do?"

"We've implanted the codecs in you: instructions for Leskov's new helicopter. All you need to do is make it work. It'll be like when you controlled the building – and that was something you weren't even designed to control. I'm also going to need some of your blood for Leskov's team to analyse."

Alex removed a case from a drawer and flipped it open. Inside was a syringe, with a needle over five centimetres long.

Tom blanched. "Are you taking the blood direct from my heart or something?"

"From near the base of your skull. We have to go deep."

"You'll paralyse me."

Marron smiled. "Not if you don't move."

Tom shook his head. "Why are you doing all this?"

"I believe this technology is a gift. I'd trade places with you in an instant to have what's inside your head."

"If you actually had it in your head, you might be saying something different."

Marron flexed his shoulders. "I saw what you did with this building. The interface works, even if the nanites have diverged from their original programming."

"The fact that they're operating outside their remit doesn't worry you?"

"We never could work out how to program them fully. In the

end we just gave them an approach and a series of guidelines because no one could foresee all the challenges they would face."

Tom shook his head. "Just tell me one thing. Why me? And I don't mean 'now'. Why me originally?"

Marron shrugged. "Your mother was a... *contact* of Bern's.

"What? Are you saying she gave consent?"

"You'll..." He coughed. "*You'd* have to ask Bern. And of course it's too late for that. Besides, whatever the risks, it has worked. Look at how you turned out."

"You're acting like this has been a success. Eighty percent of your subjects have died."

"But not you." Marron shook his head. "You're not grasping what this means, Tom: how important this project is."

"You keep saying that, but I doubt you would have volunteered your own child."

Marron smiled a curious smile. "It was all rendered moot when Bern agreed to close us down."

"Because he saw sense?"

"Because of pressure from the government. It's taken so long to get back to where we were, but now... now we've finally reached our goal."

"And you feel that justifies the body count?"

"There's a lot about this you don't understand; Bern is fond of saying this project is bigger than any one person."

"*Was* fond," Alex said.

Marron nodded. "Yes, that. Now, sit still while we get our blood sample."

"You keep saying 'we'. Are you and Alex more than a team? Are you an item?"

Marron glanced at Alex. "Clever. But not *that* clever."

And in a flash Tom *knew*. "*She's* your daughter." He swallowed. "And she has a chip as well."

Alex moved up to Marron and put her hand on his shoulder. "Nearly that clever."

"And you're OK with what he did to you?"

"He's my father."

Marron grunted. "It's needle time. Are you ready?"

"Just get it over with."

They laid him flat, face down, and lifted the back of his shirt. Alex leaned close and whispered, "Hold still now."

Tom felt the needle go in: a brief white-hot pain. Then the sensation repeated.

"All done," said Marron, holding up the two syringes, full and red. "A proportion of the nanites are programmed to make their way to a specific location at the base of your neck so we can harvest them, analyse the instructions: see what worked and what didn't."

Tom stood, adjusting his shirt. He watched as Marron eyed the vials of blood then looked at his daughter. And suddenly it became clear. "You want to use this on Alex. You still want the interface for her. Getting me was always about testing it for Alex."

Marron turned away. "We need to get upstairs."

"If this is all so amazing, why give it to anyone else?"

"Further development of the project will require significant funding. Given our path to this point, that is unlikely to be available through traditional channels. We'd obviously rather get the money and not hand the files over to Leskov, but I haven't worked out a way to persuade him to accept that yet. Help us and we get the money; help us and your journalist friend goes free."

"And Lentz?"

Marron shrugged. "We can discuss it later."

Tom ground his teeth. He tried to feel the electronics around him, tried to reach for the network. But without the collar and the hub nothing happened.

Marron cleared his throat. "Do we have a deal?"

Tom closed his eyes. "Let's just get this over with."

NINETY-THREE

LENTZ AND KATE SAT CROSS-legged on the floor of the lift. Lentz placed her phone in between them with a sigh. "If I tinker with it to boost the signal, I can get a message past the screening, but it will have to be *very* short."

"How short?"

"Just a few words. Maybe five."

Kate gave a snort. "You're joking? Surely you can send more than that in a fraction of a second?"

"Normally, yes, but I'm piggy-backing on old cell towers, using undisclosed back channels, so there's very little bandwidth available. The jamming system will react almost instantly. Now, we could try to use another form of compression, but there's no guarantee the recipient would be able to interpret it. So five words it is. Any more than that and we risk the whole data-packet being blocked."

"How am I supposed to convey the situation and location in five words?"

"You're the journalist. Come up with a headline."

"Fine." Kate took the phone and typed rapidly then handed it back.

Lentz frowned down at it then laughed. "*Prisoner at CERUS Tower. Help.*" Lentz held her own phone over Kate's and launched an app. She tapped a sequence. The message vanished from the screen. "Well, I've done everything I can. I really hope this Croft isn't playing you."

"Look at it this way: could we be any worse off?"

"I find it best not to tempt fate with that kind of language."

Kate started to reply but the lift lurched and began moving upwards. Kate's phone beeped angrily.

Lentz looked at it and scowled. "I was afraid of that."

"Afraid of what?"

"The message didn't send. And they know we tried. If you have any other ideas, now would be the time to mention them."

Kate scowled. "I think I'm out. Unless..." Kate started running her hands over her clothes. "What if you're right and we can't trust him. Maybe he bugged me."

"Something that Marron's people didn't detect?"

Lentz tapped an icon on her phone then began running it over Kate's body. As she reached Kate's neck, there was an angry squeal. Lentz narrowed her eyes and ran her fingertips over Kate's coat, stopping with a smile as they brushed a metal pin jammed into a thick collar-seam. "It has to be a passive device, but if I overload it enough I think we can send your message."

NINETY-FOUR

THE CONCEALED DOOR SLID OPEN and Marron, Alex and Tom walked out of Marron's secret room into his office.

Alex frowned down at her phone. "Lentz has been trying her hand at escapology."

"What did she do?" Marron asked.

"She had a go at hot-wiring the lift controls. It didn't work. Then she tried to send a short text message from her phone before the adaptive firewall blocked the frequency. That didn't work either." Alex held up her tablet to show Marron the message.

Marron snorted. "How subtle. Who did she try and send it to?"

"I'm running a trace. Maybe it's someone the journalist knows. Do you want me to get them in here so we can ask them?"

"Send them up to the roof. Have a team waiting to secure them."

"Understood." She looked up from her screen. "Also we have a visitor."

The door handle turned and Neil Bradley strode into the room. He stopped, staring at Tom. "You? What are you doing here?"

Marron walked over and patted him on the shoulder. "Allow me to introduce Subject Zero."

"You're kidding? Did you hire him to use him or the other way round?"

"Now's not really the time to talk about the details, Neil. Leskov will be here soon and I see there's been a change. He's flying in?"

Bradley nodded. "ETA five minutes."

"It would have been nice to have more notice. I need to arrange security." He took a slow breath. "We need everything to be perfect. Speaking of which, is everything OK? You seem tense."

"I don't want there to be any mistakes." Bradley paused. "Celia said she was coming here, but she didn't arrive."

"I'm sure she'll turn up," Marron said. "We need to focus on Leskov for now. And I'm starting to question whether we can trust him."

Bradley's eyes narrowed. "Why do you say that?"

"Could he have been behind Chatsworth's death? And Armstrong's?"

"I'm not sure that makes sense. Do you have any proof?"

"No. He's simply a very wealthy, very suspicious man."

"Then we just need to be careful. I'm sure everything will unfold correctly."

Marron nodded. "You know what, Neil, you make a good point. And if we're going to be careful, I think you should be armed."

"What?"

"I'd rather we can all defend ourselves, if necessary." Marron pulled an automatic pistol from a holster inside his jacket. "You know how to handle a gun?"

"I've been to a shooting range a few times. Rifles mostly."

"Good." Marron placed it in his hand. "Just point the dangerous end at anyone you don't trust. This model has special lightweight ammunition so it's virtually recoilless. Now let's not keep our guest of honour waiting. There are a couple of things I need to take care of, so I'll let you escort Tom to the roof."

Marron waited until his office door had closed again then turned to his daughter. "I don't like this."

"Leskov?" Alex asked.

"I meant Bradley." He rubbed his fingers over his temples. "Something is wrong. Call up the logs."

Alex's fingers flew over her tablet. "He's mostly been busy in Bern's office. He had three conversations with Leskov. Ran some searches for Celia Bern."

"When?"

"Twenty minutes ago. They came back as negative."

"As they should, for his level of access."

"Wait, this is strange," said Alex. "He went down to Level Minus 5 about ten minutes ago. He was down there for five minutes."

"Did he, indeed? I wonder how he knew where to look. I hadn't credited Neil with the technical chops to hack the system."

Alex shook her head. "That wasn't what happened. It was the reboot. It gave him temporary Administrator Access as he was in Bern's office at the time." She paused. "Why do you think he went down to Level Minus 5? Surely Celia Bern couldn't have been down there... Or did you lock her up?" She quickly started pulling up information on her tablet, but Marron put his hand over hers.

"Don't worry about her," he said. "Celia's not going anywhere."

"Are you sure..." She trailed off, eyes widening. "Oh."

Marron scratched his head. "In the circumstances, it was necessary."

"But Bradley might be a problem now. And you've just given him a gun."

"Actually that was on the basis that he *had* become a problem."

She frowned. "I don't follow."

"When you show people you trust them, it throws them off their guard. And who knows when that might come in handy. Now, we'd better get upstairs. Our money will be arriving in a minute."

NINETY-FIVE

CROFT WAS DRIVEN ACROSS THE RAF airbase. Through the open doors of a huge hanger, he saw a long row of black helicopters, all gleaming in the spotlights. Each aircraft was swarming with support crew. Croft's jeep pulled up outside a smaller hangar.

Reems was inside, talking in hushed tones with a heavily-armed black ops team.

"What's going on?" he asked. "You have an operation under way?"

She looked up. "Above your level of clearance. What did you want?"

"A few moments of your time. They've taken the journalist, Kate Turner."

"You mean CERUS? You have actionable intelligence?"

"I tagged her. Twenty minutes ago the device, an encrypted passive tracker, sent a message."

"I don't recall authorising any tagging. And what do you mean, it 'sent a message'? That's not how passive trackers work."

"There was an enormous signal spike – no way it was a fault: the device has no power source of its own. Somebody worked out how to use its feedback function to send a message." He held out his phone, showing the message: *Prisoner at CERUS Tower. Help.*"

"*That's* your evidence? Five unverified words." Reems sucked in her top lip and regarded him carefully. "Come with me." She gave a hand signal to two of the covert team then walked towards the back of the hanger, where a number of portacabins were installed. She opened the door on the smallest one and gestured Croft to precede her. He stepped inside.

Moving faster than he would have given her credit for, she slammed the door shut.

Croft spun, grabbing at the handle, just as she locked it. "You won't get away with this," he shouted.

Reems sighed. "That's the thing, George. I didn't."

Then she walked away.

NINETY-SIX

TOM STOOD ON THE ROOF of CERUS Tower, watching night fall. Bradley had refused to engage in conversation and had simply handcuffed Tom to a pipe, before speaking with Holm. Lentz and Kate had been led away, out of sight. Marron arrived, flanked by four guards - he joined Bradley and Holm, casting wary glances over at Tom. Alex stood next to the service lift, her arms folded.

The helicopter was so quiet Tom almost missed its arrival. Like a whisper of a breeze, the sleek black craft emerged from the night and touched gently down on the helipad. The rotors stopped almost immediately and four heavily-armed soldiers jumped out.

"I don't like this," Holm said, shrinking back.

"Just let me do the talking," Marron said.

A man wearing dark glasses and an immaculate pale-grey suit emerged from the aircraft and walked towards them. The four soldiers shadowed his every step.

"Peter Marron, I presume," he said softly. "And Mr Bradley. I trust you have everything ready."

"We do, Mr Leskov," Marron replied. "To be blunt, do you

have our payment?"

Leskov gave a hand signal and two large men, each carrying a briefcase, stepped out of the helicopter. They walked up and set the cases on the ground, opened them and stepped back. Alex crouched to inspect the contents. In each Tom saw five black phone-like devices with keypads tightly packed in foam padding.

"Coded bank account keys," Leskov said, "as per my agreement with Mr Bern. One hundred million on each. They're connected to randomly-generated escrow account numbers allowing a one-time transfer to a bank of your choosing."

Alex pulled a scanner from her pocket and passed it over each of the keys then she ran her hands over them. Finally, she nodded.

Marron picked up one of the devices and switched it on. He smiled and nodded at Leskov. "You're a man of your word."

"I've built my reputation on it. Now, where is the subject?"

Bradley walked over and removed Tom's handcuffs, then pushed him forward. "This is Tom Faraday."

Marron put the remote back in the case and gestured to Alex to close them. "These are the latest test results," he said, taking the small laptop Alex was proffering and handing it over.

Leskov passed the laptop to one of the briefcase carriers then turned to stare at Tom, his eyes unblinking. "Is he in good health?"

"Why don't you ask me?" said Tom. "I'm standing right here."

"How are you feeling today, *Mr Faraday*?"

"Like killing half the people on this roof."

Leskov looked at Marron with mild amusement. "He sounds well enough." He gestured to the man on his right. "What about the data?"

The man was scrolling through a report on the laptop, nodding to himself. "We have the full diagnostics and an analysis run less than half an hour ago. It supports their claims."

"We're ready to run a demonstration for you," Holm said.

Leskov coughed and glanced at each of his men in turn, giving them a nod. "That's excellent, but it won't be necessary. Load Faraday onto the helicopter."

"Do what?" Tom spun to Marron. "What's going on?"

Marron raised an eyebrow. "That wasn't the deal, Mr Leskov."

"The *deal* was done with Mr Bern. And you are not he." Leskov nodded to his soldiers, who raised their weapons.

Immediately Marron's five guards lifted their own rifles. Alex picked up the two briefcases and moved out of the line of fire.

"What about you being a man of your word?" Marron asked through gritted teeth.

Leskov shrugged. "At the moment I'm not sure if you've kept yours. I don't trust you enough to rely on a computer file or a demonstration you could have rigged."

"So we'll have to shoot it out?" Marron shook his head. "Four guns versus five doesn't seem particularly conclusive in your favour."

Leskov smiled and nodded to the helicopter. A compartment at the front slid aside and a cylindrical canon emerged, its multiple barrels spinning with an ominous timbre. "The mini-gun will deliver six thousand .50 calibre rounds per minute, with pinpoint accuracy at a range of up to eight hundred metres. You are standing much closer."

Marron cleared his throat and turned to his men. "Lower your weapons."

"Always wise," Leskov said, "to know when you are out-gunned."

"In which case," Marron said, "might I make an alternative proposal?"

"Make it quickly."

Marron nodded to Alex. She walked over to the service elevator and placed her palm over an access panel. The doors slid open. Inside were Lentz and Kate, glowering. They were tied to a metal railing, a guard standing with a gun pointed at them.

Tom hissed. "Leave them out of this."

"Do you know who this is?" Marron asked, pointing at Lentz and looking at Leskov. "Dr Dominique Lentz, the original brain behind Tantalus."

Leskov frowned, glancing at Bradley. "The file I read said she was dead."

"Those reports," Marron replied, "were mistaken. You should take her instead. I guarantee she can get the interface working for you."

Leskov's eyes narrowed. "If that is true, why do you offer her?"

"Lentz and I aren't destined to work together again. Not with our history."

"If you don't trust her then *I* trust her even less." He turned towards his helicopter. "Get the money," he barked at his men.

Marron scratched his nose. "With the greatest respect, do you think I'm going to just let you fly off with everything?"

Leskov turned back toward Marron. "And how will you stop me?"

"You land on my building and assume I have no defensive measures?"

"Whatever measures you had were targeted at my arrival by ground. I have you off balance, Mr Marron." Leskov smiled.

"If you fly off, my people will shoot you down."

"You have no weaponry capable of locking onto my helicopter."

Marron frowned. "Willing to stake your life on that, are you?"

Leskov raised an eyebrow. "I do my research." He paused. "Still, perhaps you are right. I should not underestimate you.

Perhaps I will take back just one of my cases." He snapped his fingers. The two men who had brought the money looked at Alex, who was holding the other two cases, her expression threatening. She turned to Marron, who gave a reluctant nod, and she handed one of the cases over. It was quickly returned to the helicopter by one of the men, who then hurried back with a new case, which he laid on the roof.

"What is that?" Marron asked.

"Open it," Leskov said.

Marron reached forward and flipped open the catches. Inside was a flat black device with a multitude of wires.

Leskov's smile broadened. "You won't shoot me down because if you do, that will trigger this bomb."

NINETY-SEVEN

TOM LOOKED AT THE DULL black device: its only external features were a keypad and LED display.

Marron's face was like iron. "You could just tie us up."

"I could," Leskov replied, "but maybe you do have automated systems that I didn't learn of, or other team members watching remotely. If you attempt any action against my helicopter, or against the bomb, or if anyone leaves the roof, I will detonate. The Tower will be fine." He hesitated. "Well, perhaps not the top two floors or anyone on them. It's set for twenty minutes. Once we get safely away, I'll send the code to switch it off. Now, Mr Bradley, I suggest you get onboard."

"Ah," said Marron. "I wondered how our buyer was so well-informed."

Bradley shrugged. "I was never working for you. I *was* working for Celia."

"She was going to stop the project. She thought her husband's death had changed everything."

"You didn't have to kill her. You could have persuaded her--"

Marron laughed. "You say that like you'd never met her."

Bradley's cheek twitched and he pulled out the handgun

Marron had given him. "You think you can just deceive and manipulate everyone. That you can do whatever you like to whoever you like." He raised the weapon and aimed it at Marron's face. "Perhaps I should show you that isn't the case."

Marron stared back, unblinking. "I don't think that's Mr Leskov's style."

"No," Leskov said. "I would prefer that you didn't. Pursue revenge on your own time. Now, the clock is ticking, quite literally." He gestured to two of his guards. They grabbed Tom and pulled him across the roof. Tom struggled, but they were far stronger than him and pushed him into the helicopter. One of the armed men inside gestured with his weapon and, teeth gritted, Tom reluctantly buckled himself into the seat by the door, watching the stand-off between Marron and Bradley.

For several moments, they stood frozen. Then Bradley lowered the gun.

"Can I come too?" asked Holm in a frail voice. "I'd like to see this project through and I'm getting the feeling that science is finished here."

Leskov raised an eyebrow. "Bradley speaks highly of you, Dr Holm."

"Ed," Marron said, "think very carefully about what you're doing. Your life could depend on making the right decision."

Holm shrugged. "I'm following the money. And I don't think I can work with a murderer."

Marron smiled. "Then you may be out of options."

Leskov cleared his throat. "Let's move."

He, Holm and Bradley hurried over to the helicopter and climbed in, along with the rest of the guards.

"Have a pleasant flight, Neil," Marron shouted.

Tom watched one of the guards slide the door closed then the huge rotors began to spin. In seconds, the craft had lifted off.

NINETY-EIGHT

MARRON LOOKED UP AS THE helicopter receded into the distance, then turned to Alex. "Apart from them taking Faraday, I think that went pretty well."

"I'm sorry, did I miss something?" called Kate. "Leskov just robbed you and left us here next to a bomb that he could detonate at any moment."

Marron didn't reply. Instead, he walked over to the bag Alex had left next to the lift and opened it, taking out a small briefcase. He put it next to the other briefcase that Alex had already placed on the ground and flipped them both open.

Inside each case were five coded bank account keys.

"Alex switched the briefcase," Lentz said. "You have all the keys."

Marron nodded. "Did you think I'd really let them fly off with half a billion pounds of my money? Leskov brought us a little gift. I just returned the favour." He held out his hand and Alex placed a tablet computer in it. "Nobody outplays me. And certainly not Neil Bradley."

◇ ◇ ◇

The helicopter quickly gained height, its rotors whispering in the cold night air. Bradley stared out the window, watching the rooftop recede into the darkness. Everything had gone perfectly: they had everything, on their own terms. Yet Marron had not looked dejected.

"Why were you carrying a gun, Neil?" Leskov asked.

"Marron gave it to me, in case of emergency. Sorry, I let him get to me there." He held the weapon out. "I should probably let someone who knows how to use it look after it."

One of the soldiers took it from him and hefted it. "It's not loaded," he said in a thick accent.

"No, it has special lightweight ammo."

The soldier pulled out the clip. It was empty.

"But... I don't understand."

"Why would Marron give you an empty gun?" Holm asked.

"Because he *didn't* trust you," Tom said.

Suddenly, the pilot's voice sounded in their earphones. "I'm detecting two helicopters, three kilometres out. We're going quiet-mode: no raised voices please." The noise of the blades diminished and their frequency lowered. The helicopter abruptly changed course, moving lower and more slowly.

"Amazing craft," Leskov whispered. "Worth every penny of the two hundred million it cost. Now I must thank you, Neil, for coming through for me. You're going to fit well into my organisation. I'll get you working with my son, show him how big business works--"

"The helicopters are still incoming," hissed the pilot. "I'm in stealth but they're tracking us."

"How?" Leskov asked.

There was no answer, but the helicopter descended further.

"They're still following," said the pilot.

"Our weapons are arming," said the co-pilot, alarm in his voice as he flipped switches on the control panel.

Leskov leaned forward. "I said do *something*. I didn't mean fire at them."

The pilot looked at the co-pilot. "Someone else is in control. We're locking on one of the choppers."

"What's that whirring and beeping?" asked Bradley.

"Our missile moving into firing position," replied the co-pilot, stabbing agitatedly at the console.

Suddenly the missile launched. They watched in horror as the air-to-air missile streaked away. In eerie silence it struck its target, fire blossoming in the night sky.

A familiar voice suddenly filled the cockpit. "Most impressive." Marron's loud tones reverberated around the small space. "Although I'm surprised you took the shot. It's almost like you're not in control. "

"You!" hissed Leskov. "How are you doing this?"

"You did hand over the full schematics to your craft, which rather exposed its vulnerabilities."

Leskov shouted at the pilot. "Trigger the bomb. Do it at once!"

A different voice broke over the radio. "THIS IS ROYAL AIR FORCE HELICOPTER TANGO WHISKY SEVEN NINER, HAILING UNDESIGNATED ENEMY CRAFT. LAND IMMEDIATELY OR YOU WILL BE SHOT DOWN."

"The bomb isn't responding to our signal," shouted the co-pilot. "Another of our missiles is arming!"

"DISARM YOUR WEAPONS. REPEAT: DISARM YOUR WEAPONS. YOU HAVE TEN SECONDS TO COMPLY OR YOU WILL BE FIRED UPON."

Holm suddenly bent down and yanked one of the briefcases towards him. He ripped it open. There were no bank keys, but instead an electronic device, awash with blinking LEDs. "Oh crap," he said. "That's my control box."

"*Your* control box?" Leskov shouted.

"I built it as a demo for the Tantalus interface, to connect to the helicopter systems. Marron must have reconfigured it."

"Can you shut it off?" asked Tom, struggling with his seatbelt.

"It's broadcasting our whereabouts on every conceivable frequency." Holm pulled open a side panel. "If I can just remove the--"

Under their feet they felt the whirr of another missile moving into place.

"Shut it off!" shrieked Leskov. "Shut it off or throw it out!"

The RAF helicopter fired.

Marron's voice rose in volume. "It was always the plan that you come by helicopter. And, Neil, just to be clear, I selected you specifically for this role. I always knew about Celia. I always knew about you and Leskov."

But the occupants of the helicopter weren't listening. Leskov's pilot threw the helicopter into a dive, a sudden blast of cold air and noise filling the interior. But he was not quick enough.

Bradley's last thought, as he looked around the helicopter, was: *where is Faraday?*

Marron and Alex stood on the top of CERUS Tower. Up in the sky, they saw the RAF missile strike Leskov's helicopter. The explosion was instantaneous. A blossoming flower of fire and destruction filled the air. Debris began to rain down.

"A pity Leskov changed the plan, but if we couldn't have Tom, then it's better that nobody does." Marron glanced at Kate and Lentz, who had watched in stunned silence, then walked away, Alex joining him. They stopped at the stair access point and

Marron spoke to guards. "Clear the building. Get all our people out of here."

The man nodded. "What about the two prisoners?"

"They're fine where they are."

Tom glared at the device as Holm frantically tried to deactivate it, idly wondering if he could control it. But he had no collar. And no time.

In the confusion, nobody was watching him. There was only one thing he could do that might make any difference. He could try to do what he had been designed to do: control the helicopter. He closed his eyes and felt for the system. It was there. And it felt familiar.

But without his collar, the connection was weak, tenuous. There were protocols that did not flow and others that reset as his connection continued to drop in and out. He couldn't break through the firewalls, and the weapon systems were the most heavily protected of all.

He didn't have enough time.

He felt the targeting system lock onto the RAF helicopter. He could see it and *feel* it, but he could do nothing about it. There was only one system he could interface with. It was basic, designed for the saving of human life rather than protecting secrets – though if he activated it incorrectly, it would probably kill him.

He heard the pilot shout that they'd been fired on.

With a wrench in his mind, he sent the signal and the door blew out. At the same time, a sharp force thrust him sideways and away. Still strapped to the ejector seat, he tumbled over and over as the cold night air enveloped him. Above, he caught sight of the helicopter as it was hit by the missile.

NINETY-NINE

TOM FELL THROUGH THE AIR, tumbling sideways and downwards, the heat from the explosion burning above him. He *knew* that the ejector seat should automatically fire the parachute: that was how the system worked. Yet it hadn't happened.

As he tumbled, he realised he was not very high above ground. At free-fall speed, he would plummet a mile in thirty seconds. But he was lower than that.

Time seemed to slow. In a bizarre moment of clarity, he found himself puzzling over why the chute wasn't deploying. The ejector seat was a fully automated system. Was the problem that he had overridden it? Had he confused the program? He scrabbled behind him for anything that might be a physical trigger. Then he felt it, but not with his hand.

There *was* a trigger system. It was electronic and designed to be jacked into a computerised altimeter. But, Tom realised, he didn't need one of those. Time sped up again and he looked down and saw the ground rushing up to meet him. He reached out in his mind, through the noise and the cold.

He would find a way. He would not die here, in this manner.

He found he was able to concentrate: to find calm in the storm of noise and pressure. His mind touched the trigger.

Flapping and shrieking like a flock of angry swans, the parachute opened.

Lentz watched the countdown continue. Neither Marron nor Alex had returned and a stillness had fallen over the roof. "If you have any sharp objects to hand," she said, "now would be the time to bring them into play." She tugged at the plastic ties holding her wrists to the metal railing. "It would be so nice not to spend our last fifteen minutes completely helpless."

Kate didn't even move, just stared ahead. "Marron planned all this? To get rid of Bern and take over? How can you work for someone for twenty-five years and then betray them?"

"Perhaps something changed?"

"Or perhaps nothing changed. Maybe Marron's been playing this game all along."

"I don't buy it." Lentz pursed her lips. "Marron never struck me as someone who was driven by money. I think he really wanted to see Tom's interface work."

"Even so, did he not consider that it was a two-way street? An interface is two things coming together and affecting each other. But Marron just seems interested in Tom controlling the computer. Did he – did you – ever stop to think how it might affect him?"

Lentz sighed. "I never chose him for this."

"But it was always going to be someone. Going down this path made it inevitable."

Lentz shrugged. "Speaking of inevitability..."

They stared at the counter. It was approaching fourteen minutes.

ONE HUNDRED

MARRON MARCHED INTO HIS LEVEL 88 command centre, closing the door after Alex had followed him in.

"You're actually going to leave them up there?" she said. "With the bomb? I didn't think you really would."

"Going soft on me?"

Alex scowled. "Lentz might have some uses, especially now our scientists are dropping like flies."

"We can replace them."

"Not with people like Lentz."

"In most ways that's a good thing." Marron scratched his nose. "She would never have been *our* scientist. Now we need to get out of here."

Alex picked at a fingernail. "I promised the journalist I would kill her."

"Oh she's going to die. But so will we if we don't get further away." Marron walked over to a section of wall and typed a long string of numbers into a control panel. The panel hissed and swung out, revealing a large wire-frame cradle-cage. "Your chariot."

Alex walked forward and looked down. "Have you actually

tested it?"

"No time like the present."

Marron and Alex's cage dropped in near free-fall down the fitted tracks, far faster than the turbo lifts and considerably less comfortably. As it dropped below ground level it slowed, curving sideways until it was travelling horizontally along a tunnel no longer shown on any plans.

Finally, the cage glided to a halt in a small dimly-lit room. The floor dropped away just beyond the tracks, water glinting darkly a few feet below. Marron and Alex released their harnesses and started putting on wetsuits and scuba-gear from a box by the end of the tracks. They placed their electronics in watertight containers and sealed them shut.

Marron turned to the two small submersibles docked just below where they were standing. "Ready to get out of here?" He reached into his bag and withdrew a control board. They climbed into the narrow confines of the submersible on the left and Marron plugged the control board into the dash. With a surge, the motor started and Marron directed the craft into a long metal tunnel leading out into the Thames. From there they turned east and, staying close to the river-bottom, they chugged towards the ocean. As getaway vehicles went it was pretty slow, but it did the job.

"You left the other sub?" asked Alex.

"It will be destroyed when the Tower comes down," replied Marron.

"Can we tell when the bomb goes off?" asked Alex.

"We'll miss the fireworks down here. On the off-chance that the military are minded to start sweeping the area, I've gone dark with almost every instrument."

"Shame."

"Be patient. We can watch a recording at our destination."

"You checked the Thames Barrier is open?"

Marron smiled. "Do you honestly think I didn't plan for that?"

They leaned back in their seats as the craft methodically made its way out to sea. They stopped just once to make one essential call on the radio: a tight, point-to-point, beam transmission with a maximum potential audience of one.

Twenty kilometres out in the English Channel, a luxury yacht received a call for assistance.

ONE HUNDRED ONE

"I HAVE AN IDEA," KATE said suddenly. "We need to get a signal to the other helicopter: the one that shot down Leskov."

"I'm sure they'll turn up here – though maybe not quickly enough."

"Someone must be monitoring this roof." Kate stretched forwards and kicked the side panelling of the lift. It boomed loudly. "Let's just make some noise. Know Morse code? All I know is SOS."

"Anything wrong with SOS?"

"I was thinking something more specific, from your MI5 days."

Lentz smiled. "Good point." She started kicking.

The helicopter landed three minutes later. Six armed figures clad in black emerged, weapons drawn. The first shone a torch at Lentz and Kate.

"Who the hell are you?" he demanded. "Identify."

"Former Security Service agent Dominique Lentz," shouted

Lentz. "Identify yourself."

"Special Air Service Commander Jonas."

"Well Commander Jonas, there's an explosive device on a timer just over there."

Jonas turned and stared at the display. It read eleven minutes remaining. "Do you have the code?"

"The only person who did was in the helicopter that you just shot down."

"Untie them." Jonas tapped his earpiece and turned away, speaking in clipped tones. One of the other men cut through the ties on Lentz and Kate and they stood, stretching stiffly. Jonas cleared his throat. "We're to evacuate."

"We're not going to try to defuse it?" Kate asked.

"No time for our specialist to get here. Now get on board."

The pilot called out. "The building is asking for a code?"

"What do you mean the *building*?"

"An automated system has tapped into my comms. It says I have ten seconds to respond."

"Or what?" Jonas turned to Lentz. "What is going on?"

"This is a highly-computerised facility," Lentz replied. "It may have systems that supervise the use of the helipad."

"Time's up," the pilot called.

A series of rods emerged from the rooftop and rose smoothly in a circle around the helicopter, rising inside the rotors' turning radius. The pilot leaped out and began pushing at one of the rods. "Reinforced steel. I can't take off with this here."

"Then we'll cut through it."

"Not enough time."

"How big is the bomb?" asked Jonas. "Any idea of its yield?"

Lentz frowned. "Leskov said it would take out a couple of floors, but the building's structure will hold."

"Actually I think the explosion will be bigger than that," Kate said. She pointed at one of the grey drums.

Lentz walked over and stared at it. She frowned and sniffed deeply. "It's TNT. How did you know?"

"I studied chemistry. But why would someone store TNT on the roof of an office building?"

"Because they knew there'd be a bomb here and wanted to massively increase the yield of the explosion. It'll still only take out the top third of the building," Lentz said. "But the collapse will take the remaining two thirds with it."

"Can we move the drums?"

"I should think they weigh at least 250kg each and there are perhaps fifty of them. We don't have enough time."

"Do we have any chance of disarming it?"

"The code had more than 15 digits, so we can forget trying to guess it. And I expect the device will have a number of anti-tamper measures."

"Can we move it?"

"Movement sensors would be among the most likely anti-tamper measures."

Jonas looked around. "Where is Marron now? Perhaps we can make him talk."

"He left the roof several minutes ago. He may no longer be in the building."

Jonas stared at the display. It now read *9:28*. There was a sudden squawk from his radio. He tapped his earpiece and spoke quickly, then he turned to the group, his eyes bright. "We have ground forces in the vicinity. They just intercepted a man landing a parachute in the building forecourt - his name is Tom Faraday and he says he needs to get back to this rooftop to input a certain code."

Five minutes later a small helicopter hovered awkwardly at the edge of the roof, while Tom slid down a rope. His eyes locked on the digital countdown and he swallowed.

4:22...

"Why didn't they take anyone away?" asked Lentz, glaring at Jonas as she gestured towards the new helicopter.

The Commander put his hands on his hips. "It's a support chopper, so there's no hoist or winch on board. Getting people up would be hazardous. Anyway, it can only take two passengers and there are eight of us." He nodded at Tom. "Nine now."

"Better two of us live than none."

"I'm hoping *everyone* gets to live," Tom said, as he dropped to his knees next to the bomb. Kate ran to his side and he felt her hands on his arm and shoulder.

"I can't believe you're still alive," she said.

"I'm not quite sure I believe it either." He felt an odd tingling as one of her fingertips brushed his neck. "Are you OK? What did Marron do to you?" He glared at the bomb.

"What are you waiting for?" Lentz hissed. "Put in the code."

"I don't know it."

"What?" Jonas demanded.

"Ssh. I need to listen." He brushed his fingers slowly over each key in turn. Each emitted a beep with a slightly different tone. "I *heard* Leskov punching in the code," Tom explained.

"And you're going to remember all fifteen digits like that? You'll blow us all to kingdom come unless you've got some sort of eidetic memory," Jonas said.

"It's 20 digits, actually," Tom corrected him. He opened his eyes and started pressing buttons before Jonas could reply. He finished the sequence and waited.

Nothing happened.

Tom turned to Lentz, eyes wide. "I got it right. I know I did."

She knelt down and examined the keypad. "There's what looks like an 'enter' button." She pressed it. There was no sound. "That's why you didn't recall it."

The counter paused on three minutes then the numbers vanished.

A line of text scrolled across the screen.

ARMING CODE RE-ENTERED. TWO MINUTES REMOVED FROM COUNTDOWN.

The text blinked then vanished and the counter reappeared, set at one minute. It flashed then continued counting down.

"Oh crap," Kate said, gritting her teeth. "Maybe don't do that again."

Tom hit his head with his open palms. "How could I be so stupid? To assume that the same code would disarm it." He looked up at the night sky. To fail now simply was not acceptable.

"Tom. You're not wearing the collar," Lentz said.

"Marron took it away from me."

"But how did you remember the code?"

"I never needed the collar to remember stuff. It was when I wanted to connect that..." He trailed off, remembering the ejector seat, the parachute and the electronic release. He had somehow activated them. He moved his head next to the box, staring at the numbers, trying to reach out. It wasn't like when he had the collar and was plugged into the network; then, the building system was effectively a supercomputer, whereas now he was trying to interface with something that had the processing power of a pocket calculator. But he could still do it. He had to do it. He wasn't going to let them all down.

His mind reached out. He felt the circuits in the device. He could almost see the code flowing through them. This thing had rules. This thing had laws. He could understand how it operated:

how he might bend its rules to his advantage. He looked at the steady countdown. And he began talking to the bomb.

Stop. Now.

The device bleeped. The numbers stuck on *0:05* then vanished. A message scrolled across the screen.

DEVICE DISARMED.

There were cheers and shrieks of delight from all around him, but Tom was only vaguely aware of it all as exhaustion took him.

ONE HUNDRED TWO

TOM WOKE FEELING DIFFERENT. HE was lying on a hospital bed, but in a room that looked like a science lab. Lentz was looking down at him, concern on her face.

"I'm hungry," he said.

Lentz snorted. "Not the first words I expected you to say, but I guess it means you're doing OK." She pulled a chocolate bar from her pocket.

He took it from her, tearing off the wrapper. "How long have I been out?"

"Just an hour. We're still at the Tower." She glanced over her shoulder at two SAS guards standing either side of the door. "The big problem is that the SAS saw you defuse the bomb. They know that you either used the interface to stop it or you already knew the code. Both possibilities have set them thinking."

"They know about the interface?"

"So it seems."

Tom frowned. "Where's Kate?"

"She's being accommodated on the floor below. She's... been through a lot."

"I want to see her."

"I know, but there are government people here rather keen to talk to you."

"To thank me for saving everyone?"

"Not exactly." She leaned closer, dropping her voice to a whisper. "I don't think they know whether they should arrest you or give you a medal."

"Arrest me?" He sat up in bed. "Why?"

"As I said, your diffusing the bomb has got them thinking. Which is a problem." She looked down at her phone. "I ran a quick scan. The nanites have spread throughout your body. They're not just in your blood: they're everywhere. Heck, if you spat they'd be in your saliva."

Tom swung his legs off the bed. "What difference does that make?"

"Once they begin studying you and see what's in your head, what's in your body – not to mention what you can do – they're never going to stop. They might decide to disappear you to some laboratory."

There was a cough from the doorway. Jonas stood there. "If Tom is awake, the Director would like a word."

"She's actually here? In person?" Lentz looked at Tom. "Are you up to this?"

Tom nodded. "Let's get it over with."

ONE HUNDRED THREE

TOM AND LENTZ WALKED INTO CERUS's Level 90 boardroom. A severe-looking woman in an immaculate grey suit sat flanked by bodyguards. Two other agents stood in the corners of the room.

Lentz folded her arms. "Stephanie. It's been a while."

The woman did not smile. "You're looking well, Dominique. Particularly since you're dead."

"You know each other?" Tom asked.

"We worked together in another life," Lentz said. "This is Stephanie Reems. When I last knew her, she was one of the youngest ops managers in MI5 history. Now, she's the Director."

"We can catch up on our careers later. How did Tom deactivate the bomb?"

Tom smiled. "I got lucky."

"That's lucky enough to win three consecutive lottery jackpots, even before we consider that the black ops team said the device did not respond to the code you entered."

"How about focusing on the actual bad guy," Tom said. "Peter Marron."

Reems' left eye flickered. "We'll have him and his daughter

soon. This building is a finite area."

"Actually," Tom said, "it's a finite volume, but Marron believed the Tower was going to blow up. He'll be long gone."

Reems placed her hands on the table. "We have the entire building cordoned off and locked down. Stop worrying about Marron and focus on your own situation." She leaned forwards. "Dominique, you know how this works. You help us, we help you. Both of you. We want your unqualified cooperation. We need to understand Tantalus."

"And what if," Tom said, "we don't cooperate?"

"Don't underestimate the importance of this project to the British Government."

Tom leaned forward. "I'm confused. Don't you normally shut down CERUS projects?"

"There's a lot I can do in the name of national security. I have leeway to circumvent usual legal process." Her gaze became more intense. "Most of those involved in the development of this technology have died in the last few days. Those who remain are expected to be forthcoming."

Lentz frowned. "You don't have the data, do you? What did Marron do? Hide everything?"

"You," Reems said, "clearly know where it is."

"If I did, why would I want to give it to you?" She paused. "*If* I did."

Tom looked at Lentz and said pointedly, "There's no reason not to cooperate: we're on the same side here. We have to trust them, just like I trusted you the very first time I met you."

Lentz's eyes flickered. "All I'm concerned about is your well-being. It's up to you Tom. You have to do what you think is best."

Tom turned to Reems. "I know where CERUS keeps the project data. I can show it to you."

ONE HUNDRED FOUR

BERN'S YACHT WAS HOLDING POSITION in the English Channel. Now known as the Phoenix, it looked very different from when it had been docked in Monaco. Along with a different name, it had completely changed its external livery and internal colour scheme. Instead of an ostentatious rich-man's play thing, it was now a floating command centre.

Marron and Alex's underwater cruiser docked quietly at the rear of the craft and they climbed out, greeted by the yacht's crew. They changed out of their wetsuits and into casual clothes. On the top deck, Marron opened a bottle of champagne and poured two glasses, handing one to Alex. "To evolution," he said.

"To winning," she replied.

"Did you record the explosion?" he asked one of the crewmen.

"Explosion, Sir?"

"On the television. The CERUS Tower explosion."

The crewman looked at him blankly. "I'm sorry, Sir, I don't understand."

Marron's eyes narrowed and he put down his glass. "Get me a computer." He tuned through every major news channel. There was nothing. "It should have happened thirty minutes ago. The whole *world* should know by now. Somehow they stopped the bomb."

"Could it have been a fault?" asked Alex.

Marron shook his head. "With Leskov? Unlikely in the extreme."

"Then someone entered the disarm code."

Marron swore. "Dammit, I have to see." He typed in a long sequence of numbers and a grainy image appeared on the screen. CERUS Tower was lit up against the night sky.

"Where's that coming from?" asked Alex.

"Live feed from one of my CCTV cameras on the building opposite." Marron closed his eyes, rubbing his fingers over his forehead. "I'm sure they're busy at the Tower, looking for answers, but I'd rather not take chances. He'd better get here soon."

"He's not going to be happy."

"He rarely is."

ONE HUNDRED FIVE

TOM FORCED HIMSELF TO BREATHE slowly. Lentz had collected some equipment from the Level 75 laboratory and they now stood in Marron's office, next to the entrance to his secret control room.

Reems stood aside, arms folded, as Commander Jonas attempted to open the door. "It's locked," he said, as he pulled on the concealed handle.

Lentz held up a scanning device. "It's just a question of determining the right wireless frequency."

"CCTV footage shows him entering but not leaving," Jonas said. "Our best guess is that Marron is still inside."

"I very much doubt it," Tom said, walking up and pulling on the handle, blinking as he did it. "As I keep telling you, Marron thought the building was going to blow up. He wasn't going to hang around."

"Try it again," Lentz said.

Tom twisted and pulled. The door hissed and swung out.

The room looked as if someone had left it in a hurry. Items of equipment were strewn across the floor. Tom walked over to one of the computer terminals. "This is Marron's command centre. It's a completely separate system to the main building."

"So this is where he watched the Tower, playing God?" Reems asked.

"He was playing a lot of people," Tom said. "And he liked to play a long game. He's been playing *me* since I was a child."

Reems raised an eyebrow. "I'm very much looking forward to debriefing you, Mr Faraday."

Lentz moved next to him. "I'll get connected," she said, giving Tom a tight look.

"Use the port here," he replied.

Lentz flipped open her modified laptop. "Are you sure you know what you're doing, Tom?" She ran a long cable into the port he had indicated and started typing rapidly.

"There's no alternative. You, of all people, realise that."

"We're on the clock here, people," Reems said.

"When you're ready, Dominique." Tom closed his eyes. The computer screen went off.

Lentz cleared her throat. "Here we go. Although this may be a bit hit or miss."

The screen flickered back on and the login box appeared.

"Anyone have any ideas?" asked Tom, opening his eyes.

Jonas shook his head. "We'll have to bring in specialists. It could take some time, but--"

"Never mind," said Lentz. "I'm in." The password screen faded and the display filled with a number of data windows.

"What's she doing?" Reems asked.

Jonas looked at the screen. "Parsing the data." He squinted. "It's moving too fast to read."

The screens scrolled faster and faster.

"Now that's interesting," Tom said. A floor plan popped up and then zoomed in on Floor 90. A pink light lit up in one corner.

"It's in Bern's office," Reems said. "What is it?"

Lentz shrugged. "I didn't say I'd get answers *immediately*."

"Look at the north wall of this room," Tom said, crossing to it and pressing against a panel. There was a soft alarm, a hiss and a panel swung inwards.

"What on earth?" Reems asked, walking over to look for herself.

"I'd be careful," Tom said. "It's a long way down."

Reems peered into the cavity then reflexively pulled back.

"I think," Lentz said, "that is an emergency escape route."

Reems reached her hand out and touched the metal track. "It's vibrating?"

"Wait," Jonas said suddenly, "Lentz isn't just streaming this. She's deleting it!" He lurched forward and snapped Lentz's laptop shut, yanking the network cable from it.

"What are you are doing?" cried Lentz.

Reems turned to Jonas. "Just get her out of here."

But Jonas wasn't listening. "That didn't stop it," he said. "Look. I can see dialogue boxes appearing and vanishing."

Files continued flickering across the screen.

"What's being deleted?" Reems shouted.

"It looks like building data. Corporate accounts. Project files."

Reems turned red. "Stop it right--"

A fire alarm sounded: not the type of alarm fitted in houses and offices. This one was a mind-numbing beast of an alarm, designed to terrify occupants into leaving as soon as humanly possible.

Jonas looked up sharply. "Fire suppression systems have been triggered. Halon gas: we get out or we die. Everybody move!"

◇ ◇ ◇

In seconds, they had scrambled back into Marron's office, the heavy door slamming behind them. From inside came the terrible white-noise hiss of the gas.

"What set it off?" asked Reems as they stumbled to a halt.

"Something she tampered with maybe?" suggested Jonas. He looked around. "Where is Faraday?"

Reems spun around. She went to run back in, but Jonas' strong arms caught her. "You have to wait ten minutes for it to disperse. It's too late for him."

Reems shrugged him off and turned on Lentz. "I don't know what just happened, but I'm pretty sure that was all planned." She narrowed her eyes. "You were never the one deleting the files, were you? That was Tom, using the interface."

Lentz shrugged. "It's a theory. Good luck proving it."

"What is he up to?" Reems swore. "We have a chance to seize breakthrough technology and you..." She nodded to Jonas. "Get her out of my sight." Reems' phone chimed and she glanced at it then at Lentz. "I have a message from Tom. He says we should look in the safe in Bern's office." She paused, her brow creasing. "He says you're the only one who can open it and," her expression turned thunderous, "I'd better keep you closely involved if I want to see inside."

"Is that right?" said Lentz, not hiding a smile. "Then I suggest we go have a look."

ONE HUNDRED SIX

TOM WATCHED THE OTHERS RUN from the command centre. He waited until they were all outside then activated the pressurised air-con system. It sounded convincing enough to pass as the halon gas.

He closed the outer doors to the room then shut his eyes and extended his senses. The building was operating smoothly: power, lighting, air conditioning. He reduced the security systems to the lowest possible level. No sense in obstructing the good work of the rescuers.

He flicked his attention back to the vast volumes of data he had been deleting, stripping the CERUS servers of the data that would allow someone else to do all this again. The experiment had to stop here. In amongst the scientific data, he found several files implicating various team members in things that had happened – and things that had not. Marron clearly liked to keep a hold over people. But there was nothing on William Bern. There was even a file with Tom's mother's name on it, but it was empty. What was that about?

Tom's eyelids fluttered as he continued processing. The chip in his head was gone now, the nanites spread throughout his system, distributing their heat so he barely noticed. There was nothing to distract him. Nothing to slow him down. And, as his perception shifted, he started to see things he could never have seen before.

There was an *anomaly*.

He forced himself to slow, drawing back to consider. It was a ripple in the pattern of CERUS' financial records. There was something there. He focused his thoughts, throwing his mind at the numbers, sifting and filtering. The pattern clarified.

Money had been diverted from certain accounts. At first glance, it looked like it had been done randomly. But, when he followed the chain, he saw it was, in fact, a thing of beauty. CERUS had not been failing: someone had been gutting it. There was a plan behind all the other plans: something only a computer could have seen, if properly instructed.

Or me, thought Tom. Because he was both human and computer now.

But was he the best of both, or the worst?

The vibrating of the track in the cavity reached a peak and the metal cradle appeared in the gap. But he couldn't go yet. First, he had to understand what had been happening at CERUS and he finally had the key. There was video-footage from cameras even Marron did not seem to know about. Marron had appeared to hold all the cards, but there was someone behind even his shoulder and now Tom knew who it was.

He sucked in his breath and rescanned the files. And then he found it, buried in two different places, but linked by context.

Of course it was ridiculous, impossible, unbelievable. And yet he knew it was true: only Tom Faraday could have been chosen for this role, because only he was a fit.

So many questions filled his mind that he was almost overwhelmed. So much betrayal and injustice that he could not voice.

Not here. Not now.

But finally he knew who he had to talk to. And where to find his quarry. Tom glanced around the room, his eyes locking on a cabinet on the wall marked with biohazard symbols. It was electronically locked, but a quick instruction popped the door open. Inside was a case containing three syringes. He looked at the barcode labels and the interface provided a translation.

Truth nano.

Tom gritted his teeth. This was what they had used on Kate. Filled with rage, he went to throw the syringes across the room, but something made him stop. Perhaps he could find a better use for them. So he slipped the syringes into his jacket pocket. Then, with a shake of his head, he climbed into the cradle, strapped himself in and sent the instruction to start the mechanism again.

The cage dropped out of sight.

The fact that the submersible cruiser had no control panel presented no challenge to Tom. After quickly donning a wetsuit from the open box beside the end of the cage-track, he slid the submersible out of the tunnel and into the murky waters of the Thames. As he completed his final system scan of the Tower, idly realising he was very hungry, he noticed that the building's security network had been accessed off-site. Someone had used a camera on an adjacent building to look at the exterior of the Tower.

Tom smiled. He didn't need to run further analysis to know who *that* was. Within seconds, he had location data accurate to within fifty metres. He referenced the location on a map and smiled. In the middle of the sea, fifty metres would be more than good enough.

Just two minutes into his journey, he realised that the submersible was too slow. Quickly, he searched the surrounding area for something faster. It didn't take him long to find exactly what he needed.

ONE HUNDRED SEVEN

LENTZ AND REEMS ENTERED BERN'S penthouse office, leaving two soldiers waiting next to the lifts. The women ignored the view and marched through the door into his private bathroom. On one wall hung an unmemorable watercolour.

"It's always behind a painting," Lentz said, as she carefully lifted the watercolour off its hook and revealed a small wall safe. Quickly she started typing in a long sequence of digits

Reems glared at her. "You have the combination of William Bern's safe?"

"Tom gave me the code." There was a beep.

"And the finger print scan?" Reems asked, as Lentz pressed her thumb to the scanner.

"I'm told I've been added to the approved list."

"Or you were always on it. You do realise how suspicious this looks?"

The safe clicked and swung open. Lentz reached in and withdrew a few items of jewellery, a copy of a document entitled 'Last Will and Testament', the keys to a car and a stack of documents labelled 'CERUS: Highly Confidential'. At the bottom was a dusty pink folder tied with red ribbon. It was stamped

'CLASSIFIED'.

Reems reached forward and snatched it from her. "I believe your security clearance was revoked a long time ago. If any of it is shareable, I'll let you know." Reems turned and walked back into the main office. "I have what I need. Now get her out of--"

George Croft stood facing her, holding an automatic pistol. "Hands skyward," he said. "Both of you."

Reems' jaw tightened as she lifted her arms. "Where's my security detail?"

"I told them Marron had been sighted on Level 60. They'll be a few minutes, I imagine."

"How did you even get here? I thought I had you locked up?"

"I had a field toolkit with me. Broke my way out." He shrugged. "Sloppy of you not to have searched me."

"How did you know to come here, to this office?"

There was a loud cough and Kate walked in. "He just showed his Service ID and said you'd asked him to fetch me. I guess you were so busy keeping his incarceration secret you forgot to deactivate his credentials. This story keeps on getting better. I don't think I'm ever going to have to work again."

"That can be arranged very easily," Reems said.

"I'm going to include a section on wasting tax payer resources." Kate turned to Lentz. "Do you know how she got here? By helicopter. She brought five of them."

Reems sighed. "It's a security measure to travel with decoy targets – given we just lost a helicopter to hostile fire, I would think that was obvious. So just what do you think you're doing, George?"

"You've been acting erratically since I became interested in CERUS, but it was only when you locked me up that I realised you'd been compromised."

Reems walked over to Bern's desk, sitting on the edge.

"Hindering you doesn't mean I've been compromised, George. There are some people you need to speak to."

"I'm not keeping this internal. I'm taking you to Scotland Yard."

Reems shook her head. "You can't do that." She sighed and held up the pink folder. "Why don't we have a look through what I'm sure is in here and then we'll discuss it again?"

Croft waved his gun towards Reems. "You're just stalling."

"I don't think she is," Lentz said. "Only one thing makes sense. The file contains the records of the original Tantalus. Information that now exists nowhere else. I bet Bern wanted to keep them to hand in case they ever became useful. And I bet that's because they include signed authorisation from the person who originally approved the human testing. It's his trump card: leverage."

Reems nodded at Lentz. "You always had a sharp mind." She picked up the file and held it out. "But it's more complicated than that."

Lentz marched over and snatched the file, flicking it open. Her eyes narrowed as she turned the pages then she stopped. "You? I don't believe it."

"What?" Kate said. "Reems approved the testing?"

"Presuming," Lentz said, "that this signature is genuine. You were the MI5 liaison at the time. But, Stephanie, how can this be?"

"Do you want to read the rest of the file, or shall I just tell you what it says?" She looked around the room and pointed at Bern's whisky decanter. "And I don't know about you, but I could use a drink."

◇ ◇ ◇

Reems sipped from the whisky tumbler, running her free hand

through her hair. "Tantalus was always a government project. A specific commission."

Lentz shook her head. "I would have known. I was in charge."

"I know you like to think that, but you were just a component in the machine."

"But why would the government need CERUS?" Kate asked.

"We needed each other. CERUS needed the government to blow away the red tape and provide funding: the government needed CERUS to provide resources, specific expertise and, most importantly, plausible deniability."

"Because the public wouldn't like you messing with people's heads, regardless of the potential benefits," Kate said. "So you closed them down when the human trials went so catastrophically wrong."

"Yes," Reems sighed, "but it wasn't Bern who forced the trials to take place early. It was us. Despite all our precautions, word had got out. We couldn't keep the project under wraps any more. It was either run a test or flush it. It was a mistake. Too many shortcuts. The test subjects died." She closed her eyes. "If it had just been that, we might have been able to come clean: admit our mistakes and deal with the fall out. But you know it went further."

"Child testing," Lentz said, turning away.

"Why would Bern keep the records?" Kate asked. "Wouldn't they implicate him?"

"Much less than they implicate us," said Reems. "I tried to clean house, but he kept data hidden, ready to use against us. We managed to cancel all nano projects, but he's played his hand well - there have been many initiatives that he forced past us in recent years."

"But why would you accept it?" Croft asked. "Why not arrest him?"

"Because," Kate said, "I'm assuming the government wanted

what CERUS has been developing."

Reems nodded. "He knew it was a card he had to play carefully. It was an ongoing negotiation: part of a long game I couldn't share with you," she told Croft.

"I was just doing my job, but Bern was playing us all along."

Reems shrugged. "We were trying to play him back. But then he went and got himself killed. We're still trying to work out where that has left us."

Kate drained the whisky glass she was holding. "I still don't buy it. The part about experimenting on a child should have taken any deal off the table."

Reems nodded again. "There's one more thing in the file. The details of who those children were."

"*Children?*"

"Yes. There was Tom, of course, but there were also two others."

ONE HUNDRED EIGHT

"SO," LENTZ SAID, "WHOSE IDEA was it to experiment on the children? You're not saying it was yours?"

Reems puffed out her cheeks. "No, but we were aware of the initiative."

"You *knew* about it?" Kate said. "Even with everything else, I was presuming that was on CERUS."

"It's not quite how it seems. For the children it wasn't a speculative experiment. It was a treatment of last resort. We were trying to save them. All three had a rare brain condition. We hoped to do something about it through the chip."

"But you still programmed it to create the base for the interface?"

"We agreed it would only be used in ways related to the condition, but it was a way of proving the concept and so making it worthwhile to CERUS at the same time as potentially saving their lives. I thought you would understand, Dominique."

"Don't use the memory of my sister to justify your actions. Who gave you the right to make that call for these children? I don't believe you had parental consent."

"Actually, for two of them we did. And all three of them lived.

Whereas we were told they each had no chance if nothing was done."

"So you picked children with the same condition? Isn't it very convenient that two were the children of CERUS employees?"

"What?" asked Kate.

"The second child was Alexis Marron – or Alex as you know her."

"The woman who tried to kill us?" Kate cried. "She's Peter Marron's daughter?"

Reems shrugged. "The branch didn't fall far from the tree there."

"So who was the last child?"

"His name was Connor." She paused. "Connor *Reems*."

A moment of silence hung in the air.

"Your own son?" Lentz said. "Your own son had exactly the rare condition that this process could help?"

"An impossible coincidence," Kate said.

Reems shook her head. "It didn't happen that way round. Marron found out about my son – don't ask me how – and they came to me. They offered me help if I would find a way to get myself tasked with managing the government's relationship with CERUS."

"And you just assumed it was chance that they had the perfect thing to offer you to make you do what they wanted?" asked Kate.

"I believed it because I wanted to believe it. By the time I realised what had really happened, the line had been crossed."

Lentz cleared her throat. "Where is Connor now?"

Reems shook her head. "A car accident, nothing to do with the chip. But it gave him fifteen years. I can't regret that."

Lentz lowered her eyes. "Stephanie, I'm sorry."

"What about Tom and Alex?" Kate said. "If this condition is so rare, how is it possible they both had it too?"

Reems bit her lip. "They didn't. I was lied to. CERUS lured me in then, when I realised what was happening, they made it impossible for me to walk away. When things went wrong, they threatened to reveal my involvement."

"So you admit you were compromised?"

"I decided not to play their game. I went to the then head of MI5 and we formed a plan to let things play out, to be ready to pounce if they ever created anything like Tantalus again."

"Or something *exactly* like Tantalus," Lentz said.

"And you expect me to believe all that?" Croft asked.

Reems pulled out her phone and pressed a number. "Yes, Sir," she said into the handset. "I apologise, but I have a situation at the Tower. Can you verify Project CT to one of my team?" She listened then handed the phone to Croft.

"Who is it?" he asked her, taking the phone warily.

"The Home Secretary. Hopefully he can allay your concerns."

ONE HUNDRED NINE

A NUMBER OF PHONE CALLS later, Croft and Reems had been officially designated to deal with the clean-up of the 'CERUS problem'.

"Congratulations on your security clearance upgrade, George," Reems said, pouring herself a second whisky.

"I'm just pleased I don't actually have to arrest you."

"So what next?" Kate asked.

"We need to get to Tom," Reems said.

"Perhaps you should be focusing on the bad guys," Kate said. "The ones responsible for all the deaths."

"Of course we will, but that doesn't make Tom unimportant. Dominique, I'd like you to reconsider your position. I think you'll find Tom will be better off under our protection. You know the other four subjects died because of complications. Even though Tom is clearly different, who's to say he won't develop alternate problems."

"Who's to say he will?"

Reems took a slow breath. "If you help me, I'll wipe your slate clean. This is an opportunity for you to start again. And let me reassure you: we don't want to cart Tom off to some black-site laboratory and stick needles in him for the next ten years. We want this technology to *work*. The inventive step has been taken. We just want to be able to take it again. And who better to lead the work forward than the person who created it?"

"You're not seriously considering it?" Kate said. "She's bribing you!"

"It's a proposal," replied Reems. "Not a bribe."

"And what," Kate asked, "are you going to offer me so that I don't publish this story?"

"My dear, I think you have an inflated sense of your own importance here."

Lentz folded her arms. "Are you sure? She was the one who discovered the truth of what happened with Tom's abduction. She made the connection with Croft."

Reems frowned. "She should stick to publishing lies and misrepresentations and stop dabbling in areas that risk national security."

"Is that the card you're going to play?" Kate asked dismissively. "Because if you want to talk to me about lies, I'll give you a new one I could write about."

"What do you mean?" Reems asked. "And I'd warn you to tread carefully, Ms Turner, with how you answer."

Kate rolled her eyes. "Do you really believe this is all Marron's doing? Look at the mess Bern left behind. How can you believe that he simply died in an accident? A very convenient one. Not to mention dying being a very comprehensive way of avoiding taking responsibility."

"You're suggesting it was suicide?"

"No I'm not. You should have another look at Bern's body."

"You think he was murdered?"

"Actually I'm wondering if he was killed at all."

Reems folded her arms. "That's ridiculous. The autopsy said it was him."

"Based on a pathologist who made a quick check of the dental records and assumed everything else. Think about this logically. What does Bern want more than anything?"

"I don't follow," Reems said.

"I do," Lentz said. "Bern always wanted to do whatever he wanted, free from any oversight or constraint. And, as I well know, being dead is pretty helpful with that."

ONE HUNDRED TEN

MARRON STOOD ON THE DECK of the yacht, staring at his tablet computer. "Where did you get this information?"

"From MI5 comms," Alex replied. "How did Faraday do it? I didn't think the interface worked like that."

Marron looked up as a crewman waved to him.

"A small motor cruiser is approaching our position," the man reported.

Marron smiled and nodded to Alex. "I think we're about to find out." Marron watched the motor cruiser stop for five minutes at a pre-arranged distance so that they could scan it.

Alex stood next to him, checking her own tablet. "No chatter on the coastguard or police channels. I'll tell them to proceed."

The motor cruiser began powering up its engines then slowly eased away, back towards shore.

Alex tapped the screen of her computer. "I have a small incoming submersible. Our visitor is here."

"Then we'd best go and greet him."

They made their way to the rear of the yacht and watched as the submersible docked. A man, clad in a heavy duty wetsuit and full breathing mask, pulled himself on board.

"Welcome aboard the Phoenix," said Marron.

The man reached behind his head and released a couple of heavy-duty clips on the mask.

Alex threw him a towel. "Nice boat you have here."

"Thanks. Although it's a yacht, not a boat." He lifted the mask off his head.

Marron smiled. "You look well, William, considering."

"Considering that I'm dead?" Bern replied. "Nice of Heidn to stand in for me in that regard."

"I meant considering you've been living off the grid for a week when I know how twitchy you get when your signal drops for a minute. But, yes, that too."

"It was necessary," Bern said. "Now, I want to know everything."

ONE HUNDRED ELEVEN

BERN HELD THE WHEEL, LOOKING out across the English Channel. Moonlight glittered on the water. Under his feet he felt the steady throb of the twin engines powering the yacht gently westwards. No need to get up speed just yet in these crowded waters and risk drawing attention to themselves.

"My crewman can take the helm if you want a shower," Marron said, appearing behind him.

"I think I'll stay for a bit," replied Bern. He took a sip from the champagne flute in his right hand. "It's been quite a few weeks, Peter."

"You could say that."

"Do you really think Heidn would have used the gun?"

"I read the situation as best I could. And of course he was a similar enough age and build to play your part in the car crash. Dental records were hardly a problem to modify. All in all, it was extremely convenient. I wasn't looking forward to commissioning the theft of a suitable corpse."

"I see the newspapers lost interest in my death after only a couple of days."

"It looked like an accident; the world moved on."

Bern shrugged. "Well I'm anxious to move on as well. You have the money?"

Marron smiled. "It's taken you such a long time to get to that I was half wondering if you were the real William Bern. The Leskov funds are in the process of being sanitised through a number of accounts. They'll be at their destination within twenty-four hours. As will the money we've been siphoning off from CERUS these past years."

Bern nodded, turning the wheel slightly. "That was the worst part for me."

Marron raised an eyebrow. "Stealing from your company?"

"No. Having to suggest that I had failed."

Marron reached into his jacket pocket. He produced a small padded case. "Well, we have plenty of rewards to make up for it. Like this. Handle it *very* carefully."

Bern frowned and popped open the case. Inside was a single crystal vial surrounded by a cooling unit and protective padding.

"Blood?"

"Zero's blood. The nanites didn't work as we planned. But they worked all the same."

Bern smiled.

"That's the good news." Marron coughed. "We had a few... issues that had to be dealt with."

"I always knew there would be some collateral damage."

Marron hesitated. "I had to remove Celia."

Bern sucked in his lower lip. "I'm sure she gave you no choice. Was it quick?"

Marron nodded.

"She didn't deserve to suffer. Even if she wanted that for me. What about Holm?"

"Regrettably, Ed decided to go with Leskov."

"And Bradley?"

"He couldn't wait to get on that helicopter."

Bern smiled. "So it's not all bad."

"I'm still not sure that Leskov was the right play. We will have made enemies among his circle."

"Not if they think we're dead. More to the point, it wasn't us that shot him down. It was our friendly neighbourhood government."

Marron hesitated. "Leskov changed the deal at the last minute. He tried to pay only half."

"How rude."

"I think it was because he didn't trust me like he trusted you. I don't have your charm."

Bern flashed his teeth. "Nobody does. Anything else?"

"He insisted on taking Subject Zero with him."

"We lost Zero?" Bern blinked rapidly. "Why wasn't that the first thing you mentioned? That is... a substantial set back."

"You should hear the full story first." Marron frowned. "I didn't realise you'd be so concerned. I had limited options if I was to frame MI5 for shooting down Leskov *and* frame *him* for the destruction of the Tower."

"But the Tower is still standing," Bern said, "which means there will be evidence for the government to crawl all over."

"That bomb was unsolvable in the time they had – it was far too complex. But it wasn't defused by the government."

"Then how?"

"It was Zero."

ONE HUNDRED TWELVE

BERN TURNED FROM THE STEERING wheel, an expression of relief crossing his face. "You said he was in the helicopter."

"My passive monitors intercepted fragments of a government radio communication," Marron said. "It said he landed by parachute. They then dropped him on the Tower roof. I assume he used one of the ejector seats that Leskov was so proud of – even though he was also too slow to use one himself."

"But how *did* Zero manage to stop the detonator?"

"He must have used the interface."

Bern blinked slowly. "Then we have to get him back. He's too valuable to leave in government hands."

"What we have to do is get you away from here. The beta site is the only secure location. After all our planning we cannot risk you."

"I'm overruling you, Peter."

"You should know Reems is at the Tower. They also have Lentz."

"With any luck those two will cancel each other out." Bern drained his champagne glass. "Start deploying a team."

"There may be other options. We already have a Zero 2.0

waiting in the wings."

Bern's eyes narrowed. "You mean your daughter? You want to use Zero's nanites on her? We've discussed this before – many times."

"But the situation has changed. If it worked on Zero, there's every chance she's also suitable. Wouldn't it be better to have a subject who's loyal to us – who *wants* to cooperate?"

"Or we might produce someone we could never hope to control." Bern shook his head firmly. "If something went wrong... She's your anchor: she keeps you focused, grounded. I don't think the world is ready for an *ungrounded* Peter Marron."

"I'm prepared to take that chance. As is Alex."

Bern sighed loudly. "So, what? We should kill Zero to ensure he doesn't talk."

Marron hesitated. "That might be unduly risky in all the--"

"You were happy for him to die in the explosion, but you don't want to do it yourself? I'm confused. Are you emotionally attached to the subject?"

"It's not that. With the helicopter, I had no choice, no chance to discuss it with you."

"So? We're discussing it now. Is there a problem?"

Marron shifted uneasily. "There is something you need to know. My apologies for not raising it sooner."

Bern raised an eyebrow.

"There are certain things that you've always trusted me to handle without your express knowledge. You have to remember that I've only ever acted to protect the security of your operations. I've taken absolutely no pleasure in what have been necessary measures." Marron swallowed. "When we identified Zero as a suitable candidate for the original Tantalus, there was one element I kept from you."

Bern rolled his eyes. "Cut to the chase, Peter."

"He's your son."

Bern blinked several times, then tipped his head to one side. "Subject Zero, Tom Faraday, is my son?"

"You had a relationship with his mother: Amelia Fourier."

"I remember her having a termination."

"She didn't go through with it. She kept the birth from you."

Bern nodded slowly. "How long have we known each other, Peter?"

"Nearly thirty years, since our army days, but why is that your first question?" Marron hesitated. "Wait... you knew! That's why you were upset when you thought he was dead."

"You might know *people*, Peter," Bern gave a sigh, "but I know you. I know how you operate. You keep aces up your sleeve on everyone. It would have been naïve of me to assume that I was not on that list."

"Then why didn't you do anything about it?"

"Because I wanted you to think you *did* have a card to play. I didn't want you to know that card was worthless and start looking for a better one."

"You knew you had a son? You knew I'd chosen him as a subject? Why didn't you stop it?"

"Because, in all the circumstances, it was the right thing to do." Bern gripped Marron's shoulder. "Peter, this is why you are so good at your job. I'm not sure I could ever replace you. I like to spend my time on the grand vision, whereas you make things happen, including all the things that need to happen but nobody should ever know about."

Marron took a slow breath. "So what now?"

"We get Tom back. Do I now have your support?"

"You always do."

An alarm sounded on the deck.

Alex burst through the doorway of the bridge. "We have a

problem."

ONE HUNDRED THIRTEEN

KATE FOLLOWED LENTZ INTO THE laboratory on Level 75, the special-forces soldier remaining on guard outside.

"Well," Lentz said, "I think that went somewhat better than expected. And, may I say, what a brilliant observation with regard to Bern's accident. I'm sure Reems is in a spin checking that out."

Kate folder her arms. "I've adopted a simple strategy: assume everything that happens is a lie."

Lentz frowned. "Why do I feel that some of your anger is directed at me?"

"You're considering their offer, aren't you?"

"I have to weigh all the possibilities before I can decide on the best outcome."

"Best for whom?" Kate asked. "For Tom? For you? I saw your eyes light up when Reems offered you the opportunity to be back at the centre of things. This is everything you've dreamed of for twenty-five years."

"When you're a little older, maybe you'll understand what it's like to be in hiding or for so long, pondering past mistakes, drowning in might-have-beens. Maybe this time I can do it right."

"If you really believe that then you're delusional."

"If I don't do it, someone else will try. Better me, controlling this from the inside than fighting it from the outside."

"I'm sure Tom will see it that way."

Lentz gave a sigh. "You really think he'll be fine out there on his own? He needs our help. The reality is that we can't provide it without support."

"And you think you can trust Reems? Besides, it's all moot if we can't find him."

"It would help if we could narrow down our search. Do you have any idea where he would go?"

"He never said, but I think he'd go after *them*."

Lentz nodded. "It's likely. He may feel he can outmatch them now."

Kate shook her head. "After all he's been through, he's going to get himself killed."

"You know, I don't think Tom's the one who's really in danger," replied Lentz. "Not this time."

Reems looked at her tablet computer and swore. Her team had already sent evidence that Bern's dental records had been tampered with: there could be only one reason why that would have happened. The journalist had been right. That meant Bern and Marron had been executing a plan that was years in the making. After all this time hoping to counter them, had she been outplayed?

The anonymous tip about Leskov – the reason she'd had both ground and air teams in the vicinity of CERUS Tower – was all clearly part of their scheme. They'd *wanted* her in place to shoot a helicopter down. It had got rid of Leskov *and* provided the perfect cover. Reems felt sick inside.

George Croft strode into Bern's office, looking perturbed. "We have a further problem," he said.

"We don't have enough already? I need to get back to HQ, so tell me on the way."

"Getting there will be the problem. It's your helicopters."

"Is Air Traffic Control still closing London? Just give them my clearance code."

"You don't understand. The helicopters were taken."

Reems blinked. "Taken where? By whom?"

Croft cleared his throat. "We don't know."

Reems sat forward. "Five military grade helicopters were taken from right outside this building?"

"As ridiculous as it sounds, that is exactly what I am saying."

"Was nobody guarding them? Where were the pilots?"

"Apparently all five helicopters started powering up, appropriate codes were sent and they all took off, despite the fact that the pilots were in a briefing together in the Tower's lobby. And it gets stranger. According to eye witnesses, all five helicopters took off in perfect formation: so perfect it looked like they were joined by rods."

"I know what you're suggesting." Reems stood up and walked to the window. "I know the interface was designed to fly helicopters, but do you really believe Faraday could be behind this? Surely he'd need weeks, months to train to fly even one of them, but five?"

"It's either that or five mercenary pilots, with acrobatic flying experience, just happened to be in the area."

ONE HUNDRED FOURTEEN

ALEX POINTED ACROSS THE WATER. "Incoming helicopter."
She ran across the bridge and tapped on a computer screen. "It's a
government model."

"Reems!" Bern hissed. "How did she find us?"

Marron stared at the screen over Alex's shoulder. "She
shouldn't even know to look."

"Are our weapon systems operational?" Bern asked.

"There wasn't time to test them," Marron replied, "but I made
sure we had a back-up." He pointed through the window to a
metal chest strapped to the deck.

Alex sprinted out from the bridge and flipped the chest open.
Inside was a shoulder-mounted rocket-launcher. She lifted it and
lodged it in the crook of her neck, then began flicking switches.

The tannoy system whined then crackled. "Put it down," said a
voice on the speakers.

"Faraday?" Marron asked. "How can he be--"

"There's no need for the third person. I can hear you just fine.
I'm using the speakers as a two-way channel."

"Tom?" Alex asked, lowering the weapon. "How did you find
us?"

"Using the talents you gave me. You're not the only ones who can track people. Do I have permission to land on your helipad?"

"Are you alone?"

"Thanks to you, I'm more than capable of flying a helicopter on my own."

Marron glanced at Bern, who nodded. "One wrong move and we'll shoot you down."

"Given how valuable I am to you, I consider that unlikely. Especially as I simply want to talk."

Bern cleared his throat. "Then land when ready."

"Ah, Mr Bern, back from the dead. I look forward to making your acquaintance."

The sound of the rotors grew and they could see the silhouette of the craft against the stars as it slowly approached.

"Is it a trick?" Bern asked. "Perhaps he's already given away our location?"

"If he were going to do that," Marron replied, "why come at all? Why not tip off the Air Force or Navy?" He paused. "We'll get moving, just in case." He drew a pistol from his belt. "As soon as we've secured our visitor, that is." He hesitated then reached into his pocket, producing a small remote-control device, and handed it to Bern.

"What's this?"

"The nanite remote control – the government safeguard we mentioned during implementation. Only use it if you have to, and only if you're close enough. Five metres or so and it will lock him up."

The helicopter touched down on the helipad, its rotors quickly decelerating. Marron, Bern and Alex watched and waited, but nobody climbed out.

Alex looked at Marron then called out. "Tom, come out slowly! Keep your hands where we can see them."

There was no reply.

"Go check it out," Marron said.

Alex nodded, lowering her rocket launcher to the deck and swinging the automatic rifle slung across her back to the front. She clicked a powerful torch on the barrel and shone it into the helicopter as she advanced.

Still there was no movement.

She reached the door and pulled it open, pointing her weapon inside. "There's nobody here!" she called.

Across the deck, the proximity alarm sounded again.

"What the hell now?" Marron shouted. "Tom, what are you playing at?" He moved to a computer screen. "There are four more helicopters approaching," he told Bern, frowning. "Same make and model. What the hell is going on?"

ONE HUNDRED FIFTEEN

BERN LOOKED TOWARDS THE APPROACHING aircraft. "So he did give us away."

Marron's jaw grew stiff. "Get yourself below deck before you really get yourself killed."

Bern turned and walked to the rear of the yacht and the nearest set of steps below.

"Something wrong, Peter?" asked Tom's voice, over the speakers.

The noise of the helicopters was growing.

Marron squinted in the dark. "Who's with you? Is Reems on board?"

"It's just me."

"If you're just going to be ridiculous then--"

Alex jabbed him in the ribs with her elbow. "Don't you get it? It *is* just him! He's flying *all* of the helicopters."

The four new helicopters switched their spotlights on in unison as they took up position in a horseshoe formation around the front of the yacht. Machine-gun turrets swivelled and laser-sights dotted Marron and Alex.

Marron looked up at one of the cockpits. "Tom, I know you're angry, but you have to agree that you've become something incredible."

"Nobody ever asked if that was what I wanted."

"What you have is a gift. What you are is amazing."

"What I am is your undoing."

"So you're going to gun us down in cold blood?"

Alex licked her lips. "Do you have it in you? You could have killed me before, but it's not who you are."

"I'm not who I used to be. But I probably won't shoot you. Your punishment needs to be rather more protracted."

"I thought," Marron said, "you came out here because you wanted to talk."

"Actually, I was just wasting time. Distracting you. Now I have what I want. Goodbye." The helicopters pulled sharply upwards, extinguishing their spotlights.

Marron stared at the receding aircraft in confusion. In the distance, there was the sound of a heavy crash of waves.

Alex shook her head. "Let's get out of here." The crash of waves grew louder, a harsh, discordant slap, as if they were hitting something metallic.

And then another voice boomed out of the dark. *"Attention, all aboard the Phoenix. This is the British Navy. Prepare to be boarded."*

"What now?" cursed Marron, picking up the rocket-launcher. He hefted it back onto his shoulder and turned around. And promptly lowered his weapon.

A navy destroyer was bearing down on them, its spotlights bursting into life and blinding them.

"He gave them our location," Alex said.

"The other helicopter," hissed Marron, grabbing Alex's arm. "We'll use it to escape." They crouched low and ran to the back of the yacht.

The aircraft was gone.

Alex turned to Marron. "I know why he came."

"Why?"

"For Bern."

Marron's expression turned heavy. "I did not anticipate that."

"So what now?"

He shook his head. "I think we've run out of options. There's no way out of this for us. Not for *both* of us. You understand what I'm saying?"

Alex took a sharp breath. "Will it work?"

"There's only one way to find out. Are you ready to take the chance?"

"I am."

He kissed her on the forehead. "I love you."

A tremor of a smile crossed her face. "I know."

ONE HUNDRED SIXTEEN

LENTZ PUSHED BACK FROM THE workbench, shaking her head. "I cannot find Tom. If he doesn't want to be found then he won't be."

"You're giving up?" Kate shouted. "You can't give up!"

"I'm a realist." Lentz shook her head. "He's evolving and that creates myriad other unknowns. His nanites are progressing exponentially. The interface they were designed to build was focused on a single purpose: to control a helicopter. Tom has gone way beyond that. He's connecting wirelessly, without the aid of any augmentation. Quite frankly he could do anything that involves using a computer or electronic device that he can connect to."

"What about the internet?" asked Kate.

"That is basically a big network so yes. But the more ambitious he is, the more intense his use of his abilities, the more he will drain himself at an almost cellular level as he tries to fuel and sustain the nanites. He complained about excessive hunger earlier, and I didn't think about it being symptomatic of his use of the interface. The nanites are probably multiplying within him: the situation is only going to get worse."

"What will happen?"

"He might faint. He might collapse." Lentz paused. "Or he might die. It depends on so many variables." Lentz's phone beeped. She looked at it with a frown, which turned to surprise. "It's Tom. He's given us a location. He needs help."

Kate leaned close, lowering her voice. "How are we going to get out of here without our government friends following?"

"Actually Tom's instructions are clear. He wants them there."

"Really? Why?"

"He says he has a surprise for us all."

ONE HUNDRED SEVENTEEN

THE FIVE HELICOPTERS FLEW LOW over the ocean, away from the Phoenix. Bern sat in the front passenger-seat of the lead aircraft. Behind him was Tom, pointing a gun between his shoulder blades.

"I've not seen Marron outwitted like that before," Bern said.

"It wasn't a fair fight; I had every advantage," Tom said. "Of course that's usually how you operate."

Bern shrugged. "You don't need the gun. I'm hardly going to try to overpower you, especially when you're flying."

"I'm well aware you're an experienced pilot, so I wouldn't put it past you to try."

"Alex looked in the helicopter. Where were you?"

"Hiding behind a service panel. I don't need to see out of the craft to control it. Not with the sensor arrays these things have."

Bern glanced out of the window, seeing the silhouettes of the four helicopters shadowing them. "Why did you take me and not them?"

"Because I wanted to meet you."

"How did you even know I was alive?"

"You're not as thorough as you think. So much for your

perfect crime."

"I'm not the villain here, Tom."

"Do you really believe that? I suppose nobody ever considers themselves evil, that they rationalise their actions as being for some good reason, but do you really have no doubts at all?"

"I wanted to change the world."

Tom shook his head. "Because only you know what's best for it?"

"If Henry Ford hadn't mass produced the motorcar, most people would have been happy with a faster horse. They needed his vision. People need mine now."

"I accessed the CERUS network. I reviewed the data. I made connections." Tom leaned forwards and whispered in Bern's ear. "I know who you are."

Bern swallowed. "Everyone knows who I am."

"I know who you are to *me*. I found the DNA records in the archives. And I see you know as well."

"Clearly you have all the answers already."

"Mostly I have questions: ones that only you can answer. I've often dreamt of meeting my father, but I didn't think it would happen. I was told you were *dead*."

"I know."

"Why didn't you get in touch with me?"

"Because your mother hid you from me. She wouldn't have wanted it."

"And you expect me to believe you actually listened to what someone else wanted?"

"Believe what you like. Look," Bern said, "you've either rescued me so we can have an emotional reconciliation, or you've come to kill me for what you believe I've done. Which is it?"

"Actually, I've come to give you what you never gave me. A choice."

"And what would that be?"

Tom leaned back in his seat. "Not yet. But soon."

Bern leaned back in his seat, running his fingers over the remote control tucked into his belt.

ONE HUNDRED EIGHTEEN

THE HELICOPTER QUINTET SOARED OVER the white Dover cliffs and made its way along the coast. Tom guided it to a small field and, in a storm of dust and agitated vegetation, set all five craft down. The first hints of dawn were scribbling the sky with colour.

"What's your plan?" asked Bern, looking out of the window.

"We only had so much fuel." The door opened and Tom gestured with the gun for Bern to climb out. "Let's take a walk."

They moved away from the helicopters, which were now powering down, and climbed a small hill to the south. At the top they paused, taking in the sight of the sea and the faint breaking of the waves.

"I've been trying to find out more about you my whole life," Tom said. "Even if my mother didn't want to tell me, why didn't you do something after she died? After everything I've been through – after I just saved you – I won't let you hold out on me."

"What do you mean, *save me*?"

"Two minutes after we departed, a navy destroyer arrived at the location of your yacht."

"I see. Then I guess I should thank you."

Tom waved the gun. "Don't get carried away. You have some talking to do before I make up my mind what happens to you."

"You expect me to believe that you're going to shoot me if I don't tell you about your mother? What if I run away?" asked Bern. "How would you stop me?"

Tom gave a snort. "I could always shoot you in the leg. I've seen your files. I know how you've set things up. Marron will take the fall for everything. You'll have some difficult questions to answer, but I doubt there's any proof that you haven't already removed or manipulated to your advantage. With the all-star team of lawyers you'd hire, there's not going to be any justice for you; for all the people you've had killed."

"I didn't know what Marron was doing."

"You might as well have done it yourself. But it's more than that: you don't even care."

"So, what? You're going to be the lawyer to bring me to justice?"

"Justice should be about fairness. As I said, I'm going to give you a choice. Option one: take responsibility for what you've done. Turn yourself in without hiding behind your lawyers."

"Why would I do that?"

"Because it's the right thing to do. I want to know that you *can* do the right thing."

Bern raised an eyebrow. "That's not a choice that I can make."

"Then we come to option two."

"Which is?"

"Give *me* the choice. Take this thing out of me."

ONE HUNDRED NINETEEN

BERN BLINKED. "YOU WANT ME to remove the interface?"

Tom nodded. "It would mean I could go back to my old life. You think I like being pursued by criminals and governments? Is it really that surprising I want it gone?"

"If I agree, what's to stop you turning me in afterwards?"

"We'll just have to trust each other." Tom extended his hand then hesitated. He drew it back and spat in his palm before offering it again.

Bern looked puzzled, but spat on his own hand and shook Tom's firmly. "We'd better get moving. If you've got a phone, I'll call in some emergency transportation. It would be nice if you could lower the gun now."

Tom held up a finger. "Before we get to that, I'm going to ask you those questions again."

"Why are we circling back to this?" Bern asked impatiently.

Tom reached into a pocket and held up a syringe. "Do you know what this is? It's a CERUS product I believe you call truth nano." He handed it to Bern. "Inject it please."

Bern took it slowly. He fumbled it, dropping it to the ground. "How clumsy of me."

"Pick it up. I have spares if you break it."

"This isn't necessary."

"Yes, it is. It's also unpleasant, as my friend Kate found out after Marron used it on her in order to find me." Tom tipped his head to the side. "Obviously he did all that without your permission."

Bern frowned and crouched to pick up the syringe, his hand sliding to his belt as he did so. "I guess I'll just have to live with that." He held up a small controller, pressing a button on it.

Tom's eyes flew wide open. He stumbled forwards and collapsed.

Bern bent down and took the gun from his limp hand.

"I just wanted the truth." Tom whispered. "What have you done?"

Bern waved the remote control. "All CERUS nanites have an override in them: a secret control-code that we programmed in to allow us to assert our authority in the event something went wrong. This controller allows me to instruct your nanites and, by extension, you."

Tom gritted his teeth. "I can't move."

Bern leaned closer. "I can hold you there for as long as I like."

"You were never going to take the interface out of me, were you?"

"I don't even know if it's possible. But why spend time and money going backwards? The road to the future only goes one way."

Tom grimaced. "Whatever the cost?" he asked, his voice coming in gasps

Bern snorted. "As long as I'm not the one paying it." He leaned forward and searched through Tom's pockets, quickly pulling out his mobile phone. He hefted the gun in one hand, while he started dialling with the other. There was a buzz as someone answered. "I need an evacuation. Track this phone." Then he clicked it off.

"The moment," hissed Tom, "that I'm connected to a network, I'll going to tell them where you are."

Bern frowned. "Your abilities don't scare me. We'll just lock you in a lead-lined room." He raised the gun. "Now, I'm going to release the override and we're going to start walking, put some distance between ourselves and your five helicopters. Don't try anything. I really would hate to shoot you. Even in the leg."

"I have no doubt you'd do it. But there is one thing you haven't considered."

"I doubt it."

Tom stared into his father's eyes. "I've been in your system. I know *everything*."

Bern waved the remote. "Clearly you didn't know about this."

"I had to know what you were really like. I had to know how far you would go. I wanted to believe you would help me. Now I know I should never have asked." Tom smiled. "You know something funny just occurred to me. Do you remember the Tower launch party? You talked about how no one can stand in the way of progress."

"Embrace it and change the world. I use that in most of my speeches."

"I hope it was worth it. Because I *am* progress. And *I* am going to change your world."

Bern held up the remote. "You're not changing anything right now, Tom."

"You might have control over CERUS nanites, but these are no longer CERUS nanites. They're mine," Tom replied.

And he stood up.

ONE HUNDRED TWENTY

TOM ADVANCED ON BERN. "I'M not going to be a victim any more."

Bern brought the gun up and made to squeeze the trigger, but his finger stopped. His hand started to shake. "What are you doing? How are you doing it?"

"My nanites are not just in me." Tom mimed spitting in his palm. "Since we shook hands, they're in you too."

Bern's hand shook more violently. "Doing what?"

"I wouldn't say I can control you." Tom narrowed his eyes. "But I can hold you there for as long as I like." He reached forward and plucked the gun from Bern's hand. "A taste of your own medicine."

"You never wanted the interface removed."

"It would have made things simpler. It would have been nice to have had a choice. But I guess my answer is *no*. I just wanted to see how you would respond. To see what kind of a man you really are. Now I know."

"So what are you going to do? Kill me?"

"This technology came with a price. And it's time that you paid. So let's be clear, *William*: you have no idea what I will do because even I don't."

Bern swallowed.

"Do I scare you now?"

"Yes."

"That's the first honest thing you've said." Tom smiled. "But it won't be the last." He pulled one of the syringes from his pocket then walked over and injected it into Bern's upper arm. Tom sucked his lip thoughtfully, then produced a second syringe. "Perhaps we'll give you a couple of doses. Just to be sure." He blew out a sigh, closing his eyes briefly as tiredness threatened to overwhelm him.

Bern grimaced. "So, ask your questions."

"Actually, I'm done talking to you." He pointed over his shoulder. "The truth nano's for their benefit, not mine." From behind Tom came the roar of three military helicopters.

Bern's eyes widened. "You told them where we were. You lied."

Bern's face contorted in anger, but Tom didn't have time to enjoy the moment. Suddenly, the world seemed to tilt and yaw. He staggered backwards. He felt tired, so incredibly tired.

"Then I guess we do have something in common."

"This isn't over," growled Bern. "Between you and me."

"I agree," said Tom, as his consciousness started to slip. "Because I've only just started."

ONE HUNDRED TWENTY-ONE

THREE DAYS LATER, DOMINIQUE LENTZ sat in the Level 90 boardroom of CERUS Tower, ignoring the view and staring intently at her laptop. There was a brief knock at the door and Kate walked in.

"You said you had something important to discuss."

"I do," replied Lentz, "but first, how are you?"

"Your people scanned me. Supposedly I'm clear of the nanites and my doctor has given me a clean bill of health." I don't feel the same though."

"It's just in your head." Lentz hesitated. "Sorry, bad choice of words. Why don't we talk about why I invited you here?" She pointed to a seat opposite her desk and poured coffee from a pot into two cups. "Bern and Marron are in custody, but they left behind a huge mess at CERUS. Which is a problem because the company is being considered 'too big to fail'."

Kate raised her eyebrows.

"There are thirty thousand employees and a great many smaller businesses relying on CERUS. With some new government-backed bridging finance, the company should be able to get its house in order. And there are some fascinating projects in the archives that we can soon use to turn a profit."

Kate tipped her head to one side. "They asked you to take over, didn't they? I thought they were going to put you in charge of research, but they've given you the whole damn company."

"Well, at first I said they must be joking. Then I said that, if they weren't joking, they were crazy." Lentz paused. "Then I said yes."

"I guess congratulations are due."

Lentz sighed. "Why am I not convinced that you really mean that?"

"Maybe I do. I'm certainly feeling less antagonistic since they decided not to lock Tom up. Of course I'm sure they're following him everywhere."

"I have no doubt. I note you haven't published your story."

"Reems asked me to wait a week. To be honest, I don't believe I'm going to be allowed. Or whether I should do it, even if I am. Maybe I *should* make this all public, for the sake of the people who died for these secrets, if nothing else. But I don't want to ruin Tom's life. Again." Kate shrugged. "Geraldine is calling me every thirty minutes."

"Perhaps I can suggest another way you could use this to advance your career?"

"I wasn't aware you had connections in journalism."

"I don't. Which is exactly why I need someone to fill the role of Media Relations Director at CERUS. As you can imagine, it's going to be a pretty demanding remit."

Kate narrowed her eyes. "Is this just a clever scheme you and Reems have cooked up to stop me publishing?"

"Someone's going to tell the story sooner or later. I'd rather it was you, telling the *right* story – from the inside. In return, I'll make you an offer you can't refuse."

"What about Tom? Is he coming back?"

Lentz frowned. "We certainly aren't going to fire him, but I can't see him returning to his old job."

Kate sniffed. "I guess not. Have they found any trace of Alex?"

"She went overboard when Marron was captured. They're still looking for a body."

Kate scratched her nose. "Why do you think Tom took Bern on that helicopter ride? Why not just let him get arrested with Marron?"

"He had questions to ask. And he wanted to make sure Bern would have to tell the truth about Tantalus and everything else he's done. Tom's got a lot to work through, but he'll be back in touch when he's ready."

"And what will he do until then?"

Lentz leaned back in her chair. "As he is now? That's entirely up to him."

ONE HUNDRED TWENTY-TWO

THE LARGE GOVERNMENT TEAM THAT had been tracking Tom lost him at Heathrow airport. He simply vanished into the crowds. A later review of CCTV footage provided no clues. It was like he had never been there.

In fact Tom had simply strolled up to a random long-haul flight, provided his passport and was waved on board. All his details were in the system, but then he had just put them there. Of course, five minutes later they were gone again.

He sat anonymously in economy, next to a tired-looking mother and her bored pre-teenage son. After the shake and rumble of take-off, the seat-belt sign turned off and the inflight crew moved into action. But, for Tom, it was a chance to stop: to draw breath.

He had gone through so much in the few last days. And he had survived to become something else. The interface in his head meant that he could feel the systems around him – and some of them he could talk to.

But what was there to say? And what should he do?

His world was still in pieces with Jo gone. Did he want revenge? Bern and Marron had already been arrested and it had made little difference to his pain: it hadn't brought Jo back. Nothing would. And what about Alex? Was she even still alive? The thought of her made him shiver.

He didn't know what he wanted.

Lentz had said he could come back to CERUS: he was, of course, still an employee. It was an interesting option: from trawling their systems, he knew the company had a great many projects and ideas in the works, and Lentz had said they could use his help – on pretty much any terms he might wish to dictate. But whatever she said, there were risks in going back. There were too many people he couldn't trust. And, for now, he wasn't ready for that.

His thoughts turned to Kate. She had been through a terrible ordeal in pursuit of her story and yet she now seemed disinclined to publish. For his sake, so Lentz had told him. That was no small sacrifice. He would have to balance that account.

But first he needed to get away for a while.

He closed his eyes, ready for sleep.

There was a polite cough. He blinked and saw a stewardess smiling at him. "Lunch, Sir? Chicken or beef?"

Before Tom could answer, there was a curse from the seat next to him.

"Stupid thing won't work!" said the boy, pointing at the blank TV screen in front of him. His mother sighed and closed her eyes.

"I'm sorry," said the stewardess, a practised smile on her face. "There's been a technical problem. We're looking into it."

"It's a ten-hour flight!" said the boy, his voice raising.

"Perhaps I can get you a comic," she offered, "or a magazine?"

He scowled. "I want to watch the movies. Why don't you do your job and fix it?"

Her smile hardened. "I'll see what we can do." She turned back to Tom. "Chicken or beef?"

"Chicken, please." Tom leaned closer, lowering his voice. "Don't envy you having to explain that to everyone."

She sighed. "Intercom's broken in economy so I'm having to tell people one by one." She moved to the next row of seats.

Tom stared at the screen in the seatback in front of him, testing the buttons on the side. It remained blank.

"Yeah, it's not working," said the boy. "Didn't you hear me?"

"Maybe you didn't press the right buttons," said Tom. "OK if I give it a try?"

"I know how to work it. A seven year-old could do it." The boy swallowed. "Look, I hate flying. The only reason I get through is because I have movies to watch." He glanced at his mother. "And she packed my tablet in our luggage."

"I'm sure she had a lot of things on her mind." Tom placed his palm on his screen, closing his eyes. There was a soft chime and all around the cabin screens lit up with a welcome screen.

The boy's mouth fell open. "What just happened?"

"They must have fixed it," said his mother, not opening her eyes.

"I bet," whispered Tom, "that the stewardess sorted it out. You should thank her next time she comes by."

The boy leaned closer and lowered his voice. "Seriously, did you do that?"

Tom shrugged. "Somebody obviously spoke the computer's language."

"Have you got some clever kind of phone? Are you a hacker?"

Tom raised his hands. "Nothing up my sleeves, mate."

"What *are* you, then? Some type of cyborg?"

"You watch too many movies. Or at least you can now."

The boy's mouth creased into a smile. "When I grow up, I want to be like you. I want to be able to do that."

"Maybe you will. I just hope that you have a choice."

Dear Reader

My thanks for choosing to read *Interface*. If you have any comments, questions or feedback I'd love to hear from you. I can be reached via my website www.tonybatton.com, where you can also sign up for my email newsletter to learn about forthcoming books.

If you enjoyed the book and have a moment to spare, I would really appreciate a short, honest review where you bought the book - website reviews are perhaps the most effective way to bring the book to the attention of new readers, and your help will make a real difference.

Sincerely yours

Tony Batton
London 2016

ACKNOWLEDGMENTS

I owe a great debt of gratitude to the many people who have encouraged and supported me through the long process of bringing *Interface* to completion. A special thank you to my *beta team* who so willingly read (and re-read) the manuscript and provided feedback and criticism - it was invaluable in making the book better:

Jin Koo Niersbach, Chris Turner, Maurice Murphy, Elli Murphy, Joshua Allarm, Peter Cliffin, Alicia Young, John Nicholson, Imogen Cleaver, Paul Cleaver, Scott Purchas, Joanne Theodoulou, Chris Ward, Jeremy Ward, Douglas Ashby, Alex Bott, Alistair Charleton, Petros Demetriades, Jessica Mair, Mary Loosemore, Patrick Wijngaarden, Richard McGregor and Judy Bott.

ABOUT THE AUTHOR

TONY BATTON was born in Berkshire, England. He studied Economics at St. John's College, Cambridge, and trained as a lawyer in London, before working as a consultant with a number of tech companies. He now lives in London with his wife and two sons.

When not writing, Tony likes to read, play basketball, learn about gadgets and drink coffee.

Interface is his first novel.

You can connect with Tony online at
www.tonybatton.com
https://twitter.com/thetonybatton